The Broken Realm

The Saga of Roland Inness

Book 3

Wayne Grant

For Ken and Kellye

Table of Contents

Map
The Saga of Roland Inness

Prologue

April 1191

"Who are you?"

The question hung in the air. Millicent de Laval stood in the driving rain and looked at the tall young warrior in the fine cape who had asked it. Behind him, a band of thirty men, all armed with swords and many with longbows, stood silently, waiting for an order. The place where they stood was a muddy track that ran through a cleft in the hills. It was far over the border into Wales and these were Welshmen.

The man had asked the question in his own tongue, but Millicent had lived along this border all of her life and understood it well enough. She knew that much depended on how they answered. Before she could reply, the only man in their party of three stepped forward. He spoke in serviceable Welsh.

"I am Ranulf, Earl of Chester and these are the Ladies Catherine and Millicent de Laval of Shipbrook. We are travelling to Rhyl. To whom am I speaking?"

The leader of the band showed no hint of surprise at the Earl's statement. He looked over his shoulder at his men for a moment, then turned back with a broad grin on his face. Now he spoke in decent English.

"Earl Ranulf," he nodded to the Earl. "Welcome to Wales! It is not often we get a Marcher Lord travelling these hills, except when they come at the head of an army. I have wondered what became of you. My spies tell me a new banner flies over Chester Castle these days."

"Aye—for the moment," the Earl replied with a frown. "Bad news travels fast, even in the wilderness it seems. But I ask again, who are *you*?"

Millicent studied the young warrior carefully. It did not matter much who he was—only what he was. Wales was full of bandits and cutthroats, a fact of which she was only too painfully aware. Two years past she had been carried off to a place not far from here by the cattle thief Bleddyn as a hostage.

But this man had a different bearing about him—dangerous to be sure and swagger aplenty, but none of the leering greed or craftiness of her old captors. Perhaps he was no bandit, but what then? Welshmen and Normans were enemies of old. Would they fare any better with these Welsh than with the Earl of Derby, who had seized Chester and whose men had been pursuing them for days?

The warrior took a small step back and spread his arms wide as though posing for a statue.

"Forgive my rudeness! I am Llywelyn, son of Iorwerth, grandson of Owain Gwynedd and the rightful ruler of these lands."

The Earl gave a half smile.

"My father told me many stories about your grandsire, my lord. Prince Owain and Earl Hugh were enemies to be sure, but respected one another."

Llywelyn laughed.

"Your father's name was regularly cursed at my grandsire's table, my lord, but all acknowledged he was a hard man in a fight."

Earl Ranulf nodded at this back-handed compliment.

"My lord Llywelyn, your claim to rule here surprises me. The last I heard, your uncle, Daffyd, governs east of the River Conwy and your other uncle, Roderic, holds sway in the west. You see I have spies of my own."

Now it was the Welshman's turn to frown.

"My uncles' rule is like the banner that now flies over Chester, my lord—only there for the moment. They are usurpers and will be brought down."

He turned toward Catherine and Millicent and gave them a deep bow, his hand covering his heart. "I know of the de Lavals of Shipbrook, my ladies. Sir Roger was not a man to be trifled with and your lovely little fort on the Dee was long a thorn in the side of some hereabouts."

"Was?" Millicent asked, knowing, yet fearing the answer. Llywelyn seemed to really see the girl for the first time and took a step in her direction, his gaze coolly assessing her. Despite the cold, Millicent felt her face flush at his bold stare. It made her angry.

"Aye, miss. I am sorry to tell you the walls still stand, but the buildings within have been burned to the ground. The cattle thieves on this side of the border will rejoice at the news, but I am sorry for it."

"I thought all Welshmen were cattle thieves," Millicent snapped, and instantly regretted her words. Once again Llywelyn turned back toward his men as though to gauge their reaction, then faced the girl.

"Your words wound me, my lady. Some of our folk do steal a few cows from you Normans, it's true. But you Normans have tried to steal our whole country! So who is the greater thief?"

Lady Catherine stepped forward.

"Indeed, my lord, there are grievances on both sides of the border and troubles aplenty on either side of the Dee. Perhaps we should consider making common cause against them." Catherine glanced at Earl Ranulf and the young nobleman gave her a small nod.

Llywelyn pondered her words for a long moment, and shook his head in wonderment.

"Do you suggest making an alliance between *cattle thieves* and a Marcher Lord, my lady? That would be a novel strategy indeed, though your Marcher Lord looks ill-prepared to be of much use to me."

Ranulf bristled. He moved toward Llywelyn who watched him impassively. Overhead, thunder boomed and echoed across

3

the hills. He had to shout over the storm and he did so in Welsh— loudly enough for Llywelyn and all of his men to hear.

"I have been falsely accused of treason. I go to Queen Eleanor in Normandy to remove that stain upon my honour. Then I will deal with my enemies across the Dee. I would welcome your aid and, when I come back into my own, I pledge to support your right to rule here."

"With words?" asked Llywelyn pointedly.

"With arms and men and money," said the Earl.

The Welsh leader arched an eyebrow.

"I must say, Lord Ranulf, you are not a man with a reputation for resolve, but I will think more on this. For now, you will be a guest at my humble little fortress not far from here." He motioned toward his men who began assembling on the trail.

Millicent spoke up.

"My lord Llywelyn, you should know that trouble pursues us from Cheshire. Our enemies are not far behind."

Llywelyn shrugged.

"That trouble follows you no longer, my lady. They did not like the greeting we gave them about a mile over yonder." He pointed back to the east. "Those that still live are hastening back toward the border."

He started to turn away, then pointed to her horse.

"I see that you have yew staffs strapped to your saddle. Bow staves, I believe?"

"Yes, my lord."

"We prefer elm for our bows, but either does nicely for killing Normans."

The Old Queen

December, 1191

By the highest window of the tower, Queen Eleanor sat and looked to the east. She enjoyed this view, encompassing as it did the lazy bend of the Seine as it neared the sea. If there was a flaw in the scene, it was that it included the road from Rouen—the road down which trouble usually travelled.

Soon, she would have to travel back up that road to attend Christ's Mass services in the Norman capital and she dreaded it. Once, when she was young, she would have held a festive court for weeks at the palace in Rouen, but now…now she felt old.

She hated to leave this small castle at Tancarville. It was a tranquil place, and well-positioned for her needs. Perched on a cliff overlooking the river valley below, it was close to the power centres of Normandy and near to the port at Harfleur—handy for politics and convenient for a quick escape over the Channel if events dictated. And events of late had been absorbing far too much of her time and energy.

Since his return from Crusade in late autumn, Philip of France had been a thorn in her side. No sooner had he arrived in Paris, than he began spreading slander against Richard—assigning all credit to himself for capturing Acre and accusing her son of attempting to poison him. This was to be expected, but more troubling was the gathering of French forces along the borders of Normandy.

An agreement made at Vezelay had forbidden any aggression between the two monarchs as long as either was away on Crusade, a provision Philip seemed eager to ignore. Just the week before, she had ordered the strengthening of the garrisons facing the Ile-de-France as a precaution.

If the troubles on the continent were serious, events across the Channel were hardly less so. Her son John was parading around the country as though Richard was already dead and was plundering the Midlands to fill his coffers. The one nobleman in that region who had been a counterweight, Ranulf of Chester, was now charged with treason and a fugitive, or more likely dead.

Constance, Ranulf's wife, had conspired with the King of France against Richard. Of that there was no doubt. John had made certain that Eleanor saw the letter the woman had signed seeking aid from Philip to protect her son.

Why Constance thought her son needed protection was a mystery. As King Henry's grandson, Arthur of Brittany was a legitimate pretender to the throne, and might one day be a threat to Richard or John, but the child was only three! Something about this tale of treason had a stink to it.

Constance had neither the wit nor the nerve to hatch this plot on her own, so her husband the Earl was naturally a suspect. And John had loudly proclaimed Ranulf to be the true instigator of the plot. Yet she found it hard to believe that the young Earl of Chester had turned on Richard. Surely he would not be stupid enough to stake his future on a mere babe.

Though, if not Ranulf, then *who* had guided Constance's hand? She could have used a report from the spy she had sent to Chester, but the girl had disappeared along with the Earl. There was much more to this affair than met the eye, but she simply had too many other problems gathering around her to deal with it at present.

As she surveyed the iced-over fields beside the river and the empty road, Eleanor of Aquitaine felt the full weight of her years. She was careful not to show it—any sign of weakness in these troubled times might be fatal, but she felt the cold of December right down to her bones.

Across her lap she held the materials for knitting. It was a simple activity that had always been a comfort to her—but now her hands went still—for down the road from Rouen, she saw two small figures approaching on foot. She sighed. They were not mounted. Perhaps they were local peasants.

Not likely in this weather.

She put the knitting back in the basket and prepared to be Queen.

***

On the road below, two monks trudged along, their coarse brown robes pulled close against the biting wind off the river. One was older and squarely built, while the younger was tall and broad-shouldered. Their destination loomed above them. For three months, they had sailed, ridden, and finally walked the three thousand miles to get to this place.

The two men had outrun a pirate galley off the coast of Corsica, come ashore on a moonless night at a deserted cove in Provence, evaded agents of the French king as they passed through his territory, and finally arrived at Rouen to find the object of their journey not there. But everyone knew where to find Queen Eleanor, so they had not tarried in the city.

They travelled afoot as poor monks, the better to avoid notice, though only one was a legitimate man of God.

"How do you stand these blasted robes?" asked Sir Robin of Loxley. "They itch to high heaven and are of little use when the wind can blow right up to your arse!"

The shorter man smiled. It was not the first time his companion had complained about masquerading as a monk. If it was not the clothes, it was the prohibition on wooing tavern girls that irked his friend.

"Once we deliver our message, you can burn the robe if you choose," said Friar Tuck. "But you should give it more of a chance. When the weather warms, you will appreciate the breeze."

He got only an irritated grunt in reply as they turned off the river road and started the long slog up the switchback trail that led to the castle above. The ice slowed their progress and it was near an hour before they reached the top of the hill. Two guards were waiting for them.

"We come with a message for Queen Eleanor," Tuck announced, handing over the parchment with the King's seal. The two guards seemed to be expecting them. The senior of the two inspected the parchment, which granted free passage for the King's messengers, then handed it back.

"Leave your weapons here," he said, pointing to a small alcove within the gatehouse manned by a third guard. Their status as monks did not seem to sway the senior guardsman from his duty to check all travellers, no matter how pacific they might appear.

Tuck and Sir Robin looked at each other and carefully drew forth a surprising array of blades from beneath their robes. The guards seemed unsurprised and after a thorough and intrusive inspection of their persons, the senior man jerked his head for them to follow. As they stepped through the raised portcullis, the second guard fell in behind them.

The Queen was in a small receiving room on the first level of the squat, round tower that formed the keep of the place. Sir Robin noticed with a start that boughs of spruce hung about the entrance. He had forgotten that Christ's Mass was only a few days away.

There were two well-armed guards on either side of the Queen and their two escorts remained on station by the door after they entered. Neither Tuck nor Sir Robin had seen Eleanor of Aquitaine, except from a great distance, but there was no mistaking the woman before them—a queen indeed.

"Your grace, we bring a message from your son, the King," said Sir Robin.

Queen Eleanor sat motionless for a moment conducting her own visual inspection of the two men before her. The one had the look of a monk, but one who was not that saintly. The other was younger and handsome—the sort who would have caught her eye forty years ago. *No monk he.* She smiled the smile that had won a thousand hearts over the years.

"It has been almost two months since I've received a message from my son," she said at last. "No doubt he has sent them, for he is dutiful in that way, but none have reached me. Many say it is the work of the French king—that our messengers have been detained or killed. So I would first hear from you how you have succeeded when others have failed, and what you have seen on your journey here."

Sir Robin cleared his throat. The woman was a bit intimidating. "Your grace, I am Sir Robin of Loxley and my companion is Father Augustine, a Knight of the Temple. We left the King in September, travelling by ship to the coast of Provence. We did not enter a port, as we thought it prudent to avoid passing through a place sure to be closely watched—by whoever might be interested in our journey." Robin paused and Tuck picked up the thread of the story.

"We travelled as poor friars through the land of the Franks, your grace, finding occasional shelter with Frankish Templar knights along the way. As you say, some believe the French king has been intercepting messengers, and on two occasions we were stopped and questioned by men who may have been his agents. On one such occasion, Sir Robin, having a way with words, talked us through. On the other, we had to resort to more drastic measures to continue our journey."

The Queen allowed herself a half smile at that. The priest and the young knight both looked capable of knocking heads together if it came to that. Useful to note, but she had other, more pressing, issues to contemplate.

"Tell me what you saw as you passed over the frontier from King Philip's domains to our own."

"Your grace, I would advise you to look to your defences," Tuck began. "There are troop movements all along the border and they are not fortifying their positions."

"So you believe they are preparing to attack?"

"Aye, your grace. It looks that way to me."

The Queen sat quietly for a time, silently composing orders to be issued to her frontier garrisons as soon as this interview was concluded.

"Tell me your message from Richard."

"Your grace, the King wishes you to know that he will leave the Holy Land by midsummer and return to England by Christ's

Mass next," said Sir Robin, carefully reciting the memorized message. "He said you would know what to do with that information."

"That's all of it?"

"Aye, your grace."

The Queen nodded. She tried not to let her distress show. Richard needed to come home *now,* or he might have nothing to come home to. Her son's crown was hanging by a thread and this delay in his return might prove disastrous. But at least she now knew how long she would have to keep King Philip at bay and Prince John on a leash.

At present, his enemies did not know if or when Richard might appear and this would give them pause. Philip and John both feared Richard, but they would not hesitate for long. Philip would strike soon at the Vexin or directly at Normandy and John…crafty John was threatening everything back in England.

"Sir Robin, you say you are from Loxley. Where is that precisely?"

"It's a small place, your grace, in the north of Nottinghamshire, near where the borders with Yorkshire and Derbyshire come together."

"Are you returning there?"

"Aye, your grace, just as fast as I can."

Eleanor arched an eyebrow and turned to Tuck.

"And you, Father Augustine? Where are you bound?"

"Your grace, I have yet to decide. I left behind a flock in the hills of Derbyshire when the King enlisted my services. Perhaps I will return to them." The Queen nodded.

"You both go with my good wishes," she said and the two men took this as a dismissal. They bowed and turned to leave, but the Queen was not finished with them.

"Before you take your leave, I would warn you that the Midlands, including your Nottinghamshire and Derbyshire are restive these days. I get reports that John is bleeding those counties white to fill his coffers and many outside the region are all too happy to accept his generosity. My younger son seems to believe that his brother will never return from Crusade and he is…let me put this charitably…*positioning* himself for that eventuality." She paused to gauge how these men would react to her news. She could read little in their faces. Finally, Tuck spoke.

"Those that think Richard will die across the sea do not have the measure of the man, your grace."

This brought a smile to the Queen's lips.

"Well said, Father. Richard will come home, but not, you tell me, for a year. That gives his enemies a long time to make mischief. You will see when you get to the Midlands that there is mischief aplenty. There have been peasant uprisings, and I hear tales of outlaw bands attacking and robbing the gentry. You have served the King well and I tell you this so that you do not blunder into trouble upon your homecoming."

The two men stole a glance at each other. Both recognised that, with royals, little could be taken at face value. What had prompted this warning from the Queen—surely not simple concern for their welfare. What did the woman want?

"Our thanks, your grace," Sir Robin said. "We shall be on guard against any outlaws."

Eleanor frowned.

"Young man, I am not warning you about outlaws and peasants with pitchforks. For the moment I wish there were more of them in the Midlands. No, I'm warning you to be wary of those now in power there. They are not loyal to your king."

It took a moment for this news to sink in. Robin seemed stunned at the Queen's admission that there were forces in his own region aligned against the King, but Tuck was less so.

"We understand, your grace," he said, "and will tread carefully."

The Queen rose. Now there was no doubt they had been were dismissed. She watched the two leave the chamber.

Fighting men, she thought.

There would be need of such men soon, but as the new year approached, she had to wonder,—*which side would they be on?*

***

Tuck and Sir Robin walked along the icy road that led to the port of Harfleur. The wind still bit at them and a light snow had started to fall. Sir Robin was vexed.

11

"What in God's name was the woman getting at?" he groused. Tuck shook his head.

"Strange as it seems, I think she as much as invited us to join an outlaw band and oppose her younger son," Tuck offered. "Disrupt his tax collectors; keep the Prince from getting rich enough from the Midlands to buy off the rest of the country. It says much about the state of things when the Queen looks for help from a monk and a knight with but a single fief—no offense."

"None taken, but what does it matter to us if it's John or if it's Richard. After Acre, we know that Richard is a bastard. Would John be any worse?"

Tuck trudged along in silence for a long time before he answered.

"Aye, Richard's a bad man, but a strong king. From what I know, John has no scruples whatsoever. And beyond that, he's a weak man, and weak men make bad kings. With John on the throne, we would have the Franks ruling us 'fore long. I'd rather serve our own bastard, than Philip of France."

It was now Robin's turn to walk along in silence as he considered the monk's words.

Why must everything be so complicated?

"Where are the barons?" he asked, with acid in his voice. "They have the power to control the Prince, not you or I."

"That's a good question," said Tuck. "If the Queen was sure of where the main pieces on the chessboard stood, she wouldn't be talking to us pawns."

Robin snorted.

"I'll not be anyone's pawn! Queen or no, this is not my quarrel."

"Nor mine," said Tuck, "but in these times, a man may be forced to pick a side."

Robin shook his head.

"For my part, I've had enough taking of sides. I plan to settle myself in Loxley and live my life in peace."

Tuck greeted this with a deep laugh that came up from his ample belly.

"You? I think not, my friend. You are a restless man who will not be content sitting about watching crops grow."

Robin laughed in return.

"Perhaps you are right—it does sound rather boring doesn't it? But—I hope you are wrong. I've grown weary of killing men."

"Amen to that," muttered Tuck as he crossed himself.

Homecoming

The sailing cog *Sprite* ploughed into the white-capped waves barrelling out of the west toward the coast of Wales. Master Sparks had said that somewhere over the horizon there was a storm, but its only evidence here were frothy rollers and a stiff, cold December wind that made the little ship fairly fly through the water.

She had made the turn around the rocky spine of Land's End the day before, steering close to the Isles of Scilly and far out from the Cornish coast. Sparks had warned them that pirates infested these waters and might sally out from any of the many inlets that pocked the shoreline. Boda, the first mate, went about his duties, but kept a suspicious eye on the land to starboard and all hands kept their weapons close.

No enemy ventured out to meet them and for another day they sailed north into the Irish Sea toward Wales, the River Dee and home. If the winds held, they would arrive at the mouth of the river on the day before Christ's Mass. It would be a good time to make a homecoming.

Roland Inness leaned on the port railing as the little ship plunged down one roller and up the next. He gazed off to the northwest.

"Ireland is just over the horizon, Dec. Do you ever think of going back?" He directed his question to the stocky young man beside him.

Declan O'Duinne leaned on the rail and lifted his eyes to the horizon, the sharp wind sending his long untended red hair into new tangles behind him.

"Aye, I do. I wonder if my father still lives—and my two brothers."

Roland turned from the horizon to look at his friend.

"Brothers?" In all their years together, Declan had spoken often of his father, but never of brothers.

"Aye, I'm the youngest. I suppose when Father offered me up for service as squire to Sir Roger, he felt he had sufficient heirs to pass his lands to. No need for another spare."

Roland stared at the Irishman, trying to gauge his mood, but could read little in his expression.

"But still...you must wonder," he offered.

Declan turned and smiled. "Aye, I do. I'd like to see them again, though Fagan and Keiran used to beat me regularly."

Roland smiled back.

"And now?"

Declan slowly shook his head.

"Two years training with Alwyn Madawc and two more fighting Saracens? I would invite them to try!"

Roland looked down at the foam surging past the bow of the *Sprite*.

I'd put no money on Fagan and Keiran O'Duinne in that fight.

"And what of yer brother and sister, Roland?"

This was a question he had wrestled with when first he learned he would be going home. He was bound to the de Lavals by oath, but by more than oath. Sir Roger de Laval had truly saved his life when it had hung by a hair. But he had obligations to his own blood as well. Those obligations had long gone unmet.

"Dec, I spoke with Sir Roger before we left. He gave me leave to find them and bring them back to Shipbrook—after we take tidings of him to Lady Catherine. It's been nigh three years. It's time I went for them. Oren will be thirteen now and Lorea near six. I doubt the girl will even know me."

"Aye, yer brother—he would be near the same age you were when ye took that blasted deer on Kinder Scout."

Roland shook his head. Years had slipped by since the day he had killed that deer and brought down destruction on his own family. The events of that day had ripped apart the life he had known high in the mountains of Derbyshire. With his father murdered, he had fled to survive, leaving behind his younger kin. Thanks to Friar Tuck, they were sheltered by the church, but leaving them had left an empty place inside him. It was time he looked to his own.

"For now, we are bound to follow the King's command and get his message to the Queen. We have already taken liberties with our orders by coming all the way round to the Dee to make landfall, but we are bound by Sir Roger's commands as well. I doubt the King would begrudge us a detour to take news of him to his family."

"And a detour avoids whoever has been intercepting the King's couriers—we hope."

"Aye, that too."

"And after we deliver our message?" asked Declan.

"Then I will get me to the priory up Yorkshire way where Tuck says the children have been sheltered. When we get to Shipbrook, I will ask Lady Catherine if I may bring my brother and sister back there. Sir Roger has given me leave to do so, but I think it must be her decision."

"Lady Catherine will agree—of that, I'm sure," said Declan.

Roland nodded.

"I can't think of a better place for them to make a home than Shipbrook."

***

Dawn was still an hour away as the *Sprite* heeled to starboard and entered the broad estuary of the River Dee. It was the eve of Christ's Mass and a cold fog hung just above the water. Barren mud flats could be seen closer to shore, and Boda was quietly calling the depths back to Master Sparks at the helm. True to his word, the master of the good ship *Sprite* had brought Roland Inness and Declan O'Duinne safe home.

"The channel looks clear for a ways, lads, but ye'll need to take the skiff 'fore long."

"Aye, Master Sparks," Roland called back. "Let's not ground the *Sprite* at the end of such a grand voyage. I think we are close enough now."

"Drop anchor, Mr. Boda!" Sparks commanded.

Boda heaved the anchor over the side and made sure the ship was fast, then joined Sparks and the two young knights at the stern. One of the crew had pulled the tow line in and the skiff bobbed in the current just below. Sparks clasped the hand of each of his passengers in turn and spoke with his usual bluff good humour.

"Home in time for Christ's Mass! Ye lads have been too long gone from yer own hearths. When next ye need passage on a good ship, ye may find us at the port of Dover. We'll be refittin' the *Sprite* there over the winter."

Roland looked at the two men who had shared so many dangers and hardships with them on the journey to the Holy Land and back.

"Master Sparks, no matter what feats of seamanship others may boast of in my presence, I will silence them with an account of my days on the *Sprite*."

Declan reached out and offered his hand to the first mate.

"Master Boda...I thought ye an evil looking man on first meeting, and I'll confess ye look no less evil upon repeat viewing, but I count ye as a true friend and a brave one. I hope that our paths may cross again." In the dim light it was hard to tell, but Roland was sure both men's eyes had gone misty.

It was time to go.

The two men tossed their kit into the skiff. Roland had on his mail and a sword strapped to his belt. Over his shoulder was the longbow given him by Sir Robin of Loxley. Declan wore a sleeveless mail coat and carried a long broadsword at his waist. The ragged vestiges of the Shipbrook tunic, with rampant stag, hung from his shoulders. The garment had faded from black to brown and the stag was a dingy grey, but at least it had survived. Roland's tunic had been chewed by rats in the Crusader camp until it had to be discarded.

Roland grabbed the tow rope and walked backwards down the side of the Sprite until he alighted in the smaller boat. Declan followed a moment later. A crewman already sat at the oars, waiting to ferry them to shore.

"Godspeed!" a hushed voice called from above.

"Fair sailing to all aboard the *Sprite*," Roland called back and cast off the line. The man at the oars gave a strong pull and with just a few strokes they passed alongside the little cog and headed upstream. From his seat in the stern, Roland twisted around to watch the ship that had taken him to war and brought him back home again. In less than a minute, it vanished into the mists.

He turned forward and could clearly see the dark outline of Declan sitting in the bow, though his friend's face was in shadow. The Irishman watched the channel ahead, taking care to keep them in the main course of the Dee. If they wandered off into one of the smaller tributaries that emptied into the estuary, it could take hours to find their way back out.

For a long time they saw nothing but wide mudflats on either side, but then, through the mist, thick reed beds began to appear. The sky was growing lighter ahead of them. They rowed toward a pale blue dawn.

***

An hour of hard pulling against the current brought them to a ford where an ancient trail crossed the Dee from England into Wales. Roland had the oarsman drive the bow of the skiff hard in among the reeds on the northern bank. They hopped out onto the marshy path and their few possessions were quickly passed forward. Their kit secured, they shoved the little boat back into the river. The crewman from the *Sprite* expertly turned the bow downstream and disappeared on the current.

Roland looked around him. This ford was where he had once killed a Welsh raider hidden in the reeds on the far bank. Could it have been over two years since he trailed Millie de Laval into Wales? He shook his head. By his best count, he'd be seventeen in the spring. He felt much older than that.

After the awful chaos and death of the Crusades, it would be easy to forget that this borderland was still a dangerous place.

Looking across the water at the opposite bank, he stopped to string his bow. Declan gave him a curious look, but his own hand fell absently to the hilt of his broadsword.

The two gathered their kit and headed up the track that led to higher ground and to Shipbrook. Roland slung the longbow over one shoulder and over the other he carried his bedroll and a sack with the rest of his belongings. As they trudged along in the spreading glow of the sunrise, he looked about him.

The path up from the ford was pocked with small puddles covered in a thin coating of ice. The trees were bare and the fields were brown, but even in the dead of winter he could recall how green this land became in the spring. It caused a lump in his throat after his years in the barren and unforgiving hills of Palestine. He had been raised in the peaks of Derbyshire, but the marshlands and low rolling countryside of Cheshire felt like home to him now. He quickened his pace.

Looking down he saw scattered hoof prints in the spongy ground. Few riders had used the ford in recent days it seemed.

"I wonder if Sir Alwyn is still dispatching patrols twice a day to keep watch," Roland said as they hurried along.

"We'll know soon enough," Declan replied. "I wonder what the Master of the Sword will think when he finds we are knights!"

Roland laughed.

"He'll probably put us directly on patrol duty so that we don't forget our place!"

It was full daylight when they crested a rise and saw Shipbrook before them.

Everything about the scene was wrong.

The open fields that surrounded the place had been long untended. Nothing moved on the walls of the little fortress and the gate hung half open at an odd angle. A small wisp of smoke rose from somewhere inside.

Fear twisted his gut and he heard Declan whisper a quiet oath beside him. Two years of bitter war had taught them the look of trouble. It also taught them to be cautious. Roland knew they should not rush in, should scout the place first, should have a plan.

A plan be damned.

19

He dropped his kit and started forward at a run. Declan did the same. Twenty yards from the gate they slowed. Declan drew his sword and Roland slipped an arrow from his quiver. The gate was smashed, but still hung drunkenly from its top hinge. They eased through it.

Inside, the roof of the great house was gone, burned along with all of the wooden structures within the walls. The livestock were gone, but five horses were in a pen next to the eastern wall. A man, dressed in mail, was just mounting one of the horses and four others were gathered around a cook pot near the well at the centre of the cobbled courtyard. The mounted man saw them first.

"You there! Stop where ye are!" He spurred his horse out of the pen and toward them. His fellows scrambled to grab helmets and swords. The rider reined in just short of running them down and lowered a lance until it pointed at Declan's chest.

"Drop yer weapons and state yer business here!" the man ordered.

Roland glanced at Declan and gave him a nod. The Irishman opened his arms wide and broke into a broad smile as he took a step forward. The man on horseback did not expect this and hesitated. That was a mistake.

In a blur, Declan grasped the tip of the lance and yanked backwards tumbling the rider to the cobbles. The horse reared and fled back toward the pen, scattering the other four men who had started for the gate. Declan, still smiling, took another step forward and kicked the fallen rider in the head, halting his efforts to get to his feet.

The other men-at-arms, more cautious now, slowed their advance and fanned out. Roland nocked his arrow and drew the longbow. One man had a heavy shield and he sent the arrow in his direction. The arrow pierced the inch-thick oak and its tip broke the skin just above the man's heart. He yelped as though he had been struck by a serpent. Roland drew another arrow from his quiver, but before he could nock it, the man with the shield threw down his weapons and raised his hands.

Roland swung his bow toward the three men who were still armed. For a moment they hesitated, but they had no shields.

One-by-one, they let their swords and lances fall to the ground. Roland spoke to the man who was rubbing his chest where the arrow had pricked him.

"Where is the master of this place—what happened here?"

The man stood sullenly and seemed disinclined to answer until Declan sheathed his sword and drew forth a curved dagger—a memento of his time in the east. As he stepped closer, the man found his tongue.

"The Earl has ownership of this ruin. It was taken in the spring from a family of traitors."

"Traitors?" Roland snarled. "Shipbrook is no home to traitors! You say you are garrisoned here by the Earl of Chester? You are Lord Ranulf's men?"

"Not Ranulf," the man said, still trying to stop the trickle of blood from his chest. "It was him that was the traitor. He fled here when they come to arrest him. Some say he went to Wales. If he did, he's dead by now, I reckon."

Roland struck the man with the back of his hand, knocking him to the ground. Declan laid a hand on his friend's shoulder, but Roland jerked away, dragging the man to his feet.

"What of the folk whose keep this was? What of them?" he demanded.

The man flinched, but answered readily enough.

"Don't know nuthin' about that. We was just sent out here a fortnight ago...told to watch the ford. Our lord says we are to be on the lookout should the trait...." He stopped and started again. ...should Earl Ranulf come back this way."

This was wrong—all wrong.

Roland tightened his grip on the man.

"If the Earl of Chester is not your lord, then who is?" Roland demanded.

The man looked surprised by the question.

"We serve the Earl of Derby, sir. Lord William de Ferrers now rules in Chester."

21

Requiem for a Welshman

*T*he prisoners were bound and left by the well while Roland and Declan surveyed what was left of Shipbrook. Roland walked up the steps to the entrance of the great house. What remained of the roof timbers had collapsed into the cellar. Nothing was left standing but the walls, which were still charred black from the flames.

It felt like his world had been turned on its head. He had followed his master and his king to the Crusade and had returned to find his home burnt, his master's family missing or dead, and his mortal enemy triumphant. He wondered if there had ever been a more bitter homecoming.

"Sir!" Roland flinched as a shout startled him from his grim thoughts.

An old man had come through the gate and was walking toward them with an odd jerky gait. The newcomer stopped cold when he saw the five men bound by the well, then made as though to back quickly out the way he had come. With a shock, Roland recognised him as one of the swineherds that had been part of the Shipbrook household. As the man hurried back toward the gate, he tried to recall his name.

"Sigbert?" he called out, uncertainly.

The old man stopped in his tracks and turned to stare at the tall man standing in chain mail among the ashes of Shipbrook. There was something vaguely familiar there, but he could not place this person. It took him aback that a stranger knew his name. He finally spoke.

"Sir, I come to complain about the theft of a hog, but none of this lot," he jerked a thumb toward the men tied up on the ground, "know me by name. Who are ye, then?"

"Sigbert, come closer," Roland said gently. "Your old eyes have grown dim. Do you not know me?"

The old man crept forward cautiously. In truth, his eyes were not what they once were, so he had to squint at the man who had called to him. The fellow was a warrior, no doubt. His mail and sword marked him as fighting man. He looked oddly dark for a man in the dead of winter, as though burned brown by a sun stronger than any in England. He crept very close now and noticed the longbow slung over the warrior's back. It took another moment to register.

"My God. My God. Is it you? Is it Roland Inness?"

"Aye Sigbert, I've come home."

The old man began to weep and shake. He reached for Roland's arm to steady himself. He tried to speak but only wracking sobs came forth. Finally he gathered himself.

"They burned…they burned it all…all," he managed. "It was in the spring, lord, just about the time the piglets come," he said and wiped a dirty sleeve under his nose.

"And the ladies de Laval?" Roland forced himself to ask. "Are they here...among the ashes?"

"No, no, lord, they've fled…I know not where. Men came in the night. I heard later that Earl Ranulf sought refuge here and was pursued by a nobleman from Derbyshire. We was told to run into the woods. The Earl and the ladies rode out on horseback, last I seen them. Then the men came and torched Shipbrook, sir. I watched from the trees. They burned it!" He began to weep again.

Roland thought his knees might buckle. Lady Catherine and Millie had not died here!

Thank you, God…

Declan, who had been poking around on the far side of the courtyard, joined them.

"Sigbert! You're still alive?"

"Oh, lord. It is Master O'Duinne," the old man said and began to whimper again, but even as he wept his eyes swept around the ruins of Shipbrook, searching.

"Sir Roger?"

"He lives, Sigbert, but remains with King Richard. I am thankful he has not seen this..." Declan gestured at the ruins. Sigbert began to sob once more.

Roland grabbed Declan's arm.

"The ladies—they live! Sigbert says they fled with Earl Ranulf." Declan's face, which had been mournful since first sighting Shipbrook, lit up and tears came to his eyes. He wiped them away with a sleeve.

"God does answers some prayers," he said and sniffed.

Roland turned once more to the old man and pressed him for more information.

"Sigbert, you have been most helpful, but stop crying. Try to think. Which way might Lady Catherine have gone?"

"Lord, I don't know, but I'm told there was a fight down at the ford that night. Three days later, I seen a large band of knights come out of the west, riding hard toward Chester. I think it was the men what burned our place. They and their horses looked to have been roughly treated."

Roland considered Sigbert's account. If trouble had come from up the Chester road, there were but few directions the people of Shipbrook could flee—but into Wales? They must have been desperate to chance it.

"Sigbert, are many of you left? Those who did not flee with Lady Catherine?"

"Aye Lord. Three dozen families that I know of and a few strays—some of the men-at-arms that survived the fight at the ford. It has been hard. There have been none to protect us and we've been left with little to live on. What shall we do?"

Roland reached into his tunic and withdrew the money pouch given him by the King's clerk at his departure from the Holy Land. He withdrew a handful of coins.

"Take this and do what you can for the Shipbrook folk. I will be back with Lady Catherine, but God knows when."

The old man began to weep softly again.

"Thank ye, my lord. You were a kind boy and now…"

"Tell the people that we will rebuild Shipbrook. Have faith. And Sigbert…I'm a knight and only newly made. I'm no lord."

Sigbert looked him up and down.

"But you look like one, my lord."

***

They saddled the two best horses and turned the other three over to Sigbert's care. The old man went bouncing off on one of the mounts, leading the other two by a rope. Once he was well clear, Declan cut the bonds of the five prisoners. Their weapons had been tossed down the well.

"It's a long walk to Chester, lads, so I'd be on my way," he said. The men needed no urging. They scrambled out the gate and down the road to the east. Roland and Declan mounted and rode out of the ruined fortress to fetch their kits where they had left them by the woods.

"And where are we to go now, Sir Roland? To find the Queen—as we've been commanded?"

Roland looked at his friend and shook his head.

"We are Sir Roger's men first. We must look to his interests."

Declan nodded and the two spurred their horses into a quick trot and headed west toward the ford—and Wales. As they rode, Roland brooded over the ruin of Shipbrook and the fate of the de Lavals. There had been nothing but evil tidings since they set foot back in England.

De Ferrers! How could the Earl of Derby act with such impunity here in Cheshire and why would Earl Ranulf seek refuge at Shipbrook? There were questions that needed to be answered.

As they reached the ford, he recalled his first crossing of the Dee in pursuit of Millie's abductors. The man who had waylaid him that day was long dead and no one challenged them as they splashed across the river and up the opposite bank. They had just reached dry ground when a shout came from the north side of the Dee.

"Wait!"

The two knights wheeled their horses around to see a rider splash into the ford. He was mounted on one of the three horses they had given to Sigbert. He wore a helmet and carried a spear. There was a rampant white stag on the faded tunic he wore. Roland hailed him.

"I see you wear the arms of de Laval. Those are our arms as well."

The man reined in his horse in midstream and looked hard at the two men on the bank above him.

"Sigbert said ye claimed to be Sir Roger's squires, but the old man can barely see his pigs, so I put no stock in his testimony. It's been two years gone now and neither our lord, nor his squires have returned from the Holy Land. And you two don't much favour Inness and O'Duinne. I knew those boys."

Roland shrugged his shoulders.

"We are knights now—and boys no longer. It's been a hard few years."

The man removed his helmet and looked at Roland more closely. He got a shrewd smile on his face.

"Very well, I put this question to whichever of you claims to be Roland Inness. Lady Millicent once had you dress for a costume party as a jest. Surely you would remember what you wore that night?

Roland laughed. It had been such a humiliation.

"She had me dress as a stag—but you will recall there was no party. I was the only one actually in costume and you were among those who had a good laugh at my expense. Is that how you remember it, Baldric?" When the man had removed his helmet, Roland recognised him as one of Sir Roger's men-at-arms.

The rider in the stream lowered his spear.

"By the livin' God, it's you!" He turned and looked hard at Declan. "And you as well!" He then looked past the two men on the bank. "Sir Roger—has he come home?" Declan shook his head sadly.

"No, Baldric. He remains with the King, but we've been sent home. Now what happened here? Sigbert's tale gave us little to go on."

The man spurred his horse out of the river and onto the bank. They all dismounted and Baldric told his story.

"It was in the middle of the night, in the spring. Lady Millicent shows up at the keep with Lord Ranulf in tow. I later heard she helped him flee from the Earl of Derby's men when they took Chester by surprise. Lady Constance is charged with treason, and there is a warrant for Earl Ranulf's arrest—on the same charge."

Roland held up a hand.

"How did Lady Millicent come to be with the Earl—in the middle of the night?"

"Oh, a year or more ago she had gone to be lady-in-waiting to the Earl's wife. When Earl William's men swooped down on the city, it's said the Little Lady helped get Earl Ranulf away before he was caught. She brung him here, to Shipbrook, but they were pursued. We all had to flee. Our party made it to right here at the ford 'fore they caught us."

The man seemed reluctant to go on.

"Tell us what happened at the ford, Baldric." Roland said quietly, though he was not sure he wanted to hear.

"Sir Alwyn sent the ladies and the Earl on ahead. We held 'em here fer nigh an hour. Killed a fair number and lost some of our own. But there were too many. They drove us into the reeds, then passed on by—after Lady Catherine and the Earl. Three days later they come back through—moving fast. But there was only half as many and a few had wounds. They had no one with them. I think they ran into the Welsh!"

"Lady Millicent and Sir Alwyn—they were with Lady Catherine and the Earl?"

The man cast his eyes down.

"Aye, Lady Millicent was with them. She knew the way into the hills." He stopped.

"And Alwyn? What of Alwyn, Baldric?"

Tears came to the man's eyes, but he was determined not to falter.

"It was right where you now stand, Master Inness. Sir Alwyn stood there with his axe. They came at him again and again and he slew many of them. None of their knights would face him at the end, but…they had…crossbows." The man spit into the mud on the bank. "He died a warrior's death." Baldric had to stop and gather himself.

"After they'd passed on by, Cearl and I carried him up to the high ground yonder and buried him. We didn't know what to do after that, with everyone scattered or dead, so we went home."

Declan snarled a curse. Roland felt hot tears come to his own eyes. *Alwyn Madawc—dead!* There seemed no end to the evil news. He rubbed away the tears with the back of his hand.

"Baldric, show us where you laid him."

***

A quarter mile on, the trail emerged from the reeds and climbed a low bluff. At the top, a few yards off to the side of the muddy track, was a pile of stones. Roland knew that the men who had placed those stones must have ranged far from the river banks to gather them. There was a rude cross at one end of the grave that was tilted. Declan carefully straightened it and secured the base with more stones.

"Was he a Christian?" Roland asked. He had never seen the man at chapel services during his time at Shipbrook.

"Aye, he was, in his own way," said Baldric. "He never felt at ease with all the praisin' that went on at chapel, but he was a regular visitor to confession. He'd come back from tellin' the priest his latest sins with the ladies and say 'Baldric, the slate is clean,' and he'd wink at me. I think the priest enjoyed those sessions as much as Sir Alwyn."

The two young knights smiled at each other through misty eyes as they stood over Alwyn's grave. Declan straightened himself and began to sing in his clear voice. It was in Gaelic, but there was no mistaking a hymn.

> *Nuair thronaileas mo chairdean*
> *'S an uaigh 'g am charah sios*
> *Bidh 'n uaigh 'n a leabaidh thamh dhomh*
> *Gus an la an tig thu ris*

When he had finished, the Irishman turned to Roland.

"Ye've sworn a blood oath against William de Ferrers have ye not?"

"Aye."

"I swear the same."

Roland nodded and turned to Baldric.

"We go into Wales to bring back Lady Catherine and Lady Millicent." He gave the man a few coins. "How many of you survived the fight at the ford?"

"About a dozen and a half, sir."

"Have them ready when we return."

"Ready, sir?"

"Aye, armed—and ready to fight."

Christ's Mass Eve

illicent de Laval found shelter from the pelting rain in the rough timber guard tower that sat at one corner of the ancient hill fort. She had fled the smoky warmth of the rude log hall at the centre of the enclosure where celebrations on the eve of Christ's Mass were already underway. There were too many people and too much good cheer for her mood. She needed to move and release some of her pent-up energy.

The rain had started as she walked the perimeter of the earthen walls, but now it was mixed with sleet and driven by a cold wind howling down from the mountains to the west. The tower was a welcome refuge.

The Welshman who stood guard there simply nodded at her and kept watch on the valley below. He had become used to the young English woman climbing up into the tower and taking a look about. She came almost every day, though he was surprised to see her in these conditions.

Millicent looked out across the valley below the fort and saw that the bottom of the narrow gap in the hills was shrouded in an icy fog. An army could be moving down there and be invisible from this tower.

"Not much to see, my lady." The voice came from behind her. She turned to see that it was the master of this little outpost in the wilderness—Lord Llywelyn. He gave the guard a hand gesture and the man left them alone.

"There never seems to be," she replied. Her Welsh had improved markedly in the time she had spent among these people, but in any language, her frustration was plain.

Eight long months had passed since she had helped the Earl of Chester escape arrest on trumped-up charges of treason. Her mother had proven the de Laval's loyalty to Earl Ranulf by abandoning Shipbrook and fleeing with the nobleman as his enemies approached. That loyalty had cost them their home, burned by William de Ferrers' men, but that was not the most painful loss. Weeks later, Llywelyn's spies brought word of Sir Alwyn Madawc's death at the Dee ford.

The news struck them like a physical blow. It sent her and her mother into a long, bleak time of mourning, made worse by a gnawing sense of guilt that the man had died so they might live. Sir Alwyn had been more than simply her father's Master of the Sword and oldest friend. Lady Catherine loved him like a brother and Millicent...she had thought Alwyn Madawc would live forever.

That April had brought them calamity, and their only hope of undoing it lay in restoring Earl Ranulf to his rightful place in Cheshire. That would require support from the Queen. Only she could expunge the charges of treason against the man and she would need evidence to do that—evidence that only Millicent could provide.

But here she stood in the wilderness of Wales and the Queen remained across the Channel—unaware that Ranulf was even alive. Christ's Mass was upon them and they remained fugitives, while William de Ferrers occupied the city of Chester. It left a bitter taste that had grown no sweeter as the months passed.

Hearing the note of despair in the girl's voice, the young Welsh prince sought to comfort her.

"We can try again to get you into Rhyl and find you passage by ship, my lady," Llywelyn said, but Millicent could hear the lack of conviction in his voice. The man was in rebellion against his kinsmen who ruled northern Wales, and was almost as much of a fugitive as she was.

Three times they had tried to slip through the patrols mounted by his uncle, Roderic, who ruled the coastal plain, and three times they had been forced to turn back. Llywelyn might be gaining strength in the backcountry, but she had long ago concluded he had not the power to get her and the Earl safely out of Wales.

By now, everyone of note on both sides of the frontier knew that Earl Ranulf was charged with treason and had disappeared into the wild borderland. Some thought him dead and others thought him a prisoner, held for ransom. Capturing the Earl would bring a rich reward to whoever delivered him up to Prince John. While it had been William de Ferrers who put Ranulf to flight, all assumed that the Earl of Derby had acted as the Prince's cat's-paw.

The danger of having Earl Ranulf fall into the John's hands was too great to risk further attempts toward the coast. So they had remained, cooped up here in the relative safety of a remote hill fort—*waiting*. As winter set in, the weather had matched the girl's gloom.

Millicent found it curious that Llywelyn chose to hide them and not sell the Earl to the English, but the man was clever. He might be young, but he had grown up in a world of intrigue and violence and had survived. She could only guess that, when he weighed the advantages, making a disgraced Marcher Lord his ally served his purposes more than the Prince's gold.

Llywelyn waited for some response from Millicent and wasn't surprised when none came. He had come to know this English girl well in their months together. She was stubborn and headstrong, but smart. She was also growing into her beauty—a fact she was not fully aware of.

"Come back to the hall, my lady. You'll catch a fever staying out in this weather—and I would not want to lose you."

Millicent stayed silent. She knew the Welsh rebel leader found her fair, but he was not seeking a wife, particularly not one of her low rank, and she would be no tumble in the hay for him, or any man. And even had his intentions been honourable, she was in no mood for dalliance. Her home was burned, her father was…God only knew where, and her liege lord was branded a traitor.

Llywelyn might be handsome, but he was young—hardly older than her father's squires—and full of the bravado that young men seemed to have in such abundance. It did not impress her. For Millicent, he was a means to an end—and a means that had, thus far, failed her. Finally she broke her silence.

"Very well, my lord," she said, and took his arm. As he led her back to the hall, he started up his usual teasing banter, but she hardly registered his words. She had come to a decision. The time was now to take matters into her own hands.

***

By the flickering light of the small fireplace, Millicent drew forth her dagger and began to cut away the strands of her long dark hair. There could be no turning back now. The eve of Christ's Mass would be the perfect opportunity. Most of the men in the hill fort would be drunk by now and the rain and sleet had blown through, leaving only a dense fog in the valley. There was now a bright moon in the sky, and she would use its light to guide her on her path. Conditions that were ideal tonight could be gone tomorrow. It was time to act.

To her, the facts were plain. The cordon was simply too tight to risk having the Earl captured trying to get out of Wales. The man was the most notable fugitive in the land and would be a prize of enormous value to whoever might take him. And if the Earl were taken, then the game was truly up.

But she was not notable and, with luck, she could slip through where Earl Ranulf could not. It was risky, but it was her testimony, more than his, that would hold sway with the Queen. After all, she was the Queen's agent, sent to spy on the man by Eleanor herself.

She had overheard the Earl's wife being suborned into treason by the priest Malachy and knew that it was none of the Earl's doing. No doubt, a quite different picture had been presented to the Queen by Prince John and William de Ferrers, but she had to have faith that Eleanor would believe her account of events.

Months ago she had suggested the idea to her mother, but Lady Catherine had instantly forbidden it. Nor would the Earl consent to such a plan. His pride had already been too severely injured to endure the prospect of being saved a second time by the girl who had helped him escape Chester.

So she was resolved to defy her mother and to go in secret. What other choice did she have? With escape out of the question for the Earl, she would make this journey alone, but by which path?

The three attempts to get Earl Ranulf to the northwest coast to take ship for Normandy had all come to naught. The roads in that direction were just too closely watched. To the south, Prince John had allies among the other Marcher Lords, blocking the path to the ports there. The southern route would also take her through the greater part of Wales and, while she spoke a good deal of the language now, she could not pass as a native. And she well knew, the Welsh were suspicious of strangers.

No, the way out was back the way they had come—back to the Dee ford, back through Cheshire and then to Watling Street and on to London. It was risky. De Ferrers controlled Cheshire, but she knew every hidden path a horse might take through that country. If she could cross the ford of the Dee without challenge, she could make it.

Perhaps the Queen would have returned from Normandy by the time she reached London, but if not, she would travel on to Southampton or Dover and find a ship. She had dipped into the small money bag her mother had brought from Shipbrook and could afford passage.

Since a girl travelling alone would draw far more interest than she wanted, she would do her best to pass as a boy. She would dress like one and could certainly ride like one. With a final stroke of her dagger, the last of her long hair fell to the floor. She knew she would not pass close inspection, but she did not plan to let anyone get close enough to reveal her secret.

Her preparations complete, Millicent settled down to wait for the sounds of the drunken Christ's Mass eve feasting to end. She knew it would be well after midnight.

***

The songs and merriment that filled the winter night had fallen silent when Millicent made her way from her room to the muddy courtyard inside the earthen walls of the hill fort. She was dressed in her riding breeches and a hooded cloak and carried a small bundle of necessaries. Strapped to her hip was a short sword. It was a weapon she had practiced with, but she hoped her skills would not be put to the test.

The moon was bright enough to cast shadows as she made her way across the deserted courtyard to the paddock where the horses were kept. It pained her that she could not take her bay mare, but such a well-bred horse would draw far too much attention on her journey. Instead she saddled one of the tough little Welsh ponies and led the animal toward the north wall. The watchtower would be manned, even on this night, but she knew the guard up there would be looking out on the valley, not back into the fort.

There was no gate in the north wall, but there was a spot where the natural drainage of the hillside had eroded away the earthen embankment, collapsing a small section of the wooden palisade. Soil from the wall had partially filled the ditch beyond. It was a steep climb up and down, but no barrier to a Welsh pony. She scrambled up through the cut in the wall and the pony followed without protest.

She started forward, keeping to the natural depression formed by the drainage channel. At any moment she expected a challenge from the guard, but none came. In a few breathless minutes she made it into the welcoming cover of the fog that always blanketed the valley floor. Quietly she mounted the pony. The road led off into the grey mist that shone like silver in the bright moonlight. Around a bend just ahead, the road branched with a path turning off to the east. She leaned forward and whispered in the pony's ear.

"Take me home, girl."

Return of the Bowman

William de Ferrers nodded toward the hulking man who stood across the dimly lit chamber. The man had been waiting for some signal from the nobleman. He was not used to having such high-born spectators when he practiced his craft. He stolidly returned the nod then swung the knotted whip in his hand. It landed with a sickening wet crack against the bare back of a man bound by chains to the far wall. The man screamed and the whip whistled in the air once more.

After a half dozen strokes, the Earl of Derby raised his hand to halt the beating and turned to the man beside him—a priest who watched the proceedings with a touch of disdain.

"Malachy, question this man again. If he has nothing useful to offer, I want him hung beside the Northgate—and leave him there till he rots. His village lies north of here, does it not? When the folk from that village come to market, I want them to see that thieves who assault my tax collectors will not be tolerated!"

"Aye, my lord," the priest answered. He watched as his master departed the dungeon. They had only been in Chester for a week and this would be the third hanging. He shook his head. It was the eve of Christ's Mass and perhaps not the best time for a fresh execution. It was certain to put a damper on what little holiday joy there was in the occupied city.

The killing itself did not trouble him, but torture, no matter its effectiveness, revolted him. As a boy, he had watched his own father whipped to death by the English soldiers who had sacked their town in Ireland. All to make the man reveal the whereabouts of a treasure they did not have.

That day had set him on a course that was fuelled by hate. It was a fuel that he never found in short supply and one valued by his current employers, the French. No, he was happy to kill Englishmen, but not like this.

The man being whipped had, of course, gibbered nonsense to stop the pain, but it was obvious he had nothing of interest to confess. He had struck a tax collector who had taken the family's only pig. The Earl seemed to see these petty acts of violence as a personal insult, but Malachy saw only that men will fight before they will let their families starve. It worried him that de Ferrers could not see this.

All of his careful plans to strengthen the nobleman's position, and through him the position of Prince John, could be undone if there was an outright rebellion in the Midlands. And he feared that conditions were becoming ripe for a true revolt in the region. All that was needed was a spark, but the Earl of Derby was blind to the danger. It vexed him that he had to work this hard to save these English fools from themselves, but for that very reason, he could see why King Philip wanted these men to rule in England.

He wondered, for not the first time, what de Ferrers and Prince John would think if they knew that agents in the pay of France were working furiously on their behalf? These musings always reached the same conclusion. *They wouldn't care*—as long as they gained their ambitions. The man with the whip gestured toward the bound prisoner—his way of asking if he should continue his work.

"Hang him," Malachy ordered and walked out of the chamber.

He did not return immediately to his quarters in Chester Castle—he wanted to breathe fresh air after the time he'd spent in the bowels of the building. He found his way to the passage that led to the city walls and out into the cold of the December afternoon.

Christ's Mass was now upon them and he reminded himself that he would have to practice the words of the mass he was expected to say on that occasion. He was no priest, but pretences must be maintained and after three years of passing as a man of God, he did not want to get complacent. By now, de Ferrers must suspect he was no churchman, but the Earl never challenged his clerical status. It was a status that opened doors the Earl wanted him to enter, and the man recognised the value of that.

The past year had seen his plans progress more quickly than he had dared hope. News had arrived in the autumn of Earl Robert's death on the walls of Acre and no time had been wasted in formally investing the Earl's son with the titles and powers that went with his birth right.

Prince John had come to rely heavily on the new Earl of Derby to squeeze the revenues from the Midlands to fill his coffers. De Ferrers now directly controlled both Derbyshire and Cheshire and Prince John had suggested that one of the Earl's own vassals might be appointed to replace the current Sheriff of Nottingham. This would give his master a near stranglehold on the region—and de Ferrers knew how to squeeze.

The funds that flowed in allowed the Prince to buy the loyalty of barons in other parts of the realm—loyalty that would someday be called upon to secure John the throne. The fate of the Earl of Chester—branded a traitor and now a fugitive or dead—was an object lesson to those barons who remained stubbornly loyal to Richard. It was Malachy's greatest triumph.

But the victory had not been complete. Earl Ranulf should have been caught and executed by now, but somehow the man had escaped and disappeared into Wales. There had been nothing but rumours since then. Most thought the Earl had died at the hands of the Welsh. Malachy wasn't so sure. He preferred to have a body and a head to put on a pike outside the gates of Chester. The failure rankled, and de Ferrers was happy to remind him of it.

But today was not a day to dwell on failures. This very morning he had received a message from the man who commanded his own loyalty—the Bishop of Beauvais, King Philip's cousin and spymaster. The network of agents the man controlled had England teetering on the brink of outright civil war and the French king was pleased. The Bishop had extended his personal congratulations to Malachy for his success in the Midlands.

The priest broke off his reverie. He was absently walking along the rampart of the old Roman walls that still circled Chester and had come to a spot where workmen were completing repairs on a crumbled section. He smiled with satisfaction.

Failure to look to the defences of the town had cost Earl Ranulf dearly and he would not let Earl William make the same mistake. Repairs to damaged parts of the wall were almost complete and he had installed loyal men to command the garrison. No enemy would swoop down and take Chester by surprise, as they themselves had done to Ranulf.

Content with his efforts to protect what they had won, he found his way from the outer walls back to the castle and into the keep. As soon as he entered the main hall he heard a harsh voice.

"Malachy! Where have you been hiding?" William de Ferrers had just entered the front entrance of the hall and was trailed by a rather dishevelled looking man-at-arms. The young Earl moved with his usual coiled energy, but his voice carried a note of unusual urgency. He thrust the man forward.

"Tell the priest what you saw."

The man bowed his head to Malachy and began to breathlessly tell his tale.

"We was sent out to watch over the ford of the Dee a fortnight ago and seen nuthin' worth reportin' till this morning. We was breakin' our fast, when these two brigands come upon us unawares. We'd a had 'em proper, but the one, the tall one, had a bow. Never seen the like of it. Shot an arrow right through Thomas' shield, he did. Never seen the like of it."

"You said that!" the Earl blurted. "Get on with the rest."

The man flinched, but resumed his story.

"They took our weapons. Throwed 'em down the well. Said they was lookin' for the folk who lived there. We didn't know nuthin' about that. By and by, they let us go. I found a broken down horse and rode here as fast as it would carry me. The other of my men are still walking. That's my report," he concluded, then turned back to the Earl. "Forgive me, Lord William, but they come out of nowhere. One tall and dark and t'other russet-haired. They was fightin' men to be sure."

William de Ferrers paid no attention to the man's pathetic apologies. He had Malachy fixed in his gaze.

"He is back. Only a longbow could penetrate an oaken shield."

The priest knew in an instant what his master meant. He had first learned of de Ferrers' obsession with a particular young squire and his longbow when they had travelled to London for the Queen's reception a year ago. He understood that this Inness boy had won the King's archery tournament, but had never been told why the Earl feared him so. It was unseemly that a noble of his rank should spare a passing thought to such an insignificant personage, but this boy clearly haunted the man.

While in London, de Ferrers had been eager to approach the daughter of the boy's master. Malachy had advised against it, but had been ignored. Whatever the de Laval girl had said about this Inness boy had left him agitated for days. But the boy was gone off on Crusade, and even the Earl recognised he was no threat—as long as he was three thousand miles away. The matter had been dropped, but now the Earl's personal nightmare had returned—or so the man believed.

Malachy was sceptical. Only a few wounded and broken men had yet returned from the Crusade, along with news of many deaths. What were the chances this squire had survived and returned, before even the King's vanguard? That the man who attacked the fort had a longbow could easily be explained by the nearness of Wales. There, the bow was not suppressed and Welshmen had a reputation for its use.

"Might these brigands be Welsh raiders, my lord? They are well known for using the longbow."

"Welsh!" de Ferrers choked out his response. "These men spoke English and were looking for the damned de Laval women, priest. I hardly believe the Welsh would be paying a social call!"

"Aye, my lord." Malachy knew when it was no longer safe to argue with the man.

40

"Have the commander of the garrison assemble a strong force—thirty knights at least and twice as many men-at-arms. Have them ready to ride at first light—and take this fool along," he said jerking the hapless soldier forward. "He can identify the man with the longbow."

"My lord, it is Christ's Mass eve. Your men may not be fit to ride by morning."

"I will hang any man unable to do his duty, priest, so see to it!" de Ferrers snarled. "I will not have this bastard Dane return to trouble me!"

Malachy bowed hastily and hurried to do his master's bidding. He still felt sure they were dealing with Welsh raiders, but the man-at-arms had said the men who disarmed them were seeking the Shipbrook folk. That was curious. Perhaps de Ferrers' fears were not entirely irrational.

Rational or not, the Earl was once more beginning to imagine that this bowman had put a target between his shoulder blades. This was a complication Malachy did not need. He wanted de Ferrers focused on securing the Midlands for John, not on some shadowy figure with a longbow.

If Roland Inness had indeed returned from Crusade, he must die.

Christ's Mass

Roland felt strange travelling the ancient trail back into Wales—the trail he had once followed in search of Millicent de Laval. When he had last come this way, there had been clear tracks to follow. A half-dozen raiders on Welsh ponies and one iron-shod English horse had left unmistakable signs of their passage and had led him right to his quarry. Now there was nothing but a frozen muddy path that led to…*where*?

He prayed it would not lead back into the dark Clocaenog forest. He still sometimes dreamed of the place where he had tracked down Millicent and her abductors—a place of huge brooding trees and dangerous men. He had no wish to return there, but would go wherever the search for the de Laval's led him.

"Where do ye suppose they are?" Declan asked, as though reading his mind.

"Good question, Dec. I've been thinking on it and if we presume they are alive—which we must—then there are a few things we can be certain of."

Declan gave a small hoot, his breath showing white in the frigid air.

"So enlighten me, for I am surely at a loss to guess what things you can be sure of!"

Roland smiled.

"I am certain that, if they are alive, they are being sheltered by someone."

"Or held captive."

"Aye, they may be prisoners, but if they went missing in the spring, why have they not yet been ransomed? The Welsh raiders do not keep prisoners for their own amusement. For them it is a business. They would have sold the Earl and the ladies to the highest bidder by now, and the Shipbrook folk would have heard if such a thing had happened. Remember, the patrol at Shipbrook had been ordered to watch for the Earl, should he attempt to return."

"True enough. So de Ferrers, at the least, believes the Earl may still be alive and at liberty."

"Aye, so if he is at liberty, we just need to find where."

Declan frowned.

"Wales is a big place."

"Aye, but word of a Marcher Lord holing up somewhere in the land will have spread. We need to find someone who can tell us what rumours are abroad."

"So we strike up a conversation with a friendly Welshman?" Declan asked with obvious scepticism.

"No, we will have to waylay one."

There was a long silence as they rode along the frozen trail. Finally, Declan spoke.

"It's not a great plan."

Roland shrugged.

"No, it's not. Have you a better one?"

His friend's silence was answer enough.

For three hours they rode west, seeing no one. As the sun began to set, they found a place out of sight of the trail to make a cold camp. Even the ever-cheerful Declan seemed subdued.

"I wish Sir Roger were here," he said.

Roland's thoughts turned to the big Norman knight they had left behind in the Holy Land. He could still see Sir Roger de Laval waving to them from the beach as they took ship for home. He missed the man too.

"I'm not sure I would want him here, Dec. Seeing what they did to Shipbrook and to Alwyn, and fearing what might have become of Lady Catherine and Millicent—I do not wish that upon him. We must set things aright before he returns. This," he said,"…this would break his heart."

***

"She's gone!" Catherine de Laval had just stormed into the hall where a dozen Welsh warriors still lay strewn about in drunken sleep. The one man standing in the place was Lord Llywelyn, who had been walking about rousting the men up.

"Gone, my lady?"

"Aye, gone, man! I found this in her room." She held up a handful of shorn hair. "And I'll wager you are missing one of your ponies."

Llywelyn shook his head, then raised a hand to his temple with a grimace. He had a pounding headache from the previous night's festivities and little patience for a distraught English woman.

"Where would she go, my lady? My guard would have seen her leave on horseback. Surely she is somewhere around here, perhaps making more friends among the servants." There was no mistaking the mix of irritation and condescension in the man's voice.

"My lord, my daughter escaped a captured city in the middle of the night. Do you think she could not get past your guards? So, if you please, get these drunkards up and go fetch her back."

Llywelyn could see there was no placating this woman— something he had known from the very beginning, but sometimes forgot.

"My lady Catherine, I will check the horses and, if one is missing, we will indeed go fetch your daughter back—even though it be Christ's Mass day. Where do you think she would be going?"

Catherine thought back to when her daughter had first suggested her foolish plan to go alone to the Queen. The girl had hardly got the idea out of her mouth before she had squelched it. Now she wished she had at least heard the details.

"She would not go to the coast. We've failed at that three times. I doubt she would go south—her Welsh isn't good enough to pass."

44

No, she knew her daughter. Foolish she may be, but not thoughtless. She would have weighed all of these possibilities before making a decision.

"She's gone east, back toward Chester."

Llywelyn sighed.

"Your daughter is a lot of trouble, my lady."

"Yes, my lord, she is, but nevertheless, I want her back."

The young Welshman sighed.

"As you wish. If she's gone, I'll retrieve her."

***

As dawn arrived, Millicent guessed she had a good five hour start over her pursuers, though, no doubt, they would be following on faster horses than her own. The Welsh would also be travelling in daylight over ground she had covered more slowly in darkness.

She expected Llywelyn would be leading the pursuit. It was just the kind of challenge the restless Welsh nobleman seemed to relish and she knew he would particularly enjoy running her to ground. She wondered if he would be riding her bay mare. The man had long admired the horse and would not hesitate to take it, with her gone.

Still, her Welsh pony was sure-footed and tireless and, if she resisted the urge to stop and rest, there was an even chance she would make it to the Dee before the pursuit caught up. By her reckoning, the ford was no more than three hours away over this rough track. Once across the river, she doubted Llywelyn would follow. He had few enough men that he would not want to risk them on a foray into hostile territory.

Once, she guided her mount well off the road as a lone rider approached heading west. She wanted no confrontations this day. The borderland was sparsely populated and she was thankful for that. She could not afford delays.

The rain and sleet of the past few days were gone and a bright sun lit up the frost-covered country, as morning came on Christ's Mass. She was tired, but full of energy. It had been pent-up for months and its release held a kind of joy for her. Things might turn out as badly as her mother feared, but she would be damned if she would just sit endlessly by while their world fell apart.

***

The threat of hanging had produced a good muster of knights in the pre-dawn darkness at Chester. Sir Hugh Bonsil, commander of the Chester garrison, had thirty men, mounted and in armour, gathered at the Northgate. With them were twice that many men-at-arms and archers. Malachy anxiously surveyed the gathering as Earl William de Ferrers rode up on his black charger.

"Any shirkers, Malachy?" the Earl demanded.

"None, my lord. All are ready to follow you."

De Ferrers gave him a strange look.

"I have other duties to attend to, priest. These men will be under Sir Hugh's command, but I want you to ride with them. Make sure there is no mistake. I want this boy dead. I want to see his body. Am I clear?"

The look on the Earl's face betrayed him.

He's afraid to go!

Malachy quickly bowed his head, afraid his own face would betray his feeling of disgust. There was much to dislike about William de Ferrers, but until now, he had not known the man was a coward at heart.

The priest saw that Sir Hugh was forming up the ranks of knights and he mounted his own horse. As the sky brightened in the east, they rode out the Northgate of Chester and headed northwest on the road to Shipbrook.

***

Roland crawled out of his woollen blanket and stamped his feet to get the blood flowing. It had been a cold night and they had made camp a good distance off of the trail behind a jumble of boulders that broke the wind and shielded them from sight. He reached in his sack and took out a smaller bag filled with grain and carried it to the horses tethered nearby.

Declan yawned and got to his feet, turning downhill to relieve himself.

"Better quarters than we had outside of Acre," he called over his shoulder.

"Aye, no rats or fleas and no Saracens to worry about—only Welshmen."

"I'm not sure which is worse!"

"Let's hope we don't find out," said Roland as he pulled black bread from his bag and tossed it to the Irishman who had finished his morning toilet. "Perhaps they will all spend the day in bed. It is Christ's Mass."

"So it is!" Declan said as he caught the hunk of bread in one hand. He took a big bite and began to chew.

"Better food here too," he managed, after he swallowed. Then he noticed his fellow knight had gone very still.

"*Hush!*" Roland spoke in an urgent whisper.

***

As Millicent rode east, the rising sun was brilliantly reflected off the frosty ground. It was perhaps this dazzling brightness that made her a second late when the man leapt from behind a gnarled oak's trunk and grabbed her pony's bridle. She tried to spur the animal forward to trample her attacker, but the horse reared instead. She tumbled backwards over its haunches and landed hard on the frozen ground.

For a moment she could not draw breath and her vision blurred. When it cleared, there were now two men standing over her. She reached for her short sword, but a boot came down, pinning her arm to the ground.

"It's a boy," one of the men said—the one with a tangled thatch of red hair and a wispy beard.

"I think perhaps not," said the other, who was taller and dark. This one was looking at her with a curious stare. As she fought to regain her breath, she was shocked to see the man with red hair wore a tattered and faded tunic—a tunic with a rampant white stag. Finally, her lungs were able to draw breath.

"You wear the arms of Shipbrook!" she snarled. "Did you loot the place before you burned it?" As she pulled her arm free and scrambled to her feet, she reached again for the sword at her waist, but the taller of the two grasped her wrist.

"Don't, my lady."

Millicent struggled but could not break the man's grip as he reached for a cord around his neck and drew out some sort of talisman.

"I did not loot this, my lady," he said.

Millicent gaped at the man. He held a round silver object in his hand—an amulet with an intricate carving of an English yew. She knew that amulet.

"Where did you get that?" she gasped.

"You gave it to me, my lady. On the west wall of Shipbrook," Roland answered gently.

"My…my God. Is it you? Is it Roland Inness?" the girl asked in a hoarse whisper, then turned to the other man. "And Declan?"

Now it was the Irishman's turn to gape.

"Lady Millicent? Bless me, it's the Little Lady!"

Millicent glanced past them both, scanning the wood where Roland and Declan had emerged. She turned to Roland.

"Where is my father?" She demanded with fear in her voice.

"He lives, my lady, but remains at the King's side in the Holy Land," Roland said.

The words had hardly been uttered, when the girl slapped him in the face—hard.

"If he is *there*, why are you *here*? You were to watch his back. You swore it! "

The blow stung, but Roland fought the urge to raise a hand to this cheek. He looked into the girl's furious face and once more felt the guilt of leaving behind the man they all depended on.

"Forgive us, my lady. We are here at the King's command and your father is there for the same reason. We were given no choice in the matter."

His answer did nothing to soften the look on Millicent's face.

"We all have choices, Master Inness, and you chose to leave my father alone in an enemy land. What more is there to be said?"

Slowly, Roland's guilt was turning to anger that matched the girl's. He now spoke coldly to her.

"Do you think your father would have allowed us to disobey the King? If you think that, my lady, then perhaps you have forgotten the character of the man."

Millicent said nothing, but his words struck home. Roland saw it in her eyes. She turned away and spoke to Declan.

"Was my father well when you saw him last?"

Declan nodded.

"He was hardy, my lady. He commands all of the English cavalry now and speaks often with the King."

Roland broke in. "My lady, these were the exact words Sir Roger spoke when we parted, 'Be on your toes, and as soon as duty allows, get to Shipbrook. Get to Catherine and Millie. Tell them I live and not to fear. For though Saladin himself bars my path, I will come home.'" He had memorised his master's words and carefully repeated them for the man's daughter.

Millicent dropped her head so they would not see the tears that suddenly stung her eyes. Roland's words had the familiar cadences of her father's speech and it was like hearing the man himself. Oh God, how she wished he was here in the flesh.

"My lady, we did not ask for this task and we are here in Wales in defiance of the King's orders," Roland said, gently now. "He sent us to take a message to the Queen in London, but when we landed and found Shipbrook...we thought the Queen could wait."

Millicent's head came up.

"You've been to Shipbrook? What did you find?"

"The walls still stand, but it's a ruin, my lady. De Ferrers keeps a patrol there to watch the fort. We relieved them of their weapons and took their horses. Baldric told us the Earl was charged with treason and had fled into Wales, along with you and Lady Catherine. We were coming to get you."

Millicent took a deep breath and met the gaze of the boy who was no longer a boy. He was taller than she remembered and had the stubble of a dark beard along his chin. But the eyes were the same.

"Well, Roland Inness, you do seem to have a talent for tracking me down in Wales. Let's hope it doesn't become a habit."

Roland allowed himself a small grin and trotted over to where her pony was browsing on a patch of frozen grass. He led the animal back and presented the reins to Millicent.

"Your mother...she is safe and well?"

"She is safe enough, as is the Earl. They are under the protection of a man who claims to be the rightful ruler of Gwynedd, which covers most of northern Wales. His name is Llywelyn, and they are at his keep farther into the hills."

"Thank God for that!" Declan said.

"Aye, it was a stroke of luck to stumble onto Lord Llywelyn and his men as we fled. They turned back our pursuers and he has not, up till now, sold us back to the English."

Roland asked the question that had troubled him since they had stopped her.

"My lady, if you were safe under the protection of this Welshman, what brings you to be alone on this track heading back to England, and dressed as a boy?"

"That is my own affair, Master Inness, but if you must know, I go to speak with the Queen. I have evidence that will prove Earl Ranulf is not a traitor and I must present it to her in person. She may be in London, or more likely in Normandy. Wherever she is, I must go there. Until the Earl is restored to his rightful place, we have little hope of ever returning home."

Roland did not know what evidence the girl might have that would sway the Queen, but her words regarding the Earl rang true. With Earl Ranulf a fugitive in Wales and William de Ferrers ruling in Cheshire, there truly was no going home. But something was missing from the girl's reply.

"You did not say why you travelled alone—and in the garb of a boy."

Millicent wanted to lie—wanted to tell him it was all part of a plan sanctioned by Lady Catherine and the Earl, but she doubted it would be convincing.

"I travel alone because Lady Catherine refused to allow me to go and the Earl forbade it as well. I expect that Lord Llywelyn is even now hard on my trail with the intent of bringing me back." She paused and tried to gauge the response to her confession on the faces of the two men before her. She could read nothing there.

"I do not intend to allow that. My mother fears for my safety and it has clouded her judgment. There is far more at stake here than my safety. I plan to get on that horse and continue on my way to the Queen. You say the King has commanded you to take a message to her, so you may join me if you wish. Otherwise, get out of my way."

Roland and Declan exchanged uneasy glances.

"My lady, do you think that wise?" Roland asked the question, but he was speaking to the back of the girl's head as she walked over to her pony and climbed into the saddle. She turned to the two men standing in the middle of the track.

"Wise or no, I've had my fill of running and hiding, and unless you intend to take me back by force, I will be on my way." She turned her pony's head toward the north and started down the trail toward the Dee.

Roland shook his head and turned to Declan.

"Best fetch the horses."

***

Millicent did not look back as she urged her pony down the track. The shock of seeing her father's squires appear out of nowhere was still with her, and her mind was racing. She knew they could seize her and return her to her mother if they chose. She hoped they would hesitate to use force with her, but that was not certain.

These were no longer the boyish squires she had jested with in happier times at Shipbrook. They were young still, but had a fell look about them—the look of fighting men. It was a look she knew well, having grown up as the daughter of one such. Roger de Laval had a soft heart, but even as a young girl she had known there was steel in the man. And now she saw the same in these two.

What happened to them over there?

She rode uneasily, waiting for the sound of approaching hooves behind her. When it came, she slid her sword from its scabbard.

I'll not go meekly!

The trail was broader through this stretch and Roland Inness rode up beside her. She studied him from the corner of her eye. He had his longbow slung over his shoulder and a quiver lashed to his saddle. There was a sword at his waist, but he did not draw it.

Roland looked at the weapon in Millicent's hand.

"Do you plan to use that?"

"If I must, Master Inness. I won't go back."

Roland made no move to seize her. For a while they rode silently together. The hood had fallen from the girl's head and he studied her as they rode. She was taller by almost half a foot since last he'd seen her, and her face had grown to favour her mother even more than it once did—save for the raggedly shorn hair. And despite the boy's garb, there was no disguising that she now had the shape of a woman—a woman with a sword at the ready.

"What are you looking at?" she asked him sharply, breaking the silence.

For a moment he was flustered, embarrassed that he had been staring at her.

"You've grown up, Millie, but you haven't changed at all," he managed.

The girl jerked back on her reins and glared at him.

"Much has changed since you left, Roland Inness. I haven't forgotten what you did for me in the Clocaenog, or the friendship we shared, but the years since have not been good ones. Neither of us are the same, so old familiarities, once granted, no longer apply. You will address me as a squire would the daughter of his master."

Roland met her furious gaze, with a wry smile.

"No more 'Millie' then?"

"No. Too much has changed since those days."

Roland shrugged.

"As you wish, *my lady*, but know that we are no longer squires, though we remain your father's sworn men. Declan and I were knighted by the King at the siege of Acre. If you insist on proper formalities, then you may address us as Sir Roland and Sir Declan—if you please."

"You? A knight? I...I...." Words failed her. She turned her eyes forward and kicked her pony into motion.

Knights? These two? And what had he meant when he said she hadn't changed at all?

Between Hammer and Anvil

*I*t was a three hour journey to the ford and much of it passed in silence. As they descended from the hills and into the valley of the Dee, Roland spurred forward once more to speak to Millicent.

"My lady, I know your desire for haste, but we must have some agreement on a plan before we cross over into England."

Millicent started to snap back a reply but restrained herself.

"I see no need for an agreement. I have my own plans. You may come with me or go your own way."

"My lady, with respect, don't be stupid. Your chances of reaching the Queen travelling alone are small, even dressed in these boy's garments that do little to disguise your true sex. With two knights as escorts, you might at least have a chance."

Millicent scowled. She knew he spoke the truth, but did not wish to have to parlay with anyone over her plans. Others always counselled caution when boldness was called for. She feared these two...*knights*...would do the same.

"What do you propose Master...eh, Sir Roland?"

Roland gave her a beaming smile.

"See, my lady? That was not so hard!"

She did not return his smile.

"What I propose is that we cross the Dee at the Shipbrook ford and strike northeast toward the Mersey until we are well clear of Chester. Then, we turn south to reach Watling Street. It's round about, but safer that way. We will be able to learn if the Queen is in London at most any ale house as we get near the city. If she is in London, we find her there."

"And if not?"

Roland had thought on this question. Their charge was to go to the Queen, if she be in England. Sir Robin and Tuck had the task of finding her in Normandy. Still, there was no guarantee that his friends had made it safely through King Philip's domains to get to her.

"If she is not in London, we strike east to the port at Dover. I know of a ship there that can take us to the Queen."

Millicent listened carefully. The plan differed but little from her own, and was, in truth, more sound in some ways. She was disappointed that there was nothing to object to in it.

"The plan is satisfactory. I agree to it."

With that settled, she looked over his shoulder and past Declan O'Duinne. They were only a mile or so from the Dee and there was no movement up the trail behind them. It seemed they had outrun her pursuit. It gave Millicent a warm feeling to think of Llywelyn reaching the river and finding her already across and gone.

"Let's cross the Dee, Sir Roland."

***

De Ferrers' men spotted the horses as they neared the ruins of Shipbrook. There were two tied up near a hovel at the edge of a woodline. No peasant owned horses of that quality and their guide did not hesitate to identify them.

"Them's our horses! I know that brown one with the white face fer sure!"

The commander dispatched four knights and in short order, the horses and an ancient man were driven across the open field to the road. Malachy spurred his mount forward and the old man cowered.

"What is your name, grandfather?"

"Sigbert, Father. These are my horses—I swear in the name of Jesus."

Malachy stayed mounted and slowly guided his horse in a tight circle around the frightened old man.

"I'd be wary of swearing on the Saviour, old man, particularly when it is such an obvious lie."

"Please, Father. Ye can have 'em back. I found 'em wandering in the meadow."

Malachy shook his head.

"Sigbert, it seems the truth is not in you, but enough about the horses. We want to know about the men who came here and attacked the soldiers at the ruin. Who were they? Where did they go?"

"Oh, yer reverence, I surely do not know that. They were strangers to me. Outlaws, I expect."

Malachy dismounted and stepped very close to the old man. He leaned in and whispered to him.

"I will burn your hut and you inside it if you do not tell me, Sigbert."

Sigbert told.

***

Millicent saw the grave first and reined in her pony. It was where Llywelyn's spies had said it would be. She turned to Roland.

"Did you know…?"

"Aye, my lady," Roland said with a mixture of pain and relief. He had feared that she did not know and he would have to break the terrible news of Alwyn's death to her. "Baldric told us about the fight at the ford. Alwyn slew many men that night. He died a warrior."

Millicent dismounted and Roland and Declan followed. Time was pressing, but respects must be paid.

"We never knew the details of how he fell," she replied, standing beside the wooden cross, her eyes welling with tears. "Only that he had died here to give us time to escape. I wonder if he knew how much we loved him. My mother still mourns hard his passing and blames herself."

"My lady, Alwyn Madawc would not have wished a better death than the one he found here," Roland said gently. "He was not a man destined to die old and in bed."

Millicent nodded.

"Aye, I could not picture him passing like that, but I wish he were still with us."

"As do we all, my lady," said Declan, stepping forward. "And he would still be here were it not for this bastard William de Ferrers. I have counted him as my enemy because he was enemy to Roland. But now I have grievance enough of my own. He's burned Shipbrook and killed the best man among us. I'll not rest until William de Ferrers lies dead."

"Nor I," said Roland.

Millicent de Laval, looked up with a curious expression.

"I danced with him once."

Roland gaped at her.

"Danced? With de Ferrers?"

"Yes, in the autumn, after you and Father left. Mother and I were summoned to London to meet the Queen. There was a ball. He asked."

"Sounds delightful," Roland said, thinking that he and Declan had been sharing a flea and rat-infested tent at Acre that autumn while she made merry with his worst enemy. The girl gave him a withering look and there was acid in her voice.

"Much has happened while you've been gone and there is no time to tell it all with Welshmen on my trail. But know this, Sir William de Ferrers was more interested in *you* than in me. He knows you are the longbowman from Derbyshire he seeks—and one thing more."

"Yes?"

"He is afraid of you. I saw it in his eyes at the mention of your name."

Roland looked at the girl, her eyes still red from the tears she had shed for Alwyn Madawc, and was reminded of the steel he had seen in Millicent de Laval in those desperate hours in the Clocaenog. It was still there. He had many questions, but she was right. Now was not the time.

"We can speak of this later. Let's get across the Dee."

Millicent reached into her boy's tunic and drew out a small square of cloth with the white stag of Shipbrook stitched upon it. She laid it gently on the grave. Respects paid, they mounted and rode the short distance down to the ford. It was near high tide and the Dee was full, bank to bank.

"It may be too deep for your pony, my lady," Roland said, gauging the tidal surge.

Millicent surveyed the river. She had never forded it with a high tide backing up the water and did not know if her mount had ever had to swim with a rider aboard.

"I'll ride behind you and keep the pony on a lead," she said, dismounting. He extended his arm and hauled her up behind him. He had expected her to dismiss his concerns and was surprised when she didn't.

She takes more care with the horses than with herself.

Roland eased his horse off the bank and into the water. He called over his shoulder to Declan.

"Follow close, in case the pony spooks."

Quickly, the water rose to his horse's barrel, then to its flank, but it seemed to find good footing. Millicent had one arm around his waist and the other holding the reins of the pony that was now struggling to keep its head above water. With another few inches of depth, the pony could no longer reach the muddy bottom and began to swim, its eyes wide and panicky.

They were at midstream when Declan cried out.

"Horsemen!"

Roland and Millicent twisted around to see if the pursuit from Wales had caught up to them but saw that Declan was pointing to the front. Looking back toward the English shore they saw a large body of mounted men coming down the track toward the ford, only their helmets and the tips of lances showing above the brown dead reeds. They were barely a half mile from the river and coming fast. No need to guess if they were friend or foe—England was enemy territory to them now.

Without comment, Roland jerked the reins of his horse upstream and turned back toward the opposite bank. This sudden change of direction was too much for the Welsh pony, which pulled its reins free from Millicent's clutching hand. Declan tried to grab the bridle but missed and the poor animal whinnied as it was swept downstream

They reached the Welsh side of the river and Roland was urging his horse up the bank when he heard a shout from behind. He turned to see a large contingent of armoured knights spurring down the bank on the far side and entering the ford. They had been seen. Something splashed into the water twenty feet from the bank.

"Crossbows," Declan muttered.

Roland slipped off his horse and withdrew a handful of arrows from his quiver.

"No!" Millicent turned in the saddle and fairly shouted this at him. He realized that he was standing where Alwyn Madawc had died, barring the exit to the ford.

He looked up at the girl.

"Only for a moment, my lady. Just to slow them a bit, I swear." He did not plan on meeting the same fate as his old teacher. The girl gritted her teeth, but spurred the horse up to higher ground where Declan had taken up station.

Roland nocked his first arrow and drew the bow to his ear with a slow steady pull. This was the longbow that Sir Robin had gifted him as a farewell gesture on the shore at Jaffa. He had tested the bow's draw on the voyage back from the Holy Land, but had only shot it in anger once—when they surprised the guards at Shipbrook—and that was at very close range.

He took aim at the lead rider and released. He was less than a hundred yards away and the arrow carried true, but angled plate armour saved the man. The shaft struck a glancing blow that almost unhorsed him, but he recovered.

Roland took a second arrow and sent it toward a brash knight who was eagerly urging his horse through the current toward them. This man was wearing mail and seemed shocked to find an arrow piercing his chest before tumbling backwards from the saddle.

Some of the men in front now seemed to hesitate, but their commander was roaring at them as he sent his crossbowmen into the stream protected by a phalanx of armoured men and horses. Roland sent two more riders into the water then slung his bow over his shoulder and sprinted up the trail to the high ground. Without preamble, he swung up behind Millicent.

"I've slowed them a bit, but they're coming on. Damned crossbows will be in range soon. We have to run."

They spurred their horses back the way they had come. Within minutes, the pursuers came charging up the banks of the ford and into Wales. Now it was a race and Roland knew it was one they could not win. Their mounts had been taken from the common men-at-arms they had surprised at Shipbrook. They were faster than the Welsh pony they had lost in the river, but were not of the quality or speed of the well-bred horses that pursued them. It would hardly be a contest, and, with his horse carrying the weight of two, the balance was tipped even further against them.

"They're gaining. We have to dismount and get into the woods!" Roland yelled this to Declan over the drumbeat of their horses hooves on the frozen ground. The Irishman had seen the danger and was already looking for some place to flee where they could not be ridden down.

The trail took a sharp turn up a ravine and the ground rose steeply along a rocky wooded spur on the right. It wasn't perfect, but horses could not follow. It would have to do. Declan swung off his horse and gave it a sharp slap on the rump to send it on up the trail. Roland and Millicent slid off together. Roland ripped his quiver from the saddle as Millicent sent their horse after Declan's. All three began to scramble up the side of the hill as they heard the thunder of hooves grow behind them.

They had climbed almost out of crossbow range, when the pursuers came galloping around the sharp turn. There were two dozen knights in the vanguard followed by a host of men-at-arms and crossbowmen. They did not pause at the turn, but spurred on up the trail. For a moment, Roland thought they would be missed altogether, but then, at a shouted command, knights in the front reined in their mounts and the entire host halted on the track below.

He heard Declan curse under his breath as the Irishman saw his riderless horse stopped a quarter mile up the trail, cropping some green weeds that had sprouted in a sunny spot. At the same time, Millicent gasped. Riding near the front was a tall blond man in a black priest's robe.

Malachy. She tugged at Roland's sleeve.

"The priest there! Use your bow. Kill him!"

Roland saw the man and wondered why Millicent wanted him dead. He did not think she would mark him so without cause, and for him, the fact that he was a priest was no deterrent. He had seen priests aplenty kill and be killed in the Holy Land. They were men after all.

It was the range more than any concern for his mortal soul that stopped him. The man was sitting a horse at almost three hundred yards away and could barely be seen through the bare branches of the trees. It was an impossible shot and would give away their position instantly.

"No—it's too far," he whispered. "And we need to get farther up this hill before they find where we left the trail."

Millicent looked once more at the figure of the hated priest, then whispered back.

"Very well, we go, but if they get close, I want that man dead." Roland nodded and the three moved at a low crouch further up the wooded slope.

Sir Hugh Bonsil, who commanded the troop below, had chased Welsh raiders across the border before. At the sight of Declan's horse, he ordered men into the woods on either side of the track looking for signs of his quarry. One man with sharp eyes found a scraped off bit of moss that marked their passage. The alarm was raised and pursuit on foot was quickly organized.

Roland glanced back as they climbed. He saw one group of riders continue up the trail. These would be moving to cut them off further up this spur. More men spread out in the woods below and began sweeping up the slope. Very soon they would be trapped.

Declan had reached the same conclusion.

"We have to get past the bastards up above!"

Roland slung his bow over his shoulder, and began to scramble up the slope, looking for a game trail that would allow them to outrun the men coming to kill them from below. Millicent fell in behind him and Declan brought up the rear.

His years of hunting on Kinder Scout had prepared him well for seeing the high country as the game animals did. Animals knew how to pick the best paths between the sparse feeding grounds found in the mountains. As he moved, Roland took in the contours of the slope ahead and began angling to his left.

He heard a brittle clattering sound behind him and a quiet curse from Declan. A crossbow bolt had landed ten feet behind him. The range was still too far for accuracy, but a lucky shot would end the chase before it had begun. Another twenty yards uphill, he found the game trail he had been seeking and startled a yearling buck that had been moving up the spur from below, spooked by the loud thrashing of the men downslope.

He motioned for Millicent and Declan to follow the trail that led up and to the left, while he hung back. He nocked an arrow and saw one knight who had climbed far ahead of his fellows. The man was shouting as though this was some great sport. He uttered a surprised scream as an arrow took him in the stomach, then fell silent. Roland slung his bow and ran. No other knight moved ahead of the line now, but it still moved relentlessly up the spur toward them.

As he sprinted up the game trail, he came upon Declan and Millicent, stopped and crouching low. They were looking uphill.

"There are men up on the crest," Declan said, breathing hard.

"The trail swings up and over this spur just ahead and we can hear their horses up there," Millicent added. "They must be waiting to ride us down if we try to cross."

They were caught between two converging forces with no escape route, but Roland heard no surrender in her voice. She had indeed not changed. Nor had he.

"Dec, there are more behind us than in front and those people down the hill have crossbows."

"So forward it is," Declan replied, drawing his broadsword. "Thin them out a bit with yer bow, and I'll cut a bolt hole for us."

The Irishman was already up and creeping forward. Roland nocked his first arrow and turned to Millicent, beckoning her near.

"Follow me, my lady, but not too close. I may have a need for my sword."

"This is your plan?" Millicent asked, incredulously.

"Have you a better one?"

"No, I do not," she was forced to admit, and drew her own short sword.

No lack of boldness here, she thought.

Cautiously they crested the spur and saw a line of knights looking in their direction. Roland loosed his first shaft at a tall man on a dapple grey charger who had yet to notice them. He made a short whimpering sound and, arms flailing, fell backwards off his horse.

The man next to him had quicker reflexes and did not stop to gawk. He spurred his horse right at them, but was slowed by the underbrush. Too late, he realized his danger and tried to retreat, but went down with an arrow in his neck. His horse reared in a panic and fell on the man.

Now there was a small gap in the centre of the line and Declan was charging forward, his wild hair streaming behind him and his broadsword carried loosely in his right hand. From his lips came a Gaelic war cry.

"Fág an Bealach!" Clear the way.

Two knights moved to close the gap in their cordon, spurring their mounts at Declan from opposite directions. The Irishman darted to his right, leapt onto the stump of an ancient felled oak, and, from this height, unhorsed the first man with a single blow from his broadsword.

The rider had barely hit the ground when Declan swung into the saddle of the man's riderless horse and turned on the other knight, who was bearing down on Millicent and Roland. He sank his heels in the charger's flanks and barrelled into the side of the English knight, who just barely managed to stay in the saddle.

The Englishman parried Declan's first two blows, but realized he was no match for the speed of the man he faced. Prudently, he backed away, waiting for others to join him—and they were coming, from both flanks.

"My lady, now!"

Roland sprang forward toward the gap Declan had forced. The Irishman had made quick work cutting through the net set to catch them at the top of the spur, but now the men who were coming from below had closed on them. And these men had crossbows.

He had hardly formed the thought when a knight came blundering out of the bushes from below. Roland felled him with an arrow, but others could be heard nearing the top of the spur. He drew and calmly waited for a shot, knowing that Declan could fend off the mounted men, for at least a time.

He did not see the arrow, but he heard it pass from behind, just over his left shoulder. An instant later he heard it strike flesh and a scream came from downslope. As the line of pursuers emerged from the brush near the top of the spur, the air was suddenly filled with a sound Roland knew well—the angry buzz of many arrows in flight.

He saw Declan leap from his saddle to the ground and he dragged Millicent down with him. Men downslope began to fall in scattered bunches and others quickly shrank back from the summit. The air seemed to be filled with crossbow bolts and arrows flying in opposite directions. On the trail, the contingent of English knights looked about in confusion until one of their number took an arrow in the back. That was all that was required to launch a hasty retreat back down the trail.

As the rear of the last English horse disappeared over the crest, a singular figure in bright mail came riding down the trail from the west, a mad look in his eyes and an indecipherable war cry on his lips. Roland stood and half drew his sword, unsure what this new appearance might mean, but Millicent laid her hand on his arm and motioned him to hold. The Welsh had finally caught up to her and she did not know whether to cheer or weep.

It was Llywelyn, and he was riding her bay mare.

Lord Llywelyn

*R*oland saw two dozen men moving carefully down the slope toward them. They were all armed with longbows and he watched them come, fascinated, until a shaft buzzed close overhead. He ducked back down behind a deadfall tree, then to his horror, saw Millicent rise from cover and walk toward the trail.

"My lady!" he yelled, but she did not seem to hear. Her arm was raised in greeting, and the knight in the bright armour saw her. He barked a quick command to his men and no more arrows came their way. Hunkered behind the deadfall, Roland watched the bowmen swarm past him to the crest of the spur and begin to send a stream of arrows after the fleeing English force.

Off to his left, he saw Declan poke his head above a tangle of fallen trees where he had gone to cover. Roland rose and slung the longbow over his shoulder. Millicent was on the road, standing in front of the man in the bright mail. This could only be the Welshman, Llywelyn, come to fetch her back to Lady Catherine.

The knight had dismounted and Roland noted, with only slight surprise, that he seemed to be getting a tongue lashing from the girl. He walked slowly toward Millicent and the newcomer, careful not to make any threatening moves. He was aware of many eyes on him. Declan too had emerged from his cover and was walking up the track. He had returned his broadsword to its scabbard.

The threat from the English now gone, the men who had swept by them on the crest of the spur were drifting back, keeping a close watch on the two knights who were converging on the trail. Roland could see men all around them, some with half drawn longbows and others with fully drawn swords.

"Step carefully," Declan whispered to him as they met twenty paces from where Lady Millicent was just completing her rant.

"Indeed," Roland replied in a hushed voice.

This was a delicate encounter, to say the least. Both men continued forward, but kept their hands open and away from the hilt of their swords. Ahead, they could clearly overhear the heated conversation. Lord Llywelyn seemed to be having no more luck than they in persuading the girl to abandon her risky plan to go to the Queen. The tall Welshman looked over the girl's head at the two men slowly approaching.

"That would be close enough, my friends," he said in rough but passable English. "My lads are protective of me, to be sure. I wouldn't want one of them to mistake your intentions."

Roland and Declan halted where they stood.

"Who are these two?" Llywelyn asked Millicent.

"They are Sir Roland Inness and Sir Declan O'Duinne—sworn men of my father, come to escort me to London. So, as I've tried to tell you, I have guards aplenty for the journey."

Llywelyn arched an eyebrow.

"Yes, I could see that these two fellows had the English on the run when we arrived." He made no effort to disguise the amused scorn in his voice. Roland ignored the tone and spoke up.

"Your timely assistance is much appreciated, Lord Llywelyn," he said and gave a short bow. "I swear I have never seen so many longbows in one place. It's little wonder the Normans fled. I've noticed that they have no taste for the weapon."

At that, Llywelyn broke into a broad smile and, brushing aside Millicent, approached the two knights standing in the muddy track.

"They do not indeed, Sir Roland. And I see you have your own bow at hand. That's yew, is it not?"

Roland swung the bow off of his shoulder and handed it to the Welshman. Llywelyn examined it with interest, then turned and spoke to Millicent.

"The yew staves you had strapped to your horse the day we met—did they belong to Sir Roland here?"

Millicent seemed embarrassed by the question, but nodded.

"Aye, they were his, my lord. I knew they would burn Shipbrook. I...couldn't leave them."

Roland gave her a curious look, but she avoided his gaze.

Llywelyn returned to examining the bow in his hand—drawing it a little to test the pull. His men gathered close and soon it was being passed from hand to hand, with much commentary on the workmanship. As Roland watched, one man nocked an arrow and drew it back to his cheek before sending the shaft off in the general direction of the departed English. "Strong," he grunted in Welsh and handed the bow to the next man. Roland didn't need to understand the language to get the gist.

As Sir Robin's longbow made the rounds, Roland glanced past Llywelyn to see Millicent standing alone in the muddy track, watching the proceedings with growing irritation. He would have allowed himself a small smile seeing her impatience with this turn of events, but knew that this encounter could still turn deadly.

One of the archers in the group stood close to Llywelyn and whispered in the man's ear. Roland tensed and slid his hand slowly toward his sword hilt. He saw Llywelyn nod to the man then favour them with another huge smile.

"Griff here is the best archer in Wales," he said motioning to the man who had whispered to him. "He says he's never seen an Englishman with a longbow, though he heard one was used at your King's coronation to win the archery tournament. Of course, had a Welshman been invited, the result would have been different!" This last he repeated in Welsh to the boisterous agreement of the archers gathered all around.

Then a voice cut through the merriment.

"You are looking at the man who won that tournament!"

Everyone turned in surprise to stare at Millicent, who stared back defiantly.

"He shot a melon out of the air to win!" This came from Declan O'Duinne, who still liked to take credit for training his friend to take targets in flight.

A few of the gathered archers knew enough English to translate to the rest, which set off a buzz of surprised murmurs. Llywelyn turned to Roland.

"Is this true? *You* won the tournament?"

Roland didn't like the Welshman's sceptical tone, but did not think it prudent to show it.

"Aye, I won the tournament, but no doubt it would have been a better test if Griff had been there." Roland nodded to the tough looking bowman standing beside Llywelyn. "My lord, please tell him that I know the difference between shooting a melon and a man. Griff and all your bowmen proved their skill this day— when it counted most."

Llywelyn turned to his men and, with gusto, translated Roland's words into Welsh. They were greeted with growls of agreement and grim smiles all around. The Welsh lord then turned to Millicent who still stood on the muddy track, hands on hips.

"Lady Millicent—I like these lads! Your father has chosen his men well."

The girl fought the urge to scream at the man and managed to regain her composure—for Llywelyn had just presented her with the way out of her situation.

"Aye, my lord," she began, "they are good and loyal men and good fighters, so I hope you will consider carefully what is to happen next."

Her words caught his attention and he cocked his head, waiting to see where they would take her.

"I am obliged to get to the Queen and will continue on this journey unless you prevent me by force. No doubt you could do so, but not without a fight from my father's men here," she said pointing at Roland and Declan. "If it comes to that, good men, including some of your own, will likely die—and that would be a sin on Christ's Mass, wouldn't you agree?

Llywelyn paused, considering her question.

"Perhaps it would, my lady, but I've promised your mother to return you to her. Lady Catherine will be very put out with me if I let you go," Llywelyn said gravely.

"Yes, she will, but if you were to tell her that you had to kill two of her husband's sworn men—and these are men I know her to be fond of—to bring me back, well…I think you can guess how that news would be received."

"My lord Llywelyn," Roland interjected. "Tell her we will keep her daughter safe. She will not like it, but I would hate for you to stand before Lady Catherine de Laval with our blood on your hands—now that we have become such good friends."

At this Llywelyn broke into a booming laugh. It took him a moment to recover.

"Oh, you English," he said, wiping tears from his eyes, "such talkers. You could almost pass for Welsh!" He gathered himself and turned back to Millicent.

"Very well. Get on with your journey. I will face the wrath of Lady Catherine, but I think you may be right. Your eye is clearer than hers on how matters stand. Something needs to change on the other side of the border or we may all rot in these lovely hills. So go with my blessing—but go carefully."

He took the longbow from the man nearest him and handed it back to Roland. He leaned close to the young English knight and spoke quietly so no others could hear.

"Good luck to you, Sir Roland. The Lady Millicent—she is…a…"

The man seemed, for once, at a loss for words. Roland smiled and whispered back.

"That she is, my lord."

Watling Street

Three riders looked out from the cover of trees as a cold rain mixed with snow pelted the river Dee. They were a dozen miles southeast of the great bend in the river at Chester and had come to a little-used ford that crossed a deserted stretch of this river border with England. With the ford at Shipbrook watched by their enemies, they had followed the Dee upriver to get to this place.

Roland stood in his stirrups and looked across the river. It was noon, but in the miserable weather, he could barely make out the opposite bank.

"It looks clear," he said and urged his horse forward.

Millicent de Laval followed on her own bay mare. Llywelyn's men had gathered up the two horses Roland and Declan had abandoned as they fled from de Ferrers men, and the Welsh leader, with good humour, had returned the bay to Millicent. He winked at her when he handed over the reins.

"The English breed fast horses and beautiful girls, my lady. I enjoyed sampling one of the two."

Millicent mounted quickly and looked over her shoulder at the bold young Welshman.

"It is well you chose the one you could handle, my lord," she said, wheeling the horse around and digging her heels into its flanks. Down the trail, she joined the two knights who would be her escort.

The three rode back toward the Dee, then turned off on a narrow path heading southeast. It was more a game trail than a proper byway and the going was slow. Riding single file, there was little conversation. When darkness came upon them, they made a cold camp, and all fell exhausted into a restless sleep.

The following day was much the same and it took until near noon to reach this crossing, ten miles upriver from Chester. They saw no one as they passed quietly through a bare and deserted landscape. The border lands were dangerous ground and people only came here out of necessity or for mischief. It was time to cross back into England.

The river was different here than near its mouth at Shipbrook. The water ran swifter and was clear enough to see the bottom, even with the surface roiled by rain and snow. At this ford, the river had scoured down to the bedrock leaving only an occasional green slick of algae. The horses did not like the footing, but they managed to cross with no one spilled into the icy water.

Another hour on a narrow track through thick woods, and they came to a cleared field, fallow and frozen—the first sign of habitation they had seen. An hour more, and they struck the old Roman road that ran southeast from Chester to London.

"Watling Street," Declan announced. Roland was reminded of his first journey down this highway to attend the coronation of King Richard. What was it Sir Alwyn had said about the name of this road?

Londoners, in their arrogance, think this whole great country serves only as the outskirts to their city. For them, their Watling Street runs all the way to Chester!

He could almost hear the lilt of the man's Welsh accent. As he looked both ways along the deserted road, he felt none of the high spirits of that first day on Watling Street, when all had seemed a grand adventure. Now he had come home from war only to find that war had followed him. It was the day after Christ's Mass and he was once more a fugitive in his own country. The future seemed as grey and dismal as this lonely stretch of highway.

"Too cold to be gathering wool, Roland," Declan offered, pulling his hooded cloak tighter around him.

"Aye, let's be getting on to London."

As he turned the head of his horse southward he glanced at Millicent and Declan.

Fugitive I may be, but not alone this time.

***

William de Ferrers' face was a deep crimson as he screamed at Sir Hugh Bonsil, who had returned from his mission empty-handed.

"Can no one here follow a simple order? Can no one catch a mere boy?" Sir Hugh stared straight ahead, and despite the cold, rivulets of sweat began to make their way down his forehead.

De Ferrers turned on Malachy.

"You think I'm daft, don't you priest?" he yelled. "You think there is no stinking Dane out there who wants to kill me."

Malachy fought to maintain his composure. He *did* think the man was slightly daft, but daft or no, one word from the Earl and it would be his head on a pike.

"My lord, I have never doubted that this Inness boy exists or that there is murder in his heart. We would have had him, had he not fled into Wales. We lost over a dozen men trying to apprehend him. I must wonder if he has enlisted the help of those barbarians across the border, my lord. A swarm of them came out of nowhere, just as we had the boy and his companions cornered!"

"The Welsh!" de Ferrers sputtered. "Of course. It's *always* the Welsh. First they come to the aid of Ranulf when he was within our grasp, and now this. I tell you, Malachy, when affairs are set to rights in this country, I will show everyone how a *real* Marcher Lord deals with the misbegotten Welsh. I will crush them! Do you hear? Crush them!"

His venom expended for the moment, de Ferrers slumped down on a bench.

"Leave me," he muttered, motioning toward Sir Hugh. The knight wasted no time in absenting himself from his furious lord.

"Malachy, you must not fail me again. I value your counsel, but I can find other clever priests. You will use your mysterious network of informants to find this boy, even if he hides in Wales. I *will* have him killed. Do you understand?"

"Completely, my lord," the priest replied, and quickly withdrew. As he hurried through the dimly lit corridors of Chester Castle, he pondered how to keep the Earl's obsession with a single man from upsetting plans that were falling nicely into place. On the morrow, he would be travelling to London to deliver the tax revenues of the Midlands into the hands of John's treasurer. It would give him an opportunity to seek advice on this troubling matter from his true master and mentor.

The Archdeacon would know what to do.

***

The three travellers made camp at sunset in a copse of trees that gave some shelter from the brisk north wind. The rain and sleet had stopped and, having put distance between them and Chester, they chanced a fire.

While Declan stoked the blaze, Roland slipped off into the woods. He had seen something small and grey startle when they led their horses into the trees. He moved carefully in the direction it had gone and found a small grassy clearing. At its edge, he stood perfectly still for a long time, ignoring the cold that seeped into his bones.

As the last of the sun died in the west, a large hare came out to forage in the twilight. With practiced care, he drew and shot. The creature made no sound as it died. He cleaned and skinned it on the spot and returned to camp.

"Ah, meat for the spit!" Declan declared when Roland walked into camp with his prize. The Irishman took the hare and laid it on a stone while he quickly fashioned a spit, then skewered the meat and propped it over the flames. Soon its juices were sizzling and dripping into the coals, which flamed up with each spatter.

It was the first hot meal any of them had had in days and all ate with relish. As they finished the last of the meat, Roland turned to Millicent.

"My lady, we have been hard pressed since our first meeting yesterday. There's been no time to talk. You said much had changed while we've been gone. We know some of what's occurred, but it would help if you told us the rest."

Millicent wiped a bit of juice from her chin and considered the two men gathered around the fire. She had known them well as boys, but now... They did not look or act like the young squires who had gone off on Crusade and she had questions of her own about what had happened to them across the sea. They claimed to still be her father's sworn men, but could they be trusted with what she knew?

This question had plagued her during their long, silent ride from Wales. She wished, for not the first time, that Roger de Laval was there to tell her what the wise course was, but he was not. She must decide.

Trust, or no?

"In the autumn after you left, Mother and I were summoned to a reception given by Queen Eleanor in London."

Then she told them the story—all of it—her meeting with the Queen and her encounter with William de Ferrers. Roland stopped her before she had fairly begun her account.

"You said you danced with de Ferrers? Why?"

"Well, he asked me. It would have been unseemly for me to refuse."

"Unseemly? The man is a murderer!"

Millicent had never seen a look of such fury on Roland's face. She knew well the enmity he felt for this man, enmity they all now shared, but his reaction to her dancing with de Ferrers puzzled and angered her.

"What would you have had me do? The Queen charged me with gathering information on affairs in the Midlands and, at the time, William de Ferrers controlled a third of that region. Now he controls almost all of it. It was my duty—and it would have been hard to explain my refusal. Should I have told him I would not dance with a man who killed my friend's father?"

"Yes!"

Millicent had tried to be patient with this interrogation, but she had had enough.

"Think what you will!" she said, her voice rising. "I need not answer to you for my actions."

Roland fought to get his temper under control. The depth of his anger had surprised him as well. Of course, he hated William de Ferrers, but wrapped up in his loathing had been a sick feeling in the pit of his stomach at the thought of the man laying a hand on Millicent de Laval. He would have to sort that out later.

Even in the dim firelight, he could tell Millicent's blood was up, but there was a question that had been gnawing at him since she had spoken of it over Alwyn Madawc's grave. After a long silence, he spoke.

"Of course you do not answer to me, my lady—my apologies."

Millicent took a while to collect herself, but finally replied in an even voice.

"Very well. I *danced* with de Ferrers, as I said." She paused and gave Roland a challenging look. "He was quite an accomplished dancer actually, but as I said before, he seemed more interested in you than in me."

"You said de Ferrers was afraid of me."

"Aye, he did not say as much, but he was afraid."

De Ferrers, afraid of him?

Roland tried to grasp the idea. He thought back to his deadly encounter with the man on Kinder Scout. The young nobleman had run from him that day in panicked flight, but soon enough had brought the full weight of Norman power to bear against him. He had slipped from the man's grasp when he fled Derbyshire, but all the advantages remained on the side of the Earl of Derby. Why should he fear one man?

Because he knows I will one day kill him.

Roland did not realize how long he had sat in silent thought, until Declan intervened.

"My lady, please finish yer story."

Millicent nodded and went on with her account. She told of her long days of boredom at Chester and her growing suspicion of the new priest, Malachy. She spoke of Lady Constance's high treason, the capture of the town by de Ferrers and her desperate nighttime flight to Shipbrook with the Earl. She told of Llywelyn's alliance with Ranulf and the months of frustration that followed.

When she had finished, it was fully night. The clouds had departed and the winter sky was bright with a thousand stars. Roland studied her in the firelight, looking for the right words.

"My lady, forgive me for my…words before. I had no right. It seems you have been in a war, no less than we. We had thought to return home to a land at peace. I had planned to find my brother and sister and bring them to Shipbrook where they could find a real home. We did not expect to find Shipbrook burned, Sir Alwyn dead and you and Lady Catherine driven from your home. Had Sir Roger known such evil was possible, none of us would have ever left Shipbrook. My lady, Declan and I…we are not your father, but we remain his men. Never doubt that."

"Never," added Declan.

When he had finished, Millicent sat silently for a long time before she replied.

"You said when we met, that I had not changed a bit. I hope that, appearances aside, you have not either. So I will trust you. If you play me false, don't forget that I stabbed my jailer back in the Clocaenog."

Declan laughed out loud at this and gave Roland a playful shove. Now, suddenly, they looked a bit more like the two boys she had known so long ago.

"So I have told you my story," she said. "I would now hear yours. What befell you and my father across the sea?"

So they told it—most of it. The voyage of the *Sprite*, the fight at the Pillars of Hercules, the loss of Tuck, the encounter with Tancred. Declan gleefully pointed to his missing tooth.

"I lost this in that damned dungeon in Messina and would have lost much more, were it not for Master Inness here and the lovely Isabella, who flummoxed the guards." Roland was glad of the dark, for his face had flushed at the mention of Isabella. But Millicent made no comment.

They told of the long, deadly siege of Acre but made no mention of the filth of the camp, the heat, the vermin or the death. They told of the attack on the breach, the King knighting them and promptly sending them on a mission behind the enemy lines.

"We found Saladin's army and had almost won free to return to our own," Declan announced proudly. "But the Saracens spied us. I got away, but they captured Roland. Threw him in the dungeons of Jerusalem."

"Did the lovely Isabella rescue him as well?" Millicent asked sweetly.

"Oh no!" Declan declared, amused. "He crawled out through some tunnel. We put Isabella off the ship back in Italy. She almost dragged Roland along with her, but he claimed he had promised himself to a girl back in England, and thus escaped her clutches."

"That was clever, Sir Roland," Millicent said. "Was that a lie, or have you kept a secret from us? Is there a Danish girl waiting for you up in those mountains you left behind?"

Roland turned a baleful eye to Declan.

"You're enjoying this, aren't you?" he asked his friend.

"Immensely!" said Declan.

Millicent threw another branch on the fire and watched it flare up.

"And what of your message to the Queen? I've shared with you why I must seek her out. Do you trust me enough to do the same?"

Roland and Declan looked at each other in the flickering light. They had sworn to reveal their information only to the Queen, yet to honour that oath meant concealing from Millicent the news that her father would not be home for another year. That seemed wrong, but they had pledged their secrecy.

"My lady, I do trust you, but we cannot break our oath regarding this message. When we find the Queen, she may decide whether you may hear it."

Millicent poked at the fire with a branch for a long moment.

"So you will honour your oath to keep this message a secret, though you broke your oath to my mother when you left my father behind. You seem fickle regarding those oaths you honour and those you do not."

Declan started to protest, but Roland laid a hand on his arm.

"She's right. We were released from our duty by Sir Roger, but never by Lady Catherine. It's a broken oath, and we must mend it somehow."

"How can we do that?" Declan grumbled.

"I don't know, Dec."

Roland looked across the dying fire and met Millicent's eyes. They looked more sad than angry. Finally, he rose and scattered the coals of the fire..

"I'll take first watch. We'll get an early start in the morning." No one objected.

***

Lord Llywelyn ap Iorwerth stood before Lady Catherine de Laval and Earl Ranulf like a chastened boy.

"You let her go?" Lady Catherine asked, incredulously. "Have you lost your senses?"

"No, my lady. I have not," he replied calmly. "I think your daughter perhaps sees things more clearly than any of us. My campaign to gain my inheritance goes so slowly I may be an old man before I take what is mine and your Lord Ranulf here," he motioned toward the Earl, "may be a toothless elder before he sees Chester again. Something must change, and the girl has a notion of how to make that happen. Without some show of support from beyond these Welsh hills, our cause is lost. I think we must pray that our Lady Millicent finds her way to the Queen."

Lady Catherine wrung her hands as she listened to this young Welsh nobleman tell her what her mind already knew. But her heart—her heart could not contemplate losing Millie. She tried to stem the fear that was nearly overwhelming her. For good or ill, the girl was gone beyond her control.

"Perhaps my daughter does see things that have escaped me, but she cannot possibly foresee the risks she is taking. A girl on the road alone..." she stopped, unable to utter the dangers that came so easily to her mind.

"She is not alone, my lady. There were two young knights with her when we found her. They claimed to be sworn men of your husband and your daughter vouched for them."

"Knights? My husband has no knights in his service, save Alwyn Madawc, and we know he lies buried by the Dee."

Llywelyn shrugged.

"One was tall with dark hair. He went by the name of Sir Roland. The other was red of hair and called himself,"

"Declan!" Lady Catherine fairly shouted the name, then clutched at Llywelyn's arm. "My husband—was he not with these boys?"

"No my lady, your daughter said to tell you your husband lives, but did not return with these two knights."

Catherine's head was spinning. Roland and Declan—home—but without Roger? What could it mean? She was thankful that Millicent was not alone in this unforgiving border country, but that relief was tempered by a bitter thought.

If Roland and Declan have come home, who is watching my husband's back?

Alas Jerusalem

*T*he tall man slogged through the clinging mud of the camp toward the improvised barn where the horses were kept. Dark thunderheads had been building in the west all morning and now they released a torrent of hail. The icy spheres bounced off his steel helmet with a rattling sound and gathered in white patches amidst the dark mud.

Other men looked out from the shelter of their tents and wondered at the weather. How could a land so brutally hot and dry now threaten to drown and freeze them? Sir Roger de Laval gave the weather little heed, as his mind dwelled on the task before him. Today he would lead another probe up the road that ran from Beit Nuba, where the Crusader army was camped, toward Jerusalem, twenty miles away.

Only twenty miles—it might as well be a thousand.

Doubtless, the knights he led would see this as further preparation for the final march on the Holy City, but he knew it was a futile demonstration at best.

Sir Roger shook his head as he thought of his meeting with the King the night before. His ruler was a man truly torn. Richard's honour, his reputation, his Crusader oath all drove him to march on Jerusalem, but he was a veteran soldier who was not blind to the facts. His pleas for more men from the kings of Europe had not born fruit and Saladin's army had not scattered after the Crusader victory at Arsuf the previous summer.

After that battle, the King secretly opened negotiations with Saladin through the sultan's brother, El Malek el-Adel, but both sides had exchanged ludicrous offers and impossible demands. The talks had come to naught. The glow from Arsuf had faded, but Jerusalem was now almost within sight, and optimism infused the Crusader ranks this cold December. The winter rainy season would end in two months and there were calls from all the European contingents to seize the city before Easter.

When they had met in his quarters, the King had seemed animated and full of restless energy. From somewhere in the camp loud voices were raised in a marching song.

"Do you hear that, Roger?" He gestured in the direction of the rousing chorus. "Despite the mud, despite the foul weather, the men are keen to go forward! The city is less than four leagues away. How can I turn back now?"

Sir Roger shifted uncomfortably before the King's evident high spirits, but spoke bluntly.

"Your grace, shall I recount the facts on the ground? We do not have enough men to garrison Acre and Jaffa, protect our supply lines and also besiege Jerusalem. You know this. Each time we move closer to the city, Saladin shifts his forces toward our rear and threatens to cut us off from the sea."

Richard stalked around his field tent as he listened to this familiar assessment.

"What would you have me do? How can I tell them we will retreat like whipped dogs back to Jaffa?"

"You are the commander, your grace. You don't tell them. You order them."

The King whirled on him with a dark look.

"You are a knight with a single fief. Reputation is no concern of yours, but it must be the concern of a king. Damage to my reputation is damage to my empire. Don't think that defeat here won't be used by Philip and others against me!"

The King glared at him, but the knight stood stolidly and made no reply.

"Well, say something, damn you!" the King shouted.

Sir Roger remained silent for a moment then spoke calmly.

"Your grace, as a simple knight, I cannot speak to the politics of your station. That's what you have earls and bishops for. But I know this—if you take that city, you must stay and defend it. If you depart for England, as I know you must, the European knights will follow and within a fortnight, Jerusalem will be back in Saladin's hands. So I see the die as already cast. Leave now or leave months from now, the end result will be the same—except for the many more dead we will leave behind."

He knew this had sounded like a lecture, and one did not lecture Richard the Lionheart. He stood with his head held high and waited for the wrath of his king. Instead, the man slumped and shook his head.

"You don't know how to coat things with honey, do you?"

"No, your grace."

"Very well. Take your bitter tidings elsewhere. But I want a strong probe up the road tomorrow—as far as we can get. Perhaps this close to Christ's Mass, we will be granted a miracle. And Sir Roger, I do not want you at the head of that patrol. I may not always like your counsel, but I do not wish to lose it."

That meeting was still on Sir Roger's mind as he entered the barn, making for the paddock where his great grey warhorse, Bucephalus was stabled. By rights, as commander of the English heavy cavalry, he should not lead this probe. The King had ordered him not to, but he would not risk some other man's life for the King's folly.

Bucephalus whinnied as he drew near, but the knight stopped in his tracks, for approaching from the other direction was the King.

"I see you like to give advice, but not take it—even when it comes from your King."

Sir Roger hung his head, embarrassed that he had been caught in disobedience.

"Your grace…I…"

"Oh, shut up man. I pardon you. Besides, I am going as well to see first-hand how things stand."

Sir Roger wanted to protest, but did not. He knew it was a waste. The King was not just a monarch. He was one of the mightiest warriors of the age. He did not become that by shying away from danger. A groom arrived with Richard's magnificent black stallion and another was leading Bucephalus from his paddock. Together they mounted and joined a group of forty riders who had assembled near the Jerusalem road. Sir Roger dispatched four men to scout to the front and the remainder of the patrol fell in behind the big Norman and the King.

Blessedly the hail had stopped and there was even a weak sun beginning to show through the overcast as they moved up the muddy track and began the probe. On the last patrol, his cavalry had travelled almost ten miles up the road before encountering anything more than the ever-present Muslim scouts. They had finally been halted by a barricade of brush and wagons athwart the road and manned by infantry and archers.

On this day, the road was a soupy mess and soon the horses and riders that followed the vanguard were splattered with mud. The going was slow and it was nearing noon when they sighted a barricade blocking the road. It was manned only by a few scouts who retreated at their approach. It took hardly a moment to clear the flimsy barrier. A mile further on, they came to a split, with the main road continuing down the wide valley and a smaller road leading up a narrow cleft into some low hills. Sir Roger called a halt and turned to the King.

"Your grace, I think it wise to see what lies up this road before we move on. There could be a hundred cavalry concealed up there in those hills and I do not want to be cut off." The King nodded his agreement. Sir Roger dispatched ten knights to move up the main road to watch for any threat from that direction and led the remainder into the hills.

A few abandoned shepherds' huts flanked the road as they climbed, until at last they crested the highest ridge. Sir Roger reined in Bucephalus and had to stifle a gasp. For in the distance, across a rolling carpet of hills, could be seen a huge encampment of troops. Saladin had indeed been reinforced.

The King rode up beside him and reined in his horse, assessing the enemy strength with the experienced eyes of a man who had seen many hosts arrayed against him. The look on Richard's face spoke volumes. Then the King raised his eyes further, to the farthest set of hills that lay beyond the encampment. There, as though painted on a canvas, were the walls of Jerusalem.

Sir Roger heard a strangled groan and turned to see the King wheel his horse around and start back down the hill. The rest of the patrol was so transfixed by the sight of the Holy City that they did not notice the King's hasty retreat. Sir Roger rode to catch up with the man. When they were well below the crest, Richard reined in his horse and Sir Roger slowed Bucephalus to a stop.

"Sire? Shall I order the men back?" The King rocked back and forth in the saddle, his face a picture of anguish as he looked up at his knights milling about on the ridgeline.

"No...no...let them have their moment. I would not deny them that, but I have no right to look upon that city—not if God does not intend for me to capture it."

Sir Roger kept silent, for there was little that he could say to comfort this warrior king in his despair. But he realized that the King's words carried more than just sorrow. They meant that Richard the Lionheart had finally accepted the reality before him. *Jerusalem was lost.*

"Your grace, perhaps it is God's will that we end the slaughter," he offered finally.

The King took a deep breath and straightened himself in the saddle. He gave Sir Roger a weak smile.

"It would help if God just spoke to us directly—like he did with the old prophets, but instead we are left to guess. I will know on Judgment Day if I've guessed correctly. But for now, I will send for Saladin's brother and this time we shall find a way to make a peace." He looked up the hill at the excited knights who were shouting and pointing at the distant city.

"That is, if my army does not kill me."

Sir Edgar

*T*he morning dawned clear and a bit warmer. Roland, Declan and Millicent made haste to break camp and get back on the road. It would take at least five days to reach London if the horses held up. With enemies behind them in Chester, speed was advisable. As they rode, Millicent called out to Roland.

"Sir Roland, I notice you no longer sit a horse like you were straddling a log in the forest. Perhaps my early instruction did not go completely to waste."

He smiled. When he had first come to Shipbrook he had never ridden a horse. Indeed, none of the peasants in the high country of Derbyshire owned a horse. His poor riding had been the despair of young Lady Millicent back then. But he had spent many hours in the saddle over the dusty hills of the Holy Land, and riding now seemed completely natural to him.

"I still prefer a log in the forest, my lady, but I get by."

Watching her, he knew that he would never have her skill with a horse. As she rode beside him, her back was as straight as one of the arrows in his quiver and her hands were light on the reins. The motion was so smooth, it looked as though she could balance crockery on her head. As the day wore on, her grace in the saddle did not waver.

After three days of hard riding and sleeping on the ground, they decided it was time to chance a stay at an inn. They were far enough from Chester to feel it was worth the risk, and they needed news of the Queen. If any news was to be had, they would find it at an inn.

Near the end of the day, they found a lively looking establishment beside the Roman road in the village of Towcester. There was one small room left. It had two straw mattresses on the floor.

"Better than the woods," Declan observed happily. Without ceremony, Millicent dropped her kit on one of the rough beds.

"I'm sure you two are used to sharing close quarters," she said sweetly.

"Aye," said Roland with a grin. "I've become accustomed to our Irish friend here speaking Gaelic in his sleep. I hardly notice it now."

"I dream of poetry," said Declan, with an offended tone.

"I thought I heard some strange mutterings these past few nights," said Millicent

"It was Irish gibberish, my lady," Roland offered, "and it is much louder in close quarters such as these. Perhaps it will lull you off to sleep, as it does me."

Declan gave them both a sour look, then shook his head.

"Let's go have some ale. They've a good fire in the common room, and I still feel the chill in my bones."

Together they made their way to the crowded room where two travelling priests kindly made room for them at a small table. The two church men had clearly been sampling the ale for much of the afternoon and could barely speak coherently, but they made for cheerful company.

Roland caught the attention of the beefy woman who was tending to the crowd of patrons and soon bowls of stew and three tankards of ale were produced. The stew had little meat, but plenty of carrots and onions and was flavourful enough. Roland saw Millicent take a sip of the ale.

"I should have asked if you fancied ale."

"I do," she answered, "more so than wine."

As they ate their stew and drank their ale, each of them kept a keen eye on the room and listened to snatches of conversation. No mention of the Queen was heard. Roland was about to simply ask someone if Her Grace had returned to London, when he noticed a very large man across the way staring intently at their table. The man had a long tangled beard, dark as a coal pile, and a neck like a bull. Beside him on his bench rested a battleaxe.

When their eyes met, the man seemed to reach a decision. He rose slowly, reached for his axe and began to make his way toward them through the crowded common room. He dragged one leg slightly, giving him an awkward gait. Awkward or no, he covered the distance quickly and loomed over the table. His head almost reached the low ceiling of the room. Roland saw Declan's hand move to the hilt of his sword.

"I know you!" the man said, pointing directly at Roland. There was a gleam in his eye, though it did not look hostile. Roland desperately tried to recall where he might have seen this huge man before. He was hardly the kind one would easily forget, and there was something vaguely familiar about him, but...

"I feel I should know you as well, friend, but cannot place our acquaintance."

The man did not seem offended. He leaned over and placed his axe on the table, its haft clasped in two huge gnarled fists. He drew his face close. A sour mix of ale and stale breath washed over them.

"You are the squire who held the breach at Acre—are you not?"

Acre. That's where he had seen this giant before. He had been with the English host that had come ashore with King Richard. He had been hard to miss the day they had landed on the beach, being the tallest man in the army by a considerable margin. Roland could not recall encountering the man around the camp. But now a snatch of memory came to him—of a large knight with a deadly axe who had been on his right during the fight at the breach.

"Aye, I was on the wall that day, as were you, I believe. I am Sir Roland Inness of Kinder Scout."

The giant grunted.

"I was on the far right of the line in the first wave that day— into that godawful breach in the north wall—same as you and Red there." He jerked a thumb in Declan's direction. The man's gaze lifted as he seemed drawn back to that bloody day. "Nastiest fight I've ever been a part of, and I've been in a few!"

He looked back down to Roland.

"You saved us that day—you and the Irish lad. After Earl Robert fell, the men...they lost heart. I could feel it. When that last charge swept down on us, we were finished. Some had already started to run and I'll not lie, I was about to do the same. Had we broken then, I think not a man of us would have made it to the bottom of that rock pile." The big man paused for a moment and shook his head.

"But then I heard some fool call for a shield wall and saw you and Red up there alone...well, I couldn't exactly turn tail then—could I?"

"No, I suppose you couldn't." Roland rose and extended his hand to the man. Roland was taller than most men, but this giant was taller than he by half a foot. "I remember now. I saw you with that great axe holding the right flank like an anchor. You killed many a Saracen that day."

The big man took Roland's hand in a massive paw.

"Aye, the killin' business was good that day."

As Roland looked up, he saw pride, and loss too, in the man's eyes. Those dark eyes seemed to tell the story of King Richard's crusade in a single look. Roland wondered if his own eyes told the same story. Dreams of that terrible day still came to him in the night. Less often now, but they still had the power to jerk him awake, covered in sweat. There was a bond that was shared by men who had faced such a thing together.

"Any man who stood with us on the wall that day...." Roland's voice trailed off and started to crack. Declan rose and saved him from embarrassment by extending his own hand to the giant.

"The name is Sir Declan O'Duinne and I do not take kindly to being called by my hair colour. Were ye not a man who had stood with us on the wall of Acre—and were ye not as tall and broad as an oak tree—I would have to thrash you." For a moment the man's eyes flashed a challenge, then he erupted into booming laughter as he clasped Declan's hand.

"Fair enough, Sir Declan. I will watch my words with you, as I know how *temperamental* the Irish can be. And I also saw your sword work up there on the wall. I think if you and I were to fight, we might both end up dead!"

"There will be no fighting between us, friend," Roland interjected, "and I have been remiss in not introducing the Lady Millicent de Laval." He motioned toward Millicent who had been watching the man carefully. He turned toward her.

"De Laval," the man spoke the name and seemed to be turning it over in his mind.

"Lady Millicent is the daughter of Sir Roger de Laval," Roland said.

"Ah, Sir Roger! He led the second wave that day. Great warrior, Sir Roger, and a good man I've heard. My respects, Lady Millicent." He bowed his head toward the girl.

Millicent nodded her acknowledgement.

"You have the advantage of us, sir. You know our names but haven't given us yours."

The two drunk priests had already fled at the approach of the big man and he sat down heavily, completely taking up the space they had vacated.

"My name is Sir Edgar Langton. I come from the far eastern part of Derbyshire and was a vassal of Earl Robert de Ferrers—God rest his soul. I took a wound to the tendon in my leg that day in Acre. They sent me home after that. I'll never walk straight again, but I get around—and I can still use this!" He raised the axe a little way off the table, then suddenly turned toward Roland.

"Kinder Scout? Isn't that in the high country west of Castleton? Are we not fellow Derbyshire men then?"

"Aye, I come from Derbyshire," Roland replied.

"I thought only Danes lived up in those hills."

"True enough, Sir Edgar, and I am one. Does that trouble you?"

The big man grunted and slapped Roland on the back.

"Not a'tall. I'm Saxon and our old feuds with the Danes were bloody, until the Normans came and pissed on us both! Good fighters, the Danes." He turned to Declan. "And the Irish too, Sir Declan!"

He swung his free hand around encompassing all of the patrons in the small inn. "But none of this lot understand what we did over there among the Saracens and none care. I think it may have been better for me if I had fallen that day on the wall of Acre."

Roland shook his head.

"You should not say such things, Sir Edgar. Tell us what brings you to this inn on Watling Street."

Sir Edgar sighed.

"My father had been vassal to Earl Robert before me and was close to the old man. I was the same age as his son, William, and when we were young they wanted me to be the little prick's companion. They're lucky I didn't kill him before his fifteenth birthday. He was a coward and a bully—and he cheated at games. He knew none could risk besting him and offending the Earl. I wonder now if the Earl truly would have been offended had I thrashed William."

Roland, Declan and Millicent stole glances at each other, but the man seemed not to notice as he continued his story.

"I'd hoped to be in Earl Robert's company when he sailed for the Holy Land, but he took only his closest companions. So I stayed. I stayed until I could stomach Derbyshire no more and left to join King Richard's army." The man paused and drained a cup of ale left behind by one of the priests, then belched loudly.

"After the Earl left, there was no one to restrain the son. He left Sir William to govern his lands and William is…well you've already heard my views on the man. He is a weak man who thinks he can show strength by being cruel." Sir Edgar paused to take a long gulp of ale from Roland's cup.

"When I returned from the war, I found my father had died and William had given my fief to one of his favourites. When I protested, he laughed at me, and he said this…he said, 'Edgar, a stupid oaf such as you might be of some use to me, but a crippled oaf is not.' He said that to me!"

Edgar halted his account abruptly and looked at his new companions. "I say too much. A man could lose his head for such talk."

Roland looked at the huge man and laid a hand on his shoulder.

"Sir Edgar, you do speak too freely. You should take care, but you are among friends here. William de Ferrers is a coward and a bastard. So say I—so say we all at this table. We—each of us—have our own accounts to settle with Earl William de Ferrers. But tell me, what are your plans now you have no fief?"

The man spread his hands and shook his head.

"Plans? I have no plans, nor land, nor liege lord. I travelled to London when I left Derbyshire and found others there like me—damaged men back from the Holy Land. The crown now feeds them and provides a roof, but these were *fighting men*. I could see that the crown's generosity was making beggars of them. It made me sick to see it, so I left. I have been here for two days drinking away the last of my coins. *That* is my plan."

Roland stole a glance at Millicent and Declan and got small nods in return.

"Then perhaps we might offer you a better plan. We are heading to London to meet the Queen if she is in residence and if not, we travel to Normandy to find her there. Having another sword, or axe, along would be handy. Do you have a horse?"

"I sold my horse yesterday and have drunk up the proceeds."

"That is easily remedied. If you wish to join us, we'll procure you a mount. We leave for London at first light."

Sir Edgar took a moment to consider the offer.

"Very well, but I'll not join a gaggle of geese. Who leads here?" He looked between Roland and Declan.

I do. The thought came to Roland unbidden, and he would not speak it. It was something he and Declan had never discussed, but he knew it was true—had known it for a long time.

How do I answer?

"He is!" He felt Declan slam a hand down on his shoulder. "At least until he tells us to do something stupid."

"Fine," said Sir Edgar. "I am yours to command."

"Very well," Roland said, "meet us in the stables 'fore dawn ready to ride to London."

Sir Edgar spoke as they all rose to leave.

"I'm beholden to you—and perhaps I can begin earning my keep by telling you the Queen is not in London. Nor is she in Normandy. She is a day's ride south of here—in Oxford."

***

Spurred by the news that the Queen was close by, they took their leave of Sir Edgar and sought out a horse trader doing business at a nearby stable. Finding a mount suitable for a man of Sir Edgar's size was going to be a challenge, but there were few better judges of horseflesh than Millicent de Laval and she set about expertly interrogating the man about his stock. Declan drew Roland aside as Millicent dickered.

"Roland, I should not have volunteered ye as leader without yer leave, but Sir Edgar was right. There has to be one and, while I'm a good man with a blade, I've no yen to be a leader—too many decisions for my taste," he said. "But you? It comes to you naturally. I saw it all the way back on the day you tracked Millicent into Wales. I saw it too many times to recall in the Holy Land. You've got a good head for it, so I'm happy to let you use it—just don't do anything stupid."

Roland felt a rush of relief. Declan was senior to him in age and more experienced in some things, but the words he spoke were true. The instinct to lead was strong in him. He wondered if Rolf Inness had felt the same—if that's what had compelled his father to take leadership of the Danes when they rose against the de Ferrers.

He turned to Declan.

"Declan, it would be better if Sir Roger were here, but he is not. So I will lead—but you and I, we are clan. We are brothers. I will need your good counsel."

"And you will have it—probably until yer sick of it. It's why I picked you to lead. That way I can complain!"

Just then Millicent returned, leading a large black horse with massive shaggy fetlocks. She caught the end of their conversation.

"No one asked *me* who should be leader," she said fixing them both with a challenging look.

"My lady…" Roland started, but she cut him off.

"If you must know, Sir Roland, I would have agreed with Sir Declan. That giant with the axe seems to hold you in high regard, and I think we should not trifle with that. Just remember one thing."

"My lady?"

"I do not take orders from you."

The French Web

*F*ather Malachy hated London in the winter. The place seemed forever wrapped in a chilling fog and still managed to stink. Still, he welcomed the opportunity to get away from Chester, where the Earl of Derby had doubled the guard around the castle and only emerged from his quarters to order more men out to patrol the Dee ford and watch for the boy with a bow. It was madness.

His monthly duty to escort the tax revenue from the Midlands to the capital afforded him the opportunity to leave behind his master's dark fears and tend to other, more pressing business. William de Ferrers had charged him with keeping a careful accounting of all the revenue collected from his lands— and a separate accounting to be presented to the Prince's agent in London—the two ledgers not being precisely the same.

Lately, the revenues had more than doubled with the collections from Cheshire flowing in. The totals delivered to London and the amount skimmed by de Ferrers had increased accordingly. This pleased him. Wealth bought power, and it was power in the hands of weak men—men Malachy knew would be the undoing of the English. With enough wealth, John might actually topple Richard. That was the pressing business he hoped to further on this trip.

Having a weak king on the throne in London would be a victory in itself for the man he loyally served—the King of France. Beyond weakening England, Philip Augustus would take personal pleasure in humbling the man he hated above all others—Richard Coeur de Lion.

Malachy and the heavily-guarded wagon carrying the revenue of the Midlands arrived late in the evening at the gates of London and he made his delivery to the Prince's man the following morning. The two jointly went over the books and counted the wealth that had been squeezed from noble and peasant alike in the region. The Prince's agent was no cleric, but was clearly a man with considerable education and a sharp eye as well.

"Tell your master that he has done well enough, Father," he said after they had completed the accounting. "The Prince will be pleased."

Malachy smiled and began to rise.

"*And* tell the thieving bastard, we expect a tithe more next month, or the Prince will be displeased. Tell de Ferrers not to get too greedy, or my master will replace him. Understood, priest?"

Malachy bowed. It was not the first time he had been threatened by this man, and he took it seriously. He did not think John would hesitate to replace anyone who did not serve his purposes. So de Ferrers would simply squeeze all the harder to please the Prince and keep his own share of the booty.

His official work complete, the priest trudged through the nearly deserted streets of the city. There was a cold rain falling and most folk had found shelter inside. That suited him, as he had no wish to be noticed. He could have ridden, but he had much to think on and the walk would clear his mind.

His steps led him up Fleet Street and out Ludgate. To his left, the strange round church of the Templars loomed. A half mile on, he passed the sumptuous town house de Ferrers maintained in the city and a little farther on came to a dwelling almost as grand. He looked both ways and, seeing no one, hurried up the walk to the front portico.

Someone had been watching the street and the door swung open to receive him.

"Father Malachy! Welcome my friend. What news do you bring me?"

The man who greeted him at the door was dressed in the same priestly black robes as Malachy, though of much richer material. He was an old man and slightly stooped, but he had the eyes of a wolf. Unlike Malachy, Herbert Poore was truly a churchman, and more than that, he was the Archdeacon of Canterbury. He was also the chief agent of the French king in England and very well paid for his services.

He controlled dozens of men scattered around the island, all working under the direction of his own master, the Bishop of Beauvais, cousin and spymaster to King Philip. The richness of his London lodgings attested to how well King Philip rewarded his loyal servants. Malachy pictured himself one day standing where his spymaster now stood.

"The news is good, your excellency. The Midlands are restive, as you know, but de Ferrers is keeping a tight grip on things and the revenue continues to increase." He paused, considering whether he should share his concerns over de Ferrers' obsession with a lone bowman, but lost his nerve. His worth to the French had risen along with the rise to power of the Earl of Derby. De Ferrers had become their most prized chess piece after Prince John and if the Earls reputation suffered, so too would his. He held his peace.

"That's very good news indeed," the old man said as he led Malachy back to a small room with a warm fire crackling in the hearth, "but tell me more about this restiveness. No doubt your Earl has things well in hand, but who are your troublemakers?"

Malachy paused before answering. There had been serious incidents in Nottinghamshire and Cheshire—and even in Derbyshire. On de Ferrers' orders, they had tortured the few men they had caught, but the information they provided was useless. There seemed to be no organization behind the incidents in the Midlands and no leaders—just starving peasants lashing out.

Most troubling were the attacks in the high country of Derbyshire itself. The Danes were restless and that always meant trouble. In truth, the Midlands were very restive, but the truth might raise doubts in Archdeacon's mind. This he did not want.

"They are common bandits, your excellency—they've robbed some of our tax collectors and we've caught and hung a fair number. I should think this will send a message to the rest to not trifle with the Earl's business."

"Let us pray you are right, my son, but I fear that this trouble runs deeper than a few bandits, and it seems the Prince is of like mind. My agents inform me that he will dispatch his mercenary army to Nottingham soon to seize the royal castle there. With control of that fortress, along with the castles of Peveril, Lincoln and Chester, the Prince can crush any unrest in the Midlands—even if these troublemakers you speak of prove to be more than common bandits." The Archdeacon leaned forward as he spoke and placed a bony hand on Malachy's knee.

"But let me turn to more pressing issues, if I may."

"Of course, your excellency."

"Malachy, you have proven to be one of my best men. Our masters in Paris appreciate all that we've accomplished—all that *you* have accomplished. I have persuaded them that you are capable of bigger things."

"What things, your excellency?" Malachy asked, trying not to show his eagerness.

"My son, I will share a confidence with you. We are close—so very close to toppling the English crown into the gutter! But..."

He paused searching for words, his eyes feral in an old man's face.

"But *she*—she sits like a spider in the middle of her web and feels every tremble." He did not need to mention the Queen's name.

"She has stymied Philip in Normandy and now she has come, unannounced, to England! Our man in Southampton ruined a horse getting here with the news of her disembarkation there."

Malachy stiffened. News of the Queen's sudden return to England had not reached Chester, but he instantly grasped the danger of having her back in the country.

"Why has she come now?"

"Because she knows as well as we that John is gaining strength at Richard's expense. She's gone to Oxford to bully the barons into line, and enough of them may fear her to keep the throne just out of the Prince's reach. She is a most troublesome woman."

"Is there no way to thwart the Queen, your excellency?"

Herbert Poore rose slowly from his chair, moved to a nearby cabinet, and withdrew a bottle of wine.

"Malachy, I have plans for you, but for now you will return to serve your Earl. When the time is ripe, you will be summoned to London on ecclesiastical business, so be prepared."

Malachy rose as the Archdeacon produced two glasses, dug the cork from the bottle and poured. They raised their glasses in a silent toast and the old man took a deep drink.

"French," he said with a smile, "from Bordeaux in the Aquitaine."

He poured another glass, and held it up to the light.

"You know, the sweetest wines come from the Aquitaine. I wish I could say the same for the women."

Eleanor Regina

It was well before dawn when Sir Edgar appeared outside the inn at Towcester. He seemed happy with his new mount. Millicent leaned close to Roland and whispered.

"The trader claimed it was a warhorse, but I'd wager it knows the front end of a plough. Still, it's of a size to support our new friend."

Sir Edgar hung his battleaxe to the saddle by a leather loop and climbed up. The big plough horse did not seem to mind. As they turned toward the Oxford road, he told them what he knew of the Queen. It was not much. He did not know what had brought Eleanor to Oxford, but he had passed through the town three days before and the place had been abuzz with rumours.

Some said she came with news of the King's death and was meeting the barons to prepare the way for John to succeed his brother. Others said she was meeting with barons who remained loyal to Richard to counter John's arrogant assumption of royal authority in the King's absence.

"Talk. It's all just talk," Sir Edgar said, summing up what little intelligence he had on the purpose of the Queen's presence in Oxford.

Well into the afternoon they rode hard, only stopping to procure some oats and water for the horses around noon. Before the sun set, they arrived at the outskirts of Oxford. As they neared the place, the road became crowded. The news of the Queen's presence had spread quickly and every sort of peddler, horse trader, and favour-seeker jammed the main highway into town.

"Getting to the Queen may be difficult," Millicent said, looking askance at the crush of humanity ahead of them. But they fell in behind the very large and fearsome Sir Edgar and the crowds parted as if by magic. Roland patted his tunic.

"Before we left Jaffa, a clerk gave me a safe passage with the King's seal affixed. I've had no use for it until now. It should gain us entrance." He said this with more assurance than he felt.

The mob of travellers had simply overwhelmed the sentries posted at the north gate of Oxford and they had given up stopping and questioning those converging on the town. Even so, new arrivals moved in a tight throng and at a snail's pace through the arched passageway in the outer wall. Once inside the crowd eased a bit as travellers spread into the many side streets that wove through the place.

After clearing the gate and proceeding into the centre of town, they came to High Street, which led west to the castle. The fortress had been built in a bend of the River Thames, with a moat completing its outer barrier. Guarding the bridge that led from the city into the bailey was a gated barbican. There was little doubt, judging by the crowd gathered at this entrance, that this was where the Queen had taken up residence.

Roland called for Sir Edgar to dismount and all four of them pressed forward through the crowd. After much pushing and shoving, the bulk of which was handled efficiently by Sir Edgar, they arrived before the men-at-arms who barred the way. There were at least a dozen armed men posted at the gate and they were turning away most supplicants.

As they drew near, a tall guard with a lance blocked their approach.

"State yer business, and get on with ye. The Queen is done with audiences fer the day."

Roland withdrew the safe conduct from his tunic and presented it.

"That is King Richard's seal," he said, pointing to the wax impression on the document. "We are here at his command with a message for the Queen."

The man studied him for a moment, trying to judge if this might actually be a legitimate messenger.

"We can take any message to the Queen," he said, as he broke the wax seal and looked at the safe conduct pass.

"Not this message," said Roland. "I was commanded by the King to present it only to the Queen, and no other."

The man frowned and called over his superior.

"Sez they's from the King with a message for the Queen's ears only." The senior man inspected the document and shrugged.

"If it's a fake, it's a good one. Send 'em on. Let the Lord Chamberlain sort 'em out."

The guard waved them through. Roland turned to Edgar.

"Take the horses and find us lodging anywhere you can—a stable will do if there is nothing more. Rooms will all be gone by now. Wait for us here once that's settled."

He handed Sir Edgar some coins and the big knight led the horses back down High Street. Roland, Declan and Millicent walked through the barbican gate, across the moat bridge and into the bailey. Here the crush was gone and but a single, unarmed man, no more than a clerk, was on station. He politely inspected Roland's document and motioned for a page.

"Have them leave their weapons here, then take them to the Earl. This document looks authentic to me, but I will have the Earl make his own judgment."

The page led them to a small chamber built into the bailey wall.

"Weapons here," he said.

Roland leaned his unstrung longbow against the wall, unbuckled his sword belt and drew a jewelled dagger from a sheath tucked inside his boot.

"You still have the assassin's blade?" Millicent asked, as he placed the unusual weapon beside his sword.

"Aye," he smiled at her. "I carry it still, though the only time it's been put to good use was when you dug that arrow from my thigh back in the Clocaenog."

For the first time since his return, she favoured him with a small smile. It was curious how it lifted his spirits.

The page escorted them across the bailey as the sun disappeared over the west wall of the castle. There were knots of men gathered in various corners and alcoves around the open courtyard speaking in hushed voices. He led them to a large, single-storey hall that abutted the tallest tower. Stone steps led up to an arched entrance.

Inside a small antechamber warmed by a smoking brazier was the clerk who had taken Roland's safe conduct. Behind a table, sat a man studying the King's seal on the pass. Millicent recognised the Earl of Oxford, Lord Chamberlain of England. The man looked up. There was exhaustion in his face.

"What is your business?" his voice was harsh.

"My lord," Roland began. "We come both as couriers from the King, dispatched from Jaffa with a message for the Queen and," he gestured toward Millicent, "we are escorting an agent of the Queen, come to report on events in Chester."

The Earl had returned to studying the parchment in front of him, but jerked his head up at the mention of Chester.

"Chester? What new mischief is afoot in Chester?" he asked, irritation in his voice.

Millicent stepped forward.

"My Lord Chamberlain, we met last spring—at the Queen's reception. She sent me to watch over things in Chester. I've come to report."

The Earl looked up at the girl and rubbed his tired eyes. He looked again and squinted.

"Are you the de Laval girl?" The Earl's exhaustion seemed to vanish as he rose to his feet. "We thought you dead along with the Earl!"

"As you can see, my lord, I am alive and so is Earl Ranulf, but only through luck and the grace of God. I have much to tell the Queen."

"Of course, my dear, of course. Her grace will want to see you, even at this hour. Come with me!"

He turned and started for a doorway behind him.

Roland cleared his throat loudly and the Lord Chamberlain called over his shoulder.

"You two, come along as well."

***

They followed the Lord Chamberlain and the clerk down a long hallway, past four armed guards and into a large, lushly appointed room that, until the Queen's arrival, had been the Earl of Oxford's own private parlour. Now the lady used it as a retreat from the public spaces in the castle and her public duties. They found Eleanor of Aquitaine sitting in a padded chair, her chin resting on her breast. A faint snoring could be heard.

The Lord Chamberlain approached gingerly, but before he could rouse her, the woman's head snapped up. The eyes were alert and took in the visitors behind the Earl. She gave the man a slightly disapproving look, but spoke calmly.

"What have you brought me at this late hour, Lord Oxford?"

"Forgive the intrusion, your grace, but you have ordered that any messages from the King be brought to you at once."

"So I did. And what is the message?"

Roland stepped forward. For some reason, he felt more nervous in front of this woman than he ever had standing before the King himself. The Queen was shrunken with age and the burdens of ruling in her son's absence showed on her face. But it was an extraordinary face for all that. The skin was still taut over high cheek bones and the eyes were as bright and searching as a hawk's.

Roland glanced over at Millicent, who was watching him intently. Now she would know the truth.

"Your grace, the King wishes you to know that he will leave the Holy Land by midsummer and return to England by Christ's Mass next," he recited the carefully memorized message.

The Queen gave an odd little laugh.

"You've memorized your message well, eh...what is your name lad?"

"Forgive me, your grace—I am Sir Roland Inness."

"*Sir* Roland? Well, they are making knights very young these days, or perhaps I just continue to grow older! Sir Roland, your message is not a happy one for England, but I was amused because I heard its exact copy a fortnight past in Normandy from another young knight. He recited it from memory, exactly as you did."

Roland could not hide the look of relief on his face.

"You know the man I speak of?"

"Aye, your grace—Sir Robin of Loxley and his travelling companion would be Father Augustine. They are our comrades."

"Yes, both were there. It is so like Richard to send two messengers in the hopes that one will get through. He is clever that way. I only hope his lingering in the Holy Land profits his soul, because it surely is not profiting his kingdom."

Roland stole another quick glance at Millicent. She must know that her father would not return before the King—and now that return would be almost a year away. He could see the sadness in her eyes, but resolve there as well.

Having received her son's message, the Queen looked past Roland to his two companions.

"So who else do we have in this party?"

Declan stepped forward. "Sir Declan O'Duinne, your grace. I've travelled with Sir Roland to deliver the King's message."

"Another young one," the Queen observed. "My thanks to you and to Sir Roland," the Queen said. "The Lord Chamberlain will see that you are rewarded for your loyal service. I have made the same journey from the Holy Land and know it is not for the weak."

"Your grace," the Lord Chamberlain began, with a touch of excitement in his voice, "at last we may know the answer to the mysterious events in Chester last spring. Lady Millicent de Laval, your spy, has returned!"

Millicent stepped forward and curtsied to the Queen. Looking up, she saw Eleanor had a stricken look on her face.

"Good lord, girl. What have you done to your hair?"

Embarrassed, Millicent ran a hand through her ragged locks. She had forgotten that she had shorn them.

"Your grace, I…" flustered she searched for words. Seeing her discomfort, the Queen motioned her to come closer.

"Oh, no matter, my dear. It always grows back. I am glad to see you. We all thought you dead these many months. Now tell me—what has happened to Earl Ranulf and what, in God's name, happened in Chester."

Millicent had rehearsed this moment many times in the months she had languished in the wilderness of Wales. "Your grace, Earl Ranulf is alive and no traitor. There is no man more loyal to the King than he. His wife—she has committed treason, but she is more a dupe than a true traitor."

"Why do you say that she is a dupe? She signed a treasonous plea to Philip of France, did she not? I saw the letter myself!" The Queen's voice was harsh.

"Aye, your grace, and I do not stand here to defend her—only to tell you what I heard with my own ears."

The Queen sat back and nodded. "Very well then, tell us what you know."

She told it from the beginning—the arrival of the priest Malachy, his suspicious behaviour on the walls of Chester and his insinuation into the Earl's household, his currying of favour with Lady Constance and then suborning her to treason.

"How do you know he suborned her?" the Queen asked sharply. "Surely a lady-in-waiting would not be present when such things were discussed. I'll not make judgements on second hand rumours, young lady!"

"Your grace, you must believe me. I was present—in a way. There was a secret passage that led from near the Earl's chambers to Lady Constance's rooms. I hid there and overhead the priest persuade her that her son was in danger from King Richard and Prince John." The Queen held up a hand, her stern expression replaced by one of bemusement.

"Ah…the Earl's Backdoor, I believe."

Millicent was speechless. *The Queen knew?*

"Don't look so shocked, my dear. I once visited Chester—not long after your Earl Ranulf was born. This was before Henry had me put away. Earl Hugh's wife had died giving birth to Ranulf and I occupied her quarters for a single night. Earl Hugh still had his mistress, but thought it a clever jest to creep through that hidden passage and pop into my room—after a night of too much ale I presume. It frightened my ladies-in-waiting to no end."

Millicent suddenly realized that her mouth had dropped open. She closed it quickly and hoped the Queen did not notice.

"We had a good laugh, but I am quite certain the old goat would have bedded me then and there if I'd given him half a notion." The Queen laughed once more at the memory, then saw the look on Millicent's face. Her voice took on a tender tone.

"Oh, child, don't you know? Royals and nobles are not so very different. We are separated from the peasants only by our wealth and power—not by our nature. Now, tell me the rest of your tale."

Millicent gathered herself and told of the priest persuading Lady Constance that only King Philip would protect her son Arthur and frightening her into signing the treasonous paper.

"The man Malachy spoke to Lady Constance as though he was an agent of the French, your grace, and pleaded with her to sign, then two days later Earl William de Ferrers seized Chester by surprise and Malachy turned the document over to him. It beggars belief that the two did not conspire to bring down the Earl."

The Queen sat silently for a long moment.

"It does, indeed my dear. I must admit, getting rid of Ranulf profits both the Earl of Derby and perhaps the King of France. It's a shame that the Old Earl, Lord Robert, died at Acre. He was ever loyal. But his son has risen quickly under the patronage of the Prince and is ambitious in ways his father never was. It can be a dangerous thing in one so callow. But tell me," the Queen fixed Millicent with a probing gaze. "When you heard that Constance had committed treason, why did you not immediately find your way to me? After all, you were my spy, were you not?"

Millicent had feared this question ever since the day she had chosen to take her information to the Earl instead of to the Queen.

"Your grace, Lord Ranulf knew naught of these events. He and his wife hardly spoke."

"That is hardly news, girl."

"Your grace, I knew that the Earl was no traitor, but I also knew that few would believe he had no part in his wife's treachery. I felt it my duty, as the daughter of the Earl's sworn man, to warn him."

"Ah, loyalty. So rare these days. And where was Ranulf when all of this took place?"

"He was away at his hunting lodge and had just returned when the Earl of Derby's men broke into the castle and sought to seize him. We fled to my home at Shipbrook, but they followed us there. We could not hold the place against the Earl's force. The only place left for us to flee was into Wales."

"And how did you manage to survive all these months in a wilderness filled with brigands and cutthroats?"

"Your grace, we were given refuge by a young Welsh nobleman, Llywelyn ap Iowerth, by name. The man claims to be the rightful ruler of Gwynedd."

The Queen nodded and turned toward the Earl of Oxford.

"I believe Prince Owain did have a grandson of that name."

"Aye, your grace, we have heard rumours that the boy was in arms against his uncles who rule there now, but who knows the reliability of rumours coming out of Wales?"

"True enough, but we now have solid information." The Queen turned back to Millicent.

"I wish you had come to me straight away, Lady de Laval, but I would probably have done the same in your place. You've been a clever girl and a good spy, and the news you bring gives me hope. You have my thanks. I would have you and your two young knights return here before noon tomorrow. Then we will decide what's to happen next."

The dismissal was clear. Millicent curtsied, Roland and Declan bowed and all three were led to the back of the chamber, where the clerk was waiting. Once they had departed, the Queen called for the Lord Chamberlain.

"My Lord Oxford, send word to the Justiciars. I would see them immediately."

The Lord Chamberlain frowned. There were three Justiciars of the realm, appointed by Richard to govern the kingdom in his absence and to keep an eye on his brother as well. Two were in Oxford to meet with the Queen and had been in counsel with her most of the day. They would not be happy to be rousted out in the night.

"My lady, you are in need of rest. Can this not wait till the morrow."

Eleanor leaned forward, all signs of fatigue gone save for the lines around her eyes.

"It cannot wait, Oxford. Go fetch them. Now!"

The Lord Chamberlain of England hurried from the hall. He ordered the clerk who had returned to the chamber to summon Sir William Marshal and Archbishop Walter of Coutances. The clerk quickly dispatched two pages to the quarters of these eminences, then hurried himself to another address in the city. Glancing over his shoulder to be sure he was not followed, he banged on the ornate oak door of the finest house in Oxford.

"Who's there?" came a startled reply from within.

"Open up! It's Reginald, I have urgent news for the Prince!"

***

Sir Edgar was waiting for them outside the barbican of the castle and led them through the dark streets of Oxford to a stable near the east gate of the town.

"It's all I could find," he said apologetically when they arrived. There was one stall near the back that had fresh hay on the floor and no occupants. They stumbled in wearily, and each found a corner to curl up in.

For the three who had come from the Queen, sleep did not come quickly. The woman had done little to make their future look brighter. Roland turned on his side and whispered to Millicent.

"My lady, I know the message we brought the Queen is bitter news for you and for Lady Catherine. I am sorry to be the one to bear these tidings."

For a long while he heard no response from across the stall, but finally he heard her whisper back.

"A year...mother had hoped he would be back before spring. I dread telling her."

Roland felt sympathy for the girl who now bore the secret he and Declan had held for so long.

"We will tell her together."

Again, there was a long silence, then he heard her whisper again.

"Thank you, Roland. I will hold you to that."

She settled into the hay. He lay awake long into the night.

The Justiciars

Walter of Coutances was lodging near the castle and arrived first. Though he was dressed in elegant robes, befitting the Archbishop of Rouen, there was nothing striking about the man himself. At this hour he had the fuzzy look of someone freshly rousted from a deep sleep. He bowed as he entered the chamber.

"Your grace, I came as quickly as I could. Is there news?"

Eleanor watched the man stifle a yawn, and suppressed a smile at the Archbishop's discomfiture. Walter of Coutances was often underestimated by his fellows because of the distinct cadences of his speech, a product of his birth in Cornwall. In their eyes, it marked him as something of a bumpkin, but Eleanor knew him to be one of the most astute men in the kingdom.

The prelate had faithfully served King Henry for many years, but when Richard's revolt finally ended the old King's life, it was Archbishop Walter who absolved the son of the sin of rebelling against his father. Walter of Coutances was a politician in a churchman's robes and one of Eleanor's most valuable allies. The man might be sleepy, but his counsel would be thoughtful.

"Indeed there is, your excellency, but have patience. Unless I miss my guess, that noise in the corridor is Lord William." She had barely finished her sentence, when the Lord Chamberlain announced the arrival of the second Justiciar to the Queen's chambers.

William Marshal strode into the hall with his usual unconscious air of authority. He was tall, handsome, and muscular and he moved like a man much younger than one of middle years. In his youth, he had been the champion at many a joust in Normandy and France and had a reputation as one of the deadliest knights in Europe.

During Richard's last revolt against his father, Marshal had remained loyal to the old King, even as Henry's health failed and his cause grew desperate. Pursued by Richard after a defeat at Le Mans, King Henry fled north, with Marshal commanding his rear guard. In Richard's haste to capture his father, he rode far out ahead of his men. Marshal wheeled unexpectedly and unhorsed the future King, leaving him defenceless.

That he had stood by the old king, even though his cause was lost, had cemented his reputation for loyalty. That he refused to kill the helpless Lionheart, proved he was no fool. A fortnight later, Henry was dead and Richard was King.

Marshal had expected the worst from the new King, but Richard proved that he was also no fool and forgave his erstwhile enemy, confirming all of the honours and privileges Henry had earlier bestowed. As a further act of trust, he named Marshal as one of the Justiciars who would govern his realm while he was on Crusade.

Now fashioned Lord of Striguil, Marshal controlled wide holdings both in southern Wales and Ireland. He had been one of Eleanor's favourites since taking a wound protecting her from an attack in Normandy twenty-five years ago. It was Marshal who rode to Winchester to release her from captivity after King Henry's death.

The Queen watched him approach with his usual mix of formality and familiarity. In some ways the man baffled her. He was ambitious, yet held himself to a standard of loyalty and integrity that rarely prospered a man in this age of double dealing and treachery. Others clawed their way to the top—she not least of all—yet here was a man who had risen without trampling or betraying those around him.

"William, good of you to come so late."

"It is never too late to attend you, your grace." He nodded to the Archbishop then turned back to the Queen. "What news have you?"

Eleanor got directly to the point.

"You are already aware that Richard does not expect to return to these shores until the end of the year. Two more messengers arrived today to confirm that unhappy news. How we shall hold his kingdom together until then, I can't guess, but we have been all through that."

Both men nodded.

"But for the first time in months, I have a piece of hopeful news. Ranulf of Chester is alive and hiding in Wales. I also have it on good authority that he is no traitor to the King, though there are those who have attempted to paint him so.

A flicker of surprise showed on Marshal's face.

"Ranulf, alive—and in Wales? Are you sure?"

"The source is very reliable, William."

"Then I will have to make amends to the man who reported the same to me three months ago. He came to me with no proof— nothing more than the barest of rumours that the Earl of Chester was a fugitive in the north of the country. I had heard a half dozen other rumours that the man was dead, so I discounted his tale."

The Queen waived away this admission.

"No matter now. What matters is that Ranulf is alive and loyal. It gives me hope."

"What are the Earl's circumstances, your grace? He must be under someone's protection to have survived there. It is a bloody country."

"It seems he has found refuge with a pretender to the rule of Gwynedd—a man by the name of Llywelyn. Do you know of him?"

Once more, there was surprise on the face of William Marshal.

"Indeed, your grace. I have even met him. Two years ago, he arrived at my castle in Striguil with a small and rather shabby band of followers. He had proofs that he was the grandson of the old Prince and claimed his uncles had usurped his crown. He wanted my help, but he was seventeen years old and struck me as boastful. As I was newly entailed in my Welsh lands, I wanted no trouble with his uncles. I wished him luck, but gave him no aid.   I have since heard that his support grows in the back country, but he has not yet the strength to challenge his uncles to battle."

The Queen sighed.

"The game gets more complex at every turn and we must rethink our strategy once more. A live Earl of Chester, loyal to Richard, is a valuable piece on the chessboard."

"But what of the charge of treason, your grace?" asked the Archbishop.

"As Justiciars, it is within your power to dismiss the charges against him, but we will consider the formalities tomorrow. I believe, when you hear the testimony of an eye witness to the events in Chester, you will conclude, as I have, that the man is innocent. But dismissing the charges alone will not resolve our problems in the Midlands. Ranulf does us no good holed up in Wales, but if he can be restored to his power in Cheshire, it will cut off John from substantial revenues and encourage others to remember where their loyalties lie. We must find a way to get Ranulf back into play, without him falling into my son's grasp. If that happens, he is a dead man, no matter what the Justiciars say."

She turned her gaze from Marshal to the Archbishop and back.

"Do either of you see a way to do that?"

After a long silence Marshal spoke.

"We are beset on too many fronts now, your grace. As you know, John has used his revenues from the Midlands to hire Flemish and Irish mercenaries. He's seized control of the royal castle at Lincoln and his army is marching north from London to lay siege to Nottingham. What loyal forces we have, are hard pressed to check the man. His actions are outrageous, but if it comes to civil war, I am not sure we would win."

Eleanor nodded. The threat of rebellion and usurpation had been the subject of their long meetings in Oxford and several contentious confrontations with the Prince.   Sometimes she thought it would be best to just let John take the crown as he seemed more interested in the realm than Richard, with his head full of crusading glory, but she knew—as only a mother could—that her youngest son was not up to the task. So Richard's crown must—*must*—be preserved.

But how?

"Is there *no* aid we can send to Ranulf?"

Marshal fidgeted, struggling with what to tell this woman to whom he owed so much.

"Your grace, all of our regular troops are committed. All that's left is the Invalid Company. I marched them here from London, with the thought of perhaps sending them on to reinforce the castle at Nottingham, but you know of their poor quality."

The Invalid Company was the name given to the men who had returned from the wars in the Holy Land sick or gravely wounded, some beyond saving and some who seemed uninterested in salvation. They were knights and squires, and common soldiers, many of whom had served masters who now lay buried in the bloody ground at Acre or Arsuf.

When they returned home, hobbled and in need of care, most received hostile receptions from the new men who now ruled over their fiefs. The barons who had avoided service in the King's army saw little to be gained by taking in these wretched veterans.

Richard, who knew the nature of his barons, had ordered that all his returning wounded be provided for by the crown and, in time, these rootless, damaged warriors had drifted to London. Most of them, their pride stung, were looking for some redemption, but all that was provided was an abandoned barracks outside the Aldgate and a daily ration of bread and stew.

The results were predictable. Left to their own devices, sloth, drunkenness and violence soon followed. Marshal ordered them to come to Oxford because London had grown weary of their sullen presence and frequent bouts with the authorities. Legally, these men were vassals of the crown, but they were vassals without a mission.

Now, it was the Queen's turn to be surprised.

"The Invalids, Marshal? Do you think them fit?"

Marshal shook his head.

"Perhaps not, your grace, but they are all we have and the good people of Oxford are already asking when they will be going back to London."

The Queen shook her head, then shrugged.

"Well, perhaps Ranulf can make a silk purse from this sow's ear. Who do you have to lead them?"

Once more, William Marshal struggled for an answer. All of his capable commanders were in the field. He sighed.

"I have only Sir Harold FitzGibbons currently at my disposal, your grace."

"FitzGibbons? Wasn't he the Constable at Lincoln when the royal castle was surrendered to John?"

Marshal nodded wearily.

"Aye, my lady, he was. Apparently, your son sent a band of his Irish mercenaries to demand the place be yielded and FitzGibbons gave it up with hardly a fight. But he is the only man of sufficient rank we have."

The Queen's shoulders slumped.

"Very well, William. Give the orders."

Sir William bowed.

"But come back tomorrow at noon—both of you. Then you will meet my spy from Cheshire who brought us the news of Ranulf, and two knights recently home from crusade—vassals of Earl Ranulf. They are dreadfully young, but have the look of fighting men. These three will have to lead the redoubtable Harold FitzGibbons to Ranulf. We must pray he doesn't get the lot killed."

William Marshal allowed himself a wry smile.

"I will attend your grace at noon tomorrow." The Lord of Striguil bowed to the Queen then turned and left. Eleanor turned to the Archbishop.

"Your excellency, I did not bother Sir William with this, for it seemed more in your realm—but tomorrow you will hear from my spy that a priest suborned Lady Constance to commit treason. He is said to have presented himself to the lady as though he were an agent of the French king. What do you make of that?"

Walter of Coutances rubbed his chin. He had been appointed Justiciar less than a year before, and at the Queen's direction, he had continued the work she had begun of creating a network of spies and informants throughout the land.

"This information is reliable, your grace?"

"It is, Archbishop."

The prelate nodded.

"With your permission, I would interview your man from Chester myself on the morrow. This is not the first report I've had of French agents passing as clergy. Philip's own spymaster is a bishop, after all."

"As is mine, your excellency," she reminded him with a smile. The Archbishop of Rouen gave a chuckle and shook his head.

"Your point is taken, you grace."

"And, Archbishop, be aware, my spy from Chester is no man."

"Ahh, I should have known! Of course she's not."

***

Noon the following day found Roland, Declan and Millicent once more in the presence of the Queen. Behind her stood William Marshal and the Archbishop of Rouen. Millicent again gave her account of the disasters that had befallen the Earl of Chester and of his need for aid. Only a few questions were asked before the Queen stood and turned to face the men behind her.

"The Earl of Chester has been accused of treason. Given this testimony, how do you find—guilty or innocent?"

"Innocent," said the Archbishop of Rouen.

"Innocent," agreed Sir William Marshal.

The Queen nodded and turned toward the Lord Chamberlain.

"In concert with the Justiciars of England, and in the name of the King, I hereby absolve Ranulf, Earl of Chester, of the crime of treason and dismiss the charge. Lord Oxford, see that the dismissal is publically read in every county in the land with all haste."

She paused and looked around the room.

"Lady de Laval, I wonder if your liege lord fully appreciates what you have done for him. I hope your courage and loyalty won't be for naught. Absolving Ranulf of these charges will not restore him to his place among the barons of England. In fact, those who conjured up these charges will scoff at our decision today and ignore it. We are facing a growing civil war in the land and legal niceties won't keep John or William de Ferrers from hanging Ranulf if he falls into their grasp. So now, we will see if the son of Hugh Kevelioc has fight in him, for surely he will have to fight to regain his birth right." The Queen paused to let her grim message sink in.

"We have little aid to send the Earl, but are sending what we can. Lady de Laval, I must ask you to provide one more service to your Earl and to me. You must guide the force we are dispatching safely into Wales and deliver them to Ranulf. Only you know where he is. Will you do it?"

Millicent felt a surge of relief. At last something was being done to reverse the disasters that had befallen Cheshire and her family. She did not hesitate.

"Gladly, your grace!"

Eleanor smiled at the girl. Had she ever been that young and passionate? She looked at the two young knights that flanked Millicent and noted how the taller of the two never took his eyes off the girl.

I wonder if she knows the boy is smitten?

The Queen rose, signalling the end of the gathering. When she had retired from the room, the Archbishop, beckoned to Millicent and took her aside for further questioning. Roland and Declan followed Sir William into the antechamber, where the big knight pulled them aside.

"I'm told that you two were knighted by the King himself," Marshal said. "I would hear the account of how that came to pass. Our King does not grant such honours lightly."

Roland always felt uncomfortable telling this story. Many men had done their duty that day on the wall of Acre. His call to form a shield wall had been pure survival instinct, not a calculated act of courage. Fighting to survive seemed hardly worthy of recognition, but knighthood bestowed by a King was not something to be refused. Still…the telling could hardly help but sound boastful.

"My lord, we were in the first wave into the breach at Acre. Eighty of us went in and thirty-eight came back down. The living and the dead did their duty to the King that day. Why the King singled out Sir Declan and myself, I do not know. Others died to hold that breach—we lived."

The answered surprised Marshal. The Lord of Striguil had fought in many battles, but had never faced the forcing of a breach. He had long thought that those who volunteered for that dreadful task were glory-seekers, but there seemed none of that with these two.

The Queen had said they had the look of fighting men and he saw it too. Sir Roland was almost his height and he wondered if he had ever been an archer, for he had the broad muscular shoulders common to such men. He also had the air of a natural leader. He noted that the Irishman, Sir Declan, affected an indifferent slouch, but even so, there was something coiled in the young man's stance.

Hardly more than boys, but fighters—no doubt about it.

"Very well, young sirs. Perhaps I will get the story second hand someday, but now to business. Tomorrow you will join a force under the command of Sir Harold FitzGibbons, lately Constable of Lincoln. You two, and Lady de Laval, are charged with guiding Sir Harold safely into Wales and delivering this force to the Earl. Is that understood?"

"Aye, my lord," they both responded together.

"I would have sent these men to help our garrison at Nottingham Castle, which the Prince will soon have under siege, but the Queen says otherwise. So you must make good use of them. They are men you have much in common with. They too have returned from Crusade, but not unscathed. You may find some of them…less than fit. I give you fair warning."

"Can they ride and fight, my lord?" Roland asked

Marshal gave a small smile.

"If they are sober, I expect they can."

He did not wait for further questions, but gave a slight bow to the two and strode from the room.

"Who was that?" Declan asked. "I've not heard the name William Marshal before."

"Nor I," said Roland, "but I have the feeling that we will again."

***

Having finished his interview with Millicent de Laval, the Archbishop of Rouen joined the Queen who had retired to her private parlour. He could not help but notice the signs of fatigue that showed in that ancient, but striking face. The past week had been a whirlwind for the woman. She had arrived, unannounced, in Portsmouth two days after Christ's Mass and had set a pace thereafter that would have laid low men half her age. She had used the enormous force of her personality to flatter, bully, and buy the support of just enough barons to forestall John's lunge for the throne—but only just. The strain showed.

"What did you think of my spy?" she asked.

"An extraordinary young woman, your grace. She has a keen eye and a quick wit. The Earl's head would have been on a pike had it not been for her."

The Queen nodded.

"I saw something special in her when first we met in London. The girl has great potential—if she wants to be something more than a wife out on the frontier. If we didn't need her to find Ranulf, I'd keep her here at court."

"Her account of the man Malachy was thorough and troubling, your grace. It's more proof that Philip is playing a long game here, with John more of a pawn than a king."

The Queen rose.

"I think I will lie down for a bit, Walter. You know I'm counting on you to ferret out the spies and traitors in our midst."

The Archbishop bowed.

"You may depend on me, your grace."

***

Roland and Declan waited in the courtyard for Millicent to emerge from her meeting with Walter of Coutances. When she appeared, she still had the excited look of a woman on her own crusade.

"What did the churchman have to say?" Declan asked.

"He was most interested in learning all he could about Father Malachy. He believes the French have agents at work undermining King Richard's rule here and in Normandy. He suspects some of them are masquerading as priests. I told him what I knew and he had some advice for me."

"Advice?" asked Roland.

"Aye, he suggested the next time we see Father Malachy—we kill him."

Roland nodded.

"If the man ever comes within bow range, my lady, consider it done."

Nottingham

Sir Robin of Loxley guided his horse to the side of the road to let the throngs of townspeople heading north pass by. Friar Tuck did the same and both looked down the road to the city of Nottingham, where chaos seemed to reign.

When they had set sail from Harfleur a fortnight before, the Queen's warnings of unrest in the Midlands troubled them both. They had seen ample evidence of that unrest the further north they travelled from London. As they passed through the once-rich counties of the Midlands they were a shocked at the number of children begging in the streets of the villages they passed. In every hamlet, the people had a sullen, vacant look about them.

Most of the men shied away from two armed travellers, but a few were willing to talk. The story they told was of a disaster— not of God's making but of man's. The autumn harvest had been plentiful, but over the winter the church had taken its usual tithes and the Sheriff's tax collectors had come and come again. They had taken not just the grain, but milk cows, pigs, chickens and anything they thought they could trade for silver. There was hardly enough grain left for the vermin, much less for bread. And so, the people began to starve.

Still, as they made their way into Nottinghamshire, Sir Robin hoped to find his own quiet fief of Loxley, quiet still. It was not. In the two years he had been gone, his father had died and another man now lived in the stone keep he once called home. The new lord of Loxley was Sir Anthony Beauchamp, a favourite of Prince John. He did not welcome the returning crusader warmly.

The man would never know how close he had come to dying at that first meeting. And he would have been dead, had Tuck not grasped Robin's wrist as his hand reached to the hilt of his sword.

"Ye've not served King and country only to become an outlaw," Tuck hissed in his ear, as he restrained his friend's right arm.

So they had ridden away.

Tuck had once told him that he was a restless man and, as Robin put the keep at Loxley behind him on that bleak day in January, he felt a bond being broken. Could he have settled into the quiet life of a country noble, as his father had before him? He allowed himself a small smile. Of course, he could not have. He would have been bored within a fortnight. He was a man who wanted peace and quiet, but no longer knew what to do with either.

Together they rode south—through the vast royal forest of Sherwood toward Nottingham. Robin had grown up on the very edge of this wilderness and had spent many carefree days snaring rabbits and taking squirrels with a sling. The royal foresters did not object, as long as he did not bring his longbow into the woods and did not molest the King's deer.

As they rode, they kept their weapons close at hand. The forest was notorious for harbouring outlaws, though none appeared to trouble them. Sir Robin had no particular destination in mind, but Tuck had a new mission. He had seen enough of the despair in the villages.

"I go to London to speak to the Master of the Temple, and perhaps back to Tancarville to see the Queen. There is going to be mass starvation here before spring. *Something* must be done!"

Now they had reached Nottingham, where a frantic evacuation was in progress. As they drew near the city, they met an increasing number of townsfolk moving hurriedly north up the road toward Sheffield. Many drove wagons weighed down with their possessions. Sir Robin let the first few refugees pass by, but finally turned his horse and blocked the road. A man pulling a two-wheeled cart was forced to stop.

"Good day to you, sir," Robin greeted the man with a smile, but got right to the point. "Why the haste to leave town?"

The man was not reluctant to pass along news to a stranger.

"Best turn around yerself, sir. An army's marching this way from London and Prince John means to have the castle," he said, and pointed to the towering fortress on a rocky outcrop overlooking the town and the River Leen.

"So?"

"Well, sir, the commander of the garrison says that the castle belongs to King Richard and he will, noways, give it up to the Prince. He says the Prince has rights to the revenues of the county, but not to the royal castle."

As a boy, Sir Robin had visited the castle more than once with his father. Nottingham Castle was a key fortress that had helped the Normans keep their grip on this part of England—and it had lost none of its strategic value.

"Who commands the castle?"

"Sir Clarence Varley, sir. He's the Sheriff that King Richard appointed 'fore he left on the crusade, but they say the Prince has appointed a new man now."

"So there will be a fight?"

"Aye, sir. All expect it. And even if the townsfolk stand aside, the troops will be quartered among us. We've barely enough to feed ourselves, and those men from London, they are not even English. They will take what they want."

Robin looked up and saw that the trickle of townspeople had grown to a flood as they poured out the north gate of the city. He turned to Tuck.

"I know Varley, though not well. Perhaps we should see what his intentions are and what we may do to help."

Tuck looked at him sceptically.

"I thought you were looking for peace?"

Robin gave him a rueful grin.

"Aye, you have me there, but I believe you once said that 'Richard's a bastard, but John would be worse', did you not? So maybe saving this castle for Richard is our duty."

It was now Tuck's turn to smile.

122

"Perhaps we should agree to stop quoting each other, my friend, but your point is taken. Control of that castle up there," he said pointing to the fortress on the crag, "would make it very difficult for anyone to challenge John in these parts. I was heading to London, but if John has come from there with an army, they will not be needing me to tell them there is trouble in the Midlands. Let's go see your Sir Clarence."

It took them almost an hour to make their way through the crowds abandoning the city, but at last they rode through the massive arched gate of the castle. They had not yet dismounted when Sir Robin was hailed.

"Do I see Robin of Loxley before me—or a ghost?"

Sir Robin whirled around to see a tall man striding toward him with a broad smile. The man carried a longbow in his hand and could have passed for a Viking. He had a long blonde braid hanging over one shoulder and silver bands around heavily muscled arms that were bare, even in the chill of January.

Sir Robin swung a leg over his saddle and dropped to the cobbled courtyard of the bailey.

"Magnus Rask, by God, I'd wondered what became of you! I've been to Loxley."

The big blonde bowman embraced the knight, then held him at arms' length. "Did you kill the bastard living in your house?" Robin shook his head.

"I was going to, but the priest here stopped me," he said pointing to his companion. "This is Friar Tuck." The big man laughed.

"The church! Always spoiling our fun."

Sir Robin turned to Tuck.

"Meet the man who taught me to use a bow. The great archer, bowyer and warrior—Magnus Rask. He's a Dane, but otherwise, a good man."

Tuck saw the hammer of Thor hanging by a leather thong around the man's neck. He had seen others like it in the mountains of Derbyshire, where some still believed in the old, warlike Norse gods. He gave Rask a bright smile and extended a hand, which the big man took.

"I've converted more than a few heathen Danes to the true faith in my time. It's just a matter of convincing them that 'fun' does not include plundering and burning helpless villages."

For a moment the big bowman scowled, then gave a booming laugh.

"Ah, I like this priest, Rob. The first one I've met that made me laugh!"

Magnus Rask was about to say more, but was interrupted by a rumbling sound. The portcullis was being lowered to block the gate.

"It looks like there will be little fun here for a long time," he said. Tuck dismounted and the three climbed up to the wall walk in time to see the vanguard of the mercenary army arrive outside the fortress. The siege had begun.

Robin turned to Rask.

"The bows we had cached at Loxley…"

"They're here—two dozen. I've a few of our lads from up around Loxley who are handy with them, and I'm teaching some of these English how to shoot."

Sir Robin slapped the big Dane on the shoulder as he looked out at the growing mass of enemy soldiers.

"We will have need of them all."

The Invalid Company

*F*orty men sat their horses sullenly in the cold dawn outside the city gates of Oxford. They were all armed after a fashion, though few had armour and their mounts were the dregs of Oxford's stables. They were the Invalid Company.

"Cripples and castoffs!" Sir Harold FitzGibbons declared, loudly enough for all to hear, the colour rising in his face. He turned to William Marshal who stood beside him. "This is what you give me to put Ranulf back on his seat in Chester, my lord?"

Roland was mounted along with Declan and Millicent near the head of the column. Beside him, he heard a low growl from Sir Edgar, but the hulking giant did not move. Glancing down the ranks, he saw that most of the men seemed indifferent to the insult, but some bristled.

William Marshal bristled as well. He hardly knew Sir Harold, but was taking an instant dislike to the man.

"It's what we have, FitzGibbons," he hissed under his breath. "Shall I tell the Queen you are displeased?"

Sir Harold started to make an angry retort, but checked himself when he saw the look on the Lord of Striguil's face. It did not profit a man to cross William Marshal, or worse, Eleanor of Aquitaine.

"No...No..., but, my lord, look at them!"

William Marshal looked. They were a motley collection. He could see several men who were missing a hand or part of an arm and one man had a wooden peg fastened to the stump of leg. A number had wretchedly scarred faces and several looked as though they might actually be mad. One man held his horse's reins while he retched beside the road. Marshal did not let his misgivings show.

"They are veterans, Sir Harold, and loyal to the crown. You will treat them as such. I will be sorely vexed if I hear otherwise."

Sir Harold made no reply.

"Do you understand your orders?" Marshal asked, flatly.

"Aye, my lord. I am to lead this *band* into Wales, find Earl Ranulf and place myself and this force at his disposal."

Marshal grunted his acknowledgement. His orders had been as simple and direct as possible and the man seemed to grasp them.

"You will follow your guides and avoid trouble if possible," he said, and beckoned to Lady Millicent and her companions. The three rode forward and joined the two senior men. Marshal noted the longbow slung over Roland's shoulder. With a shock, he suddenly made the connection. This young knight was the same young squire he had seen win the golden arrow at the King's coronation tournament!

An archer indeed! Someday he must have a long conversation with this young fellow, but today was not that day. He turned back to Sir Harold.

"May I present Lady Millicent de Laval, Sir Roland Inness, and Sir Declan O'Duinne. They are vassals of Earl Ranulf and know where to find him. They also know what paths to take to avoid the trouble I've spoken of. I expect you to follow their advice."

"Of course, my lord," Sir Harold replied. "At least they seem to have all of their limbs," he added sourly.

Marshal's face flushed. He wanted to strike the pompous ass, but restrained himself. FitzGibbons, like the Invalid Company he now led, was all they had. He managed to utter an unenthusiastic hope that the expedition would have good luck, then wheeled his horse around and spurred back through the north gate of Oxford.

Sir Harold sat motionless, muttering to himself as Marshal departed. Behind him, two men, squires or servants of some sort, sat their horses stolidly. Each held a lead rope attached to heavily-laden pack horses. Their master was clearly not going to exist on rough provisions or accommodations on this march. Finally, the man roused himself, and without a word to his guides, rode slowly up the column to its head. There he stood up in stirrups and glared at the entire assemblage.

"For'ard!" he commanded and spurred his horse down the track toward Towcester and the Roman road that ran through that town. His servants and baggage trailed after him. He did not consult with or give orders to his guides. Roland and Declan exchanged looks.

"Appears his lordship is going to be his own guide," said Declan over his shoulder as he clucked to his own mount and set out after Sir Harold. Roland looked at Millicent, who simply shook her head and followed Declan. It was a morning full of bad portents and hardly the way to start a campaign to take back a key county for the King. Roland twisted in his saddle and looked back at the men in the column behind him. They had not moved.

He turned to Sir Edgar, who had been quietly watching events unfold. He still wore a dark scowl, but now it seemed directed not at Sir Harold but at the men who slouched in their saddles before the walls of Oxford. He turned to Roland.

"Come with me," was all he said and they rode down the line to its midpoint. There he reined in his big plough horse and wheeled to face the immobile men with a glare. Roland had hardly reached him, when the big man began to speak in a voice that must have carried over the wall and several blocks into the town.

"In the summer,' he began, his booming voice reaching to every man, "I come back to Derbyshire with naught but my axe and this bum leg to show for two years of fightin' in the heathen lands. The bastard son of my dead Earl called me 'cripple' and gave my fief to some bootlicker, so I come to London. They said 'the King'll provide for ye,', but I saw what it did to the likes of ye!" he shouted, eyes blazing. "Ye should be ashamed! Fighting men behaving like puling babes, sucking at the Crown's teat. It made me want to heave, it did!"

Sir Edgar paused and slowly cast his gaze from one end of the line to the other, as though looking for any man who wished to challenge him. None did.

"Who here was at Acre?" he demanded. Roland could see men exchanging curious glances now. "Or Arsuf?" More heads came up. "I recall seeing no puling babes on those deadly fields!"

A big man with an eye patch urged his horse a little ahead of the others. "I was at both!" he hurled back. "What difference does it make? It made none when I came home."

This produced a buzz of angry agreement from the ranks. The man with the patch was emboldened now.

"And this coxcomb they have put in charge of us? We all seen the likes of him! Stayed here fat and safe in England, while we did the King's dirty business. I say piss on Sir Harold PissGibbons—and piss on goin' to Wales!"

Sir Edgar scowled at the man, then turned back to the others.

"Fine! Piss on the man they sent to lead us and piss on Wales too, for all I care. But are ye going to piss on the last chance ye have to prove that yer not what they call ye—invalids and cripples?" He suddenly turned and pointed at Roland.

"I follow this man. He cares not that I drag a leg."

The big man with the eye patch rode closer and looked Roland up and down.

"He's a boy!"

Sir Edgar spurred the big plough horse forward, causing the other mount to back up.

"He is Sir Roland Inness. He held the breach at Acre. He is no boy!"

The two looked as though they might come to blows until, from further down the line, another man rode forward.

"I lost this at Acre," he said holding up the stump of a hand. "I was in the second wave into the breach. I saw the shield wall stop those bastards at the top—and I heard who done it. If that is Roland Inness," he said, pointing with his stump, "he is man enough."

Sir Edgar turned in his saddle and looked at Roland. He had said his piece. Roland sat quietly for a moment as every eye turned toward him. He stood in his stirrups. He did not shout, but his voice carried to every broken man in the line.

"You and I, we know about rats and flies and days so hot the air shimmers and nights so cold the horses huddle together. We know what it is to see a horde of Saracens bearing down on us with death in their eyes." He paused and saw a few heads nod. "We know what it's like, even now, to wake in the night troubled by visions in our dreams." Men fidgeted uncomfortably at this.

"England does not understand these things, but we are back in England now! We must make a new way here. We will watch each other's backs, but make no mistake. Sir Harold FitzGibbons has been placed in command by the Queen. We are bound to follow him...or they may well hang us. You've taken the King's coin, now it's time you earned your keep."

He sat back down in the saddle, wheeled his horse around and spurred toward the Towcester road. He did not look back. Declan, Millicent and Sir Harold were already out of sight. As his horse settled into a steady trot, Sir Edgar galloped up beside him.

"Are they behind you?" Roland asked without turning his head.

"Every damn one," said Sir Edgar, who sported a smile for the first time.

***

The Lord Chamberlain's clerk scrambled down from the parapet atop the north wall of the town and raced toward the house he had visited two nights past. The house was unusual, not only for the lavish richness of its furnishing, but for the private library within. The universities that were springing up outside the walls of the town would have envied the collection of books and manuscripts on the shelves of this room, but Prince John paid no attention to the volumes that surrounded him.

The report the clerk brought of the force being dispatched to Wales was not a surprise—not after the earlier news that Ranulf of Chester was alive. He had almost forgotten about the missing nobleman since the man's flight into Wales the previous spring. After months of no word, he'd assumed, like most others, that the

Earl of Chester was dead. Now it seemed, he lived, and his return from the dead posed a problem.

Since the spring, the additional revenue flowing in from Cheshire had allowed him to buy the services of the best mercenary troops from Ireland and Flanders. It was the largest army seen in Britain since William the Conqueror. He had dispatched that army to take Nottingham Castle, which would give him a string of fortresses across the midsection of the country and a firm grip on the Midlands.

He would not have worried overmuch about a fugitive nobleman were it not for his mother, the Queen. Truly, that woman was the only thing that stood between him and his brother's crown. He had never loved his mother and recent events reminded him of why. She had arrived unannounced a week ago in Portsmouth and had the nerve to summon him to Oxford to account for his actions. She and the Justiciars had brow-beaten and threatened certain wavering barons to oppose him.

Even so, her position was weak. With his mercenary army he would eventually overawe any baron who could not be bought. So it was not surprising that the Queen was now manoeuvring to restore Ranulf's power in Cheshire and cut off his funds from those lands. Without the Cheshire revenue, his Flemish and Irish soldiers would slowly melt away.

He had it on good authority that the force the Queen had scraped together was not formidable, but there was no point in allowing Ranulf any succour. He called a young man into the library and handed him an envelope secured with his seal. "Take this to the Earl of Derby with all haste." The young man bowed and hurried toward the stables.

***

Sooner than expected, Roland caught sight of Declan and Millicent on the road ahead. The two were moving at a plodding walk so as not to overtake Sir Harold, who was setting a leisurely pace. Declan seemed to be taking this in stride, but not Millicent de Laval. As soon as Roland drew even with them, he could see her usual graceful posture atop a horse was altogether rigid.

"I waited seven months to bring help for Earl Ranulf," she hissed, "and at this speed, I swear it will take us seven more to get back to Wales!"

"Aye, this will not serve. I'll have a word with Sir Harold."

He spurred ahead and hailed the Queen's commander.

"My lord, the men have closed up. You may proceed at speed now."

Sir Harold stared at him for a moment.

"I see nothing wrong with this speed, Sir…"

"Roland Inness, my lord."

"Aye, Sir Roland. Don't want to wear out the horses on the first day!" Roland could only imagine what Millicent would say to that.

"Aye, my lord. Should we not send scouts ahead to ensure our way is clear of trouble?"

Sir Harold frowned.

"Trouble? 'Tween Oxford and Towcester? I hardly think so! Perhaps when we cross over into Wales. I doubt we will be molested until then. But I do have a concern, Sir Roland. Those men behind us—no better than thieves and murderers, that lot. I want you and your companion, Sir…"

"Declan O'Duinne, my lord."

"Yes, I want you and Sir Declan to mount a personal guard at my tent once I retire for the evening. I won't have one of these bastards stealing my purse or cutting my throat!"

Roland blinked. Could the man be serious?

"Guard your tent, my lord?"

"Yes, yes, damn it, man. Can't you understand a simple order?"

"Aye, my lord. We will mount a guard."

"Good then. That will be all."

Roland turned his horse and returned to his place at the head of the Invalid Company, falling in between Declan and Millicent.

"He doesn't seem to be increasing the pace," Millicent observed dryly.

Roland nodded.

"He thinks it would wear out the horses."

"Wear out...the horses...good Lord! At this rate the horses will go as flabby as milk cows!"

Roland nodded again.

"There's more. I asked to send out scouts."

"No scouts?" Declan asked.

"No scouts," Roland replied, grimly. "He expects no trouble between here and Wales."

"No trouble? Between here and Wales?" Now the colour was rising in Millicent's cheeks.

"Oh, he does expect some trouble," Roland replied, "though not from the Prince or de Ferrers. He has assigned Declan and I to mount a guard."

"Well that at least makes sense," said Declan.

"Less than you think, Dec. He wants us to guard his *tent*. He is afraid the men of the Invalid Company will slit his throat."

"Not if I get to him first!" Millicent said with conviction.

***

"Ranulf...alive?" William de Ferrers looked again at the message just received from the Prince. He turned to the priest who stood before him. Malachy had arrived at Peveril Castle only an hour before the messenger from Oxford.

"This is your fault, priest! Your fault! You were supposed to secure the man and you let him slip through your fingers. I will not be held responsible for this!"

But William de Ferrers knew that a lowly priest would not be the one held accountable for failing to dispose of the troublesome Earl of Chester. No, the Prince would blame *him*, and him alone. He felt sick to his stomach.

"My lord, how dangerous can Earl Ranulf be as long as he is a fugitive in the wilderness? I have seen to the defence of Chester and we have patrols along the Dee. The Earl of Chester has nowhere to turn. He will rot there in Wales."

The Earl was up and pacing now.

"The Prince fears he will not! The Justiciars have dismissed the treason charges against him and now the Queen is sending a force into Wales to find the man. The Prince has ordered me to destroy this force before it reaches him." The Earl of Derby stopped his pacing and turned to Malachy.

"Send for the Fleming."

***

The column of riders continued at a plodding pace for the remainder of the morning and, after a long break for lunch, made no better progress in the afternoon. They were still a good ways from Towcester when Sir Harold called a halt for the night. He led his horse off the track and wearily swung down from the saddle. He groaned and stretched his back, then began directing his men on the proper way to set up camp. Within moments, he fell to berating them for being slow and clumsy in the performance of their duties.

Millicent was still seething over the snail's pace of the march as they dismounted and, for a moment, Roland feared she was going to confront the man. He touched her arm.

"I have an idea, my lady."

Without explanation he walked over to where Sir Harold was supervising his two servants and engaged him in conversation. In a few minutes he returned and motioned Millicent and Declan aside.

"For a man in no hurry, our commander will brook no delays in having the comforts of camp ready for him. I've told him he should send his servants on ahead of the column so that a campsite will be ready for him at the end of each day's march. I told him this was what King Richard did when on the march in the Holy Land. That is, of course a lie, but he thought it a wonderful idea. Of course we will have to send men along with the servants to protect Sir Harold's kit."

"Scouts," said Declan with a grin.

"Scouts, indeed. Declan if you would be so good as to organize the advance party for tomorrow's march?"

"Gladly."

"And, this prepared campsite—where will that be located?" Millicent asked.

Roland smiled.

"A hard day's ride from here. So, if our commander wants to find his cot before midnight, he will have to put the spurs to his mount."

Millicent smiled back.

"Well done. Perhaps I won't have to slit his throat."

That night, after posting Declan on the first watch outside Sir Harold's tent, Roland wandered back to where the men of the Invalid Company were gathered around a dozen small fires. They had been supplied with salted beef and a few days ration of bread. Thereafter they would forage on the land. Some had contributed their meat to a stew simmering in a small round pot over one of the fires. The smell drifted over him along with other smells familiar to soldiers in the field—wood smoke, horse sweat on leather and unbathed men. It was somehow comforting.

Roland saw the one-eyed man who had challenged them at the outset of the march poking at some coals with a stick. He had learned that the man went by the name of Patch—oddly embracing the wound he'd suffered. Sir Edgar was sitting beside the man and when he saw Roland, he motioned for him to join them by the fire.

"I've set a guard around the camp," Sir Edgar said, dispensing with niceties as usual. "What's our Irish friend doing sitting out front of FitzGibbons tent?"

Roland smiled. "He's making sure none of you cutthroats molest the poor man. He seemed a bit worried about that. Perhaps Sir Harold was roughly treated when he surrendered the garrison at Lincoln castle and it has made him nervous."

For the first time Patch smiled, showing off several missing teeth.

"Well then, the ass is a wiser man than I thought, for some of the men were casting lots to see who would have the honour!"

Roland nodded.

"Just tell them not to come during the midnight watch. I'll be on duty then and would prefer to not to be awakened by screams of bloody murder."

Patch slapped him hard on the back.

"I'll tell 'em sure thing, Sir Roland. They'll come on tiptoe and not disturb you."

"I will appreciate that. Patch, I've been wondering, how did you lose the eye?"

Patch shook his head ruefully.

"It was a stupid thing, it was—just a splinter. At Arsuf, when our heavy cavalry broke the Saracens, I was riding next to my liege lord, Sir Thomas Marston. One of those heathen bastards managed to get in behind us and unhorsed him. He was stunned, so I dismounted and stood over him while the battle raged all around us." Patch stared at the fire as he recounted his story.

"I thought many times that we would be trampled, but the Lord watched over us that day. Just as Saladin's men finally broke, one of them rushed at us. We traded blows and a splinter from the edge of the man's shield flew up and lodged in my eye. After the battle, one of the leeches removed it, but the wound festered and the eye had to be taken out. Of all the grievous injuries suffered on that field, it was a damned splinter from my own blow that laid me low. It was enough for Sir Thomas to send me home." He poked a long stick into the fire and absently stirred the coals, his story at an end.

"Have you had word of Sir Thomas?" Roland asked.

The man nodded.

"We heard six months ago that Sir Thomas died of the fever, so I got this," he pointed to his patch, "for nothing."

A long silence followed, broken only by the crackling of the fire. Then Roland spoke.

"Patch, what is your name—your real name?"

Patch gave a bitter laugh.

"Patch is good enough now, but if you must know, my name is Tom Marston."

"Ah.... Sir Thomas was your father."

"Aye, and I served him as squire."

Roland nodded.

"That day—the day of the battle, was your father proud of you?"

"Aye, that day, and most days before. He was a good man, a hard man. He cried like a bairn when they took my eye out."

"Then, Tom, your wound wasn't for nothing."

Tom Marston gazed across the fire at Roland, but there was no gauging the look in his one good eye. He started to speak, but a burly man, older than most of the troop, stamped into the ring of light. He had only one good leg. The other was missing at the knee. There, a tapered wooden shaft was attached that extended to the ground. He moved with surprising ease, given his missing appendage.

The man extended his hand to Roland who rose and took it.

"I am William Butler. I was a sergeant in the infantry and I think I remember ye, though not from the assault on the breach. I was back in England by then. Did ye stand with a bunch of Pisan crossbowmen the day the daft King of Jerusalem attacked Saladin's lines north of Acre? I saw the longbow over yer shoulder and there was a lad who used one to good effect that day. Thought you resembled him."

Suddenly, Roland recognised the man. He had been a popular figure around the Crusader camp outside the walls of Acre, always full of bluff good cheer despite the miserable squalor of the place.

Roland slapped him on the shoulder.

"Sergeant Billy, I believe!"

The man beamed at the use of the affectionate nickname he had been accorded by his comrades.

"The very same! So it *was* ye?

"Aye, that was me. It's a day I still dream about sometimes."

The burly sergeant shook his head.

"Me as well, and in my dream I can never outrun those damn horsemen with their scimitars. But they are gone in the morning, so all's well. Now that I lost the leg, I have joined the cavalry and, I must say, riding is better than walking."

"Glad to have you with us, Sergeant Billy," Roland said. He wanted to ask how the man had lost the leg, but suddenly all of the men around the fire leapt to their feet. Roland turned, his hand going to the hilt of his sword, but saw what had disturbed the group. Lady Millicent had joined them.

She smiled a bit nervously at the men.

"Sir Roland, would you introduce me?"

"Of course, my lady," Roland said, a bit flustered. "This is Tom Marston. Tom—Lady Millicent de Laval."

"I go by Patch," he said and bowed his head. "It's a pleasure, my lady."

"Pleased to meet you, Tom."

"And this is William Butler."

Sergeant Billy beamed at her.

"A great pleasure, my lady. If I may say, I spent my life as a foot soldier sloggin' down the road and saw many a fine horseman ride by me, but I've never seen anyone sit a horse like you."

Millicent coloured a bit at the unexpected compliment, but the yellow glow of the fire masked it.

"Thank you, William. I'm glad you are with us."

As Roland watched this exchange, he saw dark shapes start to emerge from outside the firelight. The other men of the Invalid Company were coming forward, shyly, to meet the young woman who had come to visit. Roland did not know most of their names, but one-by-one they introduced themselves to Millicent and she greeted them each with warmth and good grace.

So much like her mother.

He watched her take the hand of each of these strangers. She might be only fifteen, but she was a lady in full. As he looked at her face, softly lit by the cook fires, there was no denying her beauty. He felt his face flush.

Oh God. What would she think if she knew what he was feeling at this moment? No doubt she would laugh at him. He might be a knight, but he was three years removed from being a peasant. *Best to put this aside.*

When the last man had been introduced, Millicent spoke in a soft voice that had every one of them leaning in to hear.

"I know you men have suffered much in the war, and even more at the hands of your own countrymen on your return. It's shameful! I also know that you were given no choice but to join our force. I would not have had it so—but know this. We go to fight for the Earl of Chester. I know Earl Ranulf. He is a good man and loyal to our King. The men who have trumped-up treason charges against him are not. Those same men would rip the crown from King Richard's head. What I must know is this. Are you men loyal to the King?"

There was a low growl that rippled through the group and Patch stepped forward. He turned to the gathered warriors.

"We all fought with the King in the hell they call the Holy Land. No one welcomed us when we returned home, but the King? He did not forget! Richard Coeur de Lion is the rightful king. Will we stand by while lesser men take the throne?"

"Not I!" a man shouted from the rear. "Nor I," Sergeant Billy added. Others joined in the chorus of nays. Once the talk had died, Patch turned back to Millicent.

"We've fought with the King and he did not abandon us when we came home. We are all loyal men here, miss. If fighting for Earl Ranulf is in the cause of preserving our King, we can be counted upon."

Millicent felt the sting of tears and fought against it. It wouldn't do to show female weakness at such a moment.

"Thank you, Tom," she said, "and my thanks to the men of the Invalid Company. They've given you that name out of pity. I think they will come to remember it out of fear."

***

The next day's march was a long one. Sir Harold set his usual leisurely pace, but as the afternoon wore on with no encampment in sight, he grew increasingly agitated. By the time they reached the man's tent well after dark he was furious and turned his wrath on Declan O'Duinne.

"My lord, I do not understand how we could have got so far ahead," Declan replied innocently. "We rode at a normal pace and stopped well before sunset so we could make camp."

Sir Harold gave him an acid look, then turned on his servants, who stolidly remained silent as he berated them at length. Roland and Declan stood off to the side while the poor men received their tongue-lashing.

"It's a trick that will only work once," Declan said. "He will not let his pack horses out of his sight again, no doubt."

"Aye, but we covered twice the distance today and it was worth it to see the Constable in such a lather."

***

For another four days, the Invalid Company plodded westward without incident. They forded the Severn River at Shrewsbury and Sir Harold took his evening rest at an inn, while the rest camped outside the walls of the town. The weather had been fair for a few days, but with evening came a cold drizzle and dropping temperatures.

The next morning, the sky was clear and the ground frozen as they broke camp and prepared for the last leg of the journey to the Dee and Wales. Chester lay almost due north, but all agreed they would need to steer well clear of the place.

"I see no reason we shouldn't use the ford upriver from Chester where we crossed a fortnight ago," Millicent said. "The track is poor, but that region is fairly deserted. The going will be slow, but it keeps us clear of de Ferrers and takes us to Llywelyn's hill fort."

"I agree," said Roland, "but even though this path skirts Chester, we will need to be on our guard. Wales is a day's hard ride away, though it will take us two with Sir Harold setting the pace. If there is to be trouble on this side of the border, it will be today or tomorrow."

"I'll leave now to scout the way before Sir Harold is up and about," said Declan. "I know where the track west meets the Chester road. You be ready to come at the gallop if I ride into a hornet's nest."

"Aye," said Roland, "and, Declan, one more thing."

"Yes?"

"Don't do anything stupid."

Ambush

*T*he commander of the Flemish mercenaries pulled his fur cape closer around him as he sat motionless on his big roan charger watching the road below. The morning was bitter cold. After days of near spring-like weather, February had reasserted itself. The ground was as hard as stone and, while a bright morning sun caused the frost to sparkle, dark skies further west foretold snow before the day was done.

His horse stamped the ground and he patted its neck. It was a magnificent animal and worth a fortune. As commander of a mercenary troop, he was well paid for his services, but a bred and trained warhorse such as this could not be had for mercenary wages. Fortunately, the nobleman who had died under his sword on their last hire could afford the beast. Now it was his most prized possession.

Behind him, sixty mounted men hid in the dense wood of the hillside, waiting to spring the trap he had laid. They were hard men, well-armed and well-paid. He had told them they would be facing a troop of cripples and drunkards and the thought had cheered them. It would be an easy fight and easy money.

They had ridden hard to reach this spot. The request from the Earl of Derby had been an urgent one and the man had been willing to pay a high price to ensure that this motley host dispatched from Oxford would never reach the valley of the Dee. The Flemish commander casually wondered why the Earl would concern himself with such a pitiful force, but he did not dwell on it. He was not paid to care about such things.

The road below emerged from deep woods on the eastern side of a broad valley. It was part of the old Roman road that ran all the way from Dover to Chester and during three seasons of the year was heavily travelled. Some brave souls used it in the dead of winter, but none had passed below them since dawn.

The valley floor was cultivated land, though the fields were frozen and empty. It was the perfect spot for a force of cavalry to fall on the flank of a passing column and overwhelm it. The commander's horse stamped a huge hoof on the hard ground and he stroked the beast's mane. He loved this horse. It was a true destrier with a fiery disposition and never shied from a fight. It was the best warhorse he had ever seen and he had seen many.

Looking out toward the valley, he saw a single snowflake drift down through the dense trees just as a lone rider appeared on the road below, heading west. The man was likely a scout for the column that would be some distance behind. He considered sending a squad of his men to intercept the rider, but he could see the fellow was paying little attention to the threat of an ambush. The man seemed to be out for a pleasure ride more than a reconnaissance. As long as their position was not compromised, he would wait. Best to just let the fool pass on by, then fall on the unsuspecting main body.

So they waited.

Below, Declan O'Duinne had seen the trail of hoof prints leave the road and disappear into the trees to the north. The ground might be frozen, but a large body of mounted men left some sign of their passing. He took care not to show any interest in the dark woods to his right where the trail led, and no one broke cover from the tree line to intercept him.

Like the commander of the Flemish horsemen, he knew a good spot for an ambush when he saw one and had no doubt that he was riding through the killing zone. As he neared the centre of the valley, he reined in his horse and swung out of the saddle. Casually, he untied the fastening of his trousers and, facing the dark tree line, relieved himself on the side of the road.

The mercenary commander almost laughed to himself. If the dolt had known there were sixty men concealed in the forest only a hundred yards from him, he would have pissed with his trousers still fastened!

Declan swung back into the saddle and giving a final, bored look about, turned his horse and cantered slowly back the way he had come. Once more the mercenary leader considered sending men to kill the scout, but there was no way to know where the main column was. He would not risk a melee on the road that might alert the main body to danger. The killing business often required patience. He would wait.

As soon as Declan entered the protection of the trees, he slapped the end of his reins on the horse's flank and dug in his spurs. At a gallop, he rode the half mile back to the column and reined in as he reached Sir Harold. Roland and Millicent had seen him approach and hurried forward.

"Ambush ahead, my lord. Mounted men in the trees north of the road," he said between gasping breaths.

Sir Harold seemed to not comprehend the warning.

"Men, what men?"

The colour rose in Declan's face.

"Men who mean to butcher us, my lord. We ride into that valley ahead and none of us will ride out again!"

The former Constable of Lincoln blinked at the young knight and gathered himself.

"How many did you see?"

Declan held his tongue for a long moment, forcing himself to keep his voice even when he spoke.

"I did not see them, my lord. They were concealed in the trees, but I saw the track."

"How many do you reckon, Dec?" Roland asked.

"More than us, for sure, and no doubt on better horses and better armed. We've no chance if they catch us in the open."

Roland nodded.

"Then we take them in the trees." He turned to Sir Harold. "My lord, mounted men lose their advantage in the forest. If you have the men dismount, we can take them in the rear."

Sir Harold looked confused for a moment, then waved Roland's counsel aside. "We must ride back to Shrewsbury at once and gather more men!"

"My lord," Roland said, fighting to keep his own temper under control, "there are no men in Shrewsbury who will come to our aid. They can barely man their own walls. And if we flee now, those men in the trees will follow, and on better horses. We wouldn't reach the town before they overtake us."

Now Sir Harold's face flushed. He was a man unused to having his orders questioned.

"Enough! We will ride for Shrewsbury. Get these men turned around, and be quick about it!"

"No!" It was Millicent who spoke up. "Earl Ranulf needs these men! He has waited too long for aid to come to him. We cannot turn and run at the first sign of trouble."

The challenge enraged the man.

"Mind your tongue, girl. You have no head for these matters." He pushed past Millicent and called out to Sir Edgar, who stolidly sat his horse beside Patch.

"You there, turn these men around, immediately!"

Sir Edgar shook his head. "I take me orders from that man," he said pointing to Roland. Sir Harold whirled once more on Roland.

"I command you to get these men moving to Shrewsbury."

Roland looked at Millicent. She said nothing, but there was entreaty in her eyes. He turned to Declan, who seemed to be enjoying this turn of events.

"This is where you get to be leader," he said and grinned.

Roland gave his friend a dark look, then turned toward the men of the Invalid Company.

"Dismount!"

Forty men and one woman swung out of their saddles. For a moment, Sir Harold looked stunned. He reached for the hilt of his sword, but saw that Declan had already drawn his and was staring at him. He spit on the ground.

"I'll have your heads for this!" he growled, then turned his horse back to the east and whipped it forward. His servants obediently followed. As he passed Patch and Sir Edgar, he twisted in his saddle and snarled at them.

"I knew you cripples couldn't be trusted!" Then he was gone, off down the road to Shrewsbury.

The men of the Invalid Company gave their departing commander not a second glance. All down the line, they were checking their weapons and securing their horses. Roland turned to Millicent.

"Will you stay here with the horses, my lady? Yours is the only one we have that could probably outrun those men in the woods and, if it goes badly, word will need to get to the Queen."

The girl nodded. It rankled to be left behind, but a pitched battle was no place for her.

"Very well, but see that it does not go badly," she said.

"I will, my lady." Roland said as he was stringing his longbow. Millicent reached out and touched his arm.

"Call me Millie."

He looked up and saw her smiling at him. It was like the sun coming out.

"Aye, my lady. Millie it shall be."

Declan cleared his throat and the girl rolled her eyes.

"You too, Declan."

Roland slung his longbow over his shoulder as Sir Edgar gathered the men around him.

"What's the plan, Sir Roland?" Patch asked.

"We go up the slope here and over the ridge. We stay to the reverse side until we are behind them." He swung his longbow off his shoulder and held it up. "When you see men start to fall out of their saddles, we all go in at once. And mark this—I need at least one man alive. We should know who is hunting us." There were low growls of agreement, from the gathered men.

"Now, let us see what the Invalid Company can do."

***

The commander of the mercenaries had been on many campaigns and had survived them all by trusting his instincts. The outrider had long since disappeared back up the road and into the woods. The column should have reached the open valley by now. Had the scout seen something? Would he have stood there and pissed, if he had thought there was danger in the woods? Doubtful, but still...

Something's wrong here.

The man twisted in his saddle to look behind him and took an arrow in the chest. He tried to shout a warning, but his voice no longer seemed to work. As he slid off the side of the big roan charger, his last sight was of another man three horses away toppling backwards from his saddle. He hit the frozen ground hard and as the world faded to dark, he heard awful war cries coming down from the slope behind them.

The Invalid Company came over the ridge with a howl of pent-up fury and hit the line of horsemen like a scythe sweeping through a row of wheat. Men went down. Horses went down or bolted in panic. Roland dropped his bow and drew his sword to join the men as they rose and charged. As he ran, his roar of defiance joined with the savage cries of the men beside him.

In the first seconds, the mercenaries had lost their leader and more than half a dozen of them were dead, but these were not men who broke easily. The first rush down the slope had taken the Invalids right through the middle of their line, but they still outnumbered their attackers and so sought to rally and make a fight of it.

Seeing the futility of manoeuvring their mounts on a wooded slope, most dismounted to form a ragged defensive line. A few, seeing the shifting odds, kept to their saddles and fled down into the valley below.

The Invalids fought with a ferocity Roland had rarely seen, even in the killing grounds of the Holy Land. These were men with something to prove—to themselves most of all. Sir Edgar joined Roland and pressed the centre of the new line. The men who faced them were veteran soldiers for hire, but shied away from the giant with the wild beard and the deadly axe.

Most of the mercenaries wore chainmail, but the Invalids had none. Still, they pressed the attack relentlessly and the enemy slowly gave ground. Roland saw Sergeant Billy to his right, lurching forward with his wooden peg of a leg. He was hacking at the men to his front with a look of pure joy on his face. Down to his left, he caught a glimpse of Patch bludgeoning a man to the ground, unhampered by the missing eye that gave him his new name.

To his front, Roland saw a big man with hair as yellow as a Dane's glaring at him. The man had a handsome sword and wore new chain mail that fitted him perfectly. Many of the Flemings had rallied around the warrior, who now stared at Roland with an unmistakable challenge in his eyes. Around them, the noise of the battle seemed to fade.

Both men leapt forward. There was little room to manoeuvre as they met with a first flurry of blows, none doing damage. The Fleming was as strong as an ox, and bulled his way forward with massive slashing arcs of his broadsword, but each blow seemed to somehow miss its mark. Some hit nothing but air and others were met with an angled blade and slid harmlessly off to the side. He stepped back, breathing like a bellows from the exertion and saw that the tall, dark-haired man who faced him was simply waiting calmly.

In five years of service, the mercenary had killed many men, but had never fought against an experienced warrior. His troop had made easy work of fat garrison soldiers and poorly-trained levies, but this man to his front was neither of those. Now there was no challenge left in his eyes, only a hard knot of fear forming in his stomach.

Roland saw the fight go out of the man and moved down the slope with a series of feints and testing thrusts. Panicked, the Fleming tried to ram the tip of his blade directly into his enemy's chest. Once more, it missed and as he lurched forward, off balance, Roland's blade found its way under the man's mail shirt and up into his gut. He stepped back and wrenched his sword free as the big man fell, face down, on the forest floor.

All along the line, the men of the mercenary troop were learning what it meant to face the veterans of Acre and Arsuf. Looking to his left, Roland could see Declan had joined Patch and they were beginning to turn the exposed flank of the enemy. If that happened, the slaughter would begin in earnest and few if any of the men from Flanders would be left alive on the field.

But though the mercenaries had been outfought, they would not sell their lives cheaply—and the Invalid Company could ill afford to lose many from their ranks. Above the din of battle Roland screamed.

"Yield!"

At first no one heeded, though he could see that some of the men across the line had heard his demand and were watching him.

"Yield, I say, or we kill every man standing!"

Men in his own ranks now heard and held their sword strokes, though their blood was up.

"If we yield, do we live?" This came from a tall man with a large drooping moustache who seemed to have taken command of the surviving mercenaries. It was common practice to put captured mercenaries to the sword after a fight—or to hire them for your own forces. The man was asking which it would be.

"You'll not die by our hand if you yield, but we will have your arms and horses—and one more thing."

"What would that be?"

"I would know who sent you here."

The mercenary commander took a long moment to look around. A man whose sword was bought and sold still felt the dishonour of laying it down in surrender, but his position was hopeless and he knew it.

"If you play me false, English…" he called, "I will curse you from the grave." Then he laid down his sword. His men dropped swords, axes and lances where they stood and waited, half expecting to be cut down without ceremony. Some of the Invalid Company looked prepared to do just that, but Roland cut them off.

"These men are not to be molested. Collect their arms and gather up all the horses you can. These are good stock, better than ours." He turned to the new mercenary commander.

"I have kept my promise. Now, who sent you?"

The man did not hesitate. He gestured toward the dead mercenary commander who lay nearby with the arrow shaft still in his chest

"I never heard from Conrad where the money came from, but it was a priest who delivered it."

"A priest? Did the man have a name?"

"Aye, he did. It was Irish. Malachy, I believe."

***

Millicent had heard the sudden eruption of war cries in the still winter air. The sound swelled as the sharp clash of steel on steel joined the cries and shouts of men trying to kill one another. It echoed down the valley and into the woods, where she had mounted her horse, prepared to flee if the fight went against them.

It went on for what seemed an eternity, as the knuckles of her hands grew white from gripping the reins. For more than a year, the fate of her family had hung by a thread. Now, if the ragged band of men who had climbed the hill behind Roland and Declan did not win this fight, the thread might finally snap.

The dread she felt was that of every woman since the dawn of time who had watched her clan, her tribe, *her men* go off to fight. As she sat her horse, she reminded herself to breathe and never took her eyes off the road that led down into the valley. Finally, the noise died. She waited.

Who will come down that road?

Then she heard men shouting and calling to each other, closer now, coming her way, but which men? Finally, two jubilant members of the Invalid Company appeared trudging back up the road, loudly swapping accounts of the victory. Close behind them, other clusters of men came. Some limped from old wounds and some favoured new ones, but all walked with a new pride and swagger she had not seen before. Millicent watched them come, laughing and preening over their captured loot.

So like boys they are.

She sagged in the saddle. The thread had held for another day. Roland and Declan were the last to arrive, having kept watch while the Flemings were allowed to skulk away unhorsed and unarmed, but unscathed by the Invalids. Millicent dismounted when they finally appeared and was surprised to find her legs a bit shaky. She had the sudden urge to run to them, but would not allow herself such an unseemly display. As they neared, she could see they were more subdued than the men they had just led to victory.

"Two dead and three wounded," Roland said solemnly, "but the wounded can ride if we bandage them up."

Millicent knew this was a remarkably low butcher's bill, but also knew that the loss of even two men was a blow to the tiny force they were bringing to the aid of Earl Ranulf.

"Where are the wounded?" she asked.

"Back in the trees, where the fight was. Sergeant Billy is tending to them now and a detail is burying the two dead. Such a shame they survived the Holy Land only to die here in England."

Millicent gave him a long look, but he did not meet her gaze.

"Aye it's sad, but at least they'll lie under good English sod and not in some desert grave across the sea."

Roland's head came up and met her eyes, then nodded wearily.

"True enough, Millie."

"See to your men, Roland. I will do what I can to help Sergeant Billy. There is some cloth with the pack animals we can use for bandages."

She turned to go about her new task, but Roland touched her arm.

"Millie, the priest you wanted me to kill—the one that rode with the men from Chester when they pursued us across the Dee—you said his name was Malachy?"

Millicent felt a sinking feeling in her chest.

"Yes."

Roland nodded.

"The mercenaries say a priest by that name paid them their wages. De Ferrers knows we are here."

***

Two miles away, the unhorsed and disarmed remnants of the Flemish mercenaries tramped eastward toward Newport. Some cursed the loss of their arms and horses, but most knew they were lucky to have escaped slaughter. At midafternoon, an unfortunate and heedless man on horseback appeared on the road and made the mistake of not turning around at the first sight of forty men on foot. He was dragged from his mount and beaten.

The tall man with the drooping moustache swung into the empty saddle. It was a two day ride back to Derby, and he kicked the horse into a trot. The Earl would be unhappy, but the mercenary did not intend for his men to be held up to blame. They had failed, but it was the priest and the Earl who were most at fault. They had said the target was a band of drunks and cripples.

Whatever else they might be, the men who had beaten them this day were no invalids.

Borderland

Roland was mounted on the roan charger that had belonged to the dead mercenary commander. Sir Edgar had insisted that, as their leader, he had rights to the most valuable booty left on the field of battle and this big stallion was surely that.

The animal was not yet the size of Bucephalus, but it was young and would grow. It had a broad chest and stood fifteen hands high. More importantly, it had the temperament of a warhorse. When Declan brought his mount too near, the roan stamped a massive hoof, swung its head around and tried to bite the offending horse.

"Can you handle the brute?" Millicent asked sceptically.

Roland laughed as he jerked the horse's big head around to the front and patted its neck.

"Perhaps we will come to handle each other in time."

Declan's own mount was a much more impressive horse than the one he had taken from de Ferrers' men in the ruins of Shipbrook, but he couldn't help but give Roland's new possession an admiring inspection. The Irish had a great appreciation of good horseflesh.

"Handsome thing, but a surly beast! What shall ye name him?"

Roland hadn't thought to name the animal. The horse's former name was lost, gone with its recent master who lay dead on the hillside, but a warhorse this magnificent deserved a name.

"Dec, I think you described this horse's nature exactly. I will call him The Surly Beast, until he earns a more fitting title."

"I like it!" Declan declared. "I only pity any boy who may someday be your squire. He will be eaten alive."

The remainder of the morning was taken up with tending their wounded, burying their dead and reorganizing the pack animals and horses. It was discovered that the mule with the wages for the Invalids was missing. Roland called the men together.

"Your wages seem to have followed your commander back to Shrewsbury. Any that wish to do the same are welcome to leave. We will continue on to Wales, but I have no authority to command you to follow." He stopped, letting the men consider the choice before them. "I have seen what you can do in a fight and I would be honoured to lead such men as you. Will the Invalids follow me?"

"Aye!" the roar echoed from the sides of the valley. The Invalids had found themselves.

Roland nodded and twisted in his saddle. He ordered four riders ahead to scout the route. Behind him the men of the Invalid Company mounted the new horses they had taken from the Flemish mercenaries and awaited the signal to move.

The events of the morning had transformed them. Each man had new mail and new weapons. None slouched in the saddle. They were men who had regained their pride. And without doubt, they were now Roland's men. He must get them to Wales and to Earl Ranulf no matter what de Ferrers might send against them. He turned to Declan and Millicent who were watching him. He raised his arm and swung it toward the north.

"Forward."

The slow pace of march from Oxford was quickly forgotten as the troop moved briskly along the Roman road toward Chester. The new mounts were sturdy and well-fed and most of the men led their old mounts by a rope. They were able to cover the twenty miles to the trailhead leading west before sunset and crossed the ford with just enough light left to make a hasty camp on the Welsh shore. Guards set, they bedded down for the night.

At dawn, Millicent and Roland took the lead and the column shook out into single file as the track got narrow and hilly. Progress slowed as forty men and twice that many horses picked their way along the track. The weather conspired to make things worse as a warm spell caused frozen ground to thaw and turn to slippery mud.

Early on the third day, they reached the main path that ran from Chester, over the ford at Shipbrook and west into Wales. Where the paths met was a dozen miles from the Dee and shielded by high hills to the east. Here, they were less than a day's ride from the hill fort where Llywelyn had sheltered Millicent, Lady Catherine and the Earl.

Despite her eagerness, Millicent did not question Roland's caution as he ordered scouts out far to the front and also to the rear. These lands were formally ruled by Daffyd, Llywelyn's uncle, but his patrols rarely ventured this far into the wilderness. No hostile force had ever come near the hill fort, which lay far from any settlement. But this was Wales, and even with a well-armed company, every mile deeper they rode increased their danger. The Invalid Company was not the only well-armed band in these lands.

As they followed the ancient trading route west, they expected with each passing hour to encounter Llywelyn's patrols, but saw no one. Roland cast occasional glances at Millicent and saw that her anxiety was growing. Finally, one of the forward scouts rode in at a gallop and reported that they had spotted a hill fort ahead. As the column crested a saddle between high hills, they found the second scout looking down into a narrow valley. At its far end, on a spur, was the hill fort. No movement could be seen near it or in the valley below.

"Something is wrong," Millicent said standing in her stirrups and scanning the entire length of the valley. "Llywelyn would never allow a force this large to approach so close without challenge."

"Could he have simply moved his camp?" Roland asked.

Millicent shook her head.

"I doubt that. He felt secure here and it was well located. He has other bands scattered in the backcountry, but they stay on the move. This was his base and I think he would not abandon it willingly."

"Very well." Roland turned to see most of the Invalid Company had closed up behind him and were looking down in the valley. "Declan, take a man and see what's at the fort. I'll bring the troop into the valley and wait for your word. Don't dawdle if you smell trouble."

"You may rely on that," Declan said, as he turned and summoned one of his scouts forward. As he rode down into the valley, Roland followed cautiously with the Invalids. On the valley floor, they came to another track that came in from the northwest and intersected the old trade route. It was churned up by the hooves of many horses, and quite recently. The signs of a large mounted force continued up the valley toward the fort. He started to send someone to warn Declan, but realized his friend would have seen the same hoof prints and would be on his guard.

The troop reached a spot on the valley floor beneath the hill fort and halted. It was plain that whatever force had torn up the track from the northwest had made camp, at least briefly, below the fort. Without being ordered to, the men dismounted and drew swords. Patch and Sergeant Billy stayed on their horses near Roland and looked up at the steep sides of the valley.

"This is not a good place for a fight," Sergeant Billy observed. But that worry was short-lived when Declan came pounding back down the steep path that led up to Llywelyn's stronghold.

"No one's up there, and no sign of a fight. Looks like they abandoned the place before these lads arrived," he said gesturing toward the turned up sod of the valley floor. "Judging by the state of things, they've not been gone long. Ashes in the hearth were still warm."

"How long you reckon?" Roland asked.

"Four, maybe five hours I'd guess. I also saw sign that others came later. A few odds and ends were smashed, but these fellows were in a hurry. Didn't torch the hall or spend much time searching the place."

Roland looked at Millicent. Her face was stricken.

"What do you make of this, Millie?"

"It can only mean that one of Llywelyn's uncles has grown worried enough to root out his stronghold in the backcountry. I saw the tracks the same as you. They must have sent an overwhelming force to do it. I would guess it would take two hundred horses or more to tear up the ground like that. If a force that size approached, I believe Llywelyn would not stand and fight. He would fall back to some new hiding place, but I do not know where. He spoke of one place in the mountains further west, beyond the Conwy River. He simply called it the caer—fortress in Welsh, but never told me where it lies."

Roland nodded. He had ridden a little further up the trail while they waited for Declan to return—far enough to judge that the mounted force had continued up the valley and had not returned the way they had come.

"It would seem Llywelyn escaped before he was trapped, and these tracks say they pursued him to the west."

"Then we must follow!"

"Aye, Millie, I believe we must, but we must take care. The force that pursues Llywelyn is between us, and there are far more of them than of us."

"I can count," she said, irritated, "but if we arrive too late, we might as well not arrive at all. We must hurry."

"We would have surprise on our side," Declan offered.

"They don't know we are here," said Patch, with an evil grin.

"We're the Invalid Company," said Sergeant Billy. "They'll not know what hit them."

Roland held his peace. The morale of his new command had soared since the desertion of Sir Harold and the victory over the Flemish mercenaries, but morale is a fragile thing, he knew. He had seen that before the walls of Acre. These men had tasted victory, the first in a long time for most, and they were heady with the feel of it. He must not let that push him into something foolish.

A wrong decision here...

"We will pursue—and we'll move fast, but Dec, I want scouts a mile ahead of us, and God help them if they give us away. If these men know we are behind them, we'll be mauled." Declan nodded and rode off to give his orders.

Roland climbed aboard The Surly Beast and turned to the men who now looked to him as their leader.

"Mount up!"

***

Prince Llywelyn reined in his horse and looked back down the trail. His breath came ragged and, despite the chill, sweat ran in rivulets under the leather jerkin he wore beneath his mail. The last fight had bloodied them, but had not stopped the pursuit. Of that he was sure. Like a pack of dogs on the scent of a boar, the men who followed smelled blood. He muttered a quiet curse between deep breaths.

He had grown complacent, had thought his uncles had given up trying to control the backcountry, where his strength had been growing. So confident was he in the security of his hill fort that he had sent over a quarter of his men on a raid toward the coast the week before. They had not yet returned. His patrols in the surrounding valleys had seen nothing for months and he had let them grow lazy. This was the price of his negligence.

He wasn't sure whose men snapped at his heels. It could have been either of his uncles. Both knew the threat he posed to them and one had sent this force into the wild valleys to catch and kill him. For the moment it did not matter which. He had to find a way to break loose from their dogged pursuit.

When the frantic word reached the hill fort of the approaching threat, the enemy had been less than an hour away. He had made the hard decision to abandon his base. It was defendable against an assault, even with some of his men gone, but was not provisioned for a siege.

Another mistake.

They were fortunate to have enough mounts to carry all of his men, but there were no horses for the women and children. They had simply slipped away into the forest to hide and he prayed they would be safe until the trouble had passed.

Only forty of his men had armour and proper horses able to stand and fight against the men who opposed them—a force with more men, better horses and heavy armour. The rest of his band were bowmen, mounted on the small Welsh ponies. These little beasts could trot along all day and night, but did not have the speed of the horses that pursued them and were of little use in a fight.

It was the bowmen who had bought them time during the long flight from the fort. Wherever Griff had found a likely place for ambush, he had left behind two or three of his archers to remind those who followed that, sometimes, the boar turns on the dogs. Most of the men who pursued them had shields, but the archers were expert and found gaps to strike at. Only a few of the enemy fell, but it had the desired effect of slowing the pursuit to a crawl until mounted men could clear out each ambush site.

Many of the archers were men who had been with him since he had turned rebel, and he prayed fervently that at least some of them would survive the day. If they could scramble up the thickly wooded slopes before the enemy horsemen rode them down, perhaps some would live.

My fault…

Despite the bravery of his rear guard, the enemy continued to close the gap. It was late afternoon when they reached the edge of the huge forest that covered most of northern Wales. As his little band pushed their tired horses out of the woods and into the open country, Llywelyn swept his gaze toward the west. The open ground was the broad valley of the Conwy River. Here was civilization—tilled fields, stone walls and hamlets dotted the scene. It was a terrible place to be overtaken by heavy cavalry.

In the distance beyond the river was the massive peak of Yr Wyddfa, the grandest mountain in Wales. Across the Conwy and into the mountains lay another fortress—a place of final refuge. The twisting valleys and narrow, steep passes that led to it were a death trap for invaders. If he could get his people across the river, he doubted his enemies would follow into the dark valleys on the other side.

But even as he harboured that hope, he knew his time had run out. They were miles from the nearest ford and even now he could hear the hot pursuit approaching. There was no time left to run. It was time for the boar to turn in earnest on the dogs.

He spurred ahead to overtake his lead riders and halted them. There was a low stone wall off to the left and set back two hundred yards from the trail. He placed his forty men mounted on good horses behind it with his right flank anchored in the woods. The wall was not much of a barrier, but it would force charging riders to engage more carefully.

His remaining bowmen he sent to occupy a small rise to the rear. He looked down his pitifully short line and tried not to show his despair. The men who stood behind this wall were his most trusted followers—many had been with him from the start. Some were knights from good families and some were simply tough men who had been drawn to his vision of a single kingdom of Wales. And he had led them to this. It was a bitter thought.

One man among them had not sworn fealty to him. Llywelyn was surprised to see the Earl of Chester, wearing borrowed chain mail, in the front rank as they prepared to meet whatever came pouring out of the woods. He had not held the Earl in much regard when first he had plucked the man from the hands of his English enemies, but their long months together had produced a grudging respect.

Ranulf was a man who did not come naturally to the leadership of other men, but he was thoughtful and learned from his mistakes. Given time, he might make a formidable Marcher Lord after all.

Llywelyn twisted in his saddle and saw Lady Catherine de Laval, sitting her horse behind the small contingent of archers. She could have as easily been watching a May Day festivity on a village square. For not the first time, he felt envious of the woman's husband—a man he'd never met.

Lucky fellow.

From the woods, he heard the sounds of drumming hooves and rode out in front of his men. He could see the exhaustion in their faces and the lack of hope. But he also saw a determination to stay by their lord to the end. Had there been time, he would have wept. It's what the Welsh did at such moments. Instead, he rode along their thin ranks and rallied them to make their stand. He called to men by name.

"Gwilym! Mabon! Pedr! Make your fathers proud this day! Tomos! Owain! Show these bastards what they've cornered!" On down the line he went until he had called to each of his men in turn. When he reached the Earl of Chester, he reined in.

"My lord, Ranulf! Our fathers would probably choke on their own bile if they saw us fighting side by side. But I am pleased you are with us. If we survive this day, I will someday return the favour."

The Earl of Chester raised his sword in salute.

"I will hold you to that, Lord Llywelyn, you can be sure, but for now, I am happy to stand with you."

He had barely finished speaking when the host that had been trailing them burst out of the forest and into the open ground of the valley. The men in the lead reined in and pointed across the muddy field toward the stone wall and the small band of rebels sheltered behind it. Llywelyn now saw a familiar banner come to the head of the column.

So it is Daffyd. Welcome Uncle...

Seeing that their quarry had turned to fight, Daffyd's men took their time deploying. Llywelyn watched as men continued to stream out of the woods and into the valley. Whoever was in command did the sensible thing and simply let the head of the column continue down the trail until the tail emerged from the wood. He then halted and signalled for them to face left and move into the field to their front.

They now formed a line two deep and over half again as wide as Llywelyn's, with their left, like Llywelyn's right, anchored at the woodline and their right extending well beyond the end of Llywelyn's left flank.

Their commander rode out ahead of his armoured host and hailed Llywelyn, who jumped his horse over the stone fence and rode out ahead of his own line. As he approached, the enemy commander removed his helmet and smiled. It was Daffyd's son, Owain, who had come to capture or kill him. He called to Llywelyn as he rode up.

"Hello, cousin! It's good to see you out on such a beautiful day."

Llywelyn had to admire the young man's bravado, though with a force triple his own, bravado was cheaply had. Owain was one year older than him and they had known each other since they could walk. They played together as boys and had even liked each other—a little, but now the game was in deadly earnest.

"Aye, cousin. You are a welcome sight," Llywelyn responded. "I had feared my uncle would send someone who I could not thrash, but he has been very obliging by sending you!"

Llywelyn was close enough to see the colour rise in Owain's face. He knew the man's nature. His cousin was a man quick to anger and headstrong and he hoped to use that against him.

"We've had enough of your playing at rebel, Llywelyn. It has grown tiresome. Surrender to me and my father will be merciful. Otherwise," he gestured to the force behind him, "you and your father's bloodline will die out on this field—or have you fathered any more bastards back there in the woods?"

Llywelyn smiled. The personal insult his cousin had included in his reply showed that he had struck a nerve. It may not inflame the man enough for him to make a rash mistake, but it was gratifying nevertheless.

"No, Owain, I've no bastards. Your sisters never came to visit me!"

He watched his cousin go stiff in the saddle and he was certain the fool would have charged him then and there if one of his men had not ridden up alongside and grasped him by the arm. He jerked free, but stayed where he sat for a long moment, glaring in Llywelyn's direction.

"Enough talk!" was all he could finally muster as he turned and rode back to his own lines, shouting for his men to make ready.

Llywelyn rode back to his far left flank, if one could call the end of a pitiful line of forty men a flank. It was here that Owain would surely use his numbers to overlap his own line and roll up any men who were not ridden under by the direct assault to their front. Earl Ranulf was positioned at that flank. Llywelyn spoke to him directly.

"My lord, they will try to turn us here. When they come, behave as a Marcher Lord would and kill as many of those Welsh bastards as you can." He turned and called to eight of the men nearest Ranulf by name. "You are with the Earl. Do your duty!" Turning back to the fugitive nobleman, he gave one last command. "Hold them as long as you can." Ranulf pulled his helmet on and gave a grim nod.

Llywelyn looked to the rear and caught Griff's eye. The man lifted his bow. Griff would need no instructions from him. He would have his thirty archers pour shafts into the charging ranks as soon as they rode within range. If those heavy cavalry broke through the thin line of mounted men behind the fence and reached the knoll where the archers stood, there would be outright butchery, but he knew his longbowman would make them pay.

Across the field, he watched his cousin ride down the length of his line rousing his men for the fight. Some were banging their broadswords on their shields and others were shouting insults at the little band that faced them. Despite his sure knowledge that he could not win this battle, he felt his blood rise with the familiar urgency that came before the clash.

"Make ready!" he shouted.

A Marcher Lord

Patch had been with the forward scouts and he rode up shouting.

"Sir Roland, it's like a picture! They are all lined up and right out in the open."

"For God's sake, Patch, what are you talking about?"

"The folk we've been trailing! They have someone—I reckon it's your Earl and that Welshman—run to ground, not a mile from here! The woods end a little ways on. There's a big valley, open country. At least a hundred fifty of them, lined up like they're on parade. They were whipping themselves into a fighting mood while we watched from the woods. It's going to get nasty up there, and soon!"

Roland's mind raced. They had caught up, but now what?

"Patch, the enemy line, how did they face?"

"They were lined up just left of the road, facing south toward the smaller band." Patch described the scene with quick hand gestures that painted a better picture than his words. "The Welshman has put his people behind a stone wall, about two hundred yards south of the road, but that won't help much I reckon."

Roland could see it in his mind. One mile down the road was an enemy in an open field with their rear and left flank exposed to them. Two years of war had taught him a few indelible lessons. He had seen what a surprise cavalry charge falling on an unprotected flank could do to an enemy formation.

But he had less than forty men. Would that be enough to change the outcome?

"Dec!"

Declan rode up beside him.

"There's a line of horsemen between us and the Earl about a mile down this road with their backs to us. If we go straight in, we can strike them in the flank and rear. We'll have no time to form a line before we hit them, but there's no help for that."

"How many?"

"Too many, but they won't see us coming."

"Well, at least there's that," said Declan with a frightening smile. Roland drew his sword.

"Would Sir Roger think this stupid?"

"Perhaps," said the Irishman as he drew his own broadsword, "but he's not here. I say we go."

No command was needed. As the Invalids saw their leaders draw weapons, swords came out of scabbards and helmet straps were tightened. Roland dug his heels into the flanks of The Surly Beast and the horse lunged down the trail, its ears already pinned back.

He had never led a cavalry charge or even fought from horseback before. He had missed the great cavalry battle at Arsuf while a prisoner in Saladin's Jerusalem dungeons. But there were men behind him who had been there, Declan among them, and he hoped that would make a difference. He felt the charger gaining momentum beneath him. Somewhere ahead was the sound of swords beating on shields. One thought was centremost.

Try not to fall off the damn horse.

Roland saw the woods begin to thin, and abruptly the trees were gone, with nothing but tilled land in a broad valley to his front. Off to the left he saw a long double line of mounted men in a muddy field. Their leader had ridden out ahead of the line and was pointing his sword toward a stone wall and a ragged line of horsemen in the distance. The mass of armoured men began to move forward, spurring their mounts to gain speed, but the ground was soft and the charge was slow to gain momentum.

With no command from him, The Surly Beast veered off the road and headed straight for the mass of horses to his left, his big legs churning. Roland threw a glance over his shoulder and saw the men of the Invalid Company fanning out to either side as they bore down on the rear of the enemy. He leaned forward in the saddle and felt a war cry come to his lips, but heard no sound.

Not a man in the enemy line turned to see death gaining on them from behind.

***

Lady Catherine de Laval saw the new horsemen first and wondered if they were simply stragglers trying to close ranks as the charge bore down on Llywelyn's line. Then she saw a man in the nearer line catch sight of this second wave and viciously jerk his horse around to face to the rear. He shouted something over his shoulder, but none of his companions seemed to notice. There was no time for further warnings, as a huge roan charger rammed into horse and rider and hardly broke stride as it trampled both beneath its hoofs. She was confused.

Could these be friends?

She watched in shock and with a spark of hope as two more of the men bearing down on the stone wall caught sight of what followed them. These men tried to call out an alarm, but in the chaos and clamour of the charge, those in front did not hear. Two more of Daffyd's men were ridden down by the men who came behind, as the Invalid Company closed on the enemy's rear.

***

Griff did not miss the arrival of a new force on the field and, like Lady Catherine, half wondered and half prayed that they might be friends. He shouted a command to his men to aim for the foremost riders who were now in range and not those in the rear.

The Welsh longbowmen began sending volleys of arrows arcing over their lines and into the charging enemy. Roland saw them come, like quick sheets of rain before an advancing squall. They lashed the ranks to his front and, in ones and twos, horses and men were struck. Some went down, or were wounded and fell behind. Those that faltered were quickly finished by the Invalids, who had almost reached the rear of the enemy line.

Roland saw that none of the arrows fell on his men and felt a strange pride in the skill of these Welsh bowmen. The enemy line had been thinned by the work of the longbows and by the few horsemen who had turned, only to be overwhelmed by the Invalids. But the enemy commander still had more than twice the number of those who opposed him.

Riders on Owain's right wing began to pull ahead of the line and swing out to complete their turning movement on the flank of the horsemen to their front. Ranulf watched them come. About thirty men jumped their mounts over the stone wall fifty yards to his left and began to wheel toward him.

The Sixth Earl of Chester had never been in a battle and had never fought a man in earnest. But in his veins ran the blood of his sire, Hugh Kevelioc, and his ancestor, Hugh Lupus, who had been with the Conqueror at Hastings. These were hard men who had fought their way into power. That power had been given Ranulf as a birth right, but now he would have to earn it.

Clearing the fence and changing direction had slowed the forward rush of the flanking force, but a tall rider at the front of the group was screaming at his men and whipping his horse back into a gallop. Soon they had closed up into a solid mass bearing down on the left of Llywelyn's line. The Earl turned toward the eight men who had been given the impossible job of protecting that flank.

"To me!" he screamed and charged directly at the tall rider, not looking back to see who might follow. The eight were not the Earl's sworn men, but men in the heat of battle will follow a bold leader. They did not hesitate, but kicked their mounts into motion and followed in the wake of an English lord toward the onrushing wave of fellow Welshmen.

The eight pulled into a tight formation around Ranulf, riding almost knee-to-knee, and slammed into the middle of the flanking force. By staying tightly bunched they formed an irresistible spear point and hacked their way completely through the enemy line, taking out five men in their passage and losing two.

The Earl had slashed savagely at whoever was to his front as they pierced the formation, but did not know if he had done any damage. He had no time to notice the bright blood on his broadsword as they burst into open ground behind their enemies.

Ranulf jerked his horse's head hard to the left and the animal slewed around to face back toward their own lines. For perhaps the first time in his life, the man's blood was up and he dug his heels into his horse's flank, charging back toward the men they had just fought through. Six of his men were still in their saddles and they closed up on the Earl, hurling insults at their countrymen.

As the uneven clash continued on the flank, Owain's main force was nearing the stone wall. Some tried to adjust their horse's gait to clear the barrier. It slowed the charge just as the Invalids slammed into the rear of the formation.

Taking an enemy in flank is a devastating tactic, but surprising your enemy from the rear is crushing. Men do not know which way to turn to defend themselves, and even the most disciplined troops will panic under such an onslaught. Owain's men were no exception. They were brave warriors, but what had looked like a sure victory was now chaos, with enemies in front and behind.

Llywelyn saw their confusion and roared a command that few of his men heard, but they knew what to do when their lord kicked his horse toward the stone fence. They followed. Now it was butcher's work.

Roland and Declan fought side-by-side, as they had at Acre. And despite the cool season, it was hot work. Oddly, the words of Alwyn Madawc came to Roland as he slashed and parried with the man to his front.

"When swords are crossed ye'll need more than skill. Ye must...and I mean must, have the will to destroy the other man— or he will certainly destroy you."

If that advice had been hard for Roland to accept when given so long ago, it had saved his life in the Holy Land more than once and he had come to embrace it. He relentlessly kept up the attack as the man in front of him tried to match him thrust for thrust.

But the Welshman's will was breaking, as fear and fatigue sapped the strength of his right arm. Hemmed in, he had nowhere to flee and after a last desperate lunge, Roland's blade found the gap between helmet and mail and the man fell.

Beneath him, The Surly Beast stamped on anyone and anything that fell under its hooves and bit savagely at any horse that came near enough. One unhorsed rider tried to drag Roland from his saddle and took a massive rear hoof to his head. He was dead before he hit the ground.

To his left, Declan was standing up in his stirrups and hammering a man senseless through his helmet. Beside the Irishman, he caught a glimpse of Sir Edgar aboard the big black plough horse. The huge horse was showing surprising spirit for the fight, churning forward into a knot of mounted men as Sir Edward cleared a path with his battle axe.

The men who had been sent to turn Llywelyn's flank, saw the melee at the stone wall and hesitated. At that moment, had they charged in behind Llywelyn's men, the day might have been saved. But they had just lost five men to a bold charge and the small band that had hacked through their line was now charging at them from the rear.

They hesitated and their hesitation caught Griff's eye. He no longer had a clear target among the brawling men near the stone fence, but here were twenty or more of the enemy a hundred paces away sitting their horses in confusion.

Within seconds, thirty shafts struck horses and riders, dropping eight. That was all that was needed to convince the remainder that the battle was lost. The survivors of Owain's right flank turned and fled down toward the River Conwy, with longbow shafts galling their retreat.

Ranulf reined in and watched them go. He looked down at his bloody sword and at this small squad of Welshmen who waited for his next command. The thought struck him that he might actually outlive this day. He had not thought that possible and had been determined to die like a Marcher Lord.

Perhaps now, I might live like one.

He pointed his sword toward the bloody fray by the stone wall and kicked his horse toward the chaos. His Welshmen fell in obediently behind.

***

Millicent de Laval watched it all from the treeline. It was sickening. She had seen men die before, had perhaps killed one herself during her escape from Clocaenog, but this was death on a new scale. This was a pitched battle with all of its brutal chaos. Hundreds of men were hacking madly at each other in a swirl of flashing steel and splattered blood.

Amidst the din, she heard horses squeal and men scream. She watched riderless mounts galloping away wildly in panic and unhorsed men staggering or crawling away from the fight. Many more lay still on the cold ground. It was madness. It was a horror.

"My God, my God..." she shuddered at the sight.

"My lady?" It was one of the men of the Invalid Company, wounded in the ambush the week before, and too weak to fight. He had stayed beside her as the rest of their band had charged behind Roland Inness into the rear of the enemy force.

"It's nothing, Fergus. I'll be alright."

But she wasn't alright—she was nowhere near to being alright. For months, she had bent all of her efforts to right the wrongs that had befallen her family and it had led to this—a bloodbath on a sunny winter's day in a far corner of Wales. She did not doubt the *rightness* of her actions, but the price?

Must everything be paid for in blood?

As she watched the ghastly scene unfold, she came to a shocking realization. Men all across the field were fighting and dying, but she could not tear her eyes away from the young man on the huge roan charger who had plunged into the centre of the enemy line. She found herself frantically searching for a glimpse of Roland Inness in the hellish jumble of men and horses. Whenever he disappeared from view, her heart lurched.

Oh God, please don't die!

It seemed the carnage would go on for an eternity, but then the fighting ebbed. Knots of men broke clear of the melee at the stone fence and galloped off the field. Others were throwing down their weapons. Finally, she caught a glimpse of Roland leaning far out from his saddle with an arm thrown around Declan's neck. The young Irishman held his bloody broadsword high over his head. She sucked in a huge lungful of air, unaware that she had been holding her breath. She lowered her head.

Thank you, God.

Raising her eyes, she caught sight of a woman sitting a horse on a small knoll far across the field. Even at this distance, she would not mistake the figure of her mother. Never had she felt her need for the woman more. She kicked her horse into a trot and, skirting the edges of the dwindling fight, rode to Catherine de Laval.

The woman on the knoll saw her daughter come and rode down to meet her. Both swung out of their saddles before their mounts had fully stopped, the older woman almost as gracefully as the younger. They held each other silently in a fierce embrace for a long time until Millicent found words.

"Mother, I'm so sorry…"

"Shush, Millie, shush baby," was all Lady Catherine could manage at the moment.

Down by the stone wall, Llywelyn was trying to make sense of what had just happened. Even as his charger was leaping the stone wall to meet Owain's charge, he had seen an unlooked-for band come out of the woods to strike at the rear of his cousin's men. He had no idea who they might be, but he sent up a quick prayer of thanks to his patron Saint David for their miraculous appearance.

Now, as some men fled and others threw down their weapons, he knew that the battle he had no right to win had been won. He looked around at the frightened remnants of the men his Uncle Daffyd had sent out to end his rebellion and did not see his cousin. Of course—Owain would run, would live to fight another day, and that was well. He did not want to kill his kinsman.

The day was coming when he would unite all of Wales and he would find uses for members of his family that now opposed him. For the present, he must deal with the Welshmen he now had in his power. He had eighty or more captives and men such as these he could sorely use.

The defeated men had been ordered to dismount and Llywelyn rode calmly through their midst. Most had dropped their weapons, but not all, and, had they chosen to, they could have dragged the young noble from his horse and killed him before loyal men could come to his aid. But they did not. He reined in his stallion and spoke to them like they were his children.

"You all know my name and my lineage. I am of the senior line from Owain Gwynedd—and my uncles are not. My father, may God preserve him, was the King's first born and I am my father's first born. By our ancient laws, I am your rightful ruler, but you have made war against me. By those same laws you deserve death."

He slowly let his gaze sweep across the prisoners. "But I grow tired of killing my countrymen. I would rather kill Saxons and Normans, when they trouble our land. Those of you who feel the same, kneel now and do homage to me. Those who prefer to fight Welshmen—you may go."

For a moment no one moved. Then, one-by-one, they sank to their knees, leaving only a handful of the older men standing. Llywelyn spoke to these.

"Your loyalty is wasted on a small man, but go with my blessing, and tell your wives and brethren that Prince Llywelyn welcomes all in a united Wales. Tell my Uncle Daffyd the same. But mark it well, if you fight me again, I will kill you all." He jerked his head and the half-dozen men who would not submit mounted and rode away. He turned to the others.

"Do you swear fealty to me and to Wales?" he roared.

"Aye, lord!" came back their answer as one.

"Then rise." That duty done, he now edged his horse toward the road and sought out the men who had saved his dream.

Roland had drawn the Invalid Company back toward the road where they watched with interest Llywelyn's recruitment of his former foes. Now they watched him come, riding with the bearing of a monarch through the ranks of the men he had just defeated. Roland could not help but be slightly awed by the young nobleman. Llywelyn reminded him of nothing so much as Richard the Lionheart.

"That is how a rebel becomes a king," he said to Declan.

As the Welshman drew near, he reined in and laughed.

"My young English and Irish friends! Can it be you? I took a fair hiding from Lady Catherine for letting you go, but it would seem I made a wise choice."

Awed he might be, but Roland now commanded a fighting force sent here by the Queen of England. That honour may have come to him by process of elimination, but it was his now. Whatever else he might be, at this moment he represented the British crown—and he needed to act like it.

"My lord, Llywelyn, Queen Eleanor sends you her greetings and her wishes for your good health," Roland began. "We have come, at her command, to aid Earl Ranulf, if he should still live, and, if by so doing we aid you, then all the better."

Llywelyn beamed.

"The Queen herself sent you? Now there is a woman I would like to meet someday! Woman she may be, but she's the boldest man in England! Is she as fair as the legends say? She must be as old as the hills now, but still…"

He paused and looked at the men gathered around Roland and Declan, saw the scars and the missing limbs. "And these are the legions of England? Few in number and hard-used by the look of them, but I've seen their worth in a fight, by God!"

"The Queen is fair still, my lord, and these men? These are the men of the Invalid Company—veterans all, and no better men in England."

He was about to continue, but Llywelyn cut him off. The Welsh Prince was staring at Roland's horse with undisguised admiration.

"Sir Roland, I see you have found yourself a new mount!" He rode closer to inspect The Surly Beast. As he came near, the big roan bared its teeth and snapped, causing Llywelyn's horse to rear back in a panic. For a terrible moment, Roland feared the Prince was going to topple off into the mud, but he managed to recover his balance and a bit of his dignity with a laugh.

"Where did you get such a wonderful horse?" he asked.

"I killed the man who owned him, my lord."

This caused Llywelyn to smile even more broadly. He seemed oblivious to the signs of carnage that everywhere filled the field around him, transfixed by this snorting and pawing warhorse.

"I will buy him from you! Name your price."

"My lord, with apologies, the horse is not for sale."

Llywelyn frowned and seemed ready to attempt a haggle right there on the field of battle, when a man rode up beside him. He ripped off his helmet and ran a hand through sweat-matted hair. On his face was a look of pure triumph. It took a moment for Roland to recognize that the young man sitting his horse and holding a blood-smeared sword was his own liege lord, Ranulf, of Chester. He nudged Declan and both dismounted. They bowed quickly toward the Earl and Roland spoke.

"My lord, we are the sworn men of Sir Roger de Laval, lately having been sent home from crusade on the King's orders with a message for the Queen. Queen Eleanor sends you her affection and the services of these men who fought with us today." Roland motioned toward the men of the Invalid Company.

"She has issued a decree finding you innocent of treason and wishes that you be restored to your rightful place in Cheshire." He paused as he saw the spreading look of shock on the Earl's face.

"I'm declared innocent, by the Queen?" Ranulf shook his head in disbelief. "How did this happen?"

"My lord, it was the testimony of Lady Millicent de Laval that convinced Her Grace that you were not complicit in any treason. She and the Justiciars have had the decree of innocence read aloud in every county."

Now the Earl raised a hand to his eyes, as though to shield them from the sun, but his voice cracked a bit when next he spoke.

"Lady Millicent. She is the bravest girl I know—no, the bravest person I know, but I thought her a fool for running off alone. Thank God she did!" He paused to gather himself.

"You must be Inness and O'Duinne. Lord Llywelyn said you were escorting Lady Millicent to London, but privately he confided his doubts you'd make it that far. I remember you from the archery tournament, Master Inness. I won a nice sum from that bastard de Ferrers by betting on you. Had I known what was to come, I would have ordered you to put an arrow through his heart!"

"And I would have gladly obliged you, my lord."

Earl Ranulf looked at the young man standing before him. He vaguely remembered him as a tall slender boy with big shoulders when they had met briefly at the King's coronation. He was still young, but his body had filled out in the intervening years and whatever he had endured on the crusade had taken most of the boy out of his bearing.

"Yes, I understand from Lady Catherine that your grievance with the Earl of Derby predates my own. It would seem that we all have scores to settle with William de Ferrers."

"I will kill him one day," Roland said simply, and no one gainsaid him.

"And where *is* Lady Millicent?" the Earl asked. "Is she here? It would seem I once more have her to thank for whatever good fortune comes my way."

Roland looked past the Earl toward the knoll where the longbowmen still stood. The two women were embracing there. He pointed to where they stood.

"Perhaps we should hold our thanks for later, my lord. I expect they have much to discuss."

Llywelyn and Earl Ranulf both winced just a bit. Each man had, on occasion, run afoul of Lady Catherine de Laval. It was not a pleasant way to pass an hour and they wondered what Millicent was enduring for defying her mother.

Up on the hill, the two women finally released their embrace.

"You were foolish, Millie," Lady Catherine said, but there was relief and tenderness in her voice.

"I did what I was compelled to, Mother. It pained me more than you know to make you suffer, but something had to be done."

Lady Catherine looked out on the field below. Over thirty bodies were strewn over the bloody ground, but it had been a victory. Llywelyn had more than doubled his strength with the defection of Daffyd's warriors and a new force, sent by the

Queen, had come to aid the Earl of Chester. To her utter shock, this force was led by her husband's own vassals, two men she had last seen as boys and squires. Millicent's defiance of her had all led to this.

"Aye, I will concede that it turned out well—this time. But it could just as easily have ended differently. Do not let this make you reckless, Millie."

Millie gave her Mother a brilliant smile. It was the kind of smile her husband used on her when he wanted to make amends. *Roger.*

"Millicent, go fetch Roland and Declan. I would have a word with them."

***

The ride back to Llywelyn's hill fortress was long, and Lady Catherine's interrogation of Roland and Declan lasted for most of the journey. Roland gathered the courage to tell her that Sir Roger would not return for almost a year and she had ridden in silence for a long time, a stricken look on her face.

Roland could not help but feel sorry for this formidable woman who so longed for her husband's return. After a bit, she resumed her questions and they were rife with urgency and barely-concealed fear.

Was he healthy when you left him? Had he taken wounds? Had he been eating well? Had he grown thin? Who served him now as squire? Tell me again of the King's decision to send you home and keep Roger there.

Roland and Declan withheld nothing. It would have been impossible to do otherwise, faced with her need. Finally, the questions dwindled and she rode for long periods in silence. Roland realized that she had not asked if her husband had sent her a message.

"My lady, Sir Roger's last words to me on the beach in Jaffa were for your ears. He said to tell you that he would come home, even though all the hordes of Saladin stood in his way."

She allowed herself a weak smile.

"Just like Roger to try to cozen me, but I know that good men sometimes don't come home...that..." Her voice cracked. Roland reined in his horse and grasped her reins as well.

174

"My lady, he *will* come home!"

"How can you know that?" she asked, angry for the first time.

"I know because he is Sir Roger de Laval and the devil himself could not keep him from coming back to you."

They sat silently on their horses for a long time as the survivors of the battle in the Conwy Valley rode past. Finally Lady Catherine spoke.

"Thank you, Roland. You spoke my husband's message so well, it sounded very much like him. It took me aback." She sighed. "I have been a soldier's wife for a score of years, and I should know by now how to wait for my man to come home."

Roland realized he was still holding her reins and released them.

"We'll wait for him together, my lady."

The Bargain

*I*t was two days before Lent when El Malek el-Adel, brother to Saladin, rode into the gates of Jaffa on a magnificent white stallion. He led seven fine camels behind him—gifts for the Christian king. El Malek was familiar with the way to King Richard's headquarters, having made this trip far too many times over the past month. He wondered if this meeting would be different.

Negotiations had been re-opened in February. Then, the proposals exchanged had been as insincere as a harlot's affection. Now it was March and he hoped the infidels had something more to offer this time, for in truth, his brother's position was weaker than any here knew.

Jerusalem they could hold, but Arsuf had shown that their army was no match for the Europeans in the open field, not with Richard of England in command. Most worrisome was the threat to Saladin's base in Egypt. If the English king chose to march down the coast toward the Nile, there was little they could do to stop him. And if Egypt should fall, so too would Saladin. He wondered if the Europeans understood this simple fact. He prayed that they did not.

King Richard emerged from his pavilion to personally greet the emissary from Saladin. Beside him stood his close companion, Sir Baldwin of Bethune, and a tall, balding knight El Malek had come to know over the months of negotiations. Sir Roger de Laval was the leader of the Christian's feared heavy cavalry and reputed to be a fearsome man in battle, but he was no zealot. More than his king, he seemed to recognize the costs of continuing the war, and El Malek was pleased he was in attendance. After the exchange of gifts, Saladin's ambassador was ushered inside for an evening of feasting—and bargaining.

As El Malek el-Adel worried over Egypt, King Richard worried over England. More news had arrived of Philip's belligerence in Normandy and John's disloyalty at home. Entreaties from the Queen that he hasten home had grown more urgent with each new correspondence. Time was growing short if he was to keep his word to his mother to return to England by Christ's Mass.

As dawn began to show in the east, a deal was struck. There would be a three year truce. The Christians would keep the cities they now held and Saladin would keep Jerusalem. Europeans would be allowed pilgrimages to the Holy City and all prisoners would be exchanged. It would take months for the provisions of the peace to be completed and only then would King Richard and his army go home—home to England.

As El Malek rode out of the gates of Jaffa taking the news back to Saladin, Sir Roger climbed to the seaward parapet of Jaffa's wall and stared west across the dark waters. It had been nearly two years since he'd last seen England. Back home, the buds would be showing on the trees and the reed beds would be greening down by the Dee. By now, Roland and Declan should have delivered their message to the Queen and made their way to Shipbrook—to Cathy and Millicent. Now, he would be going home at last. He lifted a prayer of thanks to God.

The Third Crusade was over.

Bowstrings

Millicent made her way down the muddy path from the hill fort to the small encampment in the valley below. February had turned to March, and she noticed the first buds beginning to appear on the trees. The approaching spring brought alternating days of rain and winter chill, but this day was sunny and she walked with a light step, despite the muck of the trail.

The small group of rude huts that now sat along the stream on the valley floor had been thrown up by the men of the Invalid Company in a few days after Roland decided to billet them there. The dwellings were draughty, but at least his men were not being jammed together in the fort.

They may have been allied with the Welsh in a common purpose, but the long history of ill will between the men on the hill and the English below made a bit of separation prudent. The Invalids had been more than happy to make their own living arrangements. Within a week, they had settled into camp life while waiting for the noblemen on the hill to decide what to do.

Roland had no stomach for the endless disagreements between Llywelyn and the Earl over strategy and was relieved to be half a mile down the hill. The nobles did not seek his counsel in any event. For Millicent, the past month had been yet another frustrating wait.

The days had brought an increasing stream of new adherents to Llywelyn's cause, as word spread of his unexpected victory in the Conwy Valley. Within a week, men had begun to arrive in twos and threes at the Prince's wilderness stronghold. The sudden influx made quarters on the hilltop cramped. This did not bother the girl, but the daily bickering of the lords did.

Each day, Prince Llywelyn and Earl Ranulf debated future plans in light of their new strength. The Welsh Prince favoured a campaign of raids and plunder into Cheshire, arguing that it would provide him with needed finances to support his growing rebellion, while weakening Ranulf's enemy, the Earl of Derby.

"Spoken like a true Welsh cattle thief!" Ranulf had shouted that very morning. "You would have me impoverish my own people? How will that serve to restore me to my rightful place?"

"Cattle thief?" Llywelyn snarled back. "Might I remind the Earl of Nowhere, that he is the guest of this cattle thief? And what is your plan, my lord? Oh yes! I recall it now. Simply march out on the field before the walls of Chester and invite the Earl of Derby to sally forth for honourable combat. Brilliant! Even if I gave you all of my men—which I will not—you would be outnumbered four to one and slaughtered. Your plan is no plan at all."

And thus, the disagreement that had lasted a fortnight had resumed with neither man persuading the other. Millicent had had enough. Now, as she stepped lively down the hill, she felt her spirits rise. The men of the Invalid Company were up and about—some gathering wood, some tending fires and a few practicing their sword work. She felt a special bond with these damaged men who had proven to be so surprisingly lethal in a fight. And she knew they felt the same.

"My lady!" Patch hailed her from just off the path where he was taking an axe to a deadfall oak. "Good morning to you!"

"And to you, Tom." She smiled at the wiry man with one eye who had worked up a healthy sweat in his morning labours.

"What brings you down amongst us poor valley-dwellers, my lady? Looking for Roland?"

She was far enough away that she hoped he couldn't see her blush.

Roland Inness.

Ever since the battle with Daffyd's men, she had struggled with the problem of Roland Inness. On that terrible day, she had been unable to tear her eyes away from where he was on the field.

The battle had been ghastly and all of their hopes had hung on its outcome, yet it was the fate of one person that had gripped her with an unexpected panic. The thought that Roland might be killed or hurt filled her with an overwhelming dread. She tried to convince herself that it was simply fear for a friend, but knew that was a lie.

Roland Inness. This was a problem.

After the Clocaenog, there had been a bond between them, but they were children then. She had thought about him during the years he was gone to war—but that was only natural. Now he was back and no longer a boy. These new feelings were a complication she could not indulge in their current circumstances and she had done her best to disguise them. There was simply too much at stake for her to be acting like some giddy peasant girl. But on a sunny day in early March, it was hard not to.

"As a matter of fact, that is exactly who I am looking for, Tom!"

"Well, he is down at his hut. I heard him cursing over something a bit earlier, so follow the sound of bad language to find him. But watch your ears, my lady."

She had to laugh. They were all so protective of her.

"Damn it!"

Patch had not been jesting with her. She came around the corner of the small hut that Roland called home and found him angrily muttering as he threw what looked like a tangled ball of twine into the fire. He looked up, saw her, and smiled sheepishly.

"Sorry, Millie. Didn't see you there."

"I expect not. Patch warned me that you were in a mood this morning."

Roland shook his head and reached down to grasp a handful of long fibres that were draped over a rude bench.

"This is what's vexing me. It's very fine flax and I am ruining it! I've botched three sets of bowstrings this morning. He picked up his longbow. "This is my last string, and it's shot," he said, laying the weapon down. "If I can't get this right, I'll soon have to bludgeon game with a stick."

"I'm sorry to hear that. We have all enjoyed the venison you've been providing."

Her words made him beam.

"The red deer hereabouts are shy, but they carry a lot of meat, even in the spring. You should dine with us soon. Sergeant Billy makes a fine stew."

"I would be pleased to join you," she said, suddenly feeling the conversation grow awkward. "I should be getting back now."

"Wait," he said, gently grasping her arm. "I've been working on one of the staves you saved for me. Let me show you."

He ducked into the low hut and returned holding a longbow in his hands. He handed it to Millicent.

"It isn't finished, but it will be soon. It needs tillering, and, of course, a proper bow string."

Millicent turned the yew staff over in her hands. It was longer than the bow that rested against the hut—over six feet she guessed, and just a bit taller than the man who would use it. It was rough, with bumps in several places and with dark bands of colour that ran the length of the shaft, curving around like snakes. Rough it might be, but oddly beautiful.

"Once it's tillered, I will need to work the wood with bone to harden it a bit, but I'm almost there. It's been four years since I crafted a bow, but my father taught me well. It's a thing you don't forget."

Millicent handed the staff back to Roland.

"It's beautiful, Roland. Your father would be proud."

She had a sudden urge to say more. To say something a giddy peasant girl might say. But she did not.

"I must go now. Send word to me when Sergeant Billy makes his next stew."

"Of course. Can I walk you back?"

"No, no, you have work to do here. I'll be fine."

She turned and started back up the trail. Roland watched her go and shook his head. Somewhere on the journey from Wales to Oxford and back again, something had changed in the way he saw her. He wasn't sure when he had first sensed it, but the night she had come to meet the Invalids had settled the matter for him. He had watched the way she treated them with grace and compassion. She was no longer the girl who made jests of squires. She was something else entirely.

Since the fight in the Conwy Valley, Millicent had made regular visits to the encampment of the Invalid Company below the fort. The men all treated her as something between a princess and a favourite daughter. She, in turn, treated all of them like favourite uncles—but not him. With him, she was cordial enough, but there was a distance she kept that did not exist with the other men. It hurt more than he wished to admit.

Millicent de Laval. How did this happen?

He watched her until she was lost to sight on the trail.

When Millicent reached her small quarters in the fort, she called for the young servant girl Llywelyn had provided to attend to her needs.

"Alis, send for the archer Griff—and find me a bundle of good flax.

***

Roland and Declan lay on their backs looking up at the sky, a warm spring sun on their faces. They had finished their morning chores and strolled together along the creek to the clearing where the horses were pastured. After a lean February, the spring grass had come in lush and the thin animals were starting to look fitter.

Declan had carved a crude comb out of wood and they had spent a pleasant hour combing the manes of their mounts and picking the burrs out of their tails. As was his nature, the big roan charger stamped and snorted, but otherwise allowed his new master to groom him.

"Is Llywelyn still bargaining with you for The Surly Beast?" Declan asked.

Roland laughed.

"Of course, though I've taken care not to call the animal that in his presence! Two days ago he offered me five of his horses, a fine mail shirt and three gold coins."

"Good God, he lusts after that horse like it was a woman."

"I honestly believe that if he had a woman of his own, he would throw her into the bargain for the horse."

"But you won't trade, will you?"

"Perhaps I will, if the price is right."

"And what is your price?"

Roland turned on his side and poked his friend.

"More than you can afford!"

Declan scowled.

"It is a magnificent animal, I'll concede, but it almost bit my leg off twice this week. I wouldn't want it. Tell me though, what could Llywelyn offer that you would accept?"

Roland yawned and shrugged, the warm sun making him drowsy

"I'll know it when it's offered."

***

He had taken a large doe at dawn. After field dressing the carcass, he slung it over his shoulders and started the long hike back to camp. With an ever-growing number of men to feed, game had become scarce near the hill fort. To find a spot with better prospects, he had risen long before first light and hiked a good five miles to the east. There he had struck a game trail with fresh tracks.

The sun had not yet risen above the hills further east when a red deer doe trotted down the trail, stopping to browse on some new greenery only fifty feet from where he stood. It was at moments like this that he felt like his true self. He was raised as a woodsman and a hunter and the time he spent alone in the forest, tracking and taking game for the table, was the best.

In the years he had been squire to Sir Roger, he had been well-trained in the Norman way of fighting. He had learned to ride, use a sword and wear mail—all valuable skills. But it did not come naturally to him.

The Norman way had conquered most of Europe. Their skilful use of heavily armoured knights along with strategically placed castles and forts was a lethal combination, but not without weaknesses. The uprising of the Danes in his father's time, even though it ultimately failed, had proven that. The longbow had exposed the vulnerability of the armoured knight.

Regardless of his new status within the world of the Normans, he knew he would always be a longbowman, no matter what he might be called.

It was late morning when he returned to camp. He dumped the meat with Sergeant Billy to butcher and walked down to the stream. Dressing a fresh kill was bloody work and he was fairly well covered. He tore off his shirt and began plunging it into the water, which turned a faint pink. He left it to soak and had just begun scrubbing the blood from his hands when he saw Millicent de Laval coming through the woods toward his hut.

Damn!

He jerked his wet shirt from the stream and pulled it over his head. It still had stains from the blood of his kill, but at least he was no longer half naked.

Millicent saw him standing, dripping wet, in the stream and stopped abruptly. She had grown used to the rough necessities of a soldier's encampment in the wilderness and had seen things a lady typically did not, but she had not yet surprised Roland Inness in such an awkward position. It was too late to turn back now.

"Roland, I'm sorry to interrupt your toilet. I will come back another time."

"No, Millie, please stay. I'm just cleaning up. I took a nice doe this morning and Sergeant Billy will have the pot on the boil soon. Will you not join us?"

"Well, I suppose I could." She stopped and searched for something more to say, then remembered why she had come. "I have something for you." She held out both hands. Stretched between were two perfectly woven bow strings.

Roland stepped out of the stream and took the strings from her. Each had a sturdy Flemish loop at one end and a light coating of wax. They were flawless.

"Where did you get these?"

"I made them...I've had nothing useful to do for weeks. I got help from Griff. I didn't know how long your bow was, so we only did the one loop. I..." She realized she was prattling. "I hope they will do."

Roland beamed at her.

"These will do most nicely. I've never seen better. Shall we test them with my new bow?"

He led her back to his hut and ducked inside. Frantically he dug through his few belongings to find a dry shirt and quickly changed. He emerged carrying his new longbow. With the ease of long practice he slipped the loop of one string around the bottom notch, bent the bow and tied off the other at the top notch. He would measure and adjust the length later. He grabbed up a quiver and reached out his hand to Millicent.

"Come with me, Millie?"

She took his hand.

Swords at Easter

*T*he trouble began on Easter morning. A priest had been found to conduct mass and all had jammed into the open field inside the hill fort to hear the message of resurrection and peace. The Welsh now numbered over two hundred strong and they were joined by the forty men of the Invalid Company in the muddy enclosure.

Only Ranulf, Catherine and Millicent understood the meaning of the Latin words the priest spoke, but all were familiar with the age-old cadences of the mass. The ritual included communion and the sun was almost overhead when the final prayer of thanksgiving was lifted heavenward.

As the only noblemen in attendance, Prince Llywelyn and Earl Ranulf stood in the front of the assembled men. With the mass complete, the worshipers had started to drift away from the field when a loud argument broke out between the two. Men stopped and began to edge closer as heated words rose to shouts and insults. All knew that there had been contention between these leaders, but none had heard it reach this level.

"I swear to God, Llywelyn, if I hear that even one of your men so much as steals a chicken in Cheshire, I will…I will…" The Earl seemed to choke on his rage and could not get out the dire threat he wished to hurl.

"You will what, my lord? Besiege my fort with your forty men down in the valley? You forget yourself, sir." Llywelyn greeted Ranulf's tirade with a cold calm, though it had been his words, whispered quietly to the Earl at the end of the service that had set the man off.

He had merely pointed out that Wales was a poor country and could not afford to feed so many Englishmen indefinitely— not with prosperous Cheshire just across the Dee. Surely the Earl could not object to rounding up a few head of cattle and some pigs to keep his own men in victuals?

The Earl did object and heatedly. What happened next, men would differ on, but some swore they saw Ranulf's hand reach for the hilt of his sword. Whatever the provocation, a half dozen Welshmen drew their swords, which prompted a like number of English to do the same. The belligerence spread until the quiet of the morning was drowned out by the hissing of steel sliding from scabbards.

The two noblemen had been so taken up with their growing feud that they hadn't noticed the dangerous tension that gripped the men around them. Now they looked around in astonishment at hundreds of men who were ready to do violence. It would have taken only one wrong move to start a bloodbath. Llywelyn raised both hands over his head.

"Hold!"

Roland swung around to face his men and saw that they too had weapons at the ready.

"Stand down!" he commanded. Men began to slowly lower swords and axes around the compound.

Lady Catherine, who had been watching the frightening move toward bloody chaos, stepped directly between the two men. For not the first time, she noted that these noblemen were hardly more than boys. Neither had seen two dozen summers. She spoke to them now, like a mother to squabbling children.

"That will be enough, from both of you! How do you expect to rule men when you cannot even rule your own tempers? Look about you, my lords. All here are sick of this bickering. I tell you, it is time for it to end! Come with me." She turned and stalked off toward the wooden hall at the centre of the compound.

For a moment, the men stood frozen to the spot. Neither had been spoken to in this fashion since they were small children, and then only rarely. Llywelyn threw a glance at Ranulf and saw that the Earl of Chester was wavering.

"Hell, Ranulf, I'll follow her if you will."

Ranulf gave a curt nod and the two noblemen fell in behind the woman like chastened miscreants. Catherine did not look back to see if they followed, but as she passed by the Invalid Company, she caught Roland's eye.

"You—come with me—and bring my daughter."

As she neared the hall, she saw Griff the archer leaning on his longbow.

"You, as well. Join us in the hall."

Like an avenging angel, she burst through the doors and began issuing orders to the servants—all of whom had retreated inside when swords had been drawn.

"Bring us bread, and ale—and get a stew simmering."

She spoke to the two spearmen who were on duty at the hall's entrance.

"No one in or out without my leave. Understood?"

"Aye, my lady."

When the last of those she had summoned reached the hall, Catherine wheeled around and faced them, her anger barely in check.

"There have been a thousand times in the last year that I wished my husband were here. Roger de Laval is a man who knows how to make a decision and get on with it. With you two, it seems there is nothing but endless *posturing*." She uttered this last word with scorn in her voice.

"Prince Llywelyn, you are gaining strength, but your uncles control the settled land and have far more men than you. They also have castles, which you cannot take without the support of powerful allies. The only ally I see in sight is standing beside you, yet you continue to urge the Earl to ravage his own countryside. Is this the way to restore him to strength? You take great care not to prey on folk on this side of the Dee. Is it somehow wise to plunder the people you wish to rule in England, but not in Wales?

"I…"

Catherine cut him off.

"For one with such high ambitions, my lord, you think small." She did not wait for his reply, but turned to Earl Ranulf.

"And you, my own liege lord…" She shook her head.

"We all know how much it stings to have the Earl of Derby's banner hanging over the ramparts of Chester, but you think surviving a skirmish in the Conwy Valley has made you a warlord? Sir, you are no warlord. If you were, you would know that we do not have the strength to meet de Ferrers in open battle. To do so would be the ruination of all of our hopes."

"My lady…"

Catherine held up a hand to stop him.

"Think! All of you! Everything rests on Ranulf being restored to his Earldom. How can we make that happen?"

For a long moment there was nothing but embarrassed silence in the hall. Then a voice came from the back of the room.

"We take back Chester."

It was Roland Inness who spoke. He had been standing against the wall but now walked to the front.

"Chester is the greatest city in the west of England. Whoever rules in Chester rules the west."

No one challenged this obvious truth.

"The Earl of Chester cannot wield power while his city is held by enemies, but taking it back can't be done by assault or siege—we don't have the men or the siege engines for either course. But when Chester fell, de Ferrers used neither tactic. He took the place by guile and surprise. We must do the same."

Llywelyn was first to object.

"My spies cannot get into the city, but they watch it. They report that the walls are being repaired and the garrison is kept on good alert. Surprise seems unlikely."

Now, Millicent spoke up.

"Perhaps, my lord, but we have been no threat to them for almost a year. Vigilance will have waned. De Ferrers took the place with fewer men than we have. If he could do it, why not we?"

"Why not indeed, my dear!" It was Earl Ranulf who now spoke. "Sir Roland is right. Chester is the key. Without it, my title means little. And your mother is also right," he said turning to Catherine. "I am no warlord—not yet, but I will fight for what is mine. If there is a chance we can retake the city, we must try!"

Llywelyn shook his head.

"As I've said, we cannot get spies into the city and without them we are blind. I will not send my men into Chester to be hanged on a fool's errand!" The Welsh prince folded his arms to show this issue was decided. Millicent turned to him.

"My lord Llywelyn, you cannot safely get your men into the city because they are Welsh and reveal themselves the moment they open their mouths to speak—am I not right?"

Llywelyn nodded.

"These days, no Welsh are welcome in Chester. Even our traders stay clear of the city. It's too dangerous."

"Then the solution is obvious. Our spy must be English, not Welsh."

Lady Catherine had watched Roland and Millicent lead the conversation away from the impasse, but now realized with a sickening feeling where her daughter was heading.

"Millicent!"

Millicent saw the look of fear on her mother's face and hated that she had put it there, but she knew what must be done.

"Mother, I speak like the native of Cheshire that I am, and none here know the city as I do, save the Earl, and he would be recognised instantly. I can get into the city."

"Millicent...no."

"I'm sorry, Mother. You've told these men to think, so you must as well. You know I am right in this. Don't make me have to sneak away into the night again."

Lady Catherine, who had stood so commandingly over the assembled group now sagged.

"You never were much for listening to me, child," she sighed. "I will not try to stop you, but you must not go alone, promise me..."

"She'll need someone with her who knows how to assess a city's defences."

Millicent turned to see that it was Roland Inness who spoke. He was looking at her with a peculiar intensity.

"You?"

"Me."

Into Chester

A large salmon flopped out of the basket and into the bottom of the small boat just as it approached the narrow canal that led off the Dee and through the wall at Chester's Shipgate. A woman in the stern grabbed it by the tail and slammed its head over a thwart. The fish ceased its futile struggle and she dropped it back into the basket.

It was difficult to tell the woman's age. She was dressed in threadbare woollens and her face was dirty. The man at the oars had big shoulders as would befit a fisherman who worked the nets in the estuary. Perhaps they were husband and wife. A bored guard on the Dee bridge glanced below at the boat manoeuvring toward the canal and looked away—nothing to see there.

In the brush on the far bank two men lay concealed, watching as the fisherman shipped his right oar and pulled hard on the left, swinging the nose of the little craft into the canal. Once in the canal, the woman in the stern rose and nimbly climbed past the man to reach the bow. After a few more strokes, she hopped onto one of the weathered piers that lined the waterway outside the gate with a line in her hand.

The man pulled in the oars and secured them in the bottom of the boat. As the woman tied off the line, he steadied himself and hoisted the basket of fish onto the dock, hauling himself up behind it. Together they lifted the heavy basket by woven handles on each side. Carrying their catch up the beaten path along the canal, the two approached a narrow archway next to the larger opening of the Shipgate.

Before they reached the doorway they had to pass a crude gibbet set up along the path. A fresh corpse hung there. It was a boy, though the body had been there for a day or more and the age was hard to judge. The corpse had a sign around its neck. The sign read "THIEF."

Millicent de Laval forced herself to look at the grisly remains. In her six months living in Chester, there had been no hangings. Back then, many had thought that young Earl Ranulf was too gentle on criminals. But there was a new ruler in Chester now.

For not much longer, she vowed to herself.

Finally, they reached the archway and passed through the Shipgate. The two men across the river watched until they disappeared into the city, then slithered carefully backward into deeper cover before standing. A short scramble took them to where their horses were tethered in the forest. They mounted and rode hard to the west until the track emerged into a large clearing. There, a sizable party waited. Declan O'Duinne and Griff the archer reined in their ponies and dismounted.

Prince Llywelyn, Earl Ranulf and Lady de Laval saw them come and rose, anxious for word.

"They're in! No one gave them a second look." Declan said. He did not mention the gibbet or the hanging corpse outside the gate.

Catherine de Laval realized she had been holding her breath since she saw them ride up.

"Thank God for that," she managed.

It had been Millicent's idea to go back into Chester the way she had last come out, by the Shipgate canal. The plan was simple. Row to Chester and enter through the Shipgate by noon. Spend the rest of the day noting troop strengths, guard practices and looking for weaknesses. At dusk, return to the skiff and row downstream until they were out of sight of the city walls. Horses and an escort would be waiting for them on the Welsh side of the river. It was a simple plan. Simple was usually best.

That morning, Llywelyn's men hailed one of the many fishermen who gathered for the spring salmon run on the estuary. He was bound for Chester with a fresh catch. They paid him three times what his boat and catch would bring and he cheerfully handed over both.

Fishermen—and women—had worked the lower stretch of the Dee and its broad estuary since long before the Romans came and were a common sight in spring. It had been easy enough for Roland and Millicent to dress the part. As Roland settled himself on the centre thwart of the small boat, he picked up a fish from the basket and cheerfully handed it to Millicent.

"Never met a fisherman who didn't smell like his catch," he said, as he picked up a salmon and began rubbing it over his clothes and hands. Millicent hesitated but a second and did the same. Preparations complete, Declan shoved them into the stream and Roland bent to the oars, pulling hard against the current.

Millicent, seated by the basket of fish in the stern, turned and gave a quick wave to her mother who stood between Ranulf and Llywelyn on the bank. All three waved back.

With news that the two had secured entry into the city, the group in the clearing settled in for the long wait. Twenty men from the Invalid Company and a like number of Llywelyn's men guarded the approaches. This was the borderland and it was dangerous, even for a Marcher Lord and a Welsh Prince.

***

Inside the wall of the Shipgate, three guards stood watch over the comings and goings of the water trade. Warehouses crowded around the small basin where the official docks of the city received shipments from as far away as France and Ireland. There was a substantial fee for tying up at these docks and so the local river men had built their own along the canal outside the gate. This had always been tolerated by the Earl of Chester, but Ranulf was no longer making the rules.

"Hold there you two!"

One of the guards carried a long oak truncheon and he jabbed it in Roland's side. He flinched, but kept his eyes down, fighting the instinct to strike back.

"Where'd ye think yer goin'?"

"Pardon sir, we're to the fishmonger—to sell our catch."

"Then ye should know that ye owe a fee for passin' through that gate." He pointed his truncheon at the narrow archway they had just passed through.

"Pardon sir, we've not sold here before."

"And you'll not now until ye pay up. The Earl takes a tithe of anything we let through that gate, or are you too dim to know what a tithe is?" The guard poked him again—hard in the ribs. Roland made the mistake of lifting his head, his eyes meeting those of the guard. It was then that their simple plan began to unravel.

The guard was used to having his way with the local fishermen and was startled when he met this man's eyes and saw murder there. He reflexively raised his truncheon to bludgeon the wretch, and that was his mistake.

Seeing the blow coming, Roland's instincts and training took over. The guard found his wrist caught in an iron grip, but had no time to be shocked before Roland stepped forward and drove an elbow hard into his face, leaving his nose a bloody, broken mess. The man fell to the cobbles with a pitiful whimper.

The two guards on the other side of the boat basin had been lounging in a spot of shade watching the commerce at the docks when they saw their comrade collapse in a heap. They had missed the blow that laid him low, but saw the tall man standing over him.

"You man!" one shouted, and pointed at Roland.

Roland turned to Millicent, who had been watching the collapse of their careful plan in stunned horror. He grasped her arm.

"Run!" he shouted and started toward the Shipgate, but she pulled free.

"No, this way!" She pointed up an alley that led into a warren of warehouses and dwellings. She did not wait for him to follow, but hiked up her long dress and ran. The guards started toward Roland as he watched Millicent flee into, rather than out of, the city. He cursed under his breath and followed.

195

The docks were teeming with activity at midday. Tradesmen, fishermen, carpenters, moneylenders and even a few pickpockets had all witnessed the lowly fisherman strike down the gate keeper. As the two remaining guards took up the chase, the crowd seemed to suddenly thicken between them and their quarry. Barrels accidently rolled into their path, nimble dock hands grew clumsy and stumbled into them as they shoved through the crowd.

By the time they reached the alley, there was no sign of the fisherman or his woman. The guards whirled angrily around, but everyone in sight was back at their labours as though nothing had occurred. Their fellow guard was still curled up and moaning on the cobbles. They hauled him to his feet.

"Get him to the barracks," the senior man said. "Someone there can clean him up. Then get to the captain. Tell him what happened here." He spoke louder now so the men around the basin would all hear and take note. "We'll kick in every door in the city to find this man and then we'll hang him beside the Shipgate!"

***

Roland followed Millicent through a half-dozen twists and turns in the cramped district that surrounded the Shipgate. At each turn he looked over his shoulder. No one was following, but they were moving toward the centre of the city where two people running would arouse unwanted interest. He caught up to her and grasped her arm. She tried to tear free, but he held her firmly.

"Stop. They're not following. Walk as you normally would or someone will give chase."

She caught her breath and nodded. He released her arm and they resumed their flight, walking now, from the Shipgate district.

"What did you say to the guard?" she hissed under her breath as they walked. "Another minute and we would have been about our business!"

"I said we were taking our catch to the fishmonger."

"No, after that! You must have said something to provoke him."

"I said nothing," he replied, the heat rising in his cheeks. "These bastards need no excuse to strike a man. Perhaps he was just easily provoked. I was not going to let him split my skull."

Millicent made no reply as she led them further into the city. It was early afternoon and the weather was pleasant, so people on the street were becoming more numerous. Roland felt that at any moment someone would point at them and sound a hue and cry. Finally he leaned close to Millicent and whispered.

"What now?"

"We have to find a safe place to hide and a new plan for getting out of the city. They will, no doubt, be watching our boat."

"Aye, the boat is done. You know the city—where can we hide that will be safe?"

She kept walking, lost in thought for a time before answering.

"There is only one place they will not search."

"And where is that?"

"The castle."

***

"Pssst."

The girl turned with a start. The sound had come from a narrow space between two buildings. Even in midafternoon, the shadows were deep there, but she could see that someone was beckoning to her. She hesitated. Prudence was a good girl and a good girl did not let herself be lured into an alleyway, even if she was but a scullery maid. She made up her mind to run, but then she heard her name called.

"Prudy!"

The girl did not know what to do, so she stood still. A woman came out of the shadows. She stank of fish and had a dirty face. Once more she considered running back toward the barred gate that led into the kitchens of Chester Castle.

"Prudy, it's me, Lady Millicent." Millicent pulled the wimple from her head and stepped closer. Prudy backed up a step.

"Lady Millicent's dead. They told us she died along with the Earl, off in Wales somewhere."

"I'm not dead Prudy, and neither is the Earl, but we are in danger. Can you help us?" As she spoke, she noticed Prudy edging toward the gate. The girl did not believe her.

"Prudy, you showed me how to get into the Earl's Back Door. You remember…"

The scullery maid stopped in her tracks and took a closer look. She had, indeed shown Lady Constance's lady-in-waiting this secret passage between the Earl's bedroom and his wife's.

"Can it be you," she gasped, "back from the dead? Please don't cozen me."

Millicent stepped forward and held out her hands.

"It's really me, Prudy. I've missed you all."

Prudence took Millicent's hands in hers, a smile lighting up her face.

"I didn't recognize you, my lady, what with yer face all dirty and yer dress! Everyone will be so 'appy to see you. There were lots of sad faces when you and the Earl disappeared. "It 'asn't been the same since. The new lord, 'e 'angs too many people by the gates!"

"Prudy, listen carefully. No one must know we are here. I have a friend with me," she beckoned Roland from the shadows, "and we will be the next to be hanged by the gates if the new lord catches us. Can you find a place where we can hide until we can get back out of the city?"

Prudy did not hesitate.

"Of course, my lady." She glanced up and down the street. It was empty. "Follow me."

Millicent grasped her arm.

"Prudy, if they find you've helped us, you will hang as well. Do you understand?"

"Aye, miss, I do. Anyone can be 'ung around 'ere these days, but don't fret. We won't be caught."

She led them through the iron gate and into the scullery. At midday the place was deserted save one cook who dozed in a chair. She never budged as Prudy led them through the kitchen to the back stairs leading to the upper floors. Once on the stairs, she turned to Millicent and whispered.

"No one goes in Lady Constance's suite since she was dragged off by the new Earl. You will be safe there."

They hurried up a final flight and emerged into a hallway only a few feet from the door to Lady Constance's chambers. They entered and closed it behind them.

"Prudy, I see there is no guard at the far end of the hall by the Earl's quarters. Is no one in residence?"

"No. I'd never 'ave brung ye here if the new Earl was about. But, we've been told 'e will return in two weeks."

"You say the new Earl hangs too many people, Prudy?"

"Aye, my lady. I know they say the old Earl was traitor to the King, but we all 'ate the new one! 'is men take everything and any that don't pay up—'e stretches their necks! 'E's a bad man fer certain."

Millicent nodded.

"That's why we're here Prudy. Earl Ranulf is no traitor and we mean to put him back in his rightful place in Chester."

"Well amen to that, my lady. Amen to that. Now let me do some thinkin' on 'ow to get you and this 'andsome young feller out of the city," she said and winked at Millicent.

In their haste to find refuge, Millicent realized she had not introduced her friend.

"Prudence, forgive me. I should have introduced Sir Roland Inness."

Roland gave a small bow.

"At your service, Miss Prudence, we are deeply in your debt."

"Oh my," Prudy blushed prettily and gave a small curtsy. "I'll bring you some food right away, my lord."

Millicent gave him an acid look as she left.

"If you would have been as charming to the guard, we would not be in this situation."

Roland returned her look with a small smile.

"The guard was not as pretty."

***

Lady Constance's suite of rooms in Chester Castle provided an unexpectedly fine vantage point to observe activity within the city. The castle itself sat on the highest ground within the walls and the rooms of the Earl's wife were on an upper floor. From a north-facing window, one could see the entirety of the western wall, all the way to where it turned eastward to form the north wall of the town. From a narrow east-facing window, the centre of the town was within view. And there was much to see.

Roland's assault on the guard at the Shipgate had stirred the garrison into action. Patrols could be seen moving up and down the main avenues, stopping to question people on the street and methodically searching every dwelling and outbuilding. All afternoon they watched the patrols move through the town and were able to get a good estimate on the strength of the garrison.

"I count over three hundred men in the patrols," Roland said toward sunset. "Probably closer to four hundred men in all, if you figure those manning the gates and on other duty."

"I counted about the same," Millicent said. "It's twice the garrison Earl Ranulf had—and they are not lacking in vigilance," she added.

"No, they are not."

"When de Ferrers took the town, he and his men simply rode in through the gates. No one expected treachery. Earl Ranulf harboured none in his own heart and did not expect it in others. His men were not prepared." Millicent stopped and shook her head. "I do not think this garrison can be taken by surprise."

Roland nodded.

"No, they are watchful, and even if we could get our men into the town, they will have twice our numbers. It would be a bloody affair, and I doubt we would win."

Millicent's shoulders sagged.

"We've come so far. There has to be a way."

Roland returned to the north window and watched the patrols a while longer as the sun began to set. Along the west wall of Chester, torches were being lit and the night watch posted. He turned his eyes further west. That way lay Shipbrook, still in enemy hands. Would any of them ever watch a sunset from the walls of that little fort again?

***

Prudence brought them food from the kitchen and news.

"They're stoppin' all persons leavin' the city and searchin' carts and wagons."

They had not been able to get a good view of any of the gates from their perch in the castle, but, given the aggressive searches going on throughout the town, close inspection at the gates had to be expected.

"I feared they would do that," Roland said.

"Aye," Millicent agreed, "and there's no going back to the boat. That way will be closely watched. Have you thought of a way out, Prudy?"

Prudence gave her an uncertain smile.

"Aye, my lady, I 'ave, but I don't think you or Sir Roland will like it overmuch."

Millicent shot a glance at Roland, who only shrugged. She turned back to Prudence.

"Prudy, we are in no position to pick and choose. Tell us."

Prudence wrung her hands for a moment, then took a deep breath.

"You know of St. Leonard's, my lady?"

It took Millicent a moment to recall.

"Aye, Prudy, it's the place of refuge for lepers I believe."

"Aye, miss, that's it. Every few days, a monk comes from St. Leonard's with a cart for supplies. He goes first to the market square for foodstuffs and then to St. Mary's on the Hill, which is just outside the walls of the castle. The priests there gather old clothes to give to the poor lepers."

Roland grasped the girl by her shoulders and grinned.

"And the guards never search that wagon, do they Prudy?"

She smiled proudly.

"No, my lord. They stand well back when the leper wagon passes through the gate."

"Prudy, you are brilliant."

The girl flushed a bright red.

"It's all I could think of, my lord, though I feared you would not care to 'ide in the leper wagon yourself."

Millicent came to her side.

"If a monk can drive the wagon, we can hide in it! But why would he take the risk of helping us?"

"The new Earl, de Ferrers, does not like 'avin' lepers so near to 'is new possession of Chester. The priest, Malachy 'as ordered the monks to close St. Leonard's by Michaelmas. They despair at finding any place that will take their poor charges. The monks will be 'appy to 'elp."

Millicent took the girl's hands.

"You're a good friend, Prudy. We are in your debt once more." The scullery maid blushed again.

"You were always kind to us, my lady—not like Lady Constance and the others. That counts with folks like us. You will be safe 'ere until the monk comes."

***

On the far bank of the Dee, the light was fading fast. Declan and Griff had returned to their hiding place at midafternoon and immediately saw there was trouble. Two guards patrolled the rickety pier where Roland and Millicent had tied up their boat. Something had gone wrong.

"They would not be watching the boat, if they'd already caught them, so they must still be at freedom," Griff observed. Half the words he spoke were in Welsh, but months of dwelling with Welshmen had taught Declan enough to follow his meaning. Declan rolled over and looked at the sky, searching for an answer.

"If an alarm was raised, Roland will know not to return to the boat."

"So what will they do? Mayhaps we should get back and tell the Earl and Lord Llywelyn that there's trouble."

Declan nodded.

"We'll wait till full dark. If there is no sign by then, we will have to take word back. I'm not worried about the Earl or the Prince, but I have no wish to face Lady Catherine and tell her that her daughter has gone missing again!"

Griff grunted.

"Aye, that woman frightens me. Let's wait."

They waited until midnight, with no sign of Roland or Millicent. There was no moon and high clouds blocked the stars. The night was pitch black, but they would have seen anyone attempting to cross the river near the city. Declan sighed and nudged Griff.

"Let's get back. Bad news will not get better by morning."

***

In Chester Castle, Roland watched from the narrow window of Lady Constance's chambers until it was too dark to see. On the old Roman walls of the city and down by the market square, there were pools of light where torches burned, but all the rest was black. He stepped back from his perch into the room, which was illuminated by a single candle. It provided enough light to see, but would not show beneath the door of the chamber for any curious passers.

He was weary and discouraged and knew Millicent must be as well. The day had not gone as planned, nor had the information they'd gleaned been encouraging. The city was just too well defended to be taken and, without the city, Ranulf was an Earl in nothing more than title.

Millicent had started to step down from her own window perch when they heard a soft tapping on the door. It opened and Prudence entered, followed by an older man. He stood awkwardly behind the girl, a wool cap held nervously in his hands.

"You were not to tell anyone we are here," Millicent said, more sharply than she meant to. Prudence didn't flinch.

"Aye, my lady. I know you said I shouldn't, but you said you'd be comin' to take the city back for Earl Ranulf and this man, 'e can 'elp you."

"Why should we trust him?" Millicent asked. The man stepped forward, no longer awkward.

"Because the priest, Malachy, 'ad me son 'anged, me lady. I'm Henry Thatcher, and that's me boy out there by the Shipgate," the man said, bitterness in every word. "They won't even let me cut 'im down and give 'im a Christian burial. I'm not a man as can forgive that!"

For a moment, no one spoke. They had all seen the poor lad hung by the gate.

"I'm sorry for your boy, sir." Roland said gently, then turned to the scullery maid. "If we are to trust this man, Miss Prudence, I would know what he is to you. How do you know Master Thatcher?"

Prudence gave him a look filled with pain and a fierce pride.

"'Es me father."

Millicent drew in her breath.

"The man they hanged…"

"'E was my brother, my lady. Robert was a good lad and no *thief!*" She said her voice rising.

Henry Thatcher laid a soft hand on his daughter's shoulder.

"There, Prudy. There. We'll make 'em pay for what they done to Rob."

He turned back to Roland.

"Prudy says ye plan to take back the city and restore Earl Ranulf."

"Aye, if we can."

"Well, I would see de Ferrers and that priest hung from the same gibbet as me boy, and taking back the city would be a start. I believe I can be of help with that."

"Tell me how."

"I 'ave the guard duty on the Shipgate from midnight till dawn, me lord."

Roland arched an eyebrow.

"I struck a guard there this morning. Do you know him?"

"Aye, lord. I seen 'im back at barracks. 'is nose will never draw a straight breath again, I'd wager."

"Friend of yours?"

"'E's a bastard, lord." Thatcher stopped and his face reddened. He looked at Millicent and spread his hands. "Pardon the language, me lady."

Millicent gave him a kind smile.

"I take no offense, Henry. There seem to be bastards aplenty in Chester these days. But tell me—how can you help us?"

The man looked at his daughter.

"Tell them, father."

"Me lady, there is an iron gate that lowers from the arch of the Shipgate at night to block the canal."

"Aye, I've seen it many times."

"It takes three men to raise it—I couldn't do it alone. But the small arch next to the canal, where the poor fishermen pass through on foot, by the place where they hung me son—that iron gate is small."

"Aye, we came that way this morning."

"They lower the gate on the canal and lock the small gate at night, my lady and, as I've told ye, I have the duty from midnight till dawn."

"Yes, Henry?"

The man reached in a small pouch attached to his belt and drew out a dull metal object.

"I hold the key."

***

At noon the next day, Prudence came for them. She led them back through the kitchen and out the iron gate into the alleyway where she had found them the day before. The church of Saint Mary's on the Hill sat just around a bend in the castle wall. She took them through the small churchyard and into the nave. A priest saw them enter and Prudence went to him, speaking in low tones. The priest gave Roland and Millicent a long look, then nodded.

"The priest will say nothing," Prudence whispered when she rejoined them. 'We wait here for the monk from Saint Leonard's."

Not wanting to draw attention, all three knelt before the back bench. Some prayed. The wait was not long. They heard the sound of a horse's hooves on cobble and the rumble of wagon wheels on the narrow lane that ran between the church and the castle. Prudence peeked into the alleyway and seemed to sag a bit.

"It's Brother Cuthbert. I'd hoped he would not have the duty today."

The monk from Saint Leonard's climbed carefully down from the wagon and walked toward the church. He was a tall scarecrow of a man dressed in a rough brown robe, tied off at the waist with a rope. It was the same garb worn by Friar Tuck, but there the resemblance ended. Tuck was squarely built while this man looked rickety. What's more he moved with nervous, jerky motions as though someone or something might assault him at any moment.

Prudence went out to meet him and he gave her an eager smile, but then flinched when she began to speak.

"This doesn't look promising," Roland whispered to Millicent.

As the scullery maid spoke, the churchman began to back up toward the wagon. Roland thought he might actually turn and run, but Prudence did not relent. The man held his arms wide and shook his head. Prudence stabbed a finger in his chest.

"He's frightened," Millicent whispered.

"Aye, but is he afraid of us or Prudence?" The girl now had him backed up to a wagon wheel and the fight seemed to go out of him. A few more words were exchanged and the man wearily nodded his head. Prudence hurried back to the church.

"Brother Cuthbert will hide you in the wagon."

"How did you manage that, Prudy? The man is clearly scared out of his wits."

"Aye, as well 'e should be. Brother Cuthbert is right randy for a man of the church. I 'ad to threaten to tell 'is Prior 'ow 'e stares at the girls, and tries to get under their skirts, when 'e drives the leper wagon. If that were known, it would be back to work in the fields for 'im, and no trips into town. That was enough to overcome 'is fears."

"Well done, Miss Prudence!" Roland said.

"Hold yer praise 'till yer safe outside the walls, sir. Now, wait here until the old clothing has been loaded."

A small group of acolytes began bringing tied up bales of old clothing out to the wagon. Roland could see a large basket of cabbages in the wagon bed and another basket filled with onions. The last bale of clothing was loaded and the acolytes disappeared, back to their duties.

The monk carefully rolled out a tarp to cover his supplies, then, glancing up and down the street in obvious anxiety, he frantically gestured for them to climb into the wagon.

Roland turned to Prudence and gave her a kiss on the cheek. Millicent hugged her tightly, then they both ran and climbed under the tarp in the wagon. Prudence Thatcher touched her cheek where the young man had kissed her and gave a small sigh.

***

The trip through town took them north along Bridge Street to the very centre of Chester. Where Bridge Street met Watergate Street, the wagon rumbled to a stop for an agonizingly long time before resuming its journey. They could feel the draught horse turning right onto the large avenue that ran to the Eastgate. Passage through that gate would be the real test. After a few minutes, they felt the wagon slow to a crawl. Roland longed to see what was happening, but stayed perfectly still.

Then they stopped. Was the wagon to be searched? Roland eyes darted around beneath the tarp but found nothing that would serve as a weapon. He heard the sound of boot heels coming toward the wagon, but they stopped abruptly, then retreated. The wagon lurched forward and slowly gained speed. Beneath the tarp they could hear the sound of hoof beats echoing off the stone arch as they passed through the Eastgate. It sounded like music.

Inside the gate, Prudence Thatcher watched them go. She had trailed the wagon through the town, staying close enough that Brother Cuthbert could not miss her—or lose his nerve.

The clatter of iron shod hooves on cobbles was soon muffled as the wagon left the confines of the city and travelled east on a packed dirt road. Roland turned his head and looked at Millicent. She had bitten her lip, leaving a little drop of blood, but she looked relieved. Roland gently wiped the blood away with his thumb.

Half an hour passed before the monk hauled in the reins and the wagon groaned to a halt. They felt the bed rock as he leapt down. Then bright sunshine struck their eyes as the tarp was pulled back.

"Out!" the monk hissed. "And be quick—I've lost a year off me life because of that bitch Prudence."

Roland vaulted over the side of the wagon and grabbed the monk by the collar of his rough woollen robe. The man was taller than him, but Roland fairly lifted him off his feet. He drew the monk's face close to his and spoke though clinched teeth.

"Never...never speak ill of Prudence Thatcher, you dog turd! And if word reaches me that you have displeased her in any way, I will hunt you down and end your miserable life. Am I understood?"

"Aye…aye, my lord," the man sputtered as he struggled to break free. Roland held him for a long moment, then shoved the monk against a wagon wheel.

"Which way to the river," he snarled.

The monk pointed to a trail that led south between two fields, toward thick woods.

"There, lord. That trail leads to a ford."

"How far?"

"Two miles, lord."

Roland nodded, then slapped the horse on its rump. The animal knew the way home and headed down the road at a good clip. The monk almost fell in the dust of the road as the wagon lurched behind him, then ran to catch up, pulling up his robe to show bony legs as he ran. Millicent watched the terrified monk pelting down the road and turned to Roland.

"Was that necessary?" she asked.

"I believe it was," he answered, stung by the question. "He's lucky I only frightened him. The man's a coward, and cowards are dangerous—unless they are frightened. I didn't want him causing trouble for Prudence."

Millicent arched her brow.

"I have a sense that Prudy can handle her own affairs, though I expect she wouldn't object to having you as her protector."

"She *is* a resourceful girl," Roland said and managed a smile, his anger waning. "but protection is why I was sent on this scouting expedition and your mother is going to have my hide—even if we make it back in one piece."

"And well she should!" Millicent replied. I still wonder what you did to provoke that guard."

"Nothing at all, but what of you?" he said, exasperated. "We could have been back to the boat and clean away before they caught us, but you had to run *into* the damn town."

"You didn't have to follow me!" she shot back, her own anger starting to rise. He looked at her standing in the road, her dark eyes glaring at him. They were standing very close. She still smelled faintly of fish. She was beautiful.

"Of course I did, Millie," he said, his voice oddly husky.

She blinked, and some of the fire went out of her eyes.

"Why?"

Roland saw her lip still had a tiny drop of blood where she had bitten it. She looked up at him, her eyes no longer angry—only questioning.

I can't tell her. She would laugh.

For a long moment they stood staring silently at each other in the dust of the road, then Roland broke the spell.

"We need to get into the woods. It's not safe here." He gestured toward the trail. She followed him across the open fields toward the trees, her head filled with her own thoughts.

Can he not see?

***

The two men were in the right place through pure luck. Declan and Griff had been watching the Bridgegate and the Shipgate since dawn, hoping for some sign of Roland and Millicent, or at least some news they could take to Lady Catherine. It had been an awkward meeting with her in the small hours of the night when they had returned without her daughter.

It was past noon when Griff nudged Declan in the ribs.

"Someone coming on the river trail!"

The river trail ran sporadically along most of the length of the Dee. Now someone was on that trail and heading in their direction. The two were well-concealed in the brush along the river bank and would only be seen if the hapless traveller veered off the path. Declan quietly drew his sword and put a finger to his lips.

"Let them pass. It's probably just a fisherman and this is no spot for fishing." They sank deeper into the thick undergrowth and waited as the sound of footsteps grew closer. The walkers on the path were less than twenty feet away when they rounded a bend and came into view.

Declan sprang to his feet. Roland reflexively pushed Millicent behind him until he recognised his old friend.

"You're late!" Declan cried happily rushing forward and grasping Roland in a bear hug.

Roland could barely breathe, but managed to return the hug before breaking away. Declan turned to Millicent and lifted her off her feet.

209

"I can't tell you how happy I am to see you safe and sound, Millie. Your mother is in a high dudgeon!"

Millie smiled at the Irishman.

"So let's not keep her waiting. Put me down now. We have much to report."

"So what happened? We saw guards standing about by your boat."

"It's a long story, Dec, but with help from friends of Millie, we made it out."

"And what did you find?"

Millicent broke in.

"We have a way into the city. There is a man who is prepared to open a gate for us."

"Well done, Millie!"

"Don't celebrate just yet," Roland said, sitting on a log and taking off a boot where a pebble had lodged. "There is a man who can get us inside the walls, but there are four hundred armed men in the garrison. Even if we managed to get every man we have inside, it would not be enough to take the city from de Ferrers."

Declan felt his elation evaporate.

"Four hundred? I hadn't imagined there would be that many. You're right, we would need double our numbers if we have to fight them for control of the place."

"Aye," Millicent said, "but Chester is still the key. We have to find a way."

"I've been thinking on it," Roland said, shaking the pebble out of his boot, "and there is a way."

"Well, don't be shy," Declan said. "Tell us how we can defeat a garrison of four hundred."

Roland pulled his boot back on and stood up.

"We have them leave the city."

Return of the Earl

It was a beautiful morning in late May when a column of ninety mounted men splashed through the ford on the River Dee and into England. Bright sunlight flashed off polished mail and sharpened weapons. They had waited for weeks for the Earl of Derby to return to Chester. When their scouts reported his arrival in the city, the order was given to cross the river. There was no attempt at stealth—these men wanted to be seen—for they were bait in a complex trap.

Earl Ranulf rode at the front, sitting proudly in the saddle. On his left rode Llywelyn Ap Iowerth, Prince of Gwynedd, and on his right rode a man holding high the blue and gold banner of the Earls of Chester. It had been near a year since he had fled across this ford, a hunted man charged with treason. Now he was returning to claim what was his.

The men who followed him were a hard-looking lot. Some were men of the Invalid Company, led by Declan O'Duinne, but most were Welsh and thirty had longbows slung over their shoulders. They were in no rush as they headed straight for Shipbrook.

The column was emerging from the reed beds, when a startled rider on the high ground saw them coming. He jerked his horse's head around and spurred the animal savagely in the flanks as he fled back toward the little fort that guarded the ford. He galloped through Shipbrook's still-broken gate and raised the alarm.

De Ferrers had increased the fort's strength to thirty men after five of his soldiers had been surprised and captured there on Christ's Mass eve. The reinforced garrison had dutifully patrolled the ford for months, with no trouble to report. Now, there was trouble aplenty coming up the road from the ford.

Sir Stanley de Ver had assumed command of the fort the week after Easter and found the duty boring, but as he listened to his scout's breathless report, he wished he had not put off repairs to the gate. His predecessor had told him that any hostiles coming from Wales would be few in number and intent on avoiding Shipbrook, but if the scout was to be believed, a force of about a hundred was coming up the road from the west.

The man's instincts told him to flee, but he knew what he would face back in Chester when the Earl learned that the fort and the ford had been abandoned without a fight. He had seen too many bodies hanging outside the walls.

"Barricade the gate!" he shouted. "Archers to the walls! Hold till my command." He ran to the wall walk and peered off to the west. Nothing showed on the track leading up from the ford.

"Perhaps they will bypass us," he muttered to himself, half in prayer.

But his hopes were dashed when he caught the first glint of sun on steel. He watched with mounting fear as horsemen poured over the rise and spread out into a line in the open fields. He saw the banner of the Earl of Chester in the vanguard and knew this was no raiding party—it was an invasion.

He glanced below and saw that a wagon had been pushed against the broken gate and turned on its side. It would not hold for long. The line of mounted men approached the fort at a leisurely pace and halted two hundred yards away.

"Archers, make ready!" he shouted. The enemy was still out of bow range, but if they approached another hundred yards, he would have his half dozen archers give them an unpleasant welcome. Along the north and west walls of Shipbrook, they nocked their bows and made ready.

He turned back to see the enemy still stationary in the open field, but now a group of men dismounted. He could see they were archers and wondered why they were being deployed at such a distance. An order was shouted in Welsh and he saw the line of bowman draw and elevate their weapons. With a curt command they loosed a volley that arched toward the fort.

The arrows leapt skyward then curved back toward the earth, like a dark cloud descending. Too late, de Ver realized that they would not fall short. He started to shout a cry of warning, but before he could utter a sound, the cloud struck the top of the wall with ghastly accuracy. Four of his men went down, dead or wounded, under the onslaught.

Longbows!

He had followed Earl William here from Derbyshire. There, the weapon was banned and he had never seen one used. But he had heard tales of the Danes using the great range and killing power of these bows to nearly overthrow Norman power in that county, and not so long ago. All along the wall, men who had confidently stood tall and thought themselves safe now crouched low. Sir Stanley did the same.

He peered carefully over the rampart and saw that the archers, having drawn initial blood, were dispersing to the woodline behind the mounted men. In a short while, he heard the distinct sound of axes at work and knew what that meant. They would fashion a ram, burst through the damaged gate and likely slaughter all within. He slid back down behind the wall and wished he were back in Derbyshire.

"Commander of the fort!"

The hail had come from outside. He cautiously raised his head to see a man in armour sitting his horse less than fifty yards from the front gate. He had a shield, but was well within range of the archers on the wall. That did not seem to trouble the man, as he had removed his helmet, letting a tangled mass of red hair hang down to his shoulders. The man's confidence was unnerving.

The commander took a deep breath and stood up.

"I command here. Who are you and why have you attacked us? If you abandon the field and go back to Wales, there will be no further blood spilt here."

The man actually laughed.

"Ah, well said, but I can assure you that no more blood is going to be spilt, for you are going to throw down your weapons and open the gate."

"Bold talk for a man in bow range!" Sir Stanley retorted. "Tell me why I shouldn't have my archers kill you where you sit?"

This time the red-haired man did not laugh. Even at fifty yards, the commander could see the colour rise in his face. He drew a long broad sword and pointed it at the walls.

"The place you are standing was my home—before you bastards burnt it. I am Irish and we Irish do not take kindly to having our homes burnt! I have sworn a blood oath to kill those that done it. Now my master, Ranulf, Earl of Chester, would prefer mercy, but if you resist, he has given me leave to kill you all."

"Ranulf is dead."

"Ranulf lives! And if you want to live as well, you will open that gate before I ride back to him."

Sir Stanley slid back down behind the rampart and cursed his bad fortune.

I'll hang for this, he thought.

But best to take that chance, rather than face the more immediate threat from this deadly serious Irishman with a host at his back. He cursed again and rose, turning toward his small garrison manning the walls.

"Open the gate!" he shouted. "Lay down your weapons!" Men all over Shipbrook looked nervously at their commander and at each other. Most of them had heard the threat and knew the Irishman could back it up. In twos and threes, they threw down their swords, lances and bows.

As soon as the gate swung open, Declan led fifty mounted warriors into Shipbrook. They quickly rounded up the sullen prisoners and secured the place for Ranulf's triumphant entry. With great ceremony, the Earl had his banner raised above the walls, along with a smaller banner—the rampant white stag of de Laval.

Declan O'Duinne watched the white stag rise above the ramparts and tried not to weep. He failed.

***

With the fort secure, Ranulf rode up to the prisoners who were crowded into the centre of the cobbled courtyard. He reined in and looked at the downcast men.

"I am Ranulf, the rightful ruler of these lands. Who among you are Cheshire men?"

For a long moment, none of the prisoners moved. Then one man, a bit older than the others, stepped forward.

"I am from Runcorn, my lord, and I seen ye when you visited that town not four years past." He turned to the other men. "It's 'im, alright. It's Earl Ranulf sure enough."

Ranulf watched the ripple of low talk spread through the ranks. He knew he had been painted as traitor to the King and later declared dead. It was time to begin putting the lie to those notions.

"Men of Cheshire, hear me well. I have been acquitted of the charge of treason laid upon me by the Earl of Derby—found innocent by the Queen and the Justiciars themselves. That verdict has been read in every county in England, save those controlled by the Earl of Derby. De Ferrers would not let it be read here in Cheshire."

Now the low talk in the ranks rose to a buzz. Ranulf seized the moment.

"I've returned to claim what's mine and to drive this usurper from my land. Starting from this place, I will take back our land from this interloper. If you are true Cheshire men, I would have you join me now!"

Perhaps they remembered Ranulf's gentler rule, or perhaps it was their fear of being slaughtered that moved them, but the response from the Cheshire men was spirited.

"Hail Ranulf!" the cry went up.

Ranulf smiled and acknowledged the acclaim.

"Now, who among you is not a Cheshire man?"

The silence was palpable, but moved by their new-found loyalty to the Earl, the Cheshire men shoved seven of their fellows, including Sir Stanley de Ver out of their midst. Ranulf looked down sternly at them.

"Who commanded here?"

Six men pointed to Sir Stanley. He glared at them, but there was no use evading his responsibility. He turned to Ranulf.

"I commanded here, my lord."

"It was wise of you to surrender. I will let you live, but you will take this message back to Chester. Tell William de Ferrers that, if he wants to live, he will never show his face in Cheshire again."

"Aye, my lord."

"Now—go!"

The seven wasted no time in fleeing through the broken gate and down the road toward Chester. Ranulf climbed to the wall walk and stood beside Declan, watching them disappear into the woods to the east.

"Do you think it will work?" the Earl asked.

"I believe it will, my lord. When Roland and I took the fort back at Christ's Mass, de Ferrers sent a hundred men from his garrison to chase us back into Wales—and that was for just two men. When he hears that you have returned, I doubt he will do less."

The plan had been Roland's. Henry Thatcher had promised them a way into Chester, but to take the town back, the garrison had to be reduced by more than half. It would take a dire threat to induce William de Ferrers to strip Chester of defenders, but news of Ranulf's sudden return to Cheshire should suffice. If luck was with them, de Ferrers would move to take Shipbrook, only to find that Chester had been snatched from him in the meantime.

"How long before they come?

"Not long," Declan answered. "Word will reach Chester by nightfall. I expect they will ride out at dawn."

"Good! But will you be able to hold here at Shipbrook long enough? I'm only leaving you thirty archers to defend the place. If de Ferrers returns to Chester before we secure the town, it will be a bloody affair."

"Aye, my lord. We'll hold...until they come through the gate and over the wall."

"And what then, Sir Declan? I do not wish to lose you."

216

"Nor do I wish to be lost, my lord. The Welshmen and I—
we have a plan."

The Earl nodded.

"Then God be with you."

"And you, my lord."

They climbed down from the wall walk and hailed Prince
Llywelyn, who had dismounted and was drawing water from the
well for his horse. The Prince had received word before they
crossed the Dee that his Uncle Roderic was sending a new force
out from the coast and into the backcountry looking for him. He
had kept his promise to aid Ranulf, but now made ready to ride
back into Wales to meet this new threat.

"Lord Llywelyn, I will remember this day when you call
upon me for help."

Llywelyn smiled at Ranulf and swept his arms around to
encompass the whole of Shipbrook.

"My lord, many a Welshman has dreamed of taking this little
fort by the Dee—if even for a short while. It is a day I will
remember well. And have no fear, I won't forget the debt you
owe me, not only for the shelter I've given you but for the men I
have provided to you and Sir Roland for your assault. I shall call
upon you, and soon, for repayment."

Ranulf smiled at the young Welsh nobleman.

"I will stand ready to honour my debt, my lord, but as for the
men you have loaned us, I believe that debt has already been paid
in full."

Llywelyn laughed and nodded. He lowered the bucket he
had been using to water his horse and ran a hand along the
animal's flank. It was The Surly Beast.

"Aye, my lord. Your Sir Roland drives a hard bargain, but I
think a fair one. This horse and I were meant for each other. Just
remember, the men are yours for one month—no more! I may
be needing them if my uncles continue to be restless."

The Surly Beast swung his head around and tried to bite the
man stroking his flank. Llywelyn dodged and laughed in delight.

Declan assembled the men who would be leaving with the
Earl to join the assault on Chester. Thirty Welshmen were left
behind under his command. Llywelyn kept another thirty as his

personal guard for the journey back into Wales. The rest, including the newly converted Cheshire men, formed a column and rode out the gate.

They headed for the ford, but had barely cleared the walls of Shipbrook before another band of men approached across the fields—some mounted and others running to keep up. The Earl called the column to halt. Some men in the column drew swords, others nocked arrows.

"Hold!" Declan shouted, riding up on his own mount. He knew these men. They were the remnants of Sir Roger de Laval's men-at-arms. In the lead was the man who had hailed them at the Dee ford on their first day back in England.

"Baldric!" he called.

"Sir Declan! Ye've come back—just as Sir Roland said ye would!"

"And true to your word, Baldric, you've gathered Sir Roger's men—and they look ready for a fight!

"Aye, we are that. We knew right off that a large force had crossed the ford, but when we saw the Earl's banner go up—and the white stag of de Laval, we knew the time had come to give these bastards back some of what they've dealt. They have Alwyn Madawc to answer for."

Earl Ranulf looked at these new men, some with tattered doublets that showed faded white stags on the front. He thought of the big man who had been his loyal vassal and whose men these were. The King himself had sworn him to look after Sir Roger de Laval's interests while he took the knight off to the Crusade. The burned out fort of Shipbrook gave stark testimony to his failure to keep his promise. It was time to make amends for that. He looked up and down the column and turned to Baldric.

"Welcome, men of Shipbrook. Let's go take back my city!"

***

Twenty miles away, on the opposite side of the Dee, eighty men made camp in a dense grove of birch and buckthorn. The place was a mile from the nearest road and well concealed, but no fires were permitted. They had slipped into this remote grove in the morning and now waited anxiously for word to come of events at Shipbrook.

Roland walked through the camp past his own men of the Invalid Company and saw Griff issuing quiet instructions to a large contingent of Welshmen who were throwing together crude shelters. Some of the Welsh were archers and some not, but all were veteran fighting men. He was content that his bargain with Llywelyn was a fair one. The Surly Beast was a horse bred for a Prince, and he would never be that.

There was no way of knowing how long the wait would be. All would depend on how de Ferrers reacted to the fall of Shipbrook. If he took the bait, a large part of the Chester garrison would ride west to take back the fort and kill or capture Ranulf. It could be tomorrow or a week from tomorrow, but he did not think de Ferrers would hesitate for long. He could not tolerate Ranulf gaining a foothold in Cheshire.

Once the garrison rode out, he would wait until Henry Thatcher took up his midnight post at the Shipgate. Then, he would lead a hand-picked group across the Dee to slip into the city. Trying to bring in a large force through the Shipgate was impractical. It was too slow and required too many boats, but the Bridgegate was only a quarter mile uphill from the Shipgate.

Opening that gate would allow a mounted force to cross over the Dee bridge in a matter of minutes and ride into the heart of the city. The dozen men he took with him would need to seize the Bridgegate and open it before the garrison could stop them.

That gate was always closed at night and there was little doubt that, if the city's garrison was stripped to march on Shipbrook, all gates would be closed, day or night, and well defended. Surprise would be needed to take the gatehouse. The entire plan rested on that.

At the far end of the camp, the Invalids had taken pains to build a sturdy shelter for the two ladies who were sharing their camp and were still fussing with the roof as Roland approached. Sitting nearby and watching the men work were Lady Catherine and Millicent.

Millicent had a petulant look on her face, the result of the argument they had had that morning. He had forbidden her to come with his assault party or to ride over the bridge with the Earl when the main attack on the city began. The conversation had grown heated, but he had the final word.

"Millie, if you come, the Invalids will be falling all over themselves trying to protect you. It will get men killed. I cannot have that." She knew when she was beaten, but she was still unhappy.

Roland looked past her to Lady Catherine and what he saw worried him. This was a woman of strong will and steady nerves, but she looked worn and fretful this morning. He nodded to Millicent as he approached, but spoke to Lady Catherine.

"My lady, your shelter looks snug. I hope we will not be in need of it for too long."

She looked up at Roland and he saw that her eyes were rimmed in red, but her gaze was clear.

"I've slept in worse, Roland. The men have done a fine job."

He looked over and saw a man with one arm using a leafy branch as an improvised broom to sweep leaves and twigs from the floor of the shelter.

"Aye, my lady. They are remarkable. With them, I believe we will take the city and you and Lady Millicent will have proper beds to sleep in 'fore long."

Catherine de Laval looked at the young man before her. He had come to Shipbrook three years before, still a boy. He had a wounded spirit and had been forced to grow into manhood too fast. Her husband had seen something special in Roland Inness and from the first week she had noted that he had an intelligent and curious mind.

Back then, she had sought to give him an education in the world he had entered and, while she may have taught Roland his numbers and to read a little, it was Roger de Laval and Alwyn Madawc who had taught the boy to fight. Now he was facing the fight of his young life.

Let's hope they taught him well.

The Defence of Shipbrook

William de Ferrers was enjoying his evening meal in Chester Castle when Sir Hugh Bonsil burst into the dining hall. Sir Hugh had once been commander of the Chester garrison, but his failure to capture Roland Inness at Christ's Mass had seen him demoted to Captain of the Guard. De Ferrers lay down the slice of roast duck breast he was about to pop into his mouth and wiped the grease from his lips. His courtiers fell silent. Good news never burst in upon meals.

"My lord," Sir Hugh began, but de Ferrers raised a hand to silence him.

"Such urgent news, Captain—let's have it in my chambers and not disturb our friends."

He rose and led the man to a small room off the dining hall. "Speak."

"My lord, it is Ranulf! The Earl of Chester has crossed the Dee in strength and captured the fort at Shipbrook. The Cheshire men in the garrison went over to him. He let the others go, including Sir Stanley de Ver who commanded there. Sir Stanley reports that Ranulf rides at the head of two hundred men and has fifty Welsh longbowmen with him."

Sir Hugh saw a moment of shock play across his master's face, quickly replaced with a dismissive smile.

"The coward no doubt exaggerates the numbers, Captain, but why your distress? The traitor has finally stopped skulking in the wilderness of Wales and has ridden right into our arms! Ranulf has always been a great fool, but a thorn in my side nevertheless.

Now we will finish the man and you, Captain, will have the chance to redeem yourself."

De Ferrers saw the man flinch a bit and was pleased. Fear made men more diligent in performing their duties. He glanced out the high narrow window of the room and saw that the last of the daylight was gone.

"We will ride out at dawn tomorrow. I want every man not guarding the gates of the city ready to move. We have at least four hundred men here in Chester now. I want three hundred assembled at the Northgate at dawn. Understood?

"Aye, my lord!"

"And Captain…"

"My lord?"

"Have Sir Stanley de Ver hanged by the Northgate—tonight."

***

Declan O'Duinne walked the parapet of Shipbrook and looked to the north, toward the Irish Sea. He remembered the day he had arrived here, following Sir Roger de Laval as his new squire. It seemed a long way from Ireland at the time, but the de Lavals had been kind to him and Sir Alwyn Madawc had taken him under his wing. Those had been better times and he had been happy here, but that was five years ago. Now it was his task to defend Shipbrook long enough for the Earl to retake Chester.

He turned and looked at the burned out wreck of Sir Roger's home. He thought of Lady Catherine and Millicent—fugitives for more than a year—and of Alwyn Madawc lying in a lonely grave beside the Dee. He wondered what Sir Roger would think of all this. For once, he was glad the man wasn't here.

There were thirty Welshmen with him, most of them archers. He was counting on the range and killing power of their longbows to hold the enemy at bay for a while. Every hour they could delay de Ferrers men here, would give Roland and the Earl another hour to secure Chester. But if the enemy broke through the gate or came over the walls, the lightly armed Welshmen would be no match in close fighting. He did not intend for it to come to that.

He watched the last glimmer of light in the west and waited for the new day.

***

Just past dawn, Henry Thatcher went off duty at the Shipgate. As a gate guard, he and the eighty other men on similar duty were spared the call to ride out at dawn with Earl William. These men would bar the gates and defend the city until the Earl's return.

Thatcher climbed up to Bridge Street, but instead of turning left and trudging home as was his habit, he turned right and entered the gatehouse that guarded the end of the bridge and the entrance to the city. It was time for the changing of the guard and none questioned his presence.

He climbed to the top of the barbican and looked out across the old Dee bridge to the countryside beyond. No one was visible on the far shore, but he knew he was watched. Three times he walked between the two towers that flanked the gatehouse, then, yawning, he climbed back down to the street and walked home.

Across the river, hidden in the brush near the far end of the bridge, two men saw the old guard take his morning walk. They crept back from the bank, ran through the woods to where their horses were tethered, then rode hard back to the hidden camp in the grove of birch and buckthorn. Men in the camp saw them come and stopped their morning rituals. The two reined up in front of Roland Inness and leapt from their horses.

"They've ridden out—three hundred strong!" the breathless rider reported. "The man walked three times between the towers!"

Roland nodded. This was news he'd hoped for. The Chester garrison had been stripped. Now he must wait for midnight, when he and a dozen men would slip across the Dee and through the Shipgate, opened to them by Henry Thatcher. In the small hours of the morning, they would overpower the guards at the Bridgegate and open the city to Earl Ranulf and his men, waiting just across the bridge.

Speed was everything. The city must be taken and all four gates must be in their hands before de Ferrers and the garrison returned, or the streets of Chester would run red. He looked at the sun, still low in the eastern sky. They must now wait through a long, agonizing day and evening before they could move. While they waited, three hundred men would be assaulting thirty at the little fort down by the Dee ford.

God watch over Declan and the men at Shipbrook.

***

The sun had burned away the morning mists from the untended fields around Shipbrook, when the riders came down the Chester road. The men standing on the walls of the little fort heard the commands of the enemy leader as the column fanned out on either side of the road. The men from Chester had been warned that the defenders had longbows and stayed well beyond range.

In the centre of the formation, they saw a white banner with black horseshoes emblazoned—the banner of the Earls of Derby. It was a large host—hundreds strong—and a daunting sight. To field such a force, de Ferrers must have swept up every possible man from the garrison of Chester. It brought a smile to Declan O'Duinne's lips.

"Stand to your posts!" he roared

Welcome to Shipbrook, you bastard.

***

The morning still held some coolness from the night, but Sir Hugh Bonsil was sweating beneath his mail. He was a capable soldier, but taking a fortress, even one as small as Shipbrook, was new to him. He assumed the place would fall, given the overwhelming force under his command, but the message left by the corpse of Sir Stanley de Ver, swinging beside the Northgate of Chester, had had its effect. There must be no mistakes.

William de Ferrers rode up beside him and pointed toward the fort.

"There! See that blue banner with the sheaf of wheat flying there?"

"Aye, my lord"

"That is the banner of the Earl of Chester. Poor Sir Stanley at least had that much right!"

As the Earl of Derby spoke, a group of his personal retainers gathered close by, excited by the prospect of witnessing an actual battle. De Ferrers saw their eagerness and raised his voice so they could hear.

"Captain, we must not miss this opportunity! Ranulf is more of a fool than I imagined. He must have hoped that all of Cheshire would rise up and join him if he finally showed his face on this side of the Dee!"

He paused, then swept his arm in an arc across the empty fields.

"Do you see the legions of Cheshire assembled here to fight for their Earl?"

The retainers laughed and de Ferrers enjoyed the response to his jest, but then he grew stern once more.

"Captain, you will take that fort and kill or capture Ranulf—I care little which. He must not be allowed to slip through our fingers again. Send twenty men down to guard the ford. Let no one pass. And Captain…"

"My lord?"

"Bring me Ranulf, or you may swing with Sir Stanley by the Northgate."

"Aye, my lord," he replied, feeling the sweat now running in rivulets down his back. He called a lieutenant forward and issued his orders. The lieutenant was young and had never seen a battle. He was half disappointed and half relieved that he would not be part of the attack on the fort. He quickly assembled his force of twenty and spurred toward the ford.

He had overheard the Earl's warning to Sir Hugh and it chilled him. He had known Sir Stanley and the sight of the man's swollen face as he swung from the gibbet had made him retch beside the road when they rode out at dawn.

He would let nothing get past him.

***

Declan watched the small force split off and ride to the west. He knitted his brow. The ford was their escape route and now it would be blocked.

I should have thought of that.

The remaining force dismounted, and in a short while, the sound of axes could be heard from the woods to the east. Twenty minutes passed before the object of that labour could be seen. A team of horses dragged a thick young oak log from the woods. The log had been stripped of most of its limbs and ten men on each side lifted it and laid it atop a sturdy wagon that had been hauled here from Chester for just this purpose. The log was lashed down with ten feet protruding from the front of the wagon and another ten from the rear. It made a serviceable battering ram.

Declan looked down at the mangled gate of Shipbrook. His men had worked on it through the night. The great iron hinge was still broken, but the gate was now buttressed by beams that had been taken from the new roof de Ferrers' men had built over the ruins of the burnt hall. It was a much more formidable barrier than an overturned wagon, but would not hold for long if the oak ram came into play.

After a great deal of shouting and not a little cursing, men were assembled around the wagon and began to push the ram up the road toward the gate. To the front and sides, dismounted armoured knights marched close in with shields held aloft to counter the arrows they knew would be rained down on anything that approached the walls. Two hundred armoured men mounted their horses and waited eagerly for the ram to do its work and open the door to Shipbrook. Declan gathered his Welsh archers along the north wall and watched the ram come.

When it was within range, his thirty bowmen began to take aim and loose waves of arrows at the enemy. These were professional archers, unlike any the men around the ram had ever encountered. Using shields was a good tactic against bows, but not perfect—not against Welshmen with longbows.

There were gaps in the shields and the bowmen on the walls found them. One man, then another, then two more went down as the ram covered half the distance to the gate. The men on the walls were drawing and loosing every few seconds creating a constant rain of death on the slow-moving formation.

Finally it cracked. A man pushing the ram saw his companion take an arrow in his eye and go down screaming. He bolted for the rear. It was all that was needed to create a panicked retreat to get out of range of the damned arrows. Sir Hugh watched them straggle back with disgust and mounting fear. He rode up and down the ranks.

"Who here is man enough to break down that gate? There will be gold for the men who do it!"

There were many young men in the force who, like the lieutenant guarding the ford, had idled away months on garrison duty at Chester and were eager for action and glory. The ram was now within one hundred yards of the gate…Thirty young men stepped forward to make another attempt.

This time, the ram reached to within twenty yards of the gate before the men broke and ran, leaving nine of their number dead beside it. Sir Hugh ordered his forty archers forward with shields to guard against any attempt to sally from the fort to capture or destroy the ram. No attempt came.

It was well past noon now, and the commander was out of ideas and growing desperate. He called a council of war with his ranking men. William de Ferrers had taken up station under the shade of a spreading oak that stood alone in the middle of the untilled fields. It had been left there a hundred years ago to provide a place of respite for the planters and gleaners of the fields and provided a good vantage point to watch the proceedings—well out of range of the damned longbows. He had not stirred during the first two assaults on the gates, but now rode up and sat quietly listening to his commander's exhortations.

"It's only twenty more yards! Surely we can cross that distance," he said, almost begging his men to finish the job.

"But those damn archers can't miss at that range," a man who had been in the first assault said. "With all of them aiming at the men on the ram, it's a slaughter."

Sir Hugh Bonsil glanced up at the impassive face of William de Ferrers and unconsciously wrung his hands. Finally, Sir James Ferguson, the oldest man among them, spoke up.

"An English Earl might be in that fort, but those are Welshmen on the walls. No one else can shoot like that. I've fought the Welsh before, and you can't give those bowmen but one target to aim at—and that's what we've done!"

"What do you suggest?" Sir Hugh asked, desperate to find a solution.

"We must assault the fort from all sides. I've been watchin.' There aren't more than thirty archers in there, forty at most. There may be other men hidden inside, but only that many archers man the walls. We have given those thirty archers only one target, but now they will have to choose. If they concentrate on the ram, we will be over the walls. If they target the men at the walls, the ram will do its job. They can't shoot at everything at once, and when we get in, those bowmen and anyone else inside will have no chance."

There was a long moment of silence. Sir Hugh glanced again at the Earl and could read nothing in the man's face. He turned back to the old knight.

"And how do we get men over the walls?"

The old soldier started to make a quick retort to such a stupid question, but bit back his words.

"We build ladders, my lord." he said, trying not to sound as though he were talking to a child.

"Ladders, you say?"

"Aye, ladders."

***

Sir Hugh spared no one from the new task, save the Earl, his personal retainers and the archers keeping watch on the fort. Ten men were dispatched back to a tiny village—little more than a score of hovels clustered along the Chester road—where they seized every axe and all binding material they could gather. Through most of the afternoon the men doffed their mail and helmets and sweated as they cut saplings and fashioned rough siege ladders. The sun was low over the western horizon when they were done.

On the advice of Sir James, Bonsil divided his force into quarters—one to assault the gate with the ram and one for the east, west and north walls of Shipbrook. At the base of the south-facing wall the land sloped sharply down, almost doubling the height of the thing. From there, the ground turned boggy as it angled down toward dense reed beds that lined the Dee. It was no place for an assault, and should the garrison try to escape that way, they would be met by the force guarding the ford.

The old knight knew it was a good plan, but he also knew that nothing was assured. *The enemy makes plans of its own.* The sun was now behind the trees to the west and the light was fading, as the four assault groups moved to their positions. *Enough light yet*, he thought.

He had chosen to be with the ram. It was still the most likely way they would gain entry into the fort. He pulled the strap a little tighter on his helmet and drew his sword. He looked over his shoulder and saw the great white banner with the horseshoes dip three times signalling the assault to begin.

He also saw William de Ferrers wheel his black stallion around and ride back toward the security of the big oak tree, his retainers following close behind. He spit on the ground, then crossed himself and moved toward the fort.

***

Roland paced. He simply could not sit still. It was now twilight; still hours until he would lead his men across the Dee and into Chester, but his mind was twenty miles away. Shipbrook would have come under attack hours ago. Only thirty men against three hundred! And it was all a lure. They had pulled de Ferrers away from the city. Could Declan keep him there until it was too late to save Chester?

It was an awful risk his friend was taking, one of many that would be taken this night—all in the hope that their plan, *his plan,* would succeed. Earl Ranulf had arrived with his sixty men late the previous night and had seemed full of confidence. He would be waiting, out of sight across the Dee bridge, for Roland and his men to raise the portcullis that blocked the Bridgegate.

The Earl would then lead nearly a hundred mounted men, followed by fifty on foot, across the bridge and into the town. If all went as planned, the garrison force would be quickly overwhelmed and the city secured before de Ferrers returned from Shipbrook.

If all went as planned.

As he walked and worried, he was unaware that on this day, he turned seventeen years old.

***

They came at the fort from three sides in the fading light. Each attack force numbered eighty men and carried ten ladders. Another thirty men manned the ram. The archers on the walls of Shipbrook, who had all manned the north wall during the two attempts to breach the gate, now had to disperse to the other two walls to deal with this new tactic.

After the failed attempts to employ the ram, Declan wondered if there was anyone in de Ferrers' force with an understanding of how to take a fortified position. Now he had his answer.

"Someone over there knows what they are about," he muttered to himself, as he ordered his archers into new positions. He was relieved to see that no attack was being made on the south wall that faced the river. He had expected none, since it was almost impossible to bring heavily armoured men and ladders across that boggy ground. But men with no armour could cross it with relative ease.

So the south wall and the bog would be their escape route. Ropes were already secured along the wall walk there, ready to be dropped over the side when it was time to abandon the fort. He worried about the force sent to secure the ford, but would have to deal with that problem when it arose.

His men began to loose arrows as the attackers came within range. Now there were only ten archers on each wall shooting at eighty men dispersed across a wide front. Some arrows struck home, but not enough to stop the assaults. It took time for men in mail, carrying shields and dragging ladders, to cross the killing ground, and some died in the crossing—but not enough. They reached the eastern wall first.

Three ladders were thrust against the ten foot wall and men clustered at the base of the barrier as three of their number started to climb. The archers on the wall turned all their attention to the men on the ladders and at this range, armour was no help against longbows. The first three men on the ladders barely made it half way to the top before they died.

But the enemy archers had followed the assault waves and were now in range. They began to do their work. One man on the wall walk took an arrow in the shoulder. He ripped it out and tried to draw his own bow, but couldn't. A second Welshman was struck full in the chest and died before he fell to the courtyard below. The remaining defenders managed to topple one of the ladders, but five more were now in place.

The first attacker managed to reach the top of the wall only to have a short blade thrust into his neck. He screamed and fell back onto the men behind him. At that moment, outside the north wall, de Ferrers' men reached their abandoned ram and started it moving once more toward the gate. On either side of the road, men hurried forward dragging ladders. From the wall, the archers took a deadly toll, but there were just too many targets.

Declan saw that two of the enemy had gained the wall walk on the eastern side of the fort and others were close behind. These men had shields to protect them and were slowly forcing his lightly armed Welshmen back. Those men fought like demons, but could not hold back the tide that was starting to spill over the wall.

Below him, the ram gathered momentum and, with a shuddering boom, collided with the damaged gate. The sound of splintering wood echoed across the empty courtyard. That sound, the sound of the ram striking the gate, was the signal they had agreed upon. Men all along the wall walk loosed a final arrow and ran for the south wall.

Declan looked down and saw that the gate had held and the ram was being hauled back for another charge. As it hurtled toward the gate, he toppled a brazier full of hot coals over the wall and jumped to the ground. As he ran across the courtyard, the boom of the ram striking the gate drowned out the screams of men seared by the hot coals.

The gate gave a great groan and lurched open a crack, just enough for a man to squeeze through. Sir James Ferguson shoved at the splintered wood and pushed his way inside. In the gathering darkness, he saw his own men coming over the east wall and the last of the defenders clambering over the south wall. In the dim light he saw a red-haired man turn and look back at the fort before disappearing over the wall.

He wasn't surprised that the defenders were escaping in that direction. The ground there was boggy and ill-suited for mounted men or those with heavy armour. But men with no armour could cross that bog and there would surely be trails leading down to the Dee. Perhaps their men down at the ford would bag them.

As he looked about the fort that was now empty of defenders, he was struck by a troubling thought. Sir Stanley had reported that Earl Ranulf had taken the place with a mounted force. *But where were the horses? And where was the Earl?*

***

Declan O'Duinne was last over the wall. He had taken off his mail and the only thing beneath his jerkin was a carefully folded banner. It was black with a rampant white stag. He could hear shouts behind him on the walls of Shipbrook and ran on into the deepening darkness.

Ahead of him were the Welsh archers who had survived the assault. He had seen three men down and not stirring inside the fortress as he sprinted from the main gate to the south wall. That meant that over twenty-five had got out. It could have been much worse and might still be if they could not fight their way past the men sent to block the ford.

When he reached the far side of the bog, the archers were waiting for him. All of them were breathing heavily from the sprint across soggy ground. He looked back and saw that there was no pursuit from the fort, but they all knew that men had been sent to cut off any retreat across the Dee.

Getting past them, if it could be done, would be costly. And how long before the men at the fort were ordered back to their mounts to take up the pursuit? If he could not get his men across the Dee in short order, they were all doomed. He spoke to the Welshmen in a low voice.

"It's less than a mile to the ford, lads, and there's a good twenty men between us and your homeland. So tread lightly and follow me."

Declan led them southwest from the open boggy field through patches of scrub and finally into a dense stretch of reeds that led down to the water's edge. Narrow trails wound through the head-high reed beds and they moved in single file, each man gripping his bow and some with their short swords drawn.

Night had fully fallen and, as they neared the ford, they expected to be challenged at any second. Declan stopped every few steps to listen, but heard only the buzz of the summer insects that dwelt in the reeds. He took another step.

"Don't move." The voice came out of the darkness ahead. The words were in English, but the accent was decidedly Welsh. Declan halted in place and beckoned to the man behind him. The man had heard the same quiet command in the darkness and recognised his own countryman's voice.

"Ffrind?" he called back softly in his native tongue.

"Aye, friend," the voice called back and a torch flared in the night. "Come along, we haven't much time."

Declan led his men another twenty yards through the reeds and emerged onto the cleared path that led down to the ford. Near the water's edge were gathered fifteen men, all armed with swords and longbows. He saw at least six dead men scattered about the track and a knot of downcast prisoners bound and sitting at the edge of the reeds. The man with the torch gave him a broad smile.

"Prince Llywelyn thought he could spare a few men from his guard to look after this crossing, in case the Normans tried to block it. He did not want to lose any good Welshmen at the fort—or you Sir Declan. He says you amuse him."

"My compliments to the Prince," Declan said, "and God bless all Welshmen this night."

"God always blesses Welshmen, but not so much these Norman lads." He gestured toward the prisoners.

The young lieutenant sat on the spongy ground with his hands bound behind him. They had guarded the ford all day as the faint sounds of battle had ebbed and flowed in the distance. The area had been quiet and tranquil until the sun went down and Welshmen had appeared out of the reeds from every side.

They had tried to fight, but it was no use. Men were struck by arrows from every direction. Bodkin heads on the shafts made a mockery of their armour at this close range. Had they not surrendered there was no doubt they would all lay dead like those he saw scattered around the track in the dim torch light.

Perhaps that would have been better, he thought bitterly. He shuddered as he thought of Sir Stanley de Ver's ghastly corpse, and began to weep.

The Bridgegate

A dozen men slid two small boats into the Dee a mile below the bridge at Chester. Roland had chosen these men for his assault on the Bridgegate. Among them were Patch, Sir Edgar, and the Welshman, Griff, along with two men of the Invalid Company and a half dozen Welsh longbowmen. The group was small enough for stealth, but large enough to take the gatehouse that controlled the Dee bridge—if they achieved surprise.

The oarlocks were muffled with cloth wrappings and no sound, beyond the quiet rush and gurgle of the river, was heard. It was an hour before midnight when they struck the northern bank and pulled the boats up into the thick brush. Landing a mile west of the Shipgate meant a difficult hike through dense brush and brambles along the bank, but there had been little choice. Two boats crossing the river near the bridge at this hour would have been seen by the men guarding the Bridgegate, and that could not be risked.

Roland had waited until the last possible moment before leaving the camp and moving down to the river. He was desperate for some word on the fate of Shipbrook, but none had arrived. Any messenger from Declan would be coming down the trail from the Dee ford to the north and he had walked out that way, hoping to see a rider appear out of the darkness. Millicent found him there. She stood beside him for a moment, looking to the north for a rider that did not come. Only the barest light from the campfires reached them.

"I don't like this," she said simply.

Roland turned to look at her.

"You agreed with the plan."

"Yes, it's as good a plan as any here could devise, but I still don't like it."

"Millie, I've explained why you can't come with us," Roland said gently. "As soon as the place is secured, you and Lady Catherine may come into the city."

She shook her head.

"You think *that* is what troubles me, Roland?"

"I...well...yes."

"Idiot," she said and turned toward him. Rising on tiptoes, she kissed him on the lips, then pulled away. Even in the dim light he could see the fear on her face.

"You mustn't die tonight," she said, and there was desperation in her voice.

For a moment, worries over Shipbrook and Declan and the attack on the city were far away. He felt like he'd been struck by lightning—that an impossible thing had just happened. He pulled her close and returned her kiss. They clung together for a long time until he finally drew back.

"Millie, I..." He wanted to tell her not to be afraid, that he would survive the coming fight and come back to her. Most of all, he wanted to tell her that he loved her, but he struggled to find all the right words. He stood there, staring at her face, so lovely in the faint glow from the campfires.

She rose up on her toes and kissed him again, then put a finger to his lips before he could speak.

"Just don't die tonight," she said and turned and walked away.

***

The men huddled in a tangle of blackberry bushes, thick with small white flowers that smelled of early summer. They hid at the bottom of the dry moat and watched the path leading up to the narrow arched opening beside the Shipgate canal. The iron gate in the archway was shut and the barrier that guarded the canal itself had been lowered.

The night was dark with a high overcast blocking any light from moon or stars, but torches could be seen blazing around the small inner harbour of the Shipgate and on the Bridgegate towers a hundred yards beyond. The path by the canal was in shadow, but the torchlight reached far enough into the night to cast a ghastly glow on a near skeletal corpse swinging from the gibbet by the gate. What remained of Rob Thatcher still hung there as a warning.

They had no way of measuring the passage of time, so they waited for the iron gate to open—waited for Henry Thatcher keep his promise to let them into the city. To their left, the city wall loomed. Built by the Romans and repaired by the Normans, it made Chester a formidable fortress. Behind those walls, a few hundred men could hold off a thousand, and that is what made possession of the city a prize beyond measure for anyone who wished to wield power in the west of England.

Roland thought of the meeting with the Queen in London. She had said that the kingdom was on the verge of civil war. Sitting in the darkness, waiting to enter the city of Chester with violent intent, he knew that the war had already begun. Men would die this night and crowns might be in the balance, but he cared little for the grand ambitions of royalty.

He fought for vengeance—for his father, for Alwyn Madawc, and for the burned out wreck of Shipbrook. He fought for the Danes hanging on to their lives in the mountains and for Sir Roger de Laval, whose sworn man he was. And now, he fought for a future for himself—a future that looked a lot like the face of a girl in flickering firelight.

***

The men in the brambles stayed very still as time slowly passed; each one thinking that it was surely past the midnight hour. Then there was a sound from beyond the wall—a brief clatter of metal on cobbles. All eyes were fixed on the small gate as more time passed. Then, it swung open slowly, with a faint grinding of rusted iron. To the men in the moat, it sounded horribly loud, and they froze. But no alarm was raised.

Roland rose first and led the men out of the moat and along the base of the wall to the open gate. Henry Thatcher waited inside. As they filed quickly in, they stepped over another guard who lay unconscious on the cobbles. Roland placed a hand on the old guard's shoulder and whispered to him.

"Bind and gag this man, if he's still alive," he said, nodding toward the felled guard. Thatcher had spent a restless day trying to sleep and make ready for this night, and he had come prepared. He pulled a length of cord from his belt and a wad of cloth from inside his shirt.

"Aye, lord. He'll not make a sound."

"When you're done, get to the castle. Let Prudy know that men will be coming to secure it for Earl Ranulf. She will need to let them in through the scullery."

The old man nodded and started to go about his task, but Roland grasped him by the arm and handed him a small blade.

"When you're done, Henry, take down your boy."

For a moment he thought the old man would break into sobs, but he gathered himself.

"Aye lord, and God go with ye. Six men are in the gatehouse by the bridge."

Roland headed around the small harbour and up the side street that angled toward the Bridgegate, his men falling in behind him. The streets were empty, as it was a time when all honest men were home in their beds. They reached Bridge Street and saw the gatehouse looming to their right. There was a broad archway that ran through the place, blocked on the bridge side by a portcullis. This open lattice of heavy oak beams was faced in iron. It was this barrier that had to be raised.

The gatehouse itself was three storeys high, with two towers that thrust even higher into the sky. Torches were lit at the top of the structure, but they were placed to illuminate the bridge, not the street behind. In deep darkness, they reached the heavy door that provided access to the place. Roland grasped the latch and turned, slowly. The latch moved, but the door did not budge. It was locked.

Behind him, his dozen men were all crouched low and clinging to the shadows. There were no other doors to the gatehouse. Roland took a deep breath and pounded on the oak. He heard the sound of metal falling to the floor and guessed he had startled whoever was inside. After a few seconds, footsteps could be heard coming down stone steps, along with a stream of choice curses.

Without preamble, the door flew open to reveal a red-faced guard whose eyes had not adjusted to the darkness.

"Who…?"

The last thing he saw was a dozen men rising up out of the shadows. He started to draw his sword, but Roland lunged forward, covering the man's mouth with his hand and slamming his head into the stone wall of the passage. He made no sound as he collapsed. Roland caught him as he fell and laid him gently on the steps. Then he led his men into the gatehouse. Patch closed and latched the door behind them. They found a second man asleep by a fireplace on the second floor. He heard nothing as Patch bludgeoned him senseless with the hilt of his sword.

Roland looked around.

Four left.

On the other side of the room was a spiral stone stairway leading up. Quietly, he led his band up to the top floor of the gatehouse. No matter how stealthy men might be, a dozen on a stone stairway could not be completely silent. The men above heard them come.

"Arthur?" one called down.

"Aye," Roland replied, but this guard was fully awake and was not fooled. He turned to shout a warning as Roland sprang up the last few steps, followed closely by Sir Edgar. The space on the third floor was narrow and made more cramped by the brandishing of weapons on all sides. Two guards had swords and two had lances, and they looked ready to charge the two intruders at the top of the steps.

Roland's eyes darted to the back wall of the narrow room. Mounted along the wall was a large windlass to raise and lower the portcullis. Two heavy hemp ropes ran from the long barrel of the device up to pulleys bolted into the stone of the ceiling. From there the ropes disappeared into a slot in the floor.

A guard saw Roland's glance and did not hesitate. With a quick slash he cut the nearest rope, which slithered over its pulley and snaked out of sight through the gap in the floor. He raised his sword to sever the second rope, but died where he stood with a longbow shaft through his heart. Griff had forced himself into the small room and got off a shot before the man could do further damage.

Sir Edgar swung his huge battleaxe and took six feet off the end of a lance one of the guards was brandishing. With deliberate slowness, the big knight edged forward, dragging his gimpy leg and swinging the axe in savage arcs. As he moved further into the room the three remaining guards shrank back and more Welshmen with bows edged in.

"Quarter!" one guard cried, and threw down his sword. Sir Edgar glowered at the other two and they did the same. He turned to Roland.

"We have the gatehouse, but how will we raise the damned gate?"

Roland looked at the severed rope dangling from the windlass and shook his head.

"I don't know."

The portcullis could not be raised by a single rope—even if one rope could bear the weight of the thing. The sides of the barrier were snugly placed within stone slots on either side of the arch. Without an even pull on both sides, it would tilt and wedge solidly. They needed a second rope, but from where?

His thoughts were abruptly interrupted by a pounding from below. Patch had been left to watch the first floor entrance and after a moment he called up the spiral stair.

"It's the Officer of the Watch—he's making rounds and wants in!"

Roland's mind raced. They could not afford to be discovered. Not yet. But they could not bar the commander of the night watch if he wanted to enter on his rounds. That would surely bring an unwanted response from the garrison.

"We'll let him in, but won't let him back out," he said and followed Patch back to the second floor. The two gate guards had been trussed and were lying, unconscious, on the floor as he reached the stone steps leading down to the oak door.

"Sorry, sir," he called as he ran down the steps, "mislaid the key."

"I don't like standing about out here in the dark, damn you. Open up!"

"Aye, sir," Roland called through the door and inserted the key. As the door swung outward, Roland saw to his horror that the man was not alone. He had a patrol of three guards making the rounds with him. No time to hesitate. As the impatient Officer of the Watch stepped through the doorway, Roland stepped back and let him pass. He hoped the others would follow, but they stood stolidly outside on the cobbles of Bridge Street waiting for their leader to return.

No help for it now.

He pulled the door shut and bolted it. As he turned and bounded up the steps, he saw the new arrival standing frozen at the top of the stairs. Two bound men lay on the floor in front of him and a man with a longbow had an arrow pointed at his chest. Patch had his short sword at the man's neck.

"What...what..." was the best he could manage.

Roland stepped up behind and drew the man's sword from its scabbard. He flinched, but did not resist. He handed it to Patch.

"Tie him up and put him with the others. There were three more outside. It will take them awhile to decide what to do, but it won't be long before they will be trying to break down that door."

Roland saw Griff enter the room from the spiral stair.

"Get your archers positioned. There'll be trouble soon."

Griff nodded.

"And the gate?"

Roland frowned.

"I'm still thinking on that."

He followed Griff back up the spiral stair to the third floor, past the three bound prisoners there and up a ladder to the top of the barbican. The Welshman had placed two of his archers on the north side of the gatehouse facing back into Chester and two more he sent up to the towers that loomed on either side. He had already placed a man at each of the murder holes on the second floor that looked down into the archway of the gate. From these positions, they could harass any of the town's defenders who sought to attack them from there.

Roland walked to the north side of the gate and looked down into the dark streets below. The three guards were still there, but appeared to be arguing. Finally, one broke away and pounded on the gatehouse door. Getting no response, he returned to the group and the three hurried off toward the centre of the town—no doubt eager to alert others of the strange events taking place at the Bridgegate.

The warren of alleys and side streets that ran back into the town would provide plenty of cover for an assault by the garrison. Men could be brought within forty feet of the oak door down at street level without being exposed to the Welsh archers above. His men could take a toll in that last forty feet, but a half dozen archers would not be enough to stop a determined attack.

Roland shook his head. De Ferrers' men did not even have to retake the gate. They just had to make sure it was not opened before their master returned to the city with the rest of the garrison. Could he burn the oak and iron gate? Possibly, but it would take a long time for the massive beams to burn through and collapse—too long. His careful plan was coming undone for want of a rope.

"Sir Roland." He turned. It was Sir Edgar. "One of the prisoners wants to talk to you."

Roland followed the big knight down the ladder to the windlass room where all six of the prisoners were now sitting with their hands bound behind them. Sir Edgar walked over to the oldest and hauled him to his feet.

"What have you to say?" he demanded.

The older man looked at his bound companions. The Officer of the Watch glared at him. He seemed to hesitate under the man's gaze, but then straightened.

"St. Mary's on the Hill, sir."

Sir Edgar shook his head then lifted the man by one arm until he had to fight to stand on tiptoe.

"Speak plain, or I'll…"

"Wait!" Roland cut him off. "Let him down." Sir Edgar eased his grip. The man steadied himself.

"The belfry," he said and nodded toward the windlass.

The belfry? He didn't take the man's meaning, but then…*Of course—the belfry!"*

"The bells! They don't ring themselves. There'll be rope in the belfry—perhaps enough for our needs. Sir Edgar, cut this man's bonds and get Griff down here. We're going to church."

***

William de Ferrers rode through the shattered gate of Shipbrook. Torches illuminated the empty ruin of the place and the fury written on the Earl of Derby's face. They had not found the Earl of Chester behind the walls. Three dead Welshmen was all the evidence left that anyone had defended the place. He had lost over a score of men in the assault with nothing to show for it but a burned-out fort.

When word came that the defenders were fleeing to the south, he had dispatched Sir Hugh with a large force to join the men he had already sent to block the ford. Surely they would capture the Earl and what was left of his force.

Bored with the ruined fort, he wheeled his horse around and started back toward the gate. His retainers had dismounted to examine the aftermath of the battle and were gathered around two of the corpses, chattering about their victory. Seeing the Earl taking his leave, they scrambled to join him. The group had just passed through the smashed gate when two riders appeared over the low ridge coming from the ford.

Sir Hugh was in the lead and sat his horse rigidly, like a man riding to an execution. Beside him was the young lieutenant he had dispatched to guard the ford. The boy was helmetless and had an empty scabbard at his side. Terror was written on the young man's face. Sir Hugh displayed no sympathy. He had his own neck to save. He waved an arm at the commander of the ford patrol.

"Found this young fool trussed up like a goose down at the ford, my lord. We had six dead. No sign of Earl Ranulf or the men who fled the fort—they took the patrol horses and are across the Dee and gone, I'd reckon."

De Ferrers wanted to strike the man, but fought to retain his composure. He was aware that scores of men were now watching him. Now was a time to show calm. He would make an example out of these pitiful excuses for soldiers when the time was right.

He urged his horse forward and noticed with disgust that the terrified lieutenant had pissed himself. He spoke evenly to the man.

"Did you see the Earl of Chester, boy? Did Ranulf escape over the ford?"

The lieutenant tried to keep his voice steady, but it quavered nonetheless.

"My lord…we saw none but Welshmen, save for a red-haired knight who spoke English and seemed to lead them. I would recognize the Earl. He did not pass over the ford."

William de Ferrers raised a hand to his temple. He was getting a blinding headache. Had Ranulf not been at the fort?

If not at Shipbrook, where was the Earl of Chester?

***

The Earl of Chester sat his charger a dozen paces into the woodline that bordered the road coming up from the south. It was three hours until dawn and his eyes were fixed on the only bridge that spanned the Dee from the sea to the river's source. Across that bridge was his ancestral home of Chester and he had come to take it back.

Behind him, one hundred fifty men hid themselves in the cover of the trees and waited. At the Earl's command, they would mount and ride like hell across the bridge and into the city. But not until the gate came up, and in the guttering light of the gatehouse, they could see that it was still closed to them. So they waited.

Declan O'Duinne sat beside the Earl and watched the gate as well. He had arrived from Shipbrook with his twenty-five exhausted bowman only an hour earlier. He had ridden into the camp and spoken with Lady Catherine and Millicent—who, to his surprise, hugged him like a sister.

"We prayed for you, Declan," she said.

Declan smiled at her.

"Your prayers were much appreciated, Millie. Now say one for Roland. He must be in the gatehouse by now."

***

Three men slipped through the shadows in the alleyway that led from Bridge Street back down to the Shipgate. At any moment they expected the alarm to be raised by the three missing guards, but only silence greeted them as they skirted the inner harbour and started up the narrow street that led to the church on the hill. At this hour, no light shone from any window as they crept across the small graveyard behind the church and reached the front door. It was locked.

Patch motioned for Roland and Sir Edgar to step back as he wedged his short sword between the door and the frame. Roland watched with interest as the man from the Invalid Company worked the blade with the skill of one who had done this before. In a few seconds, there was the sound of metal sliding on metal and the big oak door popped open a crack. Patch put his shoulder to it and swung it wide.

Standing just inside the entrance was a short, white haired priest in a grey robe with a candle in hand. He did not look frightened, only curious.

"Do you come to rob us, my sons? We have little, but I'll gladly share what we have."

Roland stepped forward.

"Father, we aren't thieves, but we would borrow the rope that hangs in the belfry. It's for a good cause."

The priest looked troubled.

"There have been many hangings here, young man—too many. If you need rope for that, I will not allow it."

"We mean to put an end to all the hangings, father, and for that we need your rope."

The old priest seemed to consider Roland's reply for a long moment.

"There has been much activity of late, with soldiers riding off to who knows where. There are rumours about that Earl Ranulf has returned. Would you know anything of that?"

Roland saw no profit in lying.

"We are Ranulf's men—come to take back the city."

Now the priest smiled broadly and crossed himself.

"Thank God—and the Devil take the Earl of Derby! You may have all the rope you need, but return it when you can. If Ranulf delivers us from that man, we will need it to ring the bells."

He led the men to the belfry tower where four sturdy ropes hung to the floor. Patch scrambled up the ladder and soon two of the ropes fell into loose coils at their feet.

"Either of these should do fine," Patch said as he coiled one rope over his shoulder and Sir Edgar gathered up the other. "I thought it best to bring a spare—but that leaves you two to ring once we have the city in our hands, Father."

The old priest was beaming now.

"Very kind of you, my son, but be off now. I expect you have work to do."

"Thank you, Father," Roland called over his shoulder as they slipped back out into the night.

They had reached the inner harbour when they heard the ominous sounds of marching boots on cobbles coming from up on Bridge Street. The alarm had finally been sounded and the garrison was beginning to react. Now speed was more critical than stealth, but Sir Edgar could not run with his damaged leg. He moved forward with a jerky lurching gait as quickly as he could, but halfway up the alleyway he stopped and flung the coil of rope to Roland.

"Go! Ye'll never make it at this speed. I'll do my damage from out here."

"No! We stay together—all of us."

Sir Edgar loomed over him in the dark.

"Don't be stupid. That rope is more important than me. Besides, they'll probably kill ye all in the gatehouse anyway, while I'm hiding out here!" He raised a massive hand to Roland's shoulder and shoved him up the street. Before Roland could say more, the big knight hobbled off down the hill and into the darkness.

Roland cursed to himself, but turned and ran hard for the gatehouse with Patch a few steps ahead. As they burst onto

Bridge Street and turned right toward the sanctuary of the gatehouse a shout went up behind them.

"Halt! You there! You men! I say halt!"

The two men did not look back as they ran for the door. For a moment, Roland feared they would be trapped outside, but the big oak door swung open as they neared it. He caught a glimpse of Griff in the entrance as a spear clattered off the cobbles to his left. As they ran the last few feet, they heard the angry buzz of arrows passing near them.

Patch was first through the door and, as Roland stumbled in behind him, he felt a sharp blow to the side of his face and a sting on his cheek. The door was slammed shut and bolted.

Patch grabbed Roland's arm and lifted him to his feet. In the torchlight he reached out and turned Roland's head to the side. The arrow had ploughed an ugly furrow that ran from beneath an ear to halfway across Roland's cheek. Patch took out a surprisingly clean cloth from a pouch at his belt and began dabbing at the wound.

"That was close," he said with good humour. "Lucky it was an English archer—if he was Welsh ye'd be dead now." He dabbed harder and Roland winced.

"Be still," he said as he finished swabbing the long cut. He drew the cloth away, which was now blood-soaked. "It will sting a bit, but leave a very presentable scar."

It did sting, but Roland barely noticed. They had made it back to the gatehouse with the rope they needed, but had left Sir Edgar behind. Worse, the garrison troops had now arrived and would no doubt lay siege to the gatehouse. He made his way up the two sets of stairs to the windlass room and climbed the ladder to the top of the barbican. Below, he could see that Griff's archers had forced the garrison troops to find cover. Three bodies could be seen sprawled in the shadows on Bridge Street.

"They's hid in the alleys," one of the archers offered. Roland nodded.

They won't stay there forever.

***

The long column of riders moved slowly along the road from Shipbrook to Chester. High clouds kept the night black and the uneven road made haste dangerous. This was an ancient trade road that came up from Wales and over the Dee, but it was not built by the Romans. The Romans would have made it straight as an arrow shot and paved. This road was neither and no man wanted a horse to stumble in a rut and break a leg.

When de Ferrers' men rode out at dawn the day before, it had seemed a welcome break from the monotony of garrison life. Even the sobering sight of one of their own, swinging from a gibbet by the Northgate, had not done much to dampen the mood of excitement many felt.

But the taking of Shipbrook had turned into a hard-fought battle against a foe they had failed to corner. The whereabouts of the real prize, the Earl of Chester, was a mystery and a shocking number of their comrades now lay buried outside the captured fort with nothing to show for the sacrifice. The men now slumped in their saddles as they rode. It did not feel like victory.

The column was five miles from Chester, when a rider, heedless of the risks, came galloping up the road from the city on a lathered horse. He reined up in front of William de Ferrers.

"My lord! There's trouble in the city. Men have taken the gatehouse at the Dee bridge and barred entry to our guard. Archers on the roof killed three of our men." The man got all this out without taking a breath.

For de Ferrers, this was one more piece of troubling news on a day filled with unpleasant and unexpected turns.

"How large is this force?" he demanded.

"We don't know, my lord, but they have at least four archers on the roof and other men were seen inside when they captured the Officer of the Watch."

"They have the Officer of the Watch?" de Ferrers asked, incredulous at this additional news.

"Aye, lord. Sir Percy went in to inspect the guard three hours ago. He did not return." Seeing the stricken look on the Earl's face, he hastened to add, "We have them trapped. They have no way out."

Sir James Ferguson had edged his horse up to the front of the column when he saw the rider coming. The old soldier heard the man's report and the Earl's questions. It was all such a waste. As de Ferrers sat speechless on his horse, he spoke up.

"Out? They are not looking for a way out, boy. They are looking to let folk in!" He rode close to the messenger and bellowed at him. "Is the damn gate open?"

"The gate?"

"Aye, the bloody gate! Why else would armed men be taking over the gatehouse, but to raise the damned gate?"

"I…it…it was closed, sir. At least when I was sent with my message. It was still closed."

The old soldier turned to Sir Hugh and Earl William.

"My lords, we've been cozened! If Ranulf was ever at Shipbrook, you can be sure he was long gone by the time we arrived. I would wager he's now somewhere on the other side of the Dee bridge with enough men to take the city—if the gate is opened to him. Those men in the gatehouse are there to open it."

"But…but…," Sir Hugh stammered, "why haven't they raised the portcullis then?"

The old man rubbed his chin.

"Something's gone wrong for them, so there may still be a chance to save your city, my lords—if we reach it before that gate is raised."

De Ferrers felt a burning knot in his stomach. He had risen high in the esteem of Prince John by his bold capture of Chester a year ago. All of that could be lost if the city were snatched back from him. He could not allow that. He grasped Sir Hugh by the arm and snarled.

"Push the horses until they're blown, Captain, but get to Chester before we lose it!"

Sir Hugh gulped.

"Aye, my lord."

***

Patch had taken one of the belfry ropes and knotted it around the windlass. He ran it over the large pulley hanging from the stone ceiling and dropped it into the slot in the floor. He looked up at Roland.

"It would have been much simpler if we had secured this before the guard arrived."

249

"Aye," Roland said. "But they're here now and the gate must still be raised. We haven't much time."

Patch held up a length of the slack rope in his hand.

"This still needs attaching and ye can't get out the front to attend to that little chore—not with them archers out on the street. Ye'd never make it to the arch, much less climb the portcullis."

Roland nodded.

"Sir Roland!" The call came urgently from the roof. Roland took the ladder rungs two at a time and ran to the north side. Below, he saw a tightly grouped knot of men moving up the street toward the gatehouse. They held shields above their heads, some of which already had longbow shafts imbedded. They pulled a large cart behind them and, as he watched, they disappeared into the arched passageway that led to the portcullis and the bridge beyond.

He hurried back down to the second floor and looked down through one of the murder holes to see what new threat was there.

Damn! They were building a fire.

Someone leading these garrison troops had a plan and it seemed to be working better than his own. The fire wouldn't burn the stone gate house, but that wouldn't be necessary. As the flames caught and brightened, one of the men dropped damp straw on the blaze and thick, black smoke began to rise.

Roland motioned to the archers, who took up positions by the two murder holes. After one guard took an arrow in the shoulder, the others quickly moved their shields up to block further damage from above as they stoked the fire. Now the smoke began to rise up through the murder holes and fill the room. The gatehouse was acting as a chimney, sucking the smoke up through the stairs and out the hatch on the roof.

On all sides, men began to cough.

Roland looked around him. If they stayed inside the gatehouse, they would be overcome by the smoke. If they escaped to the roof, they could not raise the portcullis and it would only be a matter of time before the door was breached.

"Find cloth and stuff these holes. Use your shirts if you must." That would only delay events, for smoke was drifting in through cracks in the mortar. He ran up the spiral stair to the windlass room.

"Patch, with me! Bring the other rope!" he called, as he once more climbed the ladder to the roof. Patch was close behind, the rope slung over his shoulder, as Roland ran to the bridge side of the gatehouse.

"Tie it off," he ordered. Patch quickly looped the rope around a merlon and dropped it over the side. Roland looked out across the dark waters of the Dee to the deeper darkness beyond and wondered if the Earl was there—and Declan. Below, the flickering torchlight illuminated a small circle on the bridge itself.

He climbed over the crenelated top of the barbican, grasped the rope and swung out into space. Bracing his feet against the outer wall, he began climbing down hand-over-hand.

***

Declan O'Duinne knew there was trouble across the Dee bridge. In the small hours of the night, sound travelled and the unmistakable sounds of a fight could be heard within the town. It was long past midnight and Roland should have secured the gatehouse by now and raised the gate, but it stood there, closed solidly against them. Then, a bonfire had flared under the arch. Something had gone very wrong with the plan.

He wanted to charge across the bridge as soon as the fire flared up, but the Earl had forbidden it. They were not to ride until the gate came up. That was the plan. There was a hint of predawn light far to the east as Declan squinted into the darkness. For a moment, he thought his sleep-weary eyes were betraying him. But no—someone was climbing over the crenelated battlements and down the outside of the gatehouse!

***

Roland pushed off with his legs, swinging out, then letting the return swing take him underneath the arch. He smashed feet first into the portcullis, looped an arm through one of the openings and released the rope.

Looking through the beams of the gate, he was relieved to see that none of the garrison troops in the archway had noticed him clinging like a fly on the other side of the portcullis. They had sent the cart back for more wood and straw and were gathered in a loose circle around the bonfire they'd built. The murder holes had been plugged up to try to keep out the rising smoke and the rain of arrows from above had stopped, but they still held their shields up defensively.

He looked to his left.

There! The belfry rope hung loosely against the inside of the portcullis only five feet away. Carefully he moved toward it, but one of the men under the arch happened to look up and catch the small motion.

"Bloody hell!" The guard shouted, and pointed his way. For a moment, the fire was forgotten as one of them saw the dangling rope and understood, at last, why the gate had not been lifted.

"Stop him!" the guard screamed and charged toward the portcullis.

Roland had no choice. He had his short sword, but it would be useless against men coming at him from below. He released his grip and dropped fifteen feet to the bridge below, landing on his heels, then falling on his backside. From five feet away he glared through the oak beams of the portcullis at the garrison troops who glared back.

"Fetch archers," one guard ordered. Roland cursed under his breath. If they got bowmen into the archway, he would have nowhere to go but over the side of the bridge and into the Dee.

***

On the other side of the Dee, Declan watched the man climb down the bridge side of the gatehouse and disappear under the arch. Seconds later, he heard the guard's shout and saw the man drop to the ground.

The plan be damned.

"Shipbrook, with me!" he screamed spooking the Earl's horse, which almost threw him. He leapt off his horse and ran for the bridge. As he reached the south end of the span, he glanced over his shoulder to see if anyone had followed. Baldric was there along with about a dozen men in tattered Shipbrook colours. To his surprise, the Welsh archers who had stood with him to defend the little fort at Shipbrook had also joined the rush.

They pounded across the bridge, Irish, Welsh and Saxon war cries rising into the brightening sky.

Roland heard them coming, but the garrison troops were coming as well. More than a score piled out of the nearby alleys and came to the defence of the Bridgegate. Roland heard arrows thumping into the unclad oak on the other side of the portcullis as they tried to bring him down. One shaft glanced off an opening and flew into the sky above his head. Another fifty feet, and they would be able to shoot through openings in the portcullis at anyone on the bridge.

They did not make the fifty feet. A dozen Welsh longbowmen beat them to the gate. The men caught in the archway had no chance. Those that tried to stand their ground died in seconds. The rest fled from the gatehouse and back into the surrounding alleys.

Declan screamed at them through the gate as they ran. He did not see Roland scramble back up the outside of the portcullis and begin knotting the belfry rope to the top. At last it was done. He called up through the slot in the floor.

"Patch, raise away!"

"Aye, sir!" came the reply and he heard the creak of the windlass as it took up the slack. With a lurch, the portcullis began to rise. Roland climbed down a few feet then dropped back to the bridge. As the great barrier rose, men began to duck underneath and move through the arch and onto Bridge Street.

Roland heard the thunder of hooves behind him and turned to see the Earl of Chester charging at a gallop across the bridge with over a hundred horsemen at his back—his blue banner now clearly visible in the dawn light. The men who had already passed through the open gate moved aside to let the wall of charging horseflesh pass through the arch of the gatehouse.

The Earl waved a short salute with his sword to Roland and Declan as he spurred his charger through the gate and into his city. It was dawn and three more gates had to be secured against the men who would be coming from Shipbrook. When the last rider had cleared the gate, Declan laid a hand on his friend's shoulder.

"Another fine plan, Roland. I don't recall the climbing part though." Roland was almost too exhausted to grin, but he managed one.

"Sir Roger used to tell us that no plan survives its first encounter with the enemy."

Declan smiled and nodded.

"Well, I can vouch that none of yours do!"

"It would seem so," Roland said and threw an arm around Declan's shoulders, "but they seem to work out in the end. Now let's get ourselves up to the Northgate. That's where de Ferrers will be coming."

***

The thundering charge of a hundred armoured horsemen overwhelmed the garrison troops that tried to bar the Earl's entry into his capital. Within a few blocks of the gate, they melted into narrow alleys or surrendered. When the Earl reached St. Peter's church, he charged straight on toward the Northgate, while groups behind split off east and west to secure the Watergate and Eastgate. In half an hour, the main gates of Chester were in the Earl's hands.

Declan had left his mount across the river and Roland had none, so the two raced on foot up Bridge Street toward the centre of the city. They had not gone far, when, across the rooftops of Chester, Roland heard the pealing of bells. The sound came from the bell tower of Saint Mary's on the Hill. He smiled as he ran. It was the sound of victory.

Half way up Bridge Street, they were hailed. It was Sir Edgar, limping up from a narrow alleyway. The huge knight had a rare grin on his face.

"I did good damage out here, Sir Roland!" he proclaimed proudly and they saw that his dark tangle of beard and face were spattered with blood.

"Well done, Sir Edgar. I feared we had lost you. We make for the Northgate. Send Griff and his archers to join us there, and take Patch with you to the rear of the castle. There is a barred door there that leads to the scullery. There will be a girl there named Prudence and she will be expecting visitors."

Sir Edgar gave a sharp nod and lurched off to do his duty. Roland and Declan hurried through the town, which had been awakened by the thunder of hooves on the cobbled streets. Some of the more curious along Bridge Street poked their heads out of second floor windows to stare at the two men running by with drawn swords. Most just closed their shutters and bolted their doors. Who knew what new calamity was being visited on Chester?

When they reached the Northgate, they saw the portcullis was securely in place and the street was jammed with horses, their dismounted riders deployed along the wall walk on either side of the gate. They climbed up stone steps and joined the Earl, who had been staring intently toward the northeast. He turned as they approached. His wide smile fading a bit when he saw the raw gash on the side of Roland's face.

"You've been wounded!" he said, with genuine concern in his voice.

Roland absently raised a hand to the furrow that an arrow had sliced along his cheek. He had completely forgotten it.

"Nothing much, my lord. My man Patch tended it, so it should not fester."

The Earl was about to say more, but one of his men called to him.

"Lord, riders on the road."

They all ran to the rampart to see the former garrison of Chester emerge from a far tree line, riding hard for the Northgate and home.

Roland saw that a few of the Welsh bowman had made their way from the south side of town to the north wall.

"Bowman!" he shouted. "Make ready!"

A dozen men along the wall nocked their arrows and waited. If the garrison troops rode heedlessly up to the gate, they would face a nasty surprise. But someone in that host knew better. The thick column of mounted men halted a quarter of a mile from the gate and only two men came on.

"Raise my banner," the Earl commanded. His blue and gold banner was hoisted above the Northgate and the two riders reined in, turned their horses and rode back to the main force. They knew what that banner meant.

"This will not be happy news for the Earl of Derby," the Earl of Chester said with obvious relish as the riders reached the head of the column. As they watched, one rider on a huge black charger struck another man and knocked him from his saddle.

"Not happy news at all," the Earl said.

For a while there appeared to be confusion at the head of the enemy column, but then four men rode forward, carefully stopping three hundred yards from the gate, well out of longbow range. One was the man on the black charger. The Earl of Derby had come to parlay.

Two armoured knights edged their mounts close in on either side of the Earl, shields at the ready. The fourth man rode forward alone. William de Ferrers was taking no chances with his own safety and was sending a herald. The man reined in his horse fifty yards from the Northgate, stood in his stirrups and shouted up at the walls.

"Earl Ranulf! Earl William sends his greetings and good wishes. He has seen your banner above the walls and rejoices at the sight. He wants you to know that he never thought you guilty of treason. When he learned of Lady Constance's plot, he feared for your safety and only seized the city for your own protection. But you fled, my lord! Had you but stayed, none of this unpleasantness would have happened. It's not too late to make this right. Open the gate, and the Earl will intercede with the Prince on your behalf."

The Earl shook his head in disbelief, then shouted back.

"Tell your master that he is a miserable turd. Tell him *my* banner flies above *my* city and his lies in the gutter where it belongs. Tell him he will pay for the people he's hanged in Cheshire. Go tell de Ferrers that I wish *him* well when he explains to the Prince how he lost Chester!"

The rider hesitated for a moment, then recognised that the parlay was at an end. He wheeled his horse around and rode back toward the Earl's party. Above the Northgate, Griff had arrived and brought the rest of the Welsh archers with him—and Roland's longbow. Without a word, Roland took the weapon, drew three arrows from Griff's quiver and slid over the wall. Declan reached for his friend's arm to restrain him, but missed.

It was a fifteen foot drop to the edge of the dry moat, but he landed lightly. There were shouts of surprise behind him, but he paid no heed. He had waited three years to have his revenge on de Ferrers. There might never be another chance.

As Roland scrambled across the moat and climbed up to the road, he saw the Earl of Derby screaming at his herald. None in his party had seen a man go over the wall, but now Roland was sprinting up the road toward them and one man let out a startled cry of alarm.

Two knights drew their swords, unsure what to do with a single man running toward them, but de Ferrers saw with horror that the man was carrying a longbow and he knew—knew in his bones—that the man was Roland Inness. He jerked his horse's head around in a panic and spurred the animal back toward his own troops.

It had taken ten seconds for the men on the road to react, and that was long enough. Roland was now within the extreme range of his bow. He stopped, nocked an arrow, drew the bowstring back to his ear and elevated the bow. This would be for Rolf Inness. This would be for Alwyn Madawc.

He would get only one shot. The three men de Ferrers had brought with him had turned to follow their master, whipping their horses as they tried to catch up. But the Earl of Derby's panicked flight had outrun them and their shields. Roland released his breath and loosed the arrow. It arched into the morning sky

On the wall, men held their breath.

"By God, he might have the range!" Griff shouted to Declan as he watched the arrow's flight.

The shaft reached the top of its arc and plummeted toward the galloping rider. With an audible clang that could be heard by men on both sides, it struck William de Ferrers in the helmet. At such extreme range, it dented the armour but did not penetrate.

De Ferrers head lurched forward, then drunkenly backwards. He seemed to lose control of his limbs, dropped his reins and toppled out of the saddle, bouncing as he hit the roadway. His guards reached him and dismounted, using their shields to protect their lord.

Twenty riders charged toward the lone archer standing on the road, but they were soon discouraged by a hail of longbow shafts from the Welsh bowmen on the walls. They retreated, dragging de Ferrers with them off the field,

Roland Inness watched them go, then turned and walked back toward the gate of Chester.

***

The dead had been cleared from the streets, but the smell of smoke still hung over the Bridgegate when Sergeant Billy escorted Lady Catherine and Millicent into the city. Patch met them at the gatehouse.

"Welcome, my lady…Miss Millicent," he said bowing to each. "I'm told you are to take quarters in the castle. It's up that way," he said pointing to the west.

Millicent wanted to scream at the man.

Quarters? What did it matter where they lay their heads at night? She gathered herself. The man meant well.

"Tom, our men—were there losses?" She held her breath waiting for his reply.

"Aye, miss. Only two dead, four wounded," Patch said, "if you don't count the nasty gash Roland got to his face."

Now she felt like kissing the poor man.

Roland was alive. For the moment, that was all she needed to hear.

"Thank you, Tom. Can we help with the wounded?"

"Won't be necessary, my lady. Town physician is tending them."

Sergeant Billy escorted them, not to the scullery door, but to the main entrance of the castle bailey. To Millicent's joy, Prudence was there to welcome them. It seemed that, until the Earl returned to his home, the young scullery maid was acting as mistress of Chester Castle.

It was late in the day when an exhausted Earl of Chester appeared at his castle gate, bringing a score of weary men with him. Some were bandaged, several smelled strongly of smoke and all were exhausted and famished. Prudence was ready. A simple but hearty meal was quickly served and the men, as all men do after battle, told tales and got drunk.

Millicent had watched them arrive and saw Declan among them. She ran into the courtyard to greet him and resisted the urge to hug the young Irishman in front of everyone.

"Lady Millicent!" he called, as he saw her approach. He was allowed to call her Millie, but that would not do in public.

"Declan! We've done it!" she said as she reached him. "I hardly thought it possible we'd ever be standing inside these walls again." As she spoke, she cast a worried glance past him to the castle gate. Declan did not miss it. He leaned in and whispered in her ear.

"He's fine, Millie. He's mounting the first guard. I'm to relieve him when I've eaten."

"Patch said he'd been hurt," she said.

Declan grimaced a bit.

"Nothing too serious, if it doesn't fester. An arrow grazed his cheek. Should make a nice scar, though."

Men and their scars—so like little boys.

"Millie, he shot de Ferrers with his longbow! Hit him square in the helmet at over two hundred yards. Even Griff was impressed. We don't think he's dead, but the bastard will have an aching head for certain."

"Declan, where…"

"He should be near the Watergate by now," he said with a grin, "if you can't wait."

Was it so obvious?

"Thank you, Declan," she said and hurried back inside the castle. There was a passageway on the second floor that connected to the wall walk, and not too far from the Watergate. She ran past surprised servants inside, then out into the afternoon sun.

She could see the blunt turret of the gate ahead and slowed to a walk. She had almost reached the gate, when Roland came through the narrow arched doorway from the tower onto the wall walk.

He moved slowly and she could see the weariness on him as he walked toward her. His gaze was turned outward, searching for any threat to their new-won city. She stopped and waited. He was almost upon her before he looked up and froze where he stood.

"Millie."

"You've been hurt," she said, reaching up with her hand and touching the raw furrow the arrow had made in his cheek.

"Nothing much," he said, raising his own hand to cup her cheek. He pulled her close and kissed her. She kissed him back as they held each other close on the deserted wall. Finally he drew back.

"Someone will see, Millie."

"I don't care. You're alive. The rest doesn't matter."

He smiled down at her.

"Well, you told me I was not to die, and I found it to be good advice."

She kissed him again. "What are we to do?" she said, for she truly did not know.

"I am a poor match for you, Millie" he said, wistfully. "Lady Catherine will be unhappy. She expects you to marry well, and I have nothing."

She stepped back and looked at him. He was dirty and smelled of smoke. His mail was of the poorest quality, his clothes were tattered and his sword, to all appearances, was borrowed. The only thing of value he seemed to own was the dagger with the jewelled handle at his waist and the longbow slung over his shoulder.

"My father had nothing when my mother married him and she never regretted it."

Roland pulled her close and cradled her head against his shoulder.

"I am not Roger de Laval, Millie."

She looked up at him and smiled.

"You are more like him than you know, Roland Inness."

Aftermath

*T*he weary troops of the Chester garrison straggled into Derby near midnight. Riders had been sent ahead to secure space in the town's barracks and a nearby barn, to at least give them shelter through the night. Their mood was sullen and a good number had already slipped away in the night to ride back toward Cheshire.

When these men rode out of Chester four days ago to attack the little fort by the Dee, none had expected to find the gates of their city barred to them on their return. Now, those that remained entered Derby in the dark of night, humbled and beaten.

A wagon had been found to convey William de Ferrers over the bumpy roads from Chester. The Earl still lay senseless from the arrow strike to his helmet and his retainers decided to take him to his castle at Tutbury, south of Derby.

Command of the garrison force had fallen to Sir Hugh Bonsil, who did not know what to do with these men. When they reached the barracks, he simply dismissed them and left them to fend for themselves, while he went to seek an inn.

Father Malachy heard the first riders gallop into town and hurried into the street where he learned of the stunning disaster at Chester. He had been in Derby for a week attending to a host of administrative duties left in his hands by the Earl. All of that was forgotten as he tried to grasp the damage that had been done to his work in the Midlands. Somehow, de Ferrers had managed to undo a year of careful effort on his part.

How?

While it was true that the force sent by the Queen to find Ranulf in the wilderness of Wales had somehow beaten the mercenaries he'd hired, it had only been forty men—certainly not enough to carry out an attack on the city.

The accounts of the first men to arrive had been contradictory and confusing, but were alike on one key point. De Ferrers had stripped the garrison to attack a relatively worthless, burned out fort on the Dee where he thought the Earl of Chester was sheltering. In his absence, the city had been snatched back by Ranulf.

It would have to be retaken. They could not afford to lose Chester and its revenue—not to Ranulf. That the city had changed hands with little loss of life spoke to some kind of treachery from within. Once the city was back in their hands, he must ferret out whoever had helped Ranulf. When that day came, the gallows of Chester would be busy.

Malachy had a horse saddled and rode through the small hours of the night to Tutbury. When he entered the Earl's chambers, he found him awake, though barely in command of his faculties.

"My lord, I came as soon as I heard. Praise God, the physician says you will fully recover."

De Ferrers looked at him dully for a moment, then seemed to focus.

"It was the bowman, Malachy. It was Inness—I know it! You must kill him Malachy…you must."

"I will, my lord. I swear to you, I will. But you must rest and regain your strength."

De Ferrers mumbled something and seemed about to drift off, but regained his senses.

"Malachy, you must take this news to the Prince. He must bring his army from Nottingham to Chester. The city is mine now! Do you hear me? Go and tell the Prince—I need his mercenaries!"

"Aye, my lord, I'll see to it." The physician was now making disapproving noises and insisted that he leave the Earl's bedside. Malachy did not object. As he hurried out of the keep of Tutbury Castle to his still saddled horse, he considered his own prospects. The Prince would be unhappy with this news, but he had been in Derby when disaster had struck in Chester. The blame would not fall on him.

Still, the reputation of de Ferrers would suffer and by association his own. He would have to think on how to turn this situation to his advantage. He climbed onto his horse and turned its head toward the southeast and London. One thing was certain—the Prince would not be the first to hear of events in Chester.

That would be the Archdeacon.

***

Malachy wore out one horse and bought another, but made it to London at twilight on the third day of hard riding. He went straight to Archdeacon Poore's London residence only to find the man was not there. A servant said his master had not been at the house since the previous week.

Reluctantly, he turned his horse back toward the walls of the city and headed for the Tower, where Prince John had been keeping his quarters. If Poore was in his bishopric of Canterbury, he would have to wait on this news.

It was full night when he reached the forbidding stone mass of London's Tower. The guards at the one open gate questioned him at length, but allowed him entrance. Two guards guided him through a confusing set of corridors to a small sitting room. As he entered, he was shocked to find Herbert Poore there, warming his gnarled old hands by the fire. The old churchman smiled at him, but the eyes were cold.

"Malachy! You've come sooner than I would have expected."

"Your excellency?"

"I presume you bring news of Chester and I am eager to hear it. The reports I've received thus far are hard to fathom. Please tell me that your Earl had not managed to lose the city."

Malachy felt a hard knot form in his stomach with the realization that Poore had already received news of the fall of Chester. It meant the spymaster had other eyes deployed in the Midlands watching events.

Watching him.

He fought a wave of panic welling up inside him. The Archdeacon, he knew, did not look kindly on weakness.

"Your excellency, Chester has fallen to Ranulf. I was in Derby on the Earl's orders at the time, but came here straightaway to advise you when the news arrived. As you know, de Ferrers is a rash man and it appears he acted stupidly in this instance. He was lured out of Chester by reports of Ranulf's return from Wales. I suspect traitors inside the city opened the gates after the garrison had ridden out, and the city fell back into the hands of the Earl of Chester."

He stopped and waited for some response from Poore. The old man shook his head mournfully.

"It's a blow, Malachy, there is no doubt of that," he said and paused, watching to see if his agent would squirm under his hard gaze. He saw no hint of fear.

Good. He placed a hand on Malachy's shoulder.

"I'm certain you would have restrained the fool had you been there, my son, but we will undo the damage he has caused in due time. As you can see by my presence here, I have become close to the Prince over the past several months. He has come to trust my sage counsel. In a short while, we will go to inform him of the bad news. I will suggest that he order de Ferrers to join his mercenary army besieging Nottingham. I doubt he can do much damage there."

Malachy kept his features impassive, but wanted to cry out with relief. The Archdeacon was absolving him of the disaster at Chester.

"Father Malachy, I have a new task for you, one that may, in time, produce results that exceed all of our efforts thus far."

"How can I be of service, your excellency?"

"Are you familiar with Westminster Hall?"

"Aye, excellency. The Queen held a reception there—shortly after Richard left on crusade. I did not attend, but I know where it is out west of the city."

Archdeacon Poore nodded.

"It has been some time since the Queen stayed at her residence there, preferring her lair in Tancarville, but she will, no doubt, return at some point. In the hall is a small chapel. The young priest who takes confession and says Mass there has taken suddenly ill and I'm quite certain he will not survive the night. It was something he ate, I believe."

"A tragedy, excellency," Malachy said, without emotion.

"You will take his place, my son. You will watch and wait. When the time is right, you will receive instructions from me."

Malachy felt a stab of disappointment. Seeing after a chapel, even within Westminster Hall seemed a step down from being counsellor to the most powerful nobleman in the Midlands. Herbert Poore's sharp eyes did not miss the quick flash of concern on the younger man's face.

"Do not fret, my son. You have done all you can in the Midlands. Now it is time to strike closer to the heart of things. I need a man ready to change history. Are you that man?" Malachy met the Archbishop's wolfish eyes and did not hesitate.

"I am, excellency."

Civil War

William Marshal spurred his horse up the steep path that led to the castle at Tancarville. He had not wanted to come to Normandy, not with affairs in England at a tipping point, but he had news for the Queen and was in need of her sage counsel. The guards recognised the Lord of Striguil and ushered him quickly inside. Eleanor could not have known he was coming, but she showed no surprise when he was announced. Nothing seemed to perturb this woman, and for that he was grateful.

He brightened when he saw that Walter of Coutances was attending the Queen. He had first met the Archbishop of Rouen the previous January when the Queen travelled to Oxford. During those difficult encounters with John, Marshal had come to understand why Richard had appointed him as a Justiciar. He had found the Archbishop to be a steady presence and a wily judge of character.

"Your grace, I am sorry to disturb you," he said bowing low.

"You are never a disturbance, my Lord of Striguil, the Queen replied. "It's good to see you William."

"And you, your grace. I am also gratified to see the Archbishop here. I have news that will interest you both and I need guidance."

Eleanor looked down on her favourite. He looked tired, but so were they all. She tried to avoid looking at herself in a mirror of late. It was too hideous a sight.

"What do you bring us, William?"

"Your grace, a miracle seems to have occurred in Cheshire. I received word ten days ago that Ranulf has reappeared out of Wales and retaken Chester! The news came from one of your spies, your excellency," he said, nodding toward the Archbishop. "I could hardly believe the report, but the next day a courier arrived with a message from Ranulf himself. He has the city, your grace. He has Chester!"

The Queen said nothing for a long moment and Marshal was not sure she had heard him properly.

"Your grace, Chester…"

"I heard, William. I just needed a moment to let it sink in. We've had so little to cheer us these many months."

"There's more, your grace. The Earl cited the bravery of the Invalid Company in his message announcing the capture of his capital."

Eleanor slapped her hand down on the arm of her chair and released a triumphant laugh.

"So they did get through! And our great fat Constable of Lincoln, the doughty Harold FitzGibbons, is a liar on top of being a coward!"

William Marshal allowed himself a grin. Sir Harold had been their reluctant choice to command the small force they'd sent into Wales to find and aid Ranulf. A week after departing Oxford with the Invalid Company, he had ridden into Shrewsbury claiming that the men had mutinied and had been massacred in an ambush.

Marshal had sent scouts out and his men found evidence of a clash west of Shrewsbury. There were bodies buried in the woods there, but the corpses had personal items that marked them as Flemish mercenaries. In the intervening months, no further word had come regarding the mystery of the relief force. Now they knew.

Marshal watched as the Queen allowed herself a small moment of triumph, but it was only a moment.

"You would not have come yourself just to deliver good news, William. What else do you have for me?"

Marshal cleared his throat.

"Your grace, Nottingham…our relief column did not make it through. They attacked us as we were crossing the River Soar in Leicester. The men fought well, your grace, but we were outnumbered and took heavy casualties. I gave the order to withdraw to London. From what we know, the garrison will be running out of provisions soon. I think they will be forced to surrender within a month, perhaps sooner."

Eleanor nodded. This was not completely unexpected. She had ordered Marshal to break the siege of the royal castle, but she knew the forces at his disposal would probably not be sufficient. Now they had nothing left to send. Still, the loss of Nottingham would be a huge blow. With John's bold disregard of orders from her and the Justiciars to cease his attacks on the royal castle there, civil war was no longer on the horizon; it had arrived and they were losing.

A messenger from Richard had got through in May informing her that a truce had been agreed to in the Holy Land. Her son planned to sail for home by late summer. With luck, he would arrive by year's end, but she had learned in her nearly fifty years of being a queen, that luck cut both ways. He might be delayed or not survive the journey. Many didn't. Somehow they had to hold his broken realm together for another half a year—at the least. And that would take more than luck.

"So, when Nottingham falls, where will John turn?"

Marshal did not hesitate.

"I would guess Chester, your grace—though he might go north first. There are wavering barons up there and he may think to overawe them. But sooner or later—he will turn on Chester. He relies too heavily on its revenues to give it up."

The Queen gave a little sigh. Ranulf was back on the board, but for how long? And Nottingham was a chess piece they could ill afford to lose. Eleanor of Aquitaine was a woman who understood sentiment and how to use it to her advantage, though she rarely gave in to it herself. Now, for a moment, she set aside cold calculation and allowed herself to feel—feel for the defenders at Nottingham, who would soon be starving.

***

Sir Robin of Loxley ducked as a massive stone smashed into the curtain wall of Nottingham Castle. He was not concerned that the stone might strike him—he could see it coming long before it arrived. But he had seen men felled by the fragments that flew in every direction with each impact. Killed by a sliver of rock seemed a silly way to die, so he always ducked.

As soon as the shards stopped flying, he arose and looked out at the enemy campfires that circled the besieged castle on all sides. For not the first time, he wondered how he had found himself here. He had hoped to find some peace when he returned home from two years at war—that his days of bleeding and spilling blood were done.

Hope. It was a slender reed these days.

He and Tuck had ridden into Nottingham five months ago. A day later, Prince John's mercenary army had swept into the town and demanded the surrender of the castle. The commander refused and the siege engines had begun the long task of reducing the walls.

At first, the commander of the Prince's force was aggressive and mounted a number of direct assaults on the castle. But resistance proved to be much stouter than expected and the mercenaries suffered terrible losses. As winter turned to spring and then summer, the enemy changed tactics and settled into siege lines, intent on starving the fortress into surrender.

To keep up the pressure on the garrison, the siege engines flung heavy stones over the walls at unpredictable intervals and the effects could be seen in the way men scurried from one protected shelter to another within the castle.

There had been small victories for the men inside. Tuck conducted a series of lightning sallies into the enemy camp burning siege engines and stampeding horses. But that was stopped when the attackers dug a deep outer ditch the horses could not cross. Robin had taken charge of the archers and his longbows had taken a heavy toll on any mercenary soldier foolish enough to come within range.

It was starvation, more than the stones battering the walls, that finally prevailed. By early May, the horses had been butchered and the defenders were beginning to boil the soles of their boots for food. Hope had surged inside the besieged fortress when a messenger made it through the siege lines with news of a relief force coming from London. But a week later, a herald came under white flag to announce that the force from London had been driven back at Leicester. It had been their last real hope.

Robin heard someone behind him and turned to see Tuck approach. It pained him to see how gaunt the burly friar had become, but the man never complained. He stopped next to Robin and looked out at the circling campfires.

"You've heard the terms that have been offered for our surrender?"

The final offer had come just that morning. It had been a fortnight since the defeat of the relief column and men had begun to perish inside the fortress from lack of food. The new Sheriff of Nottingham had ridden up to the gate of the castle and announced that, if the defenders of the castle would lay down their arms, open the gates, and make homage to Prince John, they would be paroled. Anyone who refused would be hanged. He gave Sir Clarence a day to consider the terms.

Robin nodded.

"Aye, they could have been worse, and Sir Clarence will accept them. He has little other choice, but I cannot stomach it."

"Nor I," Tuck stated simply.

Robin offered up a grim smile. "Magnus Rask and fifteen of my archers are of like mind. They've sworn no oath to Richard, but they know who the legitimate king is. They cannot—will not, swear fealty to John."

"So what are we to do?"

Robin looked back out at the encircling fires.

"I've been thinking on that. They have us hemmed in tightly on the high ground, but not below the cliffs that go down to the river."

"And for good reason," Tuck pointed out. "Those cliffs are near sheer."

"Aye, but I've been studying them. There is a way down."

"In the dark?"

"Dangerous, but possible, I assure you."

"And once you go over the wall. What then?" Tuck asked. "No doubt they will know the name of every man in the garrison. If you do not march out with the rest, you'll be outlawed."

"Aye, but it's better than being hanged for not bending our knee to John. You told me, when I wanted to kill that fool at Loxley, that it would be a shame to become an outlaw after serving King and country on the crusade. But now, anyone in these parts who stays loyal to Richard is branded an outlaw."

Tuck nodded. "So where will you go?"

"The River Leen runs by the base of the cliffs. My archers and I will follow it downstream until we're outside the siege lines, then strike north."

"North?"

"Aye, to the forest of Sherwood. Outlaws seem to find it a congenial place. Will you join us?"

"Sherwood..." Tuck rolled the idea over. "Perhaps I will. It would not be the first time I've been outlawed."

Robin draped an arm over Tuck's broad shoulders.

"My friend, that does not surprise me."

The Gathering Tempest

*R*oland looked down the column of eighty mounted Welshmen facing south along Bridge Street. It was the end of June, and the borrowed men from Prince Llywelyn were going home. Earl Ranulf had spent the previous week trying to persuade them to stay, but couriers from the Prince had made it plain they were needed west of the Dee. Llywelyn's Uncle Roderic had launched a serious campaign into the backcountry and he could no longer spare them. Ranulf would have to make do with his own forces for the present.

Those forces had grown, but were still woefully thin. He had enough men to hold the city against raiders, but not against a large force with siege engines. The walls that encircled Chester ran for over two miles. Properly manning those walls against a determined foe required far more men than he had.

But a bargain was a bargain—The Surly Beast for eighty men for one month. Roland reminded Ranulf of this, which irritated the Earl, but it had been his bargain after all—not the Earl's, and he knew they had got more than fair value.

At the head of the column was Griff, the taciturn Welsh bowman who led the force. He gave a small smile as he saw Roland and Declan approach from the arch of the Bridgegate. War made strange allies and he had grown fond of these two.

The men he had left under Declan's command at Shipbrook had testified to the Irishman's steadiness in battle and Griff had personally seen the mettle of Roland Inness during the capture of

272

the Bridgegate. They had fought together, well and honourably. By such things, men are bound.

Roland extended his hand and the Welshman grasped it.

"Griff, you and your men go with my thanks and that of the Earl. Lady Catherine and Lady Millicent also send their affection for you and your men. Please convey to Lord Llywelyn that, if we survive the storm that is coming our way, we will be proud to fight with him against his enemies."

Griff took in this farewell solemnly. He had learned a bit of English in the months he had been among these people and had prepared his own farewell address. He cleared his throat and began.

"My respects to the ladies," he said, then paused, searching for his next line. Finding it, he continued. "You two gentlemen are always welcome west of the Dee." He paused again, grimacing as he tried to recall the words he had practiced. Then a look of relief played across his weathered face. "And piss on the Earl!" He finished with a satisfied look on his face.

"Well said!" Declan declared. "I think you've mastered the language. Too bad Welsh is such gibberish."

Griff leaned toward the man next to him, who had a better command of English, for a translation. When he heard it, he scowled then broke out in a laugh. He was wiping tears from his eyes as he replied, motioning for his companion to translate for him. The man looked uncomfortable, but Griff gave him a dark look and he spoke.

"When Irishmen speak, it has a sound like the barking of dogs."

Before the exchange of insults could go further, Roland reached to the longbow he had slung over his shoulder and held it up to Griff.

"It's yew and I fashioned it myself. It's my gift to the greatest bowman in Wales."

Griff took the bow and felt its balance. He leaned back and drew it to his ear.

"Strong," he said and reached down to take Roland's hand. "God be with you English." He slung the bow over his shoulder, stood up in his stirrups and raised his arm.

"Ymlaen!"

The Welsh rode out of Chester and back into their homeland.

***

A week after Griff and his men rode out, Roland and Millicent strolled along the south wall of Chester near sunset. From this wall they had a wide view of the Dee, which sparkled in the dying rays of the sun. They took this walk on the occasional days when their duties did not interfere. It was a welcome respite from the endless tasks of preparing the defences of this lovely city.

After Ranulf had retaken Chester, the corpses had been cut down from the gibbets and the gallows torched. The citizens of the city welcomed their old ruler back with genuine joy, though with a touch of restraint. One never knew these days when the wind might change again.

In the weeks that followed, Declan was given command of the patrols that watched the borders of Cheshire, particularly the border with Derbyshire. He was often gone for days at a time, but thus far, the borders had been quiet.

Roland was charged with rebuilding the garrison force and this task was urgent. The guards who had been left behind by de Ferrers and trapped inside the city when it fell had to be dealt with. Some had simply been doing their jobs, first under Ranulf and then under de Ferrers. Others had embraced the torture and hangings that came with the Earl of Derby's rule.

Henry Thatcher helped to sort these men out. Some of the captured garrison troops were kept on. A few were hung for egregious crimes and still others were turned out of the city to shift for themselves.

Most of the city's former garrison had ridden out under de Ferrers' command to attack Shipbrook. When Chester fell back into Ranulf's hands these men were trapped outside their own city. Many had families inside but had little choice but to follow the Earl of Derby's retreat. By late June, scores of these men had slipped away from Derbyshire and drifted back to Chester.

Among them was one man from Derbyshire, an old soldier who had faithfully served Earl Robert de Ferrers, but had had his fill of the new Earl. Sir James Ferguson had been deeply troubled by the hangings he'd witnessed in Derbyshire and later in Chester, but the outright cowardice he'd witnessed in his liege lord at Shipbrook had been the final straw. He had defected.

By the beginning of July, the Earl of Chester could count on three hundred men with some degree of training and experience. Perhaps that many more able-bodied men could be cobbled together from the citizens of Chester, but when things came to blows, the value of such men was uncertain.

Roland made use of the Invalid Company veterans to drill the new Chester garrison. Sir Edgar, Patch and Sergeant Billy proved to be demanding instructors and took pride in turning complacent garrison troops and common tradesmen into something like a real fighting force.

Roland took personal charge of the archers. The loss of the eighty Welshmen, most of them skilled bowmen, could not be replaced by raw volunteers, but Griff had made him a gift of twenty longbows before he had ridden out and Roland selected a score of the sturdiest young men in the city to train as archers. They would not soon be expert, but as the weeks went by, calluses grew on their fingers and more arrows hit their targets.

Roland and Millicent had reached the east wall and turned north along it when she stopped and looked up at him.

"You look tired," she said. "You need to sleep."

Roland smiled at her.

"Oh, I sleep, but it seems I hardly close my eyes before I hear the cock crow in the morning. There is so much to do."

"Aye, mother and I are making progress on gathering stocks for a siege, but de Ferrers stripped this entire county. There is not much food—not enough to feed a city this size."

"How long would the stores we have last?"

"Two weeks—perhaps three if they must. If they close off the Dee, there will be no resupply. Not much to sustain a siege, but the crops look bountiful this summer. If de Ferrers waits until we bring in the harvest, we could have provisions for at least three months."

Roland nodded. He could look out to the east and see the crops ripening in the fields. It gave them hope. He looked at the girl beside him and could not bring himself to dampen that hope.

The harvest was two months away, and even if they could bring in the crops, would a three month store of food outlast a determined siege? The siege of Nottingham Castle had been underway for almost six months. Chester could not survive that long. He was seeking something cheerful to say, when she spoke first.

"Riders to the east."

Roland lifted his eyes to the far woodline where the eastern road disappeared into dense forest. A group of riders had emerged from the trees and were riding hard for the Eastgate. Even at this distance, he could not mistake the man at their head. Declan O'Duinne was coming at a gallop. That could only mean trouble.

They hurried down the stone steps to the arch of the gate as their friend led his men through it and reined in. Declan swung off his lathered horse as they reached him. The Irishman took a moment to catch his breath before he blurted out his news.

"Nottingham has fallen."

***

When the news of Nottingham's surrender reached Ranulf, he called a council of war in the great hall of Chester Castle. As the Earl looked around the table, he was struck by the people who had become his inner circle. None of the sycophants who had surrounded him a year ago were present. Before him were the men and women who had stood by him as a fugitive and had restored him to his birth right.

Millicent de Laval sat directly across from him. He owed more to her than anyone in the chamber. Her mother, Lady Catherine, was there—a formidable woman who did not shrink from hard choices. To his left was Sir Declan O'Duinne. The Irishman's stout defence of Shipbrook had bought them the time they needed to take back his city. On his right was Sir Roland Inness. It had been this young knight's plan and his daring assault on the Bridgegate that had delivered Chester into his hands. Now they were faced with more hard choices.

"Sir Declan, tell us what you know of Nottingham and the Prince's army."

Declan ran a hand through his hair. He looked weary.

"My lord, since we've seen little activity at the border, I pushed this patrol well into Derbyshire—all the way to the River Dove. I could even see Roland's mountains off to the north. We dodged a few patrols and nothing more, even though we were within a few leagues of Derby itself. Then we met travellers recently come from Nottingham. They told us the garrison had surrendered three days before." He paused to see if there were questions, but none spoke and he continued.

"We've all feared where John's army might turn next after finishing with Nottingham, so I pressed on. We were able to ride right up to the siege lines around the castle without being challenged. The lines were empty, save for a few town folk picking over the refuse. They told us the Prince's men had packed up and marched north toward Yorkshire. They didn't know to what purpose, though there were rumours that John wanted to use his mercenaries to cow the barons in the north of the country." Declan paused a moment to let the people around the table digest this hopeful news.

Roland looked to his left and could see the relief written on the Earl's face and it worried him. This was a reprieve, not a pardon.

"So we trailed them north toward Sheffield and got a good look at the column before we ran into a large foraging party and had to turn back. They are marching north—for now."

The Earl slapped the table with his hand.

"God has answered our prayers!"

Roland frowned, and across the table he saw that neither Millicent nor Lady Catherine shared Ranulf's relief at the news. He turned to the Earl.

"My lord, this is good news, indeed, but we must allow that an army that marches north can march back south again—or west, if it pleases its commander. Dec, if that column turned around, how long before they would be before our walls?"

Declan rubbed his chin.

"They are slowed by their foot soldiers and even more so by the oxen pulling the carts with their siege engines. I should think the soonest would be two weeks."

"And how would you estimate their strength?"

Declan reached inside his shirt, drew out a piece of parchment and laid it on the table. Roland could see there were numbers written there and so could Lady Catherine.

"Sir Declan, I am pleased to see my instruction in mathematics is still serving you well," she said with a wry smile.

He grinned back at her.

"Aye my lady, I can use it to count men as well as your cows and goats!" He turned his eyes back to the parchment and read what he had recorded.

"Over four hundred heavy cavalry. Four times that many foot and archers. He has over two thousand men in all, Roland."

The faces around the table now were sombre as Roland turned back to Ranulf.

"My lord, with our current force, we cannot defeat an army of this size. They will have more than twice our numbers and their men are well trained. Only half of our men are. We can repel direct assaults on the walls of Chester for a time, but we only have two to three weeks of food stores. If they come before the harvest is in, it will be a short siege."

"But perhaps they will be occupied in the north until we gather in the crops," Ranulf said, hopefully.

"Perhaps, but we must not count on that, my lord. Even if that comes to pass, Lady Millicent estimates we will have food enough for only three months. Prince John has shown that he can sustain a siege for much longer than that."

Ranulf was growing more agitated as the hard truths mounted. Finally he rose to his feet and slammed a fist on the table, his voice rising.

"Three months of food can get us to Christ's Mass and by then the King will have returned. You brought that news to us yourself! Will not Richard put an end to all this?"

Roland did not flinch. His liege lord wanted hope, needed hope, but he could only offer truth.

"My lord, we will all pray that the King arrives safely and promptly by then, but you cannot...you must not, risk your city on that chance. It is a dangerous journey." He saw Lady Catherine flinch and knew she thought of her husband. She turned and whispered something to Millicent, who simply nodded.

"So what are we to do?" Ranulf asked plaintively. "Wait here for our doom—or flee back to Wales?"

Roland rubbed his eyes. Millicent was right. He needed more sleep, but there was a seed of an idea in his head that he needed to grasp. Something Declan had said...

"My lord, I would urge you to send a courier to find the Earl of Striguil, in London or wherever he may be. Tell him we mean to fight to defend the city and beg him for any aid he can send. If there are fighting men to be had, William Marshal will send them I think."

Ranulf sat back down and shrugged.

"The last time, Marshal sent us but forty men. Your Invalid Company is worth twice that number in a fight, I'll grant you, but we will need much more than that to stand against John. Where are we to get the men?"

Then Declan's words came back to him. He had ridden all the way out to the River Dove. He had seen the mountains of Derbyshire to the north. He had seen the highlands where his own people still clung to a hard existence.

"I believe I can get you the men to make a fight of it, my lord."

Ranulf looked at him, incredulous.

"What men?"

"My people, lord—the Danes."

Ranulf looked puzzled.

"You are a Dane, Sir Roland?"

"Aye, my lord—an Englishman to be sure, but a Dane as well. There are hundreds of men up there in the high country, men who bear a grudge against the Earl of Derby, and most of them can shoot a longbow as well as I."

"And you think they will come and fight for me?"

Roland shook his head.

"No, not for you, my lord. But they would fight for land. You Normans long ago pushed the Danes out of the fertile valleys in the Midlands and into the hills. It's a hard life and people starve up there. If you offer a hide of good farmland to each man who joins us, I think they will come."

All eyes around the table turned to the Earl. They did not have to wait long for an answer.

"Agreed! I will grant one hide per man, Sir Roland. When will you leave?"

***

Millicent caught up with him as he walked up Bridge Street toward the quarters he kept in the barracks near the centre of the town. She wanted to shout at him—to tell him he had done enough and did not need to risk this journey into Derbyshire, but she knew risks were still necessary and that it was an argument she could not win.

"How long a journey is it to your home?"

"Three days with a good horse, but I will confess to you that I expect it will take longer. There is a long overdue obligation I must attend to. My brother and sister are at the Priory of Saint Oswald... I should have already gone to them, but all this..."

She touched his arm.

"You've had no choice till now. Where is the priory?"

"It's south of Leeds and a little ways beyond the high country. I will go there first, but only for a day. I would have them know that I am alive and intend to bring them back here when this is all over."

"When will you return?"

He shook his head.

"Millie, I can't say for sure. I do not know how things stand among the Danes these days. For certain, they will not lightly leave their families to march to Chester, even for a hide of good farmland. I hope to be back before the harvest—a month from now perhaps. Declan will know how to find me if John loses interest in Yorkshire and turns back south."

"You will take someone with you." It was a statement not a question.

He smiled at her.

"You'll be pleased that I've decided to ask Sir Edgar to come with me. Declan can't be spared."

She looped an arm inside his as they walked.

"He's a good choice. Sir Edgar will frighten the Danes into doing whatever you ask."

He laughed, for the first time in days. It felt good.

"What did your mother whisper to you in the hall?"

She squeezed his arm.

"Right after you dashed the Earl's hopes and told him how perilous the situation was, she leaned over and said, 'He sounds like your father.' I believe it was a compliment."

Storm Warnings

M illicent stood on the wall of Chester and watched as Roland Inness and Sir Edgar Langton rode out of the city. She had met Roland earlier that morning, before many folk were stirring in the town, to say their private goodbyes. It had been painful. Now, more than ever, she understood the strength of her own mother. Lady Catherine had said such goodbyes to her father many times. She had always shrugged off the agony of parting by saying, "I'm a soldier's wife," but Millicent now understood the price she had paid for those farewells.

Since the fall of the city, she and Roland had not told anyone about their feelings for each other, though both knew Declan had his suspicions. Millicent had argued that this news should wait until her father returned at Christ's Mass and Roland had finally agreed, reasoning to himself that he might be dead by then and not have to face Lady Catherine.

So they had kept it to themselves, and she had no one to share her misery with. And it was pure misery as she watched Roland come to the last bend in the road that would take him out of sight of the city. She hated to cry, but she couldn't help herself as her eyes welled and tears streaked down her face. She saw him rein in and turn his horse. He waved toward the town.

"You should wave back, daughter."

Millicent whirled around to see her mother standing there, her expression sad.

She turned and waved a scarf over her head, then watched as Roland gave a final wave and rode out of sight.

"Mother…I"

Lady Catherine raised her hand to stop her daughter.

"I am not blind, Millicent. I've seen how you look at the boy every time he comes around—and how he looks at you. You were never one to mask your feelings, child."

"I'm sorry, mother. He wanted to tell you, but I convinced him we should wait until Father came home."

Lady Catherine sighed.

"Millie, look at me. Roland Inness is a fine boy, but he has nothing to offer you but the life of a soldier's wife. You could have so much more. Do you see how it feels to watch him ride off, wondering if he will ever come back? These will not be the last tears you shed for him."

Millicent felt her anger rise, but saw the deep sadness in her mother's eyes and softened.

"Mother, you say I cannot mask my feelings. True enough. I am in love, and I suppose there is no hiding that. Have you forgotten what that feels like? Do you remember how it was with Father? Do you regret being a soldier's wife?"

Her daughter's response set Catherine back.

Had she forgotten?

Her mind raced back twenty years to the day when a very tall man rode into her family's courtyard and asked for water for himself and his horse. He was a knight to be sure, but his clothes were threadbare and his horse a bit spavined. It was hard to remember exactly what it was about this slightly dangerous-looking young man that struck her so forcefully.

Roger de Laval was never a handsome man. In fact he looked like what he was, a dangerous man to cross, but there was something about him—something steady and gentle and even playful beneath that fearsome countenance. From that day forward she had no interest in other men. She had become a soldier's wife at fifteen and had loved her man fiercely and faithfully through the years.

She stepped forward and wrapped her arms around her daughter. Together the women stood on the wall and wept.

283

No, she had not forgotten.

***

In the harbour of Acre, two swift galleys swung at anchor. One would convey the King of England and his guard. The other carried the horses and baggage going with them. A small boat manned by two of the remaining Genoese mercenaries was pulled up on the rocky beach near the docks that the Crusaders had rebuilt.

As King Richard climbed into the boat, he could not help but look upon the sad remnants of his army, lining up on the docks to board one of the squat little cogs commissioned to take them home. Unlike his arrival upon these shores, there were no bugles sounding fanfares for Richard the Lionheart as he took his leave. There were no heroic speeches given to adoring Crusaders. It was a day for melancholy, a day for regrets.

It was late July and he was keeping his promise to Eleanor to depart these shores by midsummer. But it was the broken promises to the men there on the docks that ate at him. He had sworn to give them Jerusalem and he had failed.

His army had won every battle it had fought, but the victories were hollow—like the chimaeras so common to this accursed land. He had sworn to return, to take up the fight once the truce with Saladin expired in three years, but in his heart he knew he would never come back to this place.

He kept his eyes fixed on the vessel that would take him on the first leg of his journey home to England. He did not wish to look upon the men lining the dock, the men he had led so often into battle. But he could not help but steal a glance.

So few!

His quartermaster had informed him that he would be returning home with one tenth of the men he had come with—a melancholy day indeed.

As the King neared the galley, a tall knight leaned on the railing and watched his monarch approach. He knew better than most what this leave taking had cost the man's spirit and reputation. Sir Roger de Laval looked past the King at the men lining the wharf. Many of them he knew and not a man among them was sorry to be leaving these shores. England beckoned like a sweet green balm to these veterans, yet they too felt the sting of battles won, but a crusade lost.

Some had taken advantage of the truce and visited the holy places in Jerusalem. The King would not go, nor did Sir Roger. He had come to these lands as a soldier, not a pilgrim. The only holy place he wished to make pilgrimage to was near a ford on the River Dee. Jerusalem did not tempt him.

A sudden squall came in off the sea, lashing the harbour and the men lining the docks with sheets of rain and causing the galleys to pitch at their moorings. For a moment he feared that the King's small boat would capsize, but the wind and rain blew through quickly and the sea was quiet again.

The suddenness and violence of the squall seemed an ill omen. In another month it would be the time of storms in these seas, when wise mariners put in to port and waited for fairer sailing. It was worrisome, but he would not have wanted to be anywhere else but the deck of this ship. Catherine and Millie were waiting for him across this sea.

He was going home.

***

A summer thunderstorm blew in from the Irish Sea as the riders reached the ford of the River Dane. Behind him, Roland could see the rain advancing in rippling sheets like a dark curtain, but his eyes were drawn ahead. In the distance was a line of blue hills rising up from the Cheshire plain toward the threatening skies. Beyond those hills lay higher peaks still. Kinder Scout was there, the highest of them all, but still out of sight. He urged his horse into the river as the rain struck.

He was going home.

Historical Note

The history of events in England while Richard was on the Third Crusade are not as well documented as his campaigns in the Holy Land, but accounts of the period clearly show a country on the verge of outright civil war. Mercenaries were hired, castles besieged and plenty of blood shed as Prince John manoeuvred to seize the crown from his brother.

In *The Broken Realm* I have tried to faithfully portray the chaos and divided loyalties that roiled England during Richard's absence, though the actions and words I attribute to the actual historical figures are mostly fictional.

A fair reading of this period leaves little doubt that one person managed to hold the Angevin Empire together, and that was Queen Eleanor. In this, she was ably assisted by William Marshal and Walter of Coutances. While there is the occasional revisionist historian who seeks to rehabilitate Prince John's image a bit, he was easily as disloyal and devious as I've portrayed him here.

As for the more prominent players in this story, Earl Ranulf was one of the most loyal supporters of King Richard during this period and William de Ferrers did become a favourite of John once he became King, but most of their actions in this story are fictional. Chester was never seized by the Earl of Derby, nor did Ranulf become a fugitive in Wales. The royal castle at Nottingham, however, was besieged and taken by John while Richard was away.

Prince Llywelyn ap Iowerth was an actual contemporary of Ranulf's and went on to become ruler of Gwynedd. He was in rebellion against his uncles during this period and, like Ranulf, was only in his early twenties at the time. He comes down to us in history with the illustrious appellation of, "Llywelyn the Great," and is considered one of the seminal figures in Welsh history. While his alliance with the Earl of Chester in *The Broken Realm* is fictional, the two did form an alliance in later years, illustrating the shifting loyalties and imperatives of this volatile borderland.

For his part, King Richard did agonize over his failure to take Jerusalem. The legend that he would not look upon the city that God would not let him conquer may or may not be true, but it fairly describes the pain he felt at this failure.

The Invalid Company is fictional, though I do think it fairly describes the plight of warriors coming home from the wars—both then and now. Such men have often lost more than a limb, they've lost the powerful sense of being a part of something larger than themselves, of having comrades they trust and a mission to fulfil.

One note about time—in the medieval world, everything moved slowly, particularly travel, and that does not always serve the purposes of a ripping good adventure yarn. For that reason, I have taken a few minor liberties with the timeline of events. I have Queen Eleanor arriving in Oxford in early January, when she did not get there until mid-February. I also have Richard setting sail from the Holy Land in late July, when he did not actually depart until early October.

On a final note, a "hide" of good land in the 12th and 13th century would be about 30 modern acres, though it varied considerably in different parts of the country. This would be far more than most peasant families would have been granted. So what the Earl has offered to the Danes should be tempting. We'll have to wait and see if they take the offer.

Can William Marshal and Queen Eleanor hold England together with King Richard a captive? They must depend on Roland, Declan, Millie and Sir Roger to save the crown in:

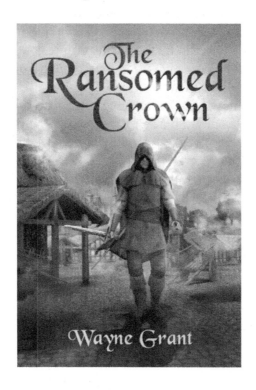

Buy it Amazon, Amazon UK or Audible

US: https://www.amazon.com/Ransomed-Crown-Saga-Roland-Inness-ebook/dp/B01LP3TGMI

UK: https://www.amazon.co.uk/Ransomed-Crown-Saga-Roland-Inness/dp/1537174525

Audible: https://www.audible.com/pd/The-Ransomed-Crown-Audiobook/B077YNHCCZ

Books by Wayne Grant

The Saga of Roland Inness
Longbow

Warbow

The Broken Realm

The Ransomed Crown

A Prince of Wales

Declan O'Duinne

A Question of Honour

The Inness Legacy
No King, No Country

ABOUT THE AUTHOR

Wayne Grant grew up in a tiny cotton town in rural Louisiana where hunting, fishing and farming are a way of life. Between chopping cotton, dove hunting and Little League ball he

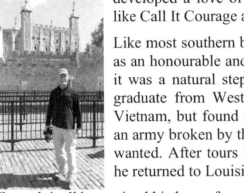

developed a love of great adventure stories like Call It Courage and Kidnapped.

Like most southern boys he saw the military as an honourable and adventurous career, so it was a natural step for him to attend and graduate from West Point. He just missed Vietnam, but found that life as a Captain in an army broken by that war was not what he wanted. After tours in Germany and Korea, he returned to Louisiana and civilian life.

Through it all he retained his love of great adventure writing and when he had two sons he began telling them stories before bedtime. Those stories became his first novel, Longbow. The picture above was taken outside the Tower of London.

The rest of The Saga of Roland Inness, which includes *The Ransomed Crown, A Prince of Wales, Declan O'Duinne* and *A Question of Honour* are now available on Amazon.

To learn more about the author and his books check out his website: www.waynegrantbooks.com or his Longbow Facebook page: www.facebook.com/Longbowbooks/

You can also follow him on BookBub: www.bookbub.com to get information on when his books go on sale and on Goodreads www.goodreads.com.

If you think these books have merit, please leave a review on Amazon or Goodreads. For a self-published writer this is the only way to get the word out. Thank you!

Made in the USA
Coppell, TX
26 November 2020

42141011R00164